HYPERSPEED

HYPERSPEED

A NOVEL

WILLIAM GROVÈRE

HYPERSPEED

iUniverse books may be ordered through booksellers or by contacting:

iUniverse
1663 Liberty Drive
Bloomington, IN 47403
www.iuniverse.com
1-800-Authors (1-800-288-4677)

ISBN: 978-1-5320-6019-9(sc)
ISBN: 978-1-5320-6018-2 (e)

Library of Congress Control Number: 2018912353

Print information available on the last page.

iUniverse rev. date: 10/23/2018

CONTENTS

CHAPTER 1

BELMULLET

C hristophe slipped off his augmented reality visor and placed it back into the pocket next to his seat. He pushed the button on his console to turn off the picture and sound. Glancing at the console, he noted the progress of his trip. The dimly lit numerals of the clock were counting down the time remaining for his short journey. He sank more deeply into his reclining seat in the darkness. There was almost complete silence except for the barely audible *click-clack* of the opening and closing air locks, reminiscent of the sound of ancient train wheels crossing the gaps between rails. Only twenty-three more minutes. He knew that in about twenty more minutes he would begin to feel the gentle tug of the deceleration of his capsule as it slowed down from its top speed of thirty-six hundred kilometers per hour. He was still about twelve hundred kilometers from the west coast of Ireland.

***

Christophe had not intended to nod off, so it startled him when the canopy of his capsule opened and his ears popped from decompression. Once his eyes adjusted to the light in the station, he saw the attendant standing on the platform next to his capsule. "I see you weren't using your AR visor. They are intended to reduce anxiety during the trip, you know." The attendant offered Christophe a hand to climb out of the capsule.

"Oh, this was my twenty-third trip. I have seen all the videos at least twice. It's time to get some new ones, don't you think?" Christophe opened the small hatch behind his seat to retrieve his briefcase and backpack. "Anyway, I was one of the builders of this system, and I can assure you that there is nothing that can reduce the anxiety!"

"Then I suppose you know where to go next. By the way, have you heard about Paris?"

"Yes." Christophe surveyed the long corridor of departure portals for all the European destinations, looking for his next portal, Paris, which was about forty meters down the hallway on the right-hand side. The queue at any of the portal gates typically never consisted of more than half a dozen persons, with capsules departing every minute or so. The days of waiting with four hundred people at a departure gate for a jet to embark at an airport were mostly history by now. From this central station located in a remote region on the west coast of Ireland, it was possible for travelers to fan out to a dozen European cities. Really, the only wait of the whole trip had been departing from the Newfoundland station at Goose Bay, where there was usually some congestion. But the wait was never more than thirty minutes.

Today was different. Arriving passengers to the Irish station were beginning to accumulate, and the queues at each portal were growing longer and longer with anxious travelers trying to rebook their reservations. There was nobody in line at the Paris portal, however. The lighted sign over the door read, "Paris portal temporarily out of service." Christophe had anticipated this because he was a member of the safety board for Hyperspeed Portal Travel. He had recently retired from the company that built the portal. He had spent his entire forty-year career with the firm as an engineering manager and senior executive, and now at sixty-six, he was ready to leave it behind. The stress of the job had taken its toll on his health, and he was worn out. He had managed the construction of the portal and knew it better than anyone else, so he had agreed to stay on the safety board because there simply was no one else more qualified.

Just before he departed from Newfoundland, he had received an alert saying that there had been an "incident" on the Paris portal. Apparently, the incident was not too serious, but anything that goes wrong in an evacuated tunnel filled with hundreds of passengers in airtight capsules going a thousand meters per second is obviously serious. The worst-case scenario would be catastrophic. The "incident" resulted in what was referred to as an "emergency repressurization." Initial reports pointed to a defective control valve, but Christophe knew this was pretty unlikely. He walked past the Paris portal and took the next elevator up several stories from the subterranean portal complex to the surface. It was the middle of the night when he walked outside into the cool Irish fog. He had departed from Los Angeles barely three hours earlier, at 3:10 p.m., so he was ready for dinner. After he'd crossed eight time zones, the time was 4:00 a.m. in Ireland. It was a marvel that one could zip around the world in just hours, but technology was never able to solve the problem of *décalage des horaires*—jet lag. It would take him a week to recover from the loss of this night's sleep.

All the portal activity was more than one hundred meters underground. There generally was not much reason for travelers to go to the surface, but there was still an enormous active airport at Belmullet attested by the muffled distant roar of jets taking off and landing in the Irish fog. The airport was built in the 2030s to serve as the European hub for all transatlantic flights. A similar airport was built in Newfoundland. After a number of jumbo jets had been shot down by terrorists using antiaircraft missiles, commercial travel had been brought to a standstill. The heavily traveled North Atlantic routes were particularly vulnerable to attack. The remote airports in Newfoundland and Ireland were built because it was the only way to provide a security perimeter against the threat. All transatlantic flights departed from one of these two airports. Initially the airports could only be reached by high-speed trains; subsequently they could be reached by way of the portals. There were no connecting passenger flights permitted. These days, the only regularly scheduled passenger flights still operating were a few westbound transatlantic jets. These would continue service until completion of the westbound North Atlantic portal, which was due to open sometime the following year.

This system of airport hubs served its purpose well for years, making it possible to travel once again without fear of being shot out of the sky. Tonight, the jets were carrying mostly freight and luggage. It was still too expensive to transport anything but people with small carry-ons through the hyperspeed portals. Luggage would arrive later by UPX at the travelers' destination. This was not as inconvenient as is sounds. Hyperspeed travel eliminated the need for people to travel with every earthly belonging. Long gone were the days of taking along steamer trunks for extended voyages. UPX guaranteed delivery of luggage within twenty-four hours. Nearly all the major airports had become freight hubs, and most of the jets had been converted into freighters. Christophe imagined that his suitcase was probably sitting in a shipping container on the tarmac in Atlanta by now.

The airport in Ireland was constructed on the site of the old Belmullet Aerodrome. It was the European terminus of almost all transatlantic commercial flights because it was located on a peninsula that was relatively easy to defend from land and sea. In its heyday, the airport terminal had teemed with restaurants and pubs. Several on-site hotels used to be almost always completely filled. Today, those that remained served mostly airport flight crews and ground staff. There was practically no reason for travelers to lay over—that is, as long as the portals were operational.

The closure of the Paris portal really threw a wrench in the works. The only restaurant still open at this time of the night was soon filled to capacity with Paris-bound passengers. Christophe knew the restaurant well from all the time he had spent in Belmullet during the portal construction project. When the portals first became operational, it morphed into more of a pub than a restaurant. The European portal system had achieved an impressive on-time performance record. Closure of portals was so rare that no one knew quite what to do with the hundred or so displaced travelers. Some would be accommodated on portals to other cities, but bookings were so tightly choreographed that there were not a lot of available capsules to any destination. It was astounding how disruptive the slightest hiccup in the system could be.

Christophe and other Paris-bound travelers began receiving notifications that passengers would be rerouted through Dublin. This was not good news, because it involved going to Dublin and on to London by train. The next train to Dublin from this remote portal hub, on the west coast of Ireland, was not due to depart for three more hours. This left plenty of time for a hamburger and draft ale. The meager staff at the all-night pub was quickly overwhelmed with grumpy travelers unaccustomed to delays and inconveniences. Once food and drink began flowing, however, the mood became rather festive. This was a new adventure for almost everyone. No sooner had

Christophe slipped into an empty booth than a couple asked if he minded if they join him. The pub was now filling up rapidly.

"By all means," Christophe said, motioning to the other side of the booth. He observed that the middle-aged man and woman were surprisingly tan for November. "Where are you coming from?" he inquired.

"We were just on holiday in Santa Monica," the man responded. "We are heading home through Paris to a town in the northeast of France." His English was perfect, but there was more than a trace of French accent.

"Bienvenue! Est-ce-que vous etês francais?" This was about the limit of Christophe's French proficiency. His mother was French, and she had managed to give him and his siblings French *prénoms*, but beyond just an elementary proficiency, his French speaking skill was woefully inadequate, although not for lack of trying. He was learning the difficult lesson that in order to really speak French, you actually had to be French.

"Ah bon. Je m'appele Thierry, et je vous présente ma femme, Sophie." Indulging Christophe in French, the man extended his hand across the table. His hands were rough, and his handshake was firm.

"Très bien. Je m'appelle Christophe. Je viens de Marina del Rey, près de Santa Monica." It was now clear that Thierry's English was much better than Christophe's "Frenglish," so it was safe for both to converse in English thereafter.

"I know it well," said Thierry. "We try to go to Santa Monica every year about this time as soon as the—"

Thierry stumbled because he did not know the English word—"*betterave sucrière* harvest is complete."

"Betterave sucrière? What is that?" Christophe opened the French dictionary app on his smartphone. "Spell it for me."

"B-e-t-t-e-r-a-v-e s-u-c-r-i-e-r-e. Did you find it?"

"Yes. Sugar beets. Do you grow sugar beets?"

"*Oui*, yes. We farm about one hundred hectares. It's not a very big farm, but it pays the bills." A server came by the table at that moment to take drink orders. "A pint of Guinness for me, please."

"Same for me," requested Christophe.

Sophie responded, "Just water, s'il vous plaît."

"Farm life is northern France can be lovely for half of the year, but I must tell you, from November until April it is intolerable—cold, dark, and dreary. We really look forward to slipping away to Southern California. My son takes over the juice extraction operation and lets us get away for a couple of weeks once the syrup is shipped off to the fermentation and distillation plant."

"You make vodka?"

"No. Actually, we make bioethanol. It is not intended for drinking. It's mostly for fueling trucks. You know," Thierry added, trying to enliven the conversation, "France has been the leading sugar beet producer in the world since Napoleon. France has always loved its sugar and the distilled spirits made from it, but now most of the sugar beet juice goes into making fuel ethanol. This has really saved the French farmer. Thirty years ago, we were still importing about 98 percent of our fuel from the Middle

East, but ever since the ban on petroleum imports, France has become practically energy independent."

"I guess I knew this," responded Christophe, "but you are the first sugar beet farmer I have met."

"There are not many of us left. Most of the ethanol these days comes from cellulose, and now that natural gas is so plentiful and inexpensive, it has put sugar beet farmers under a lot of pressure. I'm not sure how much longer we will be able to make our yearly trek to the former United States. There is still a lot of ethanol used in fuel cells—including my tractors—but other than boats and a few other niches, everything else is converting to natural gas. People in Europe seem to be willing to exchange dependence on foreign petroleum for dependence on Russian natural gas. I always expected France to be smarter about this in the long run. Anyway, we need the gas to stay warm during winter. This is a better use of natural gas, don't you think?"

"Actually, I have a sailboat in the Mediterranean that burns E95 in fuel cells. That's ethanol, isn't it?"

"Absolutely! There's actually a pretty good chance that I or one of my neighbors grew the beets."

A jovial Irish waitress appeared at the table with the drinks at that moment. No one had yet looked at the menu. The restaurant was now completely full, and people were standing around waiting for tables. "And what would ye be havin' to eat, then?" she said in her Irish brogue, holding up her order pad with pencil at the ready.

The time flew by as Christophe and the farmer exchanged views on everything from American politics to the best French cheeses. This was an unlikely chance encounter between a French sugar beet farmer and a retired American executive, but a lasting friendship was blossoming. Thierry took particular interest in hearing Christophe's fascinating stories about the construction of the North Atlantic portal. The food had arrived and was eaten with practically no awareness of the passage of time. Sophie hardly spoke, but when she finally did speak, the dreaded question came out: "Do you have any family?" Of course, everyone has family, but this is not what this question is intending to ask. What it really means is, are you married with children?

Christophe had observed that she was looking at his wedding ring. He pointed to it jovially and responded, "No, I am not married. Actually, I have never been married." After a brief pause and gulping the last of his second pint, Christophe sensed that this probably required some further explanation.

"I nearly got married once—a long time ago. I met a woman at a conference in Bordeaux. We both worked in the area of safety engineering, although there wasn't much overlap of our particular fields. I was working on emergency evacuation of high-speed subterranean transport, and she worked on safety protocols for fusion power plants. She was a fascinating and stunning Frenchwoman named Monique. When we first met, what I had interpreted as disinterest actually turned out to be coyness on her part. By chance, we ended up sitting next to each other on the

TGV to Paris after the conference. By the time we pulled into Gare Montparnasse, we both knew that something more than just a casual friendship was developing."

Sophie and Thierry were leaning forward, intent on taking in every word of the story in the noisy pub. After a long pause, Christophe realized that he had crossed the threshold of no return and had to go on. "She grew up in a lovely apartment *avec terrasse* on La Croisette in Cannes, and her parents adored me. She was the love of my life. We were going to be married in Cannes. She had been working near Warsaw at a power plant that accidentally released some low-level tritium radiation— nothing serious, but the safety procedures were not being followed, so she was called on to conduct some emergency training at the last minute, the week before our wedding. The timing was very inconvenient, but she was dedicated to her work." Christophe's mood became somber as he realized by this time that he was trapped into finishing the story. "She was flying back to France to make final arrangements for our wedding. I was at the Nice Côte d'Azur airport waiting for her with a huge bouquet of flowers, watching for the screen to announce that her plane had landed, but it just kept flashing "En attente … En attente … En attente" for what seemed like eternity. Then there was a commotion, and I knew immediately that something must be wrong. As it turned out, her jet was brought down by a bomb on approach to the airport. There were no survivors."

There followed a long, awkward silence. Finally, Christophe broke it. "She was the one and only love of my life. She was irreplaceable. Even years after the grief subsided, I couldn't bring myself to have any other woman in my life, knowing she would only be second best. So, to answer your question, I never did get married, and I have no children." He paused. "I wear this ring as a reminder of Monique. But that was forty years ago. I think it became my mission in life to make sure such a tragedy never happened to anyone else. I guess this explains my passion for hyperspeed travel and why traveler safety is all I think about almost every waking moment." When he saw tears forming in Sophie's eyes, Christophe regretted having delved into such sad things with strangers. "I am sorry. I got a bit carried away. I haven't told this story to anyone for years. I guess it is just that you remind me of my sister."

Thierry had been receiving notifications that two capsules to Brussels were now available. He and his wife were reluctant to abandon their newfound friend, but Christophe guessed what the alert sound on his mobile phone probably meant. He said to Thierry, "You need to take those capsules and get home to your farm." They finally agreed, and after exchanging contact information, they got up from the booth. Christophe paid the bill for all three of them, and they walked together toward the elevator in the main terminal. Christophe sensed that this was not going to be their last encounter. He kissed Sophie on both cheeks and waved goodbye as the elevator door closed.

Christophe walked alone in the Irish fog toward the platform where his train to Dublin was standing. The faint glow of dawn was barely visible in the east on that cold November morning. He was flooded by uncomfortable thoughts and emotions. He was ordinarily good at subverting any mention of his private life. Tonight, Sophie's query had caught him off guard. Perhaps it was because, as he'd told her, she reminded him of his own sister. Perhaps it was the stress of disrupted travel plans or two pints of Guinness, but the story of Monique Fabré just seeped out unexpectedly. Something in Sophie's eyes spoke that it was safe and necessary for him to recount the sad story. In any event, Christophe had enough time on his stroll to the train station to push the memories back into the hard case of his inner soul. He had the final random thought: *If California had been settled by France instead of Spain, would Santa Monica be called Sainte Monique?* After this, the door to his soul closed again tight.

CHAPTER 2

SLOW TRAIN

The train was mostly filled by the time Christophe boarded. Besides some other Paris-bound travelers, there were passengers for whom Dublin was the final destination, as well as commuters coming off the night shift who would get off at one of the stops along the way. There was no portal from Belmullet to Dublin, because the distance was too short. There were also a few of those skittish about traveling by portal. It was still possible to fly east across the Atlantic. There were only a few commercial flights on this route, but also most of the freight-liners maintained passenger cabins for the remaining people who preferred to travel the "old-fashioned way." The choice was fifty-eight minutes in a hyperspeed capsule or six hours bouncing around in North Atlantic air turbulence. Not everybody was ready for hyperspeed travel.

Christophe began reflecting on the factors that led to such a radical change in how people traveled around the world. The desire to get places much faster required some sacrifices. Because of demanding size restrictions, capsules could only accommodate a single passenger, confined to a nearly prone position in what resembled a coffin, which definitely took some getting used to. It was also necessary for those traveling with small children to go by traditional jets because travelers had to be at least twelve years old to go in capsules alone. This was ponderously inconvenient for families, but the times demanded it for safe travel. Consideration was currently being given to deploying capsules with four seats, but this would require a whole new portal infrastructure. The family vacation to exotic distant places had become much more difficult.

In addition to disallowing children under twelve, it was necessary to implement a weight limit of 125 kilograms. Since there was no provision for checking luggage, this also meant wheelchairs and similar items had to be shipped by plane. Passengers under the weight limit requiring wheelchairs could still travel by portal, but they needed to make suitable arrangements to be picked up upon arrival at their destination. Vital signs were monitored throughout the short trip, so in the event of a medical emergency during transit, EMTs would be standing by when the capsule with the stricken passenger arrived. Passengers were offered a mild sedative and antidiuretic if they wanted. As a frequent portal traveler, Christophe no longer found these medications necessary. One further benefit of portal travel was the dramatic drop in the spread of contagious diseases that had caused numerous worldwide pandemics during the age of passenger flight. Besides the reduction in direct passenger-to-passenger contact, capsules were decontaminated after each use.

All of these restrictions turned out to be far less controversial than expected. Much of the long-haul family travel and those needing extra assistance had already gone away. For the people who weren't in a hurry to get to their destinations, there were still plenty of cruise ships operating. The majority of the remaining traveling public was actually glad to be done with fussy babies and the added congestion at security screening from infant paraphernalia. Security screening was also mostly a thing of the past. The only real threat remaining was explosives. A wide array of sensors that could detect trace explosive residues at parts-per-billion levels eliminated this threat. There had never been a capsule explosion on any portal.

By now capsule design had become standardized to the point that any capsule would work in any portal. This had not always been the case. In the past, portal operators deployed proprietary designs and dimensions that meant capsules could only be used in their own portals. This was fine as long as portals could be operated with both inbound and outbound tunnels. But with the advent of centralized portal hubs, it became necessary to implement strict international standards. This was reminiscent of the same problem that existed in the nineteenth century when railroads had to adopt the standard gauge for track spacing.

With the advent of transoceanic hyperspeed travel, a new challenge arose. These portals had to follow a ballistic trajectory, so it was only possible to operate portals in one direction because of the Coriolis effect caused by the earth's rotation. This is the same effect that causes hurricanes to swirl counterclockwise in the Northern Hemisphere and clockwise in the Southern Hemisphere. At one thousand meters per second, the effect is substantial, and without making corrections for this effect, it would otherwise take too much energy to propel the capsules through thousands of kilometers of evacuated tunnels. The capsules in these portals were not self-propelled. Once they were accelerated to the terminal velocity, they moved along, magnetically levitated, in the frictionless high vacuum. It was the same as with a satellite in orbit around the earth. The only thing keeping the capsule in motion was the inertia of its forward velocity. Because of the torque produced by the Coriolis force, if the portals were straight, it would be necessary to apply a counterforce, like thrusters on a satellite, and there was no way to do this with any known technology at the time. Therefore, a slight curvature had to be introduced to the portal in order to compensate for this, meaning that bidirectional portals could not be made colinear. The west–east North Atlantic portal was bowed slightly upward in the direction of the North Pole, whereas the corresponding east–west return portal, which was currently under construction, was bowed toward the equator. They diverged in the middle by as much as one hundred kilometers.

There was a return portal to the Western Hemisphere operated between West Africa and Brazil. It was also possible to reach North America by continuing east through Russia and traveling across the Bering Strait to Alaska. It was also still possible to take a jet flight from Belmullet to Goose Bay. Time-wise to the West Coast of the former United States, it was a toss-up. The westbound trip to Los Angeles from Southern France would take ten and a half hours either way. Once the new portal from Ireland to Newfoundland became operational, it was expected to cut at least five hours off the journey.

There were hundreds of thousands of capsules deployed around the world by this time, but the logistical challenges of having to wait at the northern portals for capsules to come back from the other portals around the world proved to be insurmountable. Thus, a simple, although rather inelegant, solution was to ship some of the capsules arriving in Dublin by train back to Belmullet in containers and ferry them back to Goose Bay by means of a jumbo jet freighter. This also meant that lots of empty capsules were being returned by train via Dublin. The air freight system was working well enough, and the problem would be solved, in any event, once the east–west North Atlantic portal became operational.

A new hyperspeed portal going from Svalbard Island, north of Norway, to the Yukon, and passing under the Arctic ice cap, was supposed to begin construction soon. It was decided that these portals had to be bidirectional, which required a large amount of energy to counteract the Coriolis force going in either direction.

This was a massive undertaking. It would be the most extensive submarine hyperspeed portal ever attempted. It was going to be thirty-five hundred kilometers long, compared to the thirty-four-hundred-kilometer North Atlantic portal, but it would lie in shallower water. It was anticipated that capsules would reach a top speed of twelve hundred meters per second, or three and a half times the speed of sound. Numerous studies had shown that one hour is about the limit of human endurance for this mode of travel, so it was necessary to increase the speed for this longer route. Construction was now delayed due to some cost overruns. Originally, Ashleigh Systems, the company Christophe had been working for, thought they could build it for six hundred million euros per kilometer. However, the latest projections were coming in at one billion euros, meaning that the Arctic portal could cost as much as five trillion euros—a staggering sum even by the standards of 2075.

The sovereign control of Svalbard Island had been disputed for centuries given its strategic location as the northernmost inhabited island on the planet. It was also realized that it was the logical hub for international portal travel between Europe, North America, and Asia, so the entire archipelago was designated as a "world state" under the direct rule of the United Nations. Accordingly, the town of Longyearbyen had become a construction boom town, with world-class hotels and resorts for passengers wanting to enjoy the northern lights in winter and midnight sun in summer on their way to distant places. The portal from Gare du Nord, in Paris, to Longyearbyen, a distance of 3,320 kilometers, was finished and undergoing certification. Even though there would be nowhere else to go for a couple of years, it was needed for transporting the construction crews to and from the island. Ultimately, there would be two Arctic portals, one going to the remote outpost at Atkinson, Yukon, connecting to Seattle, San Francisco, and Los Angeles, and the other connecting the Siberian mining center of Mirny, which would connect to Shanghai, Tokyo, and Seoul, with portals that were under construction. The dream of being able to travel from Paris to Shanghai in under four hours would be realized within the next five years.

Christophe's journey to Dublin today, however, would not be by portal and would be glacially slow by comparison. Even on a so-called fast train, the three-hundred-kilometer journey to Dublin would still take one and a half hours. As always, trains seemed to spend much of the time waiting in stations, and his train was already late for departure. He had time now to begin reading the incident reports for a clue to the reason for closing down the Paris portal. There was nothing known yet, except there had apparently been what was being called an "emergency repressurization." While Christophe began pondering the potential implications, the freight cars of a second train entered the station and inched past his window. This train was loaded with specially designed containers backing down the track toward a jumbo jet on the airport tarmac. The track fed directly to the awaiting jet with its huge forward cargo bay doors open wide. Once the train came to a stop, a conveyor was deployed to the end car and the containers were slid into the belly of the jet almost effortlessly. It was a nice piece of engineering that Christophe had promoted in his days as an engineer with Ashleigh Systems.

The containers held capsules on their way back to Newfoundland. Each container held forty-eight capsules, and each purpose-built jet could hold twenty containers. There was a similar terminal at the Goose Bay airport in Newfoundland for offloading. In all the years Christophe had made the North Atlantic portal crossing, this was the first time he had been to the surface at Belmullet since construction of the portal was completed, so it was the first time he had actually observed the capsule transfer in action. Seeing the fruits of his labor gave him a great deal of pride.

Christophe's train was an hour late departing from Belmullet, so by the time it actually pulled out of the station, he was able to begin piecing together some details of the Paris portal incident. Apparently one of the vacuum control solenoid valves had failed, causing the entire evacuated tunnel to repressurize to one atmosphere. The tunnel had to be maintained at a vacuum pressure of less than ten millibars in order to function properly. This was equivalent to the pressure at about eighty thousand meters above the earth. Many fail-safe systems existed for maintaining the low system pressure, so emergency repressurization was a last resort. Christophe knew all about it because he had been part of the design team for the system from the very beginning and had personally had a hand in developing the emergency repressurization protocols.

A portal tunnel was typically filled with capsules going at very high speeds. The capsules resembled large gelatin vitamin pills. They were seventy-five centimeters in diameter and two meters long, spaced about one thousand meters apart. In high vacuum, the capsules were levitated electromagnetically inside the tunnel and moved along with virtually no friction or aerodynamic drag. One could easily imagine the carnage that would ensue if capsules were ever to collide. A critical fail-safe mechanism was employed to ensure that capsules never got too close to one another. The spacing between capsules was maintained dynamically by small adjustments to the vacuum pressure between them. A little more pressure aft caused the capsule to speed up a little and the following capsule to slow down. The adjustments were minute—on the order of millimeters per second—but at one thousand meters per second, just a few millimeters per second amounted to meters in distance of separation between capsules. It was the function of the vacuum control solenoid valves, spaced every ten meters or so apart along the tunnel, to make these fine adjustments. Master control solenoid valves were also placed every one thousand meters to make coarser pressure corrections. These are what made the faint click-clacking sound that one heard when traveling down the tunnel, and it was one of these that had apparently failed in the Paris portal. Since all the control systems were multiple-redundant, Christophe had difficulty believing these initial reports.

In the fifty milliseconds required to sense that any two capsules were closing in at an unsafe rate, teraflops of computations needed to be carried out to readjust the spacing of each capsule in the entire tunnel. In a one-thousand-kilometer portal, there could be as many as one thousand capsules at any time, and each one needed a minute pressure adjustment fore and aft. In the event of a system-wide malfunction, much more dramatic action was necessary.

Just like in a spacecraft, each capsule was pressurized, with breathing air delivered from a pressure tank under the seat. An onboard scrubber removed exhaled carbon dioxide and replaced it with air to maintain a constant oxygen pressure. The amount of air a capsule needed on board was determined by the trip duration with a reasonable safety margin. In the event of an emergency repressurization, the air in the tanks of all the capsules was released quickly and simultaneously into the space in front of and behind each capsule. At the same time an air bag was deployed in the capsule, because the net effect was about 30 g's of deceleration. This was not a pleasant experience for the passenger, but it beat the alternatives. Christophe had firsthand knowledge of this because he had occasionally been called upon to be a "crash test dummy" during field trials at the test track.

The portals from Belmullet to Paris, Frankfurt, and Rotterdam were all constructed at about the same time. This was well before the North Atlantic portal became operational and when the Belmullet airport was still a lively hub for transatlantic commercial passenger flights.

These three portals were based on an older technology. When the subterranean tunnels were bored, the maximum portal speed was only 520 meters per second, or one and a half times the speed of sound. This permitted more curvature than could otherwise be tolerated on longer, higher-speed portals. The Rotterdam portal was the shortest of the three at 973 kilometers. Paris was 1,042 kilometers, and Frankfurt was considerably longer at 1,351 kilometers.

At the portal station in Goose Bay, when a passenger entered a capsule in the loading bay, a safety check was completed to be sure the air pressure on the inside was nominal at one atmosphere and that there was an airtight seal to the outside. A small amount of helium was added to the capsule air so that mass spectrometers could detect any leaks. It was critical that no capsule leaked, as this would be catastrophic and bring down the whole system. Then ballast was added in order to ensure that each capsule weighed exactly 250 kilograms. This typically took about five minutes. Also, during this time, the passenger's heart rate and blood pressure were monitored to be sure that he or she could actually handle the stress of the trip. Just like with an amusement park ride, there would be no opportunity for a change of mind once the capsule was launched. Upon clearance for launch, the capsule passed through an air lock into a giant turntable facing outward. This process typically took about two minutes.

There were no windows, so the only "view" for the passenger was provided on his augmented reality visor. The purpose of the AR image was to trick the passenger's mind into thinking the trip was shorter and much slower, using familiar settings of passing scenery as if viewed from a train window. The maximum carrying capacity of the thirty-four-hundred-kilometer North Atlantic portal was four hundred passengers per hour, but more often the number was less, depending on the time of year or time of day. At maximum capacity, it was necessary to launch about six capsules per minute, so there had to be a dozen or so positions in the turntable in order to stage capsules for launch at ten-second intervals.

Once launched, a capsule was gently accelerated at about the force of gravity—1 g, or 10 meters per second squared—to the terminal velocity. Actually, the acceleration was not constant but started more slowly at first for passenger comfort. Otherwise, it would feel a bit like being shot out of a cannon. At the other end of the trip a similar deceleration profile was required. From elementary Newtonian physics, the time that it took to reach terminal velocity from rest was determined by acceleration, a, times time, t. It would take the capsule about 100 seconds to reach the terminal velocity of 1,000 m/s and the capsule would have traveled $x = \frac{1}{2} at^2$, or about 50 km in that time. On the North Atlantic portal from Goose Bay to Belmullet, this meant that most of the journey—more than 3,300 km—was accomplished at 1,000 m/s, or 3,600 km/hr. By comparison, the trip from Belmullet to Paris Gare du Nord would have taken 34 minutes at 520 m/s (1,870 km/hr), not including loading and unloading time. The original three European portals were a huge leap forward for fast and convenient travel, not to mention the much lower cost and greater safety ushered in by the advent of portal travel.

It was 7:25 a.m. as the sun was just breaking the horizon in the east, but Christophe's body clock was telling him it was bedtime. He bought double espressos at the snack bar on the train and fought the urge to sleep while he plunged into the incident reports that were starting to overwhelm his phone. It was an unusually clear fall day, and the passing Irish countryside was pristine. One of the unintended costs of portal travel was the loss of much of the direct contact with living things in nature. It required a new type of self-discipline to take some time to slow down once in a while. Christophe liked to take long walks, but this was becoming more difficult because of his deteriorating arthritic knees. Since retirement the year before, he was less and less enamored with portal transport. It was time for him to begin slowing down generally and start taking life at a slower pace. His final destination was Beaulieu-sur-Mer on the Côte d'Azur, France, where he had an apartment from which he could watch the sun rise every morning from a spacious deck and spend time on the Mediterranean in his sailboat.

From the Paris incident reports, it seemed that the emergency repressurization had gone as well as could be expected. Thankfully, there had been only a single fatality—a man had died of a heart attack while waiting to be rescued from the tunnel. Anytime there is a recompression in this type of portal, several hundred stranded capsules must be extracted manually. This basically entails sucking them out at both ends using enormous vacuum pumps. Not including the size of the capsules, the volume of 1,000 kilometers of a one-meter-diameter tunnel is almost 750,000 cubic meters. It would take two or three hours to suck all the capsules to safety. Even though the occupants were in constant video contact with the base station for reassurance, this obviously was a harrowing experience for those unfortunate souls stranded in the middle. The same procedure might require days for transoceanic portals—a procedure that fortunately, and to Christophe's credit, had never had to be carried out.

From the start, something about the reports did not add up. The vacuum control solenoid valves were ridiculously reliable. They were ultrafast-acting solid-state digital valves from Sturgeon Industries capable of opening and closing trillions of times. There had never been a reported failure. Christophe had personally certified them for use in the system. Also, two solenoids always operated in tandem so that both valves would have to malfunction simultaneously to cause the kind of fault being reported. The odds against this were astronomical.

By the time his train pulled into Dublin station, the tunnel evacuation in Paris was nearly completed, and work crews were already starting to enter the tunnel to investigate the problem. Fortunately, the faulty valve was only thirty kilometers from the Paris end, and repairs would proceed quickly. Even then, it would take a week to pump the tunnel back down to a pressure of ten millibars and recertify the portal for operation.

Christophe looked up from his reading from time to time to reflect with some remorse on a much slower world rolling by his window. Trains on the surface of the earth were disappearing rapidly, and for better or for worse, a golden age of travel by rail that had lasted more than two hundred years was slipping away forever. His unplanned train ride to Dublin turned out to be much more therapeutic than he had expected.

CHAPTER 3

LE CENTRE DES PORTALS DE PARIS

There was no direct portal from Dublin to Paris. It was necessary to take a train to London first to make a connection. It was a modern high-speed bullet train capable of a top speed of 360 kilometers per hour. It departed a few minutes after Christophe's train from Belmullet arrived, and then it headed south, where it crossed under the Irish Sea to Wales through a 70-kilometer-long tunnel. This was still the world's longest railroad tunnel in 2076, and was likely to hold that record in perpetuity since long railroad tunnels had been obsoleted by the portal technology. The 580-kilometer trip would take a little more than an hour and a half—astonishing, considering that he had traversed the entire North Atlantic in just

58 minutes. Even modern fast trains were no match for portals. Another inconvenience was that the train from Dublin arrived at the Paddington station, while the London–Paris portal departed from the Saint Pancras station, which required taking a subway. Christophe did not know London well, so what should have been an easy connection ended up taking him an hour. By the time he got to the Saint Pancras portal, he realized that he had not had anything to eat since the pub in Belmullet. It was still the middle of the night according to his biological clock, but he didn't want to wait until Paris to eat. He booked his capsule at the ticket office, where they were expecting him. His capsule would depart at 2:05 p.m. He would be in Paris by three and hopefully to Nice by six. He had a few minutes to grab a bite to eat.

Christophe finally arrived in Paris at half past three. He decided not to continue on to Nice, where he would end up arriving after dark. Rather, he thought he would just spend a quiet evening in Paris. It was Friday, and there was no particular reason to press on to his apartment in Beaulieu-sur-Mer. Anyway, he would be waking up about this time in LA, and with the cumulative effect of multiple espressos, he no longer felt like he had lost an entire night of sleep—that would come tomorrow or the next day. He thought he would pop into the administrative center for the Paris portal to see if the defective vacuum control valve had been delivered to the evaluation lab yet. The facility was next to the arrivals and departures portals at Gare du Nord. He knew it well and had been there many times. He was hoping that his friend François had not gone home from work early. Presumably, there would be a bustle of activity because of the portal shutdown. Christophe retrieved his security badge from his briefcase and slipped the lanyard around his neck as he walked through the door marked Le Centre des Portals de Paris.

He greeted the receptionist. He knew almost everyone at the center, but she was someone he did not recognize. He held his badge up to the scanner and waited for the door to swing open. Instead, there was a red light and beep. He tried it again and got the same result. He went up to the receptionist, who had been watching him intently. "Madame, the scanner does not seem to be working. Can you let me in?"

He handed his badge to her over the counter, and she scanned it into her computer. "Monsieur, ce n'est pas valide. Votre code était terminé." She searched his record again more carefully. "Ah, voilà! Je vois que vous etês à la retraite."

"I know I am retired, but I am still a member of the Portal Safety Board. My badge should still work."

"Désolé. Vous ne pouvez pas entrer." She sported a disarming official smile that told him he was not going to get any sympathy or further help from her.

Christophe was already edgy from lack of sleep and too much caffeine, so his demeanor was not exactly courteous. "*Désolé!* I have come here dozens of times, and you are obviously new. Please call your supervisor!"

She made a few keystrokes on her computer and said, "Can I offer you a cup of coffee?" Her English was just fine. She had just been toying him.

"No. I will just wait over there," he answered, pointing in the general direction of the small waiting area. His frustration was forced to give way to resignation. After a few minutes, another woman came out into the lobby. Christophe recognized her immediately. "Bonjour, Bernice. Comment ça va?"

"Monsieur Conally. What an unexpected surprise! How can I help you?"

Christophe was more than a little put out that she addressed him formally by his last name. "Apparently, my badge has been deactivated. I was hoping to take a look at the defective control valve removed from the portal this morning."

"Oh, but that would not be possible. The valve is probably on its way to the failure analysis lab in Toulouse by now."

"I need to see it before anyone takes it apart."

Bernice paused for a moment. "Anyway, even if the valve were still here, I cannot let you enter without proper clearance."

"Okay. I understand. Will you please do me a favor and see if the valve is still here? In the meantime, I will call the head office of the Portal Safety Commission in Los Angeles to find out what happened to my clearance." Bernice disappeared from the lobby, and Christophe placed his call to Los Angeles on his mobile phone. By 2076 the entire world was on a single wideband communications network. There was no longer such a thing as a "long-distance call."

"Hello, this is Dr. Christophe Conally. I need to speak with Director Simms. It is rather urgent."

"Hi, Christophe. This is Bridget. How was your trip?"

"Hi, Bridget. Not great. I got redirected from Belmullet thanks to the Paris portal closure. I only arrived in Paris thirty minutes ago. Say, I am at the Paris Portal Center. I was hoping to take a look at the faulty valve, but my security clearance has apparently expired. What do you know about this?"

"Christophe, I know the reinstatement request is sitting on Fred's desk, but he is not in the office, and I don't know when to expect him."

"Can someone else authorize it? This is really urgent."

"Oh, no. Director Simms is the only one who can do that."

"Okay. Have him call me the minute he walks in the door." Christophe knew this was futile. When Fred Simms wasn't in the office by nine o'clock on Friday morning, this usually meant he was taking a long weekend at his cabin in Big Bear. Christophe terminated the call and drafted an email to Fred. He knew that the director would at least be monitoring his messages.

Bernice returned to the lobby. "Good news. The valve is still here."

"Can I have a look at it then?"

Bernice was silent for a moment while she weighed the options. Something Christophe had never gotten accustomed to was the way the level of bureaucracy always seemed to grow disproportionately with technological progress. The more advanced things were, the more massive and convoluted the associated bureaucracy became. There was a subtle difference between American and French bureaucrats, however. In the former United States, generally no one was willing to stick out their neck to bend the rules. Bureaucracy was totally rigid. Without the director's authorization signature, there was no hope of having the necessary clearance in time to see the valve before it shipped off to the failure analysis lab for disassembly. In France, however, it was different. There was a greater feeling of empowerment among upper-level bureaucrats, who were therefore willing to take personal risks that might get them in trouble.

"Okay, Christophe. I will sign you in as my guest, but I will need to escort you at all times." Bernice was the group manager for the technical staff at the center, so she was sympathetic to his appeal and bent the rule this time on his behalf. She scanned her badge, and the door swung open. "Let's go. François is waiting."

They proceeded down a long corridor with laboratories and offices on both sides. Most of the labs were dark. Fifteen years ago, when the portals were first coming into use, these laboratories were bustling. The center was responsible for conformance testing of subcomponents, but these days there was not much need since these functions had been handed over to the system operators.

At last Christophe and Bernice reached a well-lighted lab and entered. François was waiting for them. He greeted his old friend with a customary kiss on both cheeks. They had communicated regularly by email but had not met face-to-face for a couple of years. François had been one of the principal software engineers for the portal system. By now, everything had become pretty routine—perhaps too routine—but there wasn't much demand on his time anymore, so he was just passing time for another year, after which he would be eligible to retire.

After a few pleasantries, Christophe inquired, "Where is the VCVA?" referring to the vacuum control valve assembly. François pointed to a neatly packed and sealed shipping container on a cart. It was covered with Extremely Urgent labels and a shipping slip.

"I was just about ready to take it to shipping when Bernice called. What's up?"

"I have been giving some thought to the story that this valve assembly malfunctioned. I'm not sure I believe it."

"But all the system diagnostics said it did. It got stuck in the open position. I have been studying the printouts myself most of the day."

Christophe glanced at Bernice. She seemed to be interested in hearing more. "You know these valves have cycled billions of times without a single failure, and suddenly you are trying to tell me we have a defective one? It just doesn't make any sense."

"That's exactly why we are shipping it off to the failure analysis lab in Toulouse. Once they get it apart, they will be able to determine what went wrong."

"But François, what if the valve is not defective? Once they disassemble it, we will never know if it is actually still functioning properly." There was a long silence. It was nearly quitting time, and Friday as well. Christophe could sense that François was eager to get home for the

35

weekend. He knew this involved breaking the seals on the shipping container that signified that the contents had not been tampered with while en route. It also meant that the tests would keep everyone in the lab working until at least midnight.

François stared at his old friend. "Christophe, I have plans for tonight." Then after a long sigh, he looked over at Bernice. "What do you think?"

"Christophe has a point, and this is not a difficult test to run." Bernice glanced at her wristwatch. "I will authorize it if you will stay over. But the valve must ship to Toulouse no later than tomorrow morning."

François said, "But what about the packaging seals?"

"I will take care of the paperwork. The people in Toulouse need to be informed that additional handling of the valve took place after it was removed from the portal. I will write this up in a discrepancy report. Anyway, it is too late in the day to ask for permission." Bernice flashed him a smile. "On Monday, we may both get our chance to retire early." She headed for the door and then turned around. "François, don't let Christophe out of your sight. I signed him in illegally. And don't let him touch anything!" Then she departed.

The environmental test unit (ETU) was in an adjacent lab. François fumbled for the light switch. He needed to plug the unit into the wall and turn on the power since it had not been operated for a couple of years. The unit came to life and went through a series of self-diagnostics. "It still seems to be working," François said to no one. "It will take about fifteen minutes to pump down." Christophe already knew this, as he was very familiar with this particular piece of equipment; it had played a key role in the development of portal technology. They wheeled the cart into the test room and began breaking the seals on the shipping container. The vacuum control valve assembly was neatly fitted into a foam pocket in a case inside the shipping container. The entire unit was only about fifteen centimeters long and about eight centimeters in diameter. It had a label on the outside that said, "Ashleigh Systems, Toulouse, France," followed by a lot of serial numbers.

François put on a pair of latex gloves and carefully removed the unit from the case. The ETU had a vacuum-tight load-lock door in the front, which he had vented moments before. He placed the VCVA into the test fixture, making electrical connections and hooking up the vacuum lines. He closed the load-lock door and depressed the button for pump-down. They heard the purr of the mechanical pump as it came on, and after a minute or so, the turbo-molecular pump switched on.

"Okay. Here's what I propose," Christophe said. "Program the cycle to go back and forth between ten and fifteen millibars. This should simulate a pretty realistic operating condition." François was not paying attention as he was intently watching the vacuum gauge.

"That's not good." He paused. "That's not good at all." François pressed a few more buttons and then went behind the test unit to check the plumbing connections. "It's not pumping down. I was worried that the vacuum seals may have dried out over time."

"What do you recommend?" asked Christophe.

"Other than to take the whole system apart and reapply vacuum grease to every joint?" François's sarcasm was oozing out now. Both men stared at each other in disappointment. Christophe was thinking that this was no way to spend the night.

Finally, Christophe broke the silence. "This happened to me once before. I did something totally unauthorized. Do you want to hear it?" The other scientist was skeptical. "I will tell you anyway. I pumped down the system with some low-molecular-weight silicone oil to coat all the surfaces. It worked like a charm."

"That's crazy," said François. "It would destroy the vacuum gauge and nullify the calibration."

"True," said Christophe, "but we don't care about the absolute vacuum. All we need is the five-millibar differential. Okay, so you destroy the gauge. You can install a new one next week if you want. You probably have a stockroom full of them. These instruments don't see much use anyway."

Finally, François opined, "Oh, I just hate this kind of rogue activity, but okay. I guess inaccurate results are better than no results." He shut off the unit and repressurized the load lock. Silicone oil was commonly used to lubricate moving parts in vacuum solenoids. There was a bottle in a cabinet in the next lab, which he fetched. He poured a few drops into a crucible and placed it in the load lock next to the VCVA. After repeating the pumpdown procedure, he watched the vacuum gauge inch downward toward 1 millibar, and then on to the target of

0.01 millibar, where system calibration could begin. The idea was working perfectly. After a series of green lights turned on, the system was ready to begin going through the test sequence.

"You said cycle between ten and fifteen millibars?" Francois began typing in the test parameters on the console computer. "What duty cycle?"

"How about twenty-nine seconds off and one second on. Don't forget to hook up the helium." A small amount of helium was added on the downstream side of the valve. When the valve opened, the amount of helium that passed during the one-second on cycle was determined by using a quantitative mass spectrometer. It was an ingenious piece of engineering, without which it would never have been possible to construct the portals. The data output from the mass spectrometer could be read in much the same way as an EKG, and it gave fine details of dynamic valve performance.

The computer began acquiring reams of data during the first few cycles. From what they could tell, the defective VCVA was operating just fine. Christophe proposed that two hundred cycles should be sufficient. At two cycles per minute, the run would take under two hours.

At this point, Bernice reentered the lab. "How are things going, gentlemen?" She could tell that the system was operating and logging data by the characteristic *click-clack* of the valve when it opened and closed again. "Can I gather that, perhaps, the defective valve may be working after all?"

"It will be really hard to tell until we analyze the computer printouts, but so far, so good," Christophe said. It didn't occur to him to mention the use of silicone oil to get the system to pump down. "It needs to run for about two hours, so François and I were thinking of stepping out to grab a bite to eat for dinner. Do you care to join us?"

"No thanks. I have done about as much as I can do tonight. I decided to wait for your initial findings before I complete my report. I am going home now. Forward the analysis to me tonight, and get the VCVA repackaged for shipment. I will come back in the morning to finish the paperwork and arrange for the courier."

It was seven o'clock by the time François and Christophe left the lab. The ETU had completed thirty cycles, and everything seemed to be working nominally. There was a night watchman manning the reception desk. François informed him that they would be returning in an hour or so but didn't mention that Christophe's security badge was invalid. Since they would be returning to the lab together, they could both get in by swiping just his badge.

There was a café around the corner from Gare du Nord that they had frequented during the earlier days when demands of work and tight schedules often kept everyone late at the lab. Christophe and François found their favorite table and began catching up. François was younger by six years, but this was not obvious from his appearance. He smoked heavily, was considerably overweight, and had not been exercising. His doctor told him he was heading for a health crisis if he didn't amend his habits, but he had decided that if he could just manage one more year at work, he could retire—and then he would turn over a new leaf. He called his wife to let her know it would be a late night, the news of which was not well received at home. François was typical of a man for whom his identity was not separable from his work. He had no real life of his own. Several times Christophe had invited him to the South of France for a vacation, but the plans always seemed to break down for one reason or another. François said his wife hated traveling and would not let him go anywhere without her. Christophe had never met her, but he imagined her to be rather simple and domineering. François's life seemed to be a very sad and colorless existence.

Christophe ordered a bottle of red wine while François logged in remotely to the ETU to check on the progress. "Ninety-two cycles, and everything is progressing nicely. We should have a complete data set by the time we get back." They ordered pizzas. This was always a safe bet in Paris. Nobody in Paris knew how to make a bad pizza. The meal consisted of small talk. The two men liked each other well enough but were never able to penetrate beyond the surface. After more than ten years, they still knew relatively little about one another, and a deeper understanding would not come out of this impromptu dinner.

Christophe fell into an extended silence as he ate his pizza. The very long and strenuous day had finally caught up with him. His friend seemed equally lost in his thoughts. After finishing his meal and paying the bill, he suggested that they get back to the lab. The walk back was quiet. Christophe noted that it was about nine thirty as they entered the building. There was no issue about reaccess to the facility because the security guard was barely awake. The ETU had finished its task, and the data were waiting patiently on the hard drive. François gave the test data file the name *Defective_paris_vcva_sn7345689* and sent it to another computer for data analysis. The program could resolve events in the time domain down to about one millisecond. The vacuum control valve could switch state in about thirty milliseconds, so there were about thirty data points to check for each activation cycle. If necessary, further data processing could be carried out to reveal finer details. This would not be warranted tonight, however.

Each valve actuation was shown to be completely normal. In two hundred cycles, they saw nothing out of the ordinary that would suggest that the VCVA was defective. This came as no surprise to Christophe, but this was not at all the result François was expecting. He had accepted the initial finding of a defective valve assembly. François also created a second copy of the test data file, which he named just "Conally," and sent it to his computer at home.

"Is that legal?" asked Christophe. François just grinned without saying a word.

In software, it was possible to overlay each of the two hundred switching events in time sequence and put the data into a standard form for Bernice's analysis report, which they forwarded to her along with their assessment. After packing up the VCVA and reapplying the security seals, François turned off the ETU and the lights to all his labs, and the two men walked out of the center into the main concourse of Gare du Nord at just after eleven at night. François had to catch the Réseau Express Régional (RER) to his home in the southern suburbs, which would take him an hour or so, and Christophe hoped to find a room at a hotel nearby.

CHAPTER 4

THE GLITCH

Christophe probably would have slept all day had he not forgotten to silence his phone when he'd gone to bed. A series of annoying urgent alerts finally woke him from a deep sleep at nine in the morning. He was still groggy from the sleeping pills he had taken. He checked the time and saw a long list of voice mails. "Hello, this is Fred. Please call as soon as you can"; "Christophe, this is Fred Simms. You need to call me immediately"; "This is Fred again. Call me immediately at 710-32 ..." It was after midnight in Los Angeles, so he couldn't imagine why this couldn't wait until morning. Recognizing the number as Fred's personal number, he dialed it.

"Simms here!" The voice was gruff.

"Fred, this is Christophe. What are you doing up at this hour?"

"I have had my ear chewed off for the past three hours by the director of portal safety at Ashleigh. He is fuming mad. Apparently, you diverted the defective valve from the Paris portal to run an unauthorized environmental performance evaluation? I would have denied it if I didn't know you so well. This is just the kind of rogue stunt you are capable of."

This was not the way Christophe had expected his Saturday in Paris to start out. "Fred, there was no harm done. I just wanted to see the diagnostics before the valve got disassembled."

"What you have done, Christophe, is to have placed the safety of the global portal system in doubt."

"What do you mean? I don't think the valve was even defective."

"Everyone was satisfied that there was an assignable cause for the emergency repressurization in the Paris portal, which would be confirmed in Toulouse by Ashleigh by the time the tunnel would be pumped back down later in the week and recertified for operation. Now, the Paris portal is on indefinite shutdown. This is a disaster!"

"But they would have reached the same conclusion in Toulouse. There is nothing wrong with the valve, Fred."

"It doesn't matter anymore whether or not the valve is defective. They can't reopen the portal until they can positively confirm that the problem is fixed." There was a long pause. Christophe had no immediate response while his brain tried to deal with the reality of the situation. Finally, Fred said, "If not the valve, then what?" Fred asked the question sarcastically in such a way that it was obvious that he had no serious interest in the answer.

"I am inclined to think there is a software glitch."

After an expletive, Fred exhaled deeply. "Christophe, that is madness! That is highly speculative, and you must not tell this to anyone—especially anyone at the Paris Center. Any rumor of a software problem could shut down the portals worldwide." After another long silence, he added, "Don't do anything more. Don't go to the Paris Center. Don't talk to anyone! Don't send any messages! The valve has already arrived in Toulouse, and the test engineers have been requested to come in today to begin the evaluation. In deference to you, I did request that they rerun the environmental performance test to confirm or—hopefully—contradict your assessment."

"Okay. I promise to lie low until I hear back from you."

"Christophe, I need to be sure you understand the gravity of the situation. This is an extremely sensitive matter that must be kept under wraps. Be prepared to go to Toulouse next week. I anticipate there will be an emergency meeting. I will be there as well, if I can. I will get back to you tomorrow. I need to get some sleep now." He hung up abruptly without saying goodbye.

Christophe slipped into the shower for a long, hot soak while he contemplated what he was going to do next. He had planned to go to his apartment in Beaulieu. This time of year, it was quiet and neither too hot nor too cold. But if he was going to be on call to go to Toulouse, there was no particularly convenient way to get there from the southeastern corner of France. And he didn't really want to just hang out in Paris. He decided instead to visit his sister in Bordeaux. Bordeaux was easy to get to from Paris, and Toulouse was just an hour further by train. He was still pretty rattled from his call with Fred Simms. When Fred had requested that he continue serving on the Portal Safety Board, he had agreed, but what he was experiencing did not seem much like the retirement he had in mind. A trip to Bordeaux would provide a nice opportunity to visit his sister and her husband. He checked out of his room and took the Métro to Gare Montparnasse, where he caught the next TGV to Bordeaux. It was gray and overcast in Paris, and he was glad to be leaving the city. The grayness had also permeated his soul, and he hoped to leave that behind as well.

The train wandered slowly through the switchyard and the southern Paris suburbs on its way to the high-speed track headed south. Christophe retrieved his phone from his backpack and dialed his sister.

"Allô?"

"Sandra. It's Christophe."

"Ah, Christophe. Quelle bonne surprise!"

"I am on the TGV from Paris heading your way. As soon as I check into a hotel, do you mind if I come by to say hi?"

"Hotel? That's ridiculous. Stay with us. What time do you arrive?"

"It looks like I should be there just before noon."

"*Parfait*! Today is Julien's sixth birthday. We are going to celebrate it at the fair at La Place des Quinconces.

Everyone will be thrilled to see you. Call me when you arrive, and I will meet you at the station."

"Wonderful. This sounds great, but let me just take the tram."

"It's no trouble, really," said Sandra, "but are you sure?"

"Absolutely! Just save me some food. I will call you if I can't find you at the park." Christophe knew Bordeaux well. His mother had been born there, and he visited her parents often as a child. He spent a semester during high school with his grandparents before they died. He should have picked up a lot more French than he had, but the French kids only wanted to practice their English on him.

He had given a lot of thought to buying an apartment in Bordeaux rather than in Beaulieu, but he loved the Mediterranean, and his passion was sailing. He kept his nine-meter sailboat in the marina in Beaulieu, and the muddy Garonne river in Bordeaux was just no substitute. He had learned to sail on it during summer vacations at his grandparents' house. Sandra's husband, Frederick, had lived next door and was just the same age as Christophe. One spring, the two boys took sailing lessons together. They flipped over their sailboat in the swift river water, and besides the cold, the boys discovered that the taste of the river water was something they wanted to forget. Thereafter, they were more careful when coming about in the rapids.

The Paris–Bordeaux TGV was not actually a train. The true meaning of the TGV acronym was long lost. The "train" was actually a railless maglev that looked pretty much like the older TGV trains except without wheels. It had no locomotive. The fore and aft cars, with carefully sculpted aerodynamic curvature, carried passengers rather than engines. The train followed a shallow U-shaped channel that provided the levitation and propulsion. Since Roman times, the route between Paris and Bordeaux had been a showcase for the most advanced travel technology. The maglev was no exception. It screamed along the French countryside at a top speed of just under five hundred kilometers per hour—a bit less than half the speed of sound. This represented the practical limit of travel speed in the earth's atmosphere. Higher speeds than this either required flight at high altitude or travel in evacuated tunnels near the surface of the earth. At only four hundred kilometers, the distance between Paris and Bordeaux made it attractive for developing and demonstrating high-speed surface trains. When portal travel became feasible, the distance was really too short, so the route continued to be used to prove out the most recent advances in train technology. There had been discussion of constructing an aboveground portal on the route for a long time, but in the end, the priority was low. The maglev was more than adequate. Christophe's journey would take a mere forty-five minutes, with the added advantage of being able to watch the world go by—albeit rather quickly—out of his window. This is something portal travel would never offer except vicariously with the aid of a virtual reality visor.

By this time most of the longer intercity routes around the world had converted to portal transport. Interestingly, this was not so much a matter of speed as it was of being able to procure a surface right-of-way straight enough for ultra-high-speed travel. At five hundred kilometers per hour, the tolerable centripetal g-forces placed a constraint on the minimum radius of curvature of the tracks. Urban congestion made it increasingly difficult to find routes for tracks. Just as with subways, the obvious solution was to go underground, and with the widespread deployment of fast tunnel-boring machines, long straight tunnels ushered in the possibility of also pumping down the tunnels to low pressure in order to reduce aerodynamic drag. Subterranean portal travel posed only a modest safety risk. Generally, escape shafts were located every ten kilometers or so; in an emergency, the tunnel could be cleared of passengers quickly.

Long subterranean trains began to proliferate during the 2030s. They were able to increase top speed by partial reduction of the air pressure in the tunnels. The practical limit was about 0.4 atmosphere. As the pressure in the tunnels became lower, the passenger cars needed to be pressurized in order for people to be able to breathe comfortably, and the railcars started looking more and more like the cabin of a passenger jet. Solid rails were gradually replaced by magnetic levitation and the speed steadily increased, approaching that of subsonic jet aircraft on some of the longer routes. It was widely believed that this was the future of transport. The tunnels were typically bored to a standard diameter of 7.6 meters. Although no satisfactory way had yet been perfected for intercontinental travel requiring crossing deep oceans, the technology became the standard for transcontinental travel almost universally by 2060.

In addition to relieving much of the congestion in the skies due to proliferation of aircraft during the first quarter of the twenty-first century, portal travel eliminated the need for jet fuel. Jet fuel had been predominantly made from petroleum since the beginning of the aviation age, and there was no suitable replacement. But by 2020, natural supplies of petroleum were beginning to be depleted and were replaced by synthetic jet fuel, derived from natural gas. Synthetic jet fuel was superior in almost every regard, except that it was prohibitively expensive, costing five times more than jet fuel derived from petroleum during the days of cheap oil. The result was that jet travel for ordinary people reached its zenith in about 2025, ultimately being supplanted by travel in high-speed subterranean trains. Tunnel-boring machines were autonomous and highly effective, so 7.6-meter tunnels were being constructed all over the world at a brisk pace. This trend continued until the disaster in the London–Paris Eurotunnel.

The Eurostar train had been steadily improved since the Chunnel became operational in 1994. It was the logical route to test out new technologies, and it was the first rail line to be converted to maglev and operated at low pressure. The tunnel pressure was kept at about one-tenth of an atmosphere—about the pressure at an elevation of sixteen thousand meters above the earth. The train reached a top speed of one thousand kilometers per hour, making the trip from London to Paris about twenty-five minutes—much faster, and certainly safer and more convenient, than the same trip by commercial jet. Each car could hold up to one hundred passengers in twenty-five rows of four seats, with a central aisle resembling that of a commuter jet. Because of the maglev technology, there was no need for a locomotive. Each car was propelled along by linear motors. The individual cars moved through the tunnel at ten-minute intervals, and there were two tunnels, so at any given time there were as many as six cars in the tunnel going back and forth between Paris and London. By 2033, this was the most heavily traveled route in the world and served to join the two capitals together in a remarkable way. The world was becoming smaller and smaller. Peace and prosperity were steadily increasing. Security procedures seemed to be effective, and people traveled around the world inexpensively and without fear or concern for their safety.

The jihad of the early years of the twenty-first century had largely been eradicated—or so it was supposed. In fact, jihad only went underground. Like a dormant virus, it surfaced in 2033. That is when the Eurostar was blown up. It had become routine to intersperse cargo and passenger cars on the line. The cargo-loading terminal on the London side had been infiltrated by a sleeper cell of disenfranchised radical jihadists. Mostly young men with relatives who either had been killed or had gone to prison after the collapse of the caliphate, they were bent on revenge. They managed to sneak a tactical nuclear warhead into a shipping container and send it into the tunnel as ordinary freight. It detonated under the English Channel with a yield estimated at twelve to fifteen kilotons of TNT. A passenger car in the adjacent tunnel was obliterated, and four other cars in both tunnels were extensively damaged with very few survivors. The blast shattered the tunnel casement, and seawater began flooding in. A few stunned passengers miraculously managed to find their way out of the tunnel on foot, but all in all, 437 people were killed. It was by far the worst train disaster of all time.

The Eurotunnel was completely flooded in a matter of hours and remained so for many years. Every attempt to pump it out failed before the tunnel was finally abandoned for good. Some wanted to permanently seal it as a memorial to those who had died. Others were proposing that new tunnels needed to be bored. This latter idea proved controversial. The Eurotunnel blast had exposed a critical flaw in the whole idea of how people traveled by train in tunnels. Freight, of course, was banned entirely, and much tighter security procedures were implemented, but every traveler had a growing sense of vulnerability traveling in a cabin with ninety-nine other, suspicious persons with piles of carry-on luggage. It seemed that travel would never feel safe again.

A few years earlier, a group of researchers in Canada were demonstrating the feasibility of transporting a single passenger in a small capsule at a very high speed in what came to be known as portals. It was proposed that a Paris–London portal be laid on the seabed of the English Channel as a demonstration project, essentially right above the abandoned Chunnel. Because the seafloor between

France and England is relatively flat and not too deep, the project rapidly gained momentum. Christophe, who was just finishing his graduate studies in engineering physics at UCLA at the time, had responded to an advertisement for engineers for the project. He had applied and was offered a job with the Paris-based company that was awarded the contract. After spending six months in Montreal with the company that had been developing the system prototype, he moved to Calais, where he was thrust into the role of the senior project manager for portal design with eighty engineers reporting directly to him. He had had no prior work experience beyond delivering pizzas by bicycle, but he had quickly made a positive impression on the senior management. Most importantly, he was able to grasp the intricacies of the challenges of things that had never been attempted before. This was good because practically no aspect of the proposed English Channel portal had ever been attempted before. Everything had to be developed from scratch. Christophe was responsible for constructing the systems and strategies for the fleet of undersea autonomous and semiautonomous robots required to assemble the portal segments on the seafloor. The project, the first of its kind, took a total of six years to complete. The first test runs began in 2041, and full commercial certification was achieved in the following year. The London–Paris portal, consisting of the sections above ground, below ground, and under the sea, was an overwhelming success, profoundly altering the complexion of intercity travel forever.

As a result of this success with the submarine portal, people started thinking seriously about travel by portal between continents for the first time. The idea caught on quickly. The prospect of going one thousand meters per second, or three times the speed of sound, was enticing. The undersea portals, like the North Atlantic portal that Christophe had taken the day before, posed a completely new technical challenge. The distances were such that it was only possible to traverse them at very high speed, which was only feasible using small single-person capsules. At the same time, it was necessary to construct submerged tunnels thousands of meters below the surface. And not the least of the worries was how to evacuate the passengers in the event of an emergency in the middle of the ocean and at considerable depth. This is what actually had kept Christophe awake at night. He would spend the balance of his career tackling these challenges on a grand scale with the construction of the North Atlantic portal.

Christophe's TGV pulled into the Gare Saint-Jean a little ahead of schedule at 11:36. He decided it would be a bad idea to show up at his grand-nephew's sixth birthday party empty-handed, so he chose to walk to the Lego store, which he recalled was more or less on the way to the park.

CHAPTER 5

LA FOIRE AUX PLAISIRS

Christophe retrieved his backpack and briefcase from the overhead rack and realized that he had forgotten about his suitcase, which was being delivered to his apartment in Beaulieu. He paused briefly outside the train to email a message to his apartment manager to keep an eye out for delivery of his suitcase and to be sure his cat had plenty of food and water. He also realized that he had been wearing the same shirt for about twenty-four hours and had not packed a spare. He would need to stop by a store to buy another.

Either he was getting older or the Lego store was farther from the station than he remembered. In any event, by the time he got to where he thought the store should have been, he discovered that it was no longer there, and no one he asked could remember ever seeing it. He did find his favorite men's clothing store, however, so he purchased a sport shirt, but he would have to make up with Julien in some other way for the birthday present.

By the time he had made it to the park at Esplande des Quinconces, he was worn out. The park, which was normally a sprawling vacant lot, was filled twice each year for a few weeks with the traveling carnival La Foire aux Plaisirs. The carnival had come to Bordeaux every year in the spring and fall for almost two hundred years, and Christophe had many fond memories of it from his youth. It was a particularly pleasant Saturday afternoon, and the fair was completely mobbed. Sandra had messaged him to meet at the famous Monument aux Girondins, and there she was, just as she said she would be.

"Christophe! It is so good to see you." They hugged. Sandra was younger by eighteen months, and the two had always been very close.

"Now that I am retired, perhaps I should spend more time here in Bordeaux," said Christophe. "Where's Fredrick? I can't wait to see him."

"Oh, he's off with Julien somewhere. Look, I saved you a sandwich. Knowing you, you probably have not had a bite to eat in hours. We reserved a picnic bench over there." She motioned to it. "Sit and rest your bones. I want you to catch me up on what you have been up to." She knew Christophe better than anyone, and it was she who had brought him the most solace when Monique died. She had a window on his soul. He had barely taken the first bite of his sandwich before she said, "So, what's wrong?" Christophe was silent and only grunted with a mouthful of sandwich. He continued to chew and took another bite without responding. "Christophe, I know you. You have that look when something is wrong."

He took a swig of Orangina and cleared his throat. "I'm okay." Sandra stared at him, unconvinced. Finally, Christophe opened up a little. "You know, Sandra, I always loved my work—probably too much. I guess it was my therapy after I lost Monique. I poured my life into Ashleigh for forty years. I never held back. The whole time that I ran the North Atlantic portal project, I loved every minute. Then it was over. There was nothing more to do, no more pressure, no more challenge. I was going to endless meetings at La Défense headquarters, and then I just started attending remotely from Marina del Rey and Beaulieu. I was increasingly irrelevant. They were nice to me and paid me well. My stock options alone were an indication of a successful career. But they just didn't seem to need me anymore." Christophe took another bite while Sandra's eyes bathed him with tenderness in a way only his little sister could do. "I never thought I would retire. I was sure my experience and wisdom would be valuable. But no. I was just punching a time clock. A couple of years ago, when I first started thinking of retiring, the idea incubated into an obsession. I started counting the days. I started to make plans for turning over my files and training my successor." His voice unexpectedly began to break. He took another swig of Orangina and paused to regain his composure. "You know what? There was not going to be a successor. The world had moved on, and I was a brontosaurus." After another long pause, he said, "Last year at my retirement party, they showered me with accolades and gifts. They showed videos of my North Atlantic portal being built in stages and the ribbon cutting. They showed a video of me popping out of a capsule in Belmullet on a maiden voyage. Champagne was flowing everywhere. Dignitaries from around the world were on hand!" He stopped talking as if that was all there was to say, and he leaned back, taking in the sights and sounds of the fair.

"Christophe, dear. I know there's more. You have weathered stronger storms than this in your life. You are worried about something. I can tell."

Christophe knew full well that Sandra was going to drag it out of him sooner or later. With a sigh he continued. "Well, yesterday I got myself into a bit of a jam. You probably heard about the emergency closure on the Paris portal?" Sandra nodded affirmatively. "I was supposed to take it and be in Beaulieu last night. I had plans to go sailing before winter sets in and enjoy life in Provence. You recall that the company gave me emeritus status and kept me on the Portal Safely Board. I started receiving incident reports when I arrived in Belmullet. During the train ride to London, I developed some grave concerns. It's amazing how much reflection gets done on slow trains. I guess this is how we got modern physics, when Einstein, Planck, and Bohr worked it all out coming from and going to Berlin on trains. Anyway, by the time I got to Paris, it was already too late to go on, so I decided to stop by the portal office at Gare du Nord. There was a piece of hardware that was being blamed for the shutdown. I had a pretty good idea that the faulty valve would still be in Paris. I just wanted to see for myself if the preliminary conclusions of the incident report made sense."

He finished his sandwich and Orangina, getting up to put the wrapper and bottle in the trash bin nearby. When he sat back down, Sandra showed no sign of losing interest in his story. "Anyway, I went to the office and talked them into letting me in. An old and trusted colleague was still there, and I persuaded him to unpack the faulty valve and run it through a series of routine tests. We didn't have authorization, but I assured him it was warranted due to the urgency. As I suspected, the valve worked perfectly. We wrote up the report, and I went to bed. It seemed totally harmless, really harmless. Well, as it turned out, it wasn't so harmless. I whipped up a firestorm the likes of which I have never experienced in my entire career. Now I am in real trouble. That's why I came to Bordeaux. I am expecting to be summoned to Toulouse tomorrow to meet the 'inquisition.'"

Christophe was saved from further inquiry when his brother-in-law, Fredrick, returned with his grandson, Julien, in tow, along with Julien's parents—Laurent and his wife, Audrey. Warm greetings were exchanged by all of them. "This must be the famous Julien," Christophe said. Julien was shy and peeked his head around his father's pant leg at Christophe.

"Say hi to your uncle Christophe," said Audrey. Actually, Christophe was Julien's great-uncle, but no six-year-old would know the difference.

Reluctantly, the boy extended his hand. "Bonjour, monsieur." Julien spoke practically no English.

"The girls took off for one of those death-defying rides," Laurent said, pointing toward a huge ride with rapidly spinning arms with kids either screaming or completely silent, trying not to get sick. "I think you have to be downright certifiable to go on one of those things." The girls were Julien's two older teenage sisters. Laurent was Sandra's and Fredrick's only child and Christophe's only nephew. Christophe's other sister had died suddenly from a rare form of cancer as a child. Audrey was from Strasbourg. Christophe knew her, but not well. Laurent continued. "Julien has been pestering me to take him back to the duck-fishing pool-hooking game; he has his eye on a toy model of a Concorde jet and wants to earn enough tickets to win it. We got halfway there, but that's the limit of my endurance. I think it will end up costing fifty euros for a toy we could just as well buy in town for ten."

"I'll take him!" volunteered Christophe, seeing a chance to redeem himself for not having arrived with a birthday gift. Laurent explained to Julien the offer. Julien nodded consent and took Christophe by the hand. The two disappeared into the crowd.

Julien knew exactly where to go. Christophe started shelling out euros, and the attendant handed Julien his preferred fishing pole. The game consisted of a circular water trough with a collection of yellow rubber ducks of various sizes going around in a continuous loop. The ducks had rings on their backs, and the object was to snag a duck using a pole with a hook at one end as they went by. Apparently, the smaller the duck, the more points were earned toward a prize. It was harder than it looked, especially for a six-year-old.

There is something about catching things and earning a reward, like an Easter egg hunt, that has always captured the imagination of children. Julien was in heaven. This was turning out to be an endless endeavor, however. More than once, Christophe was tempted to just grab some ducks with his hands when the attendant wasn't looking, but he knew that would fly in the face of a child's sense of fair play. Christophe was in this for the long haul.

He found a stool nearby and began studying the ducks going around and around in the water trough. There was a recirculating water pump at one end that kept the water flowing and the ducks moving. As he watched, he realized that the trough was somewhat like a portal. The ducks were like capsules going through the tunnel. Every time Julien started to hook one, it stopped the flow, and ducks began piling up behind it. As soon as he succeeded in removing it, to be placed in his trophy collector, a ten-liter paint bucket, the other ducks began to flow again until the track regained its equilibrium. It was interesting to observe that as long as no child was perturbing the flow of ducks, they spread out naturally in the trough with almost uniform spacing. This is exactly how capsules in a portal were kept from crashing into one another. It required careful balance of equilibrium, and this is what the vacuum control valves were required to do. In this same way, as when Julien upset the flow by snagging a duck, if ever a control valve in a portal were to malfunction, the capsules would careen into each other. So, were it not for the emergency procedure of recompression, disaster would ensue. Unlike the trough of ducks, however, it was not possible for the capsules to reequilibrate once the vacuum was compromised. Maybe the valve in the Paris portal really had stuck open, and the system responded exactly like it was supposed to. Christophe considered that maybe he had been wrong to question the incident report. Perhaps he had allowed himself to think he could reassert himself as having some importance like before and had made everything up in his mind to make himself look good.

Then the most remarkable and unexpected thing happened. The attendant was walking back and forth behind several troughs, trying to maintain some order in the midst of the bedlam of too many children catching too many ducks and wanting prizes all at once. She tripped on the electrical cord to the recirculating pump of Julien's trough and kicked the plug out of the wall socket. Julien's trough suddenly went still, and all the ducks began to bunch up into groups. The attendant plugged the pump back in, and all continued as before. Ordinarily, this would have gone completely unnoticed, except that Christophe immediately recognized this unexpected behavior, which he decided must be the result of surface tension, the way corks bunch together when floating in a glass of water. He couldn't believe his eyes. He held up a five-euro note and said to the attendant in bad French, "Here's five euros to do that again." She looked at him, bewildered, and was quite certain he had just gotten some words confused.

But he pointed to the wall socket with a yanking motion, moving his index finger in a circle to indicate his desire to see the effect again, while saying, "Encore." She got the message and took the five-euro note. She pulled out the plug for a second time without further questioning. The same thing happened. All the ducks started to bunch together into groups just like before as soon as the water became still. This gave Christophe an interesting idea. Julien was also pleased because the stationary ducks were much easier to hook.

At last Julien had collected enough points to win his reward. He needed one hundred tickets. The gifts were displayed on a revolving carousel behind the duck troughs. Julien waited patiently until he saw his prize—a 1/100 scale model of a sleek Air France Concorde supersonic jetliner. The plastic model was almost as big as Julien, 61 centimeters in length with a wingspan of 26 centimeters. The attendant took Julien's tickets with a big smile and happily handed him the model.

It was getting late. The girls had apparently survived their death-defying amusement rides, and Julien had his Concorde. Everyone was ready to leave. Laurent and Audrey lived just a few kilometers north of Bordeaux. Sandra and Fredrick had a small vineyard and winery about thirty minutes farther north, close to the confluence of the Garonne and Dordogne rivers. Sandra was packed up and ready to depart by the time Christophe and Julien finally returned to the picnic area. Sandra said, "The kids don't have school tomorrow, so why don't we meet at our home for an early dinner. I made a lovely lamb cassoulet.

Fredrick and I can take Christophe in our car, and perhaps Julien also if that's okay."

"That sounds great," said Audrey. "The girls have plans tonight. We will drop them off at home on the way. I suspect they also need to do some homework." The girls groaned as expected.

Fredrick had found a good parking space not too far away. He kept a car seat in the trunk for such occasions, and buckled Julien into the back seat, the boy clutching his Concorde. Sandra sat next to Julien, and Christophe was in the front with Fredrick at the wheel as they headed out of town. No sooner had they reached the outskirts than Julien was sound asleep, still holding his prize.

"Why is Julien so fascinated with that old airplane?" Christophe asked Fredrick.

"I don't know for sure. I told him a story before bed once about the Concorde. I might just as well have been telling him about fire-breathing dragons. He just seemed fascinated by the whole idea of supersonic flight."

"Did you ever see the Concorde memorial at Charles de Gaulle?" Christophe asked.

"Sure," said Fredrick. "I assume it's still there."

The Concorde's short life span of only twenty-seven years, which ended in 2003, was concluded before either Fredrick or Christophe had been born. The Concorde was ahead of its time. Transatlantic travel time had shrunk from weeks to hours in just one hundred fifty years. The Concorde had been the next logical step, making the trip from New York to Paris at twice the speed of sound in just over three hours. Many thought the fateful crash in Paris in 2000 was the reason for its demise, but the aircraft was doomed long before then. In reality, it was the enormous cost to shave a few hours off the trip. A ticket on the Concorde cost ten times more than a coach ticket on a subsonic jet. This made such travel seem elitist. It was something reserved for the rich and famous and not accessible to ordinary people. In the end, the dream of supersonic travel by aircraft died without a whimper. Many attempts were made to revive supersonic flight, including a serious program in the United States to send passengers on what amounted to ballistic space trajectories that involved reentry into the earth's atmosphere. The idea was bold and admirable, but in reality, the energy cost to shoot people into outer space just so they could get somewhere fast was never justified. The dream of supersonic travel could only be realized if outer space could somehow be brought down to earth. This is exactly what the portals did.

CHAPTER 6

OUT TO PASTURE

Fredrick and Sandra lived on a bucolic vineyard with a winery that had been in Fredrick's family for three generations. It was small, at only twenty hectares, but they managed to produce an award-winning Cabernet–Merlot blend that supported their lifestyle. Dusk was upon them by the time they pulled into the driveway. It was starting to get chilly at night, and Christophe had packed a fleece, which he pulled from the bottom of his backpack. He had been to the vineyard many times but regrettably had not visited in several years. Nothing had changed. The pungent aroma of decomposing leaves filled his nostrils, and he could smell the freshly applied compost to the rows of vines extending in all directions. Fredrick carried the still-sleeping Julien into the house while Sandra unpacked the car and started getting ready for dinner. Christophe wandered off into the vineyard for a solitary respite, soaking in the memories of happier times. A few clusters remained on the vines. He plucked one to enjoy the familiar sweetness of overripe Merlot grapes. He headed back to the house when he saw the lights of Laurent's car entering the driveway.

Sandra was in the kitchen when he entered the side door. "I made up Laurent's old room for you. There is a clean towel on the bed. I hope you will start spending more time here now that you are retired. I think it is good for your state of mind." Christophe nodded in agreement. "Everyone is in the salon having a glass of wine. Why don't you join them? Dinner is almost ready."

"Let me put my things in the bedroom first. I will join them in a minute." Christophe grabbed his backpack and briefcase and headed back in the direction of the guest room. He had not noticed the new message on his phone until then. It was from Fred Simms, and it read, "Christophe, no need to go to Toulouse. I will get back to you tomorrow. Fred." Christophe was initially relieved, but this was soon replaced by a feeling of being perturbed. He checked for any additional information about the Paris portal incident. He should have been receiving regular status updates, but there was no news. Perhaps he would have something by morning.

Dinner was lovely. Sandra was raised in the United States, but she had mastered all the charm of a refined Frenchwoman. She just had a way of making everything seem easy. Julien was insisting on having his Concorde in the center of the dining table, but she got him to put it on the coffee table instead, having convinced him the coffee table looked more like an airport runway.

Christophe sat next to his nephew, Laurent, who was a software engineer for a firm that made automation robots. He had worked one summer for Christophe as an intern during college, where he was exposed to a lot of undersea remote control technology. Christophe helped get him a job at the company that designed and manufactured some of the equipment after graduation. During a lull in the light dinner conversation, Christophe took the opportunity to engage in a more serious discussion.

"Tell me, Laurent, what happens in one of your robots when there is a power failure?"

After some reflection, he said, "Well, it's generally not any problem. The backup systems powered by batteries take over. Why are you asking? Is this a test? I'm sure you already know the answer."

"It's *generally* not a problem?" Christophe repeated for clarification.

Laurent gave his uncle a puzzled look. "Where are you going with this? I guess what I meant to say was, never."

Christophe smiled and took a sip of wine in order to keep the conversation from seeming excessively serious. "Is there no situation you worry about when there is a sudden loss of power?"

"Uncle Christophe, there are all kinds of safety protocols. You know!" Laurent thought for a minute. "Why do you want to know? Does this have to do with the Paris portal?"

"Perhaps. I'm just trying to imagine an unusual set of circumstances. Let's just say, something anticipated but so improbable that it never actually happens."

Laurent served himself another helping of his mom's lamb cassoulet while he gave the question some thought. Then he said, "Okay. Here's an idea. Fail-safe systems often contain trapdoors."

"Trapdoors?"

"Yes. Microchips in critical systems always have a large capacitor nearby on the circuit board. Besides smoothing out any transient voltages, they store enough power for the chips to execute a couple of hundred primitive machine cycles that are necessary to save the current state of the processor if the power is lost. This is called a trapdoor." By now, everyone at the table was paying close attention to the conversation between Laurent and Christophe. "But Uncle Christophe, this code never gets executed. It never gets to that point. There are too many other redundant systems."

"Go on. This is really intriguing. I know a lot about such systems, but this is the first time I have ever heard of a trapdoor."

Laurent was convinced that his uncle was the smartest man on earth, so he took delight in the thought that perhaps he might know something that Christophe did not. "The reason you never heard of it is because it is a secret trick that software designers employ. The code is never intended to actually execute. We use trapdoors when developing circuits because we are forever bumping the alligator clips off our breadboards."

"What happens to the code then?" Fredrick interjected.

"We typically just leave it in. It doesn't hurt anything, and there is no chance it will ever be executed."

Christophe nodded. An idea had just been planted in his mind that was beginning to incubate. Meanwhile, Laurent proceeded to describe a new project at his work that everyone at the table was eager to hear about.

While dessert was being prepared, Christophe excused himself from the table and went to an adjoining room to place a call. The phone rang several times before François answered at his home. "Allô?"

"François. It's Christophe."

After a pained pause, François replied, "Oh, Christophe! Bonsoir! Comment ça va?"

"François, I need a favor."

"Listen, they told me not to talk to you."

Christophe was a little shocked by this but not completely surprised. A few things were starting to make sense. "No. This time it is really simple."

"Christophe, you almost got me fired. They threatened to put me on a month of unpaid leave!"

Christophe was still not completely aware of the gravity of the situation. "Do you have access to the event spool?" The event spool was a database that showed every action and every signal of the portal system prior to the emergency recompression, down to the microsecond. It was a massive database.

"Yes, but you know I can't send it to you."

"I don't want you to send it to me. I just need you to look at it." There was no response from François for what seemed like an eternity.

"What are you getting me into now?"

"It's simple. All I need you to do is take a look at the power conditioner logs for a power bump in the control circuitry for the so-called faulty valve."

"So-called?"

"Okay, faulty valve. Just look for a power bump. Can you do it?"

François exhaled loudly. Finally he said, "If they haven't cut off my remote computer access privileges, maybe—"

"Great! Just try. I will call back tomorrow. Bye." Then Christophe hung up before François could say *non*.

When Christophe returned to the table, Sandra asked him where he had disappeared to. "Oh, Laurent gave me an idea. I had to call a friend in Paris."

François stared at the receiver. "Who was that?" his wife asked from the bedroom.

"Just an old friend." The last thing in the world he wanted was for his wife to find out he had been talking to Christophe. Without his full retirement pension, she would not be happy with the lifestyle adjustment that they would have to make. "Go ahead and go to bed. I need to check something on my computer. I'll be there in just a minute."

He logged into his account remotely, knowing that if they were going to suspend his access privileges, they wouldn't be able to do it until morning. Accessing the event spool, he narrowed the search down to the power conditioner logs as Christophe had requested. Even so, there were still about a million data entries for the output line voltage going to the control valve. The data was very noisy, so he passed it through a statistical filter program, which helped a lot. By this time, it was well past midnight. His wife was sound asleep, and he was on his fourth cup of coffee. "Easy, he says," he mumbled under his breath. François was just getting started. This would take all night.

By three in the morning, he finally had a data set worth charting. He began scrolling the plot for the 30 seconds prior to when the valve stuck open. There was nothing out of the ordinary. Then at exactly T-minus 493 microseconds, there it was, bigger than life, a three-volt dip lasting barely a microsecond. No one would have caught this. How in the world did Christophe know to expect this?! François was too excited and too wired from the coffee to sleep now. He made a backup copy of the event spool and sent the news to Christophe at 4:35.

What was supposed to be an early dinner turned into a three-hour session of catching up. Christophe was not accustomed to drinking fine wine, and by the time everyone realized it was getting late, the mood was quite relaxed. Sandra served her signature *ile flottante* for dessert.

"It turns out that I'm not needed in Toulouse after all," Christophe finally volunteered.

"Wonderful," said Fredrick. "Then you can stay with us a few more days."

"That's very kind, Fredrick, but I was looking forward to returning to Beaulieu. It's supposed to be a very good week for sailing, and now it's getting late in the season. I had some repairs done to the boat, and I am eager to take her out before winter. Say, why don't you join me?"

Sandra said to Fredrick, "That might be a good idea, dear. You haven't been sailing in years."

"Well, I certainly can't go this week. There's too much to do in the winery."

"Nonsense. You have Victor. He doesn't need your help." Victor was their master vintner and was the one who did most of the work.

"Well, let's sleep on it. Maybe I could get away on Wednesday or Thursday for a couple of days."

The group got up from the table. Laurent scooped up a soundly sleeping Julien from the sofa, still clutching his Concorde. Almost as quickly as the dinner had begun, good nights were said and everything became quiet as Sandra and Fredrick turned off lights and headed to their side of the house. Christophe was left alone in the sitting room on the same sofa Julien had occupied minutes before, in front of the last red embers of a small fire that made the house very cozy. He was reflecting on the day while sipping the last of his twelve-year-old Château de Pommerance 2064 before heading to bed.

Sandra had left a light on in the hallway, and the faint glow bathed the sitting room with a warm radiance. Christophe studied the room, which was a magnificent example of rural Bordelaise elegance. The walls were covered with built-in bookshelves containing leather-bound volumes written by long-forgotten French writers. Several small oil paintings with intricate gold frames decorated the spaces between the bookshelves. Heavy drapes with gold fringes were drawn back and held open by satin ropes. Ornate ceiling molding and wainscoting gave the room a distinctly French classical feel. There was a large landscape hanging over the hearth that might have been painted by one of Rembrandt's understudies.

Christophe finally went to bed. He didn't think he was sleepy, but he was out by the time he pulled up the covers. He did not wake up until nine o'clock the next morning, refreshed and invigorated. He saw the text from François: "Christophe, there was a power bump just like you said. How did you know? What should I do next?"

Christophe's instincts were usually good, and he was pleased with himself that they served him well again this time. Also, thanks to the tip from Laurent and the way the rubber ducks behaved when the water pump was shut off, he was beginning to piece together a plausible scenario in his mind. He sent the cryptic message back, "Start looking for a trapdoor." He figured if Laurent knew what it was, surely François would also.

After his shower, Christophe found Fredrick in the den drinking morning coffee and reading the Paris newspaper. "Good morning, Fredrick. Is there anything in the news about the Paris portal incident?"

"Only to describe it as a minor incident, and saying that the portal will be back in operation by the end of the week. There is coffee in the kitchen. Sandra has gone to the boulangerie for croissants."

"As soon as she gets back, I think I would like to be on my way," Christophe said. "Is that all right with you?"

"Certainly. I have a lunch meeting in town later this morning. I can drop you at the Gare if you like," said Fredrick without looking up.

"That would be perfect. I checked, and there is a train to Nice at 12:50. Are you sure you don't want to come with me?"

CHAPTER 7

MONIQUE II

Christophe got into his apartment just in time to see the sun drop below the hills above Cap-Ferrat. His suitcase had been placed inside the door, and his cat came out to greet him as if he had not been gone at all. She weaved in and out of his legs meowing. Mignon, or Minnie as he called her, greeted him this same way whether he had been gone a week or just fifteen minutes at the store. He had brought her with him to France on his previous trip two weeks earlier. Small pets were permitted as carry-ons in portal capsules subject to gross weight and size constraints. She had been in a soft carrier behind his seat and barely made a peep the whole trip.

Minnie was a cream-colored American shorthair that Christophe had picked up at an animal shelter in Los Angeles the previous year. She was his first pet since childhood. When he got her, he was expecting to spend more time in Marina del Rey and to be traveling less. He actually went to the shelter looking for a dog, but when he walked past her cage, she meowed as if to say, *What took you so long?* At the shelter, they told him she didn't get along with other cats and was indifferent to people, but she perked up when she heard Christophe's voice as if she had been waiting for him to come get her all along. So far, she was adapting well to her new home in France. Christophe was finally back in France after the last trip to Marina del Rey to remove a few remaining things from his condo and turn the keys over to the real estate agent. Beaulieu was going to be his permanent home from now on.

The apartment, stuffy when he entered, needed to be aired out. Christophe raised the shutters and opened up the glass doors leading to the patio. His fourth-floor apartment was on the corner of the building facing southwest with a large wraparound patio. The 270-degree panoramic view from his 65-square-meter apartment was spectacular, taking in everything from Cap-d'Ail to Cap-Ferrat. A magnificent orange half-moon was just breaking the horizon. He could see most of the brightly lit marina, but the slip where his boat was berthed was just out of sight. The only drawback of the apartment was that it was right above the railroad tracks. The trains were mostly quiet, but they occasionally blasted their horns upon entering the Beaulieu-sur-Mer station, and this took some getting used to. He had liked living in California, but he was now ready for a change.

Turning on the computer on his desk, he checked for messages. There was a new message from Fred Simms waiting to be opened.

Dear Christophe,

Apparently, it caused quite a stir in Toulouse when they discovered that you had coated all of the control valve surfaces with silicone oil, but everything is now under control. Fortunately, I did not have to make the trip to France. The Paris portal should be back in operation by the end of the week. Everyone appreciates your concerns and wanted me to extend the company's gratitude for your long and faithful service on the Portal Safety Board. Your participation on the board will no longer be needed, however. Enjoy France and retirement. I am really jealous.

Best regards,
Fred

Christophe stared at the computer screen in stunned disbelief. This was a whitewash—they were sweeping the whole thing under the carpet! He was hungry and tired and was starting to get angry. There was nothing more he could do that evening, so a *demi-bouteille* of rosé and a light Mediterranean dinner would have to suffice to sustain his sanity. His favorite place was not open on Sundays, so he decided to explore the village for some place new to eat. By late November there were not many options.

Christophe slept well. It was nice to be back in familiar surroundings. Minnie slept on his pillow next to his head, which is where she preferred to stay whenever she was insecure about how long he would remain. He awoke at his favorite time of day, just as the first streaks of dawn appeared. He made a large cup of instant coffee and wrapped himself in a blanket on his favorite deck chair on the patio to sip his coffee and watch the sunrise. The faint pink glow on a few fluffy clouds at the horizon soon gave way to a palette of brilliant orange and red hues, giving notice that the sun would break the horizon at any second. He could hear his friends cooing in a nearby palm tree. They were Mr. and Mme. Onze-heures-deux, a pair of *tourterelles*, turtledoves, who got their name from their characteristic staccato dove-speech—*Onze heures deux, onze heures deux*. It wouldn't be long now before they would realize that Christophe was back, and they would show up on his railing cooing for breakfast. Sure, enough, as soon as the full sun was above the horizon, there they were. He couldn't tell them apart, except that one was slightly larger. He had decided that she must probably be Madame Onze-heures, but he was never quite sure which was which. He kept an old instant coffee container filled with oatmeal handy and spooned out a little onto the ledge. Minnie sat frozen on his lap, watching the birds intently. One tablespoon was never enough, so when finished, the doves would stand together on the ledge while the larger bird begged for more. Today was going to be a perfect day for sailing.

The weather was ideal, and the forecast indicated that it would be nice all week. The marina was a short walk from his apartment. He stopped by the grocery store on the ground floor of his building to get some lunch supplies and then headed for his boat. The marina was bustling with fellow sailors who also realized the day would offer perfect sailing conditions. His slip was near the end of the pier, and when he finally saw it, his heart began to race with excitement. Emblazoned across the stern was the name *Monique II*. It was a nine-meter sloop that he had purchased brand new a couple of years earlier, about the time he began contemplating retiring in France. Christophe was not an experienced sailor, with much still to learn. He had been considering taking more lessons and moving up to a bigger yacht, but *Monique II* was perfect for short sails, and he could handle it without difficulty by himself as long as the seas were calm and the winds were gentle.

It had been more than a month since the last time Christophe had taken it out. He checked the level of E95 ethanol in the fuel tank. It showed three-quarters full. The charge on the battery was a bit low, but it was sufficient to heat up the fuel cells. It would take thirty minutes to bring the fuel cells up to operating temperature. He could leave port under battery power if he wanted to, but he needed to check in with the marina office regarding a repair done while he was gone. By the time he had the boat ready, the fuel cells would be at full power, ready to deliver thirty kilowatts to the direct current inboard motor that powered his single retractable propeller. This was a wonderful invention. The DC drive made it possible to pivot the propeller up and out of the way when under sail in order to reduce the drag.

A fellow boatman helped him cast off, and he was under way. The fuel cell electric drive made no noise and put out no fumes. He passed the end of the seawall and headed under power into the unusually calm Mediterranean waters. There was barely enough wind for sailing, but he took advantage of this opportunity to test the mechanism for unfurling the mainsail. The drive motor had burned out on his previous voyage, and a new one had just been installed. The replacement seemed to be working just fine, so he put out the entire sail. Pleased with the result, he decided to deploy the jib and began to feel the boat's gentle heel as he tightened the sheets and headed into the wind, which was starting to pick up a little. He retracted the propeller and leaned back in the captain's chair, applying the necessary force to the helm to maintain the tack. By now, the wind was stronger than he was expecting, but he could handle it with ease. He had completely forgotten how much he loved sailing.

His intention was just to be out an hour or two, but everything was going so well that he decided to sail around Cap-Ferrat and head west, perhaps going as far as Antibes. He was unaware of the changing weather conditions. An unexpected storm was forming in the hills behind him, and clouds were beginning to billow up in the vicinity of

Èze Ville. As he passed Cap de Nice, he became aware that the wind was changing direction. Instead of a gentle onshore breeze, it began gusting from his stern. When he looked back, he realized that a squall was heading his way. Antibes was certainly out of the question now. He came about and reeled in his jib sail. The waves were getting bigger, and he now had too much mainsail out. He reefed it back in and deployed his propeller to gain steerage. He could tell it was going to rain before long, so he retrieved his rain gear from under the seat. The sea off Cap-Ferrat had whitecaps by now, so he decided to duck for cover in the protected *rade* of Villefranche-sur-Mer until the storm passed. By the time he had passed the lighthouse and was sheltered from the strongest wind, it was raining hard, and he was soaked despite his rain gear, so he decided to enter the marina at Port de la Santé to see if there was somewhere to tie up his boat. He soon discovered that he was not the only sailor to have this same idea; four or five other boats were also hunting for a place to tie up. He would have to drop his anchor out in the rade since the marina was completely filled up by the time he got there.

The sea was heaving, which made setting the anchor difficult. He finally got the boat secured and the sail put away. The anchor seemed to be holding, so he opened the hatch and went below to get out of his wet clothes. The lights and a small electric heater were powered by the fuel cells. He retrieved a bottle of rosé wine from the refrigerator and took out the lunch supplies he had purchased that morning to make a sandwich. He lay out on the berth and watched the rivulets of rainwater stream down the windows. The boat was pitching wildly, and he was glad not to be out in the open sea. His glass of wine was in a gimbal that swiveled with every movement, keeping it upright. This was just what Christophe needed to clear his mind. He was comfortable and safe in the cabin of *Monique II* with his homemade smoked salmon sandwich and a glass of his favorite wine.

He began thinking of Monique and their times together in Cannes. Her father had had a boat that was quite a bit bigger than his that could comfortably accommodate four adults. One summer, they sailed on it to Corsica. Christophe's boat was better suited for solitary voyages. When people saw the name *Monique II*, sometimes they would ask whatever happened to *Monique I*. There never had been a sailboat named *Monique I*. He always shrugged off the question, but in his heart, he knew that Monique would always be his one and only "*Monique I*."

The wind whistled through the stays and shrouds, and the driving rain beat on the carbon composite deck. The violent pitching reminded him of the times he had spent on ships in storms in the North Atlantic during the portal construction. Although the ships were enormous, the pounding they took in twenty-meter seas and hurricane-force winds felt about the same as his pitching in the rade of Villefranche.

Construction of the London–Paris portal was scant preparation for the challenges of building the North Atlantic portal. It was one thing to work at ocean depths of two hundred meters, but working at two thousand meters was quite another matter. Much of the technology for deep-sea construction had been developed by his team for the shallower English Channel. Adapting the equipment, designed for operation at a pressure of twenty atmospheres, to work at two hundred atmospheres turned out to be more of a challenge than anyone had imagined. This would become Christophe's crowning achievement. Digging tunnels under the ocean floor at depths below about five hundred meters was not possible because of the extreme pressure. The original concept for the transatlantic portal was to bore a tunnel. Such a tunnel would have needed to be more than thirty-five hundred meters below sea level to go under the deepest part of the Mid-Atlantic Trench. This idea was quickly abandoned. Actually, what ultimately scuttled this concept was that a rigid tunnel would need to traverse the rift zone where the North American and European plates collided south of Iceland. Besides being seismically active, the transverse sheer of the plates of about two and a half centimeters per year would put an unacceptable kink in the portal, a problem for which engineers were never able to come up with a solution. Several undersea portals were operational around the world in shallow water, but the idea of transoceanic portal travel seemed quite out of reach.

Then a French company by the name of Les Tunnels d'Aubrey was created in the 2050s to exploit an invention for deploying large, semirigid underwater "pipes." The company had been demonstrating such tunnels using a special high-strength concrete they developed that contained small air pockets that served to make the tunnel segments neutrally buoyant in water at any depth. This basically meant that "floating" tunnels could be constructed with cable anchors to the seafloor. The number and size of air pockets in the concrete could be tailored for the intended operating depth. Christophe was managing a team at Ashleigh's Versailles Design Center at the time, trying to come up with a concept for constructing deep-water portals. The Aubrey idea immediately caught his attention. Aubrey's company was located in Toulouse. Christophe initiated a dialogue with the owner and founder of the company only to find out that Ashleigh's principal competitor, Portals Inc., was already engaged in acquisition talks. PI was a US company that was planning to build a portal across the Strait of Gibraltar, where the maximum depth was nine hundred meters. Such a portal would open up the entire African continent with routes that would compete directly with Ashleigh's portals. Christophe had succeeded in convincing top executives at Ashleigh to tender an offer for Aubrey of their own. Things got messy in a hurry, but after threats of a lawsuit, Ashleigh managed to acquire PI, as well as Aubrey, thus obtaining exclusive rights to their technology. As it turned out, PI was about out of cash anyway, so it was doubtful if they could have completed the Gibraltar portal on their own. But Ashleigh was able to take over the PI design, which was quite far advanced by then, and use the Gibraltar portal as a demonstration project for the new Aubrey technology. Christophe had assumed responsibility for this project. He completed it in just under three years, for which he earned a great deal of recognition in the company.

Philippe Aubrey was the inventor of the neutral buoyancy concrete and founder of the company that bore his name. By sheer coincidence, he had been a classmate at L'École des Mines with Monique's father, Pierre. Christophe had discovered this in discussions with Philippe years later, but he had not talked with Pierre since Monique's funeral and had never had a chance to mention the mutual acquaintance. That chapter of his life in Cannes with the Fabré family was closed. Reminiscing about Monique and her lovely apartment on the Promenade de la Croisette caused him to drift off into sleep.

He was awakened some time later in the afternoon by the blast of the harbormaster's air horn. Christophe went up on deck to see him waving his arms and pointing in the direction out to the sea. Christophe's boat had been dragging anchor, and he had entered a swimming area where boats were forbidden. It was a good thing that he was awakened when he was, because in another hour, he would have been on the rocks. The wind had moderated and the rain had stopped, but there was still quite a bit of swell from the storm. Also, it was getting too late in the day to sail back to Beaulieu, so he found a guest slip vacated after the storm had passed and decided to come back for his boat the following day. He took the short train ride back to Beaulieu.

CHAPTER 8

METHANOGENESIS

It was dark by the time Christophe got back home. Minnie greeted him in her usual fashion the moment he walked through the door. The electricity in his apartment was off again, and he was unable to turn on the lights until he reset the circuit breaker in the main panel by the door. This had become an all too common annoyance. The electrician had told him that his new water heater was malfunctioning intermittently and tripping the breaker. It was easy enough to restore the electricity, but there would be no hot water for a while, and the frozen pizza he planned to microwave for dinner was no longer frozen. He also needed to reboot his computer. Until he had reliable electricity in the apartment, there wasn't much point in buying groceries. He would have to dine out again tonight. He changed into dry attire from his still-damp clothes and fetched a light jacket and scarf from the hall closet. Before leaving, he scrolled through his messages to see if there was anything from François. There was nothing from him, which came as no surprise, since finding a trapdoor, even if he should happen to know what one was, could not be done quickly. There was, however, one message that caught his eye:

Dear Dr. Conally,

You probably don't remember me, but you knew my father, Philippe Aubrey. I thought you might like to know that he passed away recently. Having retired after his company was purchased by Ashleigh Systems, he had been grooming me to take over the business. However, I saw this as an opportunity to return to academia to study geophysics, which became a passion for me while I was working at his company.

The reason for contacting you is that I came across a paper you published some twenty years ago in a rather obscure geology journal on the topic of abiotic methanogenesis. Judging by the lack of impact, I suspect you were just way ahead of your time. I find your conclusions compelling, and in hindsight, I don't know why your ideas did not get more attention at the time.

I am on the planning committee for the International Conference on Breakthroughs in Earth Science that will be held in Lausanne next June. We would be honored if you would consider delivering a keynote address on a topic of your choosing. Information on the conference is attached to this message.

Please consider this invitation, and let me know as soon as possible of your availability.

Best regards,

Prof. Philippe Aubrey II
Dept. of Earth Physics
Université d'Avignon

The unexpected email buoyed his spirits immeasurably and made him completely forget about the tribulations of the day. The restaurant on Place de Charles de Gaulle that Christophe frequented was just around the corner. It was dark outside, and the evening air was crisp. The restaurant had just opened at seven in the evening, and he was the first patron. The owner recognized him immediately and seated him at his favorite table in the corner. Christophe settled in and ordered the two-course plat du jour and a *pichet* of rosé. While waiting, he contemplated the message from Philippe Aubrey and reflected back on his discovery of methanogenesis.

During the construction of the North Atlantic portal, fifty-meter-long tunnel segments had been brought to the worksites. These were behemoth things delivered by specially designed ships. The tunnel segments were too heavy to be managed by traditional boom cranes. Rather, a gantry crane hoisted the segments off the deck in a cradle and lowered them down through a gap between twin hulls two thousand meters to the worksite below, as the tunnel progressed above the seafloor. Similar worksites existed at both ends with the last segments connected in the middle of the Atlantic. This event was celebrated with great fanfare reminiscent of the nineteenth-century Golden Spike at Promontory, Utah, when the two ends of the First Transcontinental Railroad were finally joined. The tunnel segments used the neutral-buoyancy concrete technology developed by Aubrey and were oval in cross section. They contained two one-meter diameter portals side by side with two additional smaller service portals. The one-meter portals had cutouts in the floor to accommodate the maglev track, which would be installed after completion. The entire portal used more than seventy thousand of these segments.

Working at depths of thousands of meters could only be accomplished by a fleet of autonomous and semiautonomous machines. Since the tunnels had to be very straight, it was necessary to excavate the route through ridges and submerged mountain ranges. More challenging, actually, was the system of tethers to valley floors that were in some places more than one kilometer deeper than the portal. Anchoring these tethers was where Christophe had encountered methane clathrates for the first time. These clathrates were a hydrated phase of natural gas that became a crystalline solid at extreme pressure.

In order to secure the tethers to the seafloor, it was necessary to drill holes deep enough to reach the underlying rock formations that were strong enough to support the tension of the support cables. Once securely anchored, the tethers had dynamic tensioning mechanisms to maintain a constant force on the tunnel section that was attached. The tethers also had powerful ultrasonic beacons to warn off whales and submarines. In certain cases, particularly in areas where there was geothermal activity, it was found that it was often necessary to drill through several hundred meters of soft, friable surface layers. If drilling was carried out too quickly, bubbles of what turned out to be methane gas came to the surface. In the early days of the project, before anyone understood the danger, a fire was ignited around a control vessel at the surface, and several workers were badly burned. This resulted in a lengthy shutdown of the project on the west end. The simple solution was to add shrouds to the drilling machines and capture the gas in large balloons, which would float harmlessly to the surface for retrieval. In the meantime, Christophe had authorized a project to study these unusual mineral formations more thoroughly.

It was a routine procedure to continuously analyze drilling core samples from the anchor boreholes, but it was not possible to just bring samples up to the surface for study because the pressure drop could introduce crystallographic phase changes, and in the case of methane clathrates, they would decompose completely by the time they reached atmospheric pressure. So, a system of high-pressure containers was used to store the samples at the same pressure as that of where they had been removed from the seafloor before being brought to the surface. This also involved constructing a laboratory aboard the control ships equipped to handle the necessary analyses, such as x-ray diffractometry and mass spectrometry, at pressures of several hundred atmospheres. One of the tests was to analyze certain isotopes in order to determine, if possible, the age of the rock. Since the predominant minerals in many places were carbonates, the test for isotopic abundance of ^{13}C was particularly informative, because from this it was possible to identify whether or not the carbon was of recent biological origin.

The portal construction proceeded outward from both the North American and European continents simultaneously. The origin of the methane from the shallower waters near the respective continental shelves was clearly from clathrates, or hydrated methane, but as drilling approached the Mid-Atlantic Ridge, the character of the samples began to change. What was thought to be methane clathrates turned out to be something totally different and never observed before prior to that time. Unlike with methane clathrates, no water was found in the crystal structure, and the nature of the methane was a gooey solid phase. The soft rock was actually metamorphosed quartzite and feldspar that would have ordinarily been quite strong, but solid methane had diffused along grain boundaries causing them to fracture. The result was like grains of beach sand glued together by this gummy methane phase. Perhaps the most startling observation of all was that, unlike clathrates, the carbon in the methane was not biological in origin. In fact, the age was characteristic of ancient carbon in the surrounding strata of carbonate minerals, even though those very carbonate minerals were absent from the methane-containing core samples. At one atmosphere, the methane quickly vaporized, leaving behind a crumbly material that could be reduced to fine powder simply by rubbing it between one's thumb and index finger. As far as anyone knew, Christophe's team was the first ever to observe this material.

He had requested that Ashleigh send in a team of specialists to study the phenomenon, but they had shown no interest in the discovery. They were preoccupied with production schedules and finishing the portal. Christophe asked for, and received, permission to disclose the discovery in a publication, which article he drafted and submitted to the leading journal in the field at that time. After several weeks, he was notified by the editors that his article had been rejected out of hand. The comments were dismissive and generally insulting. As was the case with many reputable scientific journals, this one had become a closed society with a narrower and narrower focus, which was hard to penetrate by outsiders. After all, even though Christophe held a PhD in engineering physics, he had no credentials in anything resembling earth science. He did not have the time or the inclination to fight the decision, so he submitted his article instead to a lesser-known journal with a reputation for publishing almost anything just to fill the pages. They were delighted to have it. They published it almost immediately with hardly any revisions—and then it was forgotten. In twenty years, it was only ever cited twice, and one of these was by accident.

In reality, although Christophe was the first to publish such results, the discovery was inevitable. The technology of drilling from fixed platforms on the seafloor was proliferating because of advances in autonomous control. By 2040, most of the world's terrestrial and shallow-water petroleum reserves had been depleted, and deep-sea exploration was the only remaining option. US and Russian oil exploration teams had also discovered the same strange new methane-containing mineral. A geophysics professor in Saint Petersburg, Russia, had submitted a manuscript one month later to the very same journal that had rejected Christophe's. Peer review in that case was almost effortless because that particular professor was well-known to the editors. That particular professor was to receive the notoriety of the discovery. Christophe would have liked the recognition, but fortunately, his livelihood never depended on publications. Philippe Aubrey's message was a sign that perhaps his earlier paper might finally be getting the recognition it deserved.

Also, at the time, Christophe's conjecture of how methane was formed was highly controversial. Up to that point, it was generally believed that methane was an ordinary fossil fuel just like crude oil and that, like crude oil, it was being depleted from the earth. One of the mysteries of the time, however, was that long after oil wells stopped producing petroleum, they continued to produce methane gas at nearly a constant rate for years and years. A fossil origin could not explain this. Christophe had proposed that natural gas was actually a renewable resource, which idea could be explained by the natural reduction of carbonate minerals under heat and pressure in the earth's crust. He suggested that the mechanism was the result of codiffusion of protons from water and electrons in claylike minerals deposited on top of layers of diatoms and the remains of shellfish in ancient shallow seas. Methane was synthesized at high pressure and temperature from the decomposing carbonate under the small electric field and oxygen concentration gradient in the earth's crust. In order to reduce carbonate, the simultaneous oxidation of surrounding oxides to a higher oxidation state was necessary. This explained why no carbonates were typically found in the methane-rich minerals showing up in the deep-sea core samples and why the remaining minerals were all fully oxidized. By the end of the decade, the debate was largely settled. Methane was being found almost everywhere, and there was no longer any concern that it would ever run out. The mechanism had been proven conclusively in the laboratory, but again, Christophe would not receive any credit for being first to propose the idea.

By the time he had finished eating, the restaurant was completely filled with French locals for whom dinner before eight o'clock was unthinkable. He was hoping that he would have hot water by now, as he was feeling a bit chilled. He just needed to get an email off to Fredrick before he went to bed to see if the latter was still considering making the trip to Beaulieu for a day of sailing.

CHAPTER 9

CONNECTIONS

Christophe had been under more physical and mental stress than he had realized. He awoke refreshed late the next morning after ten hours of deep sleep. He had left the door to the patio open, and it had been a chilly night, so Minnie had managed to squeeze under the covers and was sleeping motionless by his side. M. and Mme. Onze-heures were on the railing cooing away for breakfast. The sun was brilliant through the windows. Christophe discovered that the electricity had gone off again during the night, which meant there probably was not much hot water. He reset the circuit breaker and texted Henri, the apartment manager, about it. He made a large cup of instant coffee, grabbed a two-day-old *pain au chocolate*, and proceeded out to the terrasse to enjoy the warmth of the autumn sun. There was not a cloud in the sky, so it would be a good day to retrieve his sailboat.

Throughout his life, he had been driven to perform at peak efficiency in a very competitive work environment, and it had recently made him feel like sand going through an hourglass. This was the first time he could recall that he did not have the sense that he was just running out of time. Being removed from the Portal Safety Board came as a bigger relief than he had expected. He was no longer angry about being dismissed. The Paris incident was no longer his problem. Just as he came to this conclusion is when his phone rang.

He did not recognize the Paris-based number. "Hello. Who is this?"

"It's François. I am calling on my wife's phone from home." His voice was very animated. "Christophe, how in the world did you know to look for a trapdoor? How did you even know what a trapdoor is?"

It would have been too complicated to explain the epiphany he had had while watching the ducks when the recirculating pump went off or the discussion he had had with his nephew over dinner. "I just had a hunch. What did you find out?"

"Christophe, your hunch was spot-on. It looks like there was a trapdoor, and I am pretty sure it got executed even though that would have been totally impossible. The power bump alone could not have triggered it."

"I agree," said Christophe. "There had to be at least two, and maybe three, simultaneous events, not to mention that it would have been necessary for both valves to malfunction concurrently."

"You know, Christophe, they only sent one of them to the lab. Don't you find that a bit strange?" There was a long silence while both men pondered this. "Christophe, I'm not sure it was an accident." As unthinkable as this was, the possibility had been simmering in the back of Christophe's mind.

"Do you have any idea of the implications of what you just said?"

"Well, why do you think I called you on my wife's phone?" There was another long pause. "Christophe, yesterday my computer access privileges at the center were completely revoked. I can't even sign in to record my work hours. They told me this morning to take the week off." There was another long pause. "Christophe, there is more going on here than either of us ever imagined."

Finally, Christophe said, "Even so, without access to the computer, I guess there isn't much more we can do."

"Well, not exactly." Christophe's interest was now piqued. "Do you remember at the lab when I saved the data file? Well, I also sent an encrypted version to my home computer."

"Yes, I saw you do that. I'm sure that will get you into trouble."

"It just seemed important at the time. I thought I might want to be able to look at the data over the weekend, and I just thought it would be easier if I didn't have to log in to get it."

Christophe took a moment to clear his senses. "This is more than my brain can handle right now. You need to give me a chance to think about it. I will call you back this evening. Can I reach you at this number?"

"Yes."

Christophe started to hang up, then suddenly spoke more quietly. "François?"

"Oui?"

"I am concerned now for your safety. Is there any possibility that you and your wife could disappear for a while?"

There was another long pause. "That might be wise. Let me think about it. Let's talk later." François hung up the phone.

Christophe stared into space with his phone still at his ear. The mere speculation that the Paris incident might have been deliberate was more than he could process. His entire career had been focused on preventing an accident due to natural causes. Sabotage had always been a possibility, but this thought now had his stomach in knots. How could it happen? Who might know about it? How much did Ashleigh know?

Christophe needed air. He went back out on the terrasse, spooned out some more oatmeal for M. and Mme. Onze-heures, and reclined in his favorite chair. Minnie jumped up on his lap and nuzzled his hand to have her ears scratched as if she knew that something was wrong. She could sense by the tone of his voice that he would be going away again soon.

He took up his phone and dialed Fredrick. Sandra answered. "Allô."

"Sandra, it's Christophe. Can I speak to Fredrick?"

"Sure. He's just in the den. Let me get him. By the way, it was really wonderful seeing you this weekend. You made a real impression on Julien. Here's Fredrick."

"Fredrick? Christophe."

"Oh, Christophe! I'm sorry I didn't respond to your email yet. There is just no way I can get away to go sailing with you this week."

"That's not really why I am calling. Something has come up." Christophe cleared his throat. "Do you by any chance remember Monique Fabré's father?" Fredrick didn't answer right away. Christophe was expecting a just simple yes or no. "His name was Pierre Fabré. If he is still alive, he must be in his nineties by now."

Fredrick finally responded, "Yes, he is still alive, and I know him well. We have stayed in touch for the past forty years. We never told you, because we knew the memory was too painful for you, but Sandra and I continued to visit Pierre and Monique's mom regularly after Monique died. And we have kept up with Pierre since her mom passed away a few years ago."

This was now just one more piece of news Christophe would have to process later. "Didn't he work for the French intelligence service?"

"Yes. I think he actually ran it for a while."

Christophe took a deep breath. "Fredrick, I need your help. I may have gotten myself into something way over my head. Do you think you and I could visit Pierre together?"

"Sure," replied Fredrick. "He lives in Nice now. What do you mean, 'over your head'?"

"Could you meet me there? This is rather urgent. I am going to need some connections, and Pierre seemed to know everybody important in France."

"Pierre would be thrilled to see you again. I'm sure I can arrange it. When did you have in mind?"

"Tomorrow."

"That doesn't give me much time."

"And would it be possible to come with Laurent?"

"Laurent? Christophe, what is this all about?"

Christophe replied, "I will fill you in, just not over the phone. I need access to someone high up in the government, and Pierre Fabré is the only one I could think of who may still have those kinds of connections."

Fredrick breathed out with a whistle. "Let me see what I can do. I will call you back in a while."

"Thanks, Fredrick. I appreciate this more than you can imagine."

Only an hour earlier, the most demanding decision Christophe had faced was the choice of wine with lunch. Now with full adrenaline pumping in his veins, his thoughts were jumbled by all kinds of conflicting demands. His first priority was to retrieve his boat. Just then there was a knock at the door. It was Henri, the apartment manager. He said, "I have arranged for an electrician to come look at your hot water. I will let him in if you'd like."

"Yes, thank you. I left my boat in Villefranche yesterday, and I need to bring it back to the marina."

"But what about your cat? She keeps trying to sneak out," replied Henri.

"Good point. I will just take her with me. Thanks a lot for all you do for me, Henri."

Christophe got dressed and loaded Minnie into her soft-case carrier, which she really hated, letting Christophe know it by biting his hand. He and Minnie caught the train and got back to his boat by early afternoon. The harbormaster was glad to see him. Another day and his boat would have been towed and he would have had to pay a fine to get it back.

The Mediterranean was like glass, and there was not a breath of wind. It would be necessary to return to Beaulieu under power. At his top speed of four knots, this would take at least a couple of hours. After he cast off, he let Minnie out of her carrier. Boating was not her favorite thing to do, so she promptly went to explore all the nooks and crannies belowdecks. There was a large gray yacht at anchor that had not been there the day before. Christophe passed it a little too closely, and a couple of armed security guards signaled to him to move away. It was not unusual to see this kind of yacht in those waters. The rade of Villefranche, providing cover and seclusion for the international business tycoons who owned these yachts, and the presence of armed guards was not out of the ordinary. What did impress Christophe about this particular boat, however, was its large array of satellite dishes and radars, which were more characteristic of a military vessel than a private yacht. Christophe swerved away as requested, proceeding around Cap-Ferrat without giving the matter any more thought.

It was three o'clock by the time Christophe and Minnie docked in Beaulieu and secured the boat. Henri was waiting for him to return and met him in the lobby. "The first electrician came here this morning after you left, and he could not find the problem. I wasn't very impressed by him, so I called in a second electrician. It turns out that when they installed your new water heater, they wired it to the same circuit breaker as your bathroom space heater. It didn't become a problem until the weather got colder and the heater started to switch on. Why the first electrician didn't spot the problem is beyond me. How that guy ever got a license as an electrician is a mystery to me. It's a good thing I brought in a second one, or you would still be tracking down the problem." Henri peeked into the carrier. "How did Minnie like her boat ride?"

"Not much," Christophe replied, stepping into the elevator. "Thanks again for your help." The elevator door closed.

Christophe dropped Minnie off in the apartment and went back down to the supermarket to stock up on some groceries. Finally, his refrigerator was working reliably so he could start cooking at home. He dialed François from the phone in the lobby. There was no answer and no answering service. Thinking he had dialed the wrong number, he tried calling once again when he got back into his apartment and got the same result. Without being able to contact François, there was no point in having Fredrick and Laurent make the trip. Everything of importance was in François's head and on his computer. Christophe needed to send a message to Fredrick to hold off on coming to Nice for at least another day.

He made spaghetti and a tossed salad. He didn't mind cooking, but he really disliked cleaning up, so he tended to settle for simple meals to prepare, which more often than not meant precooked microwavable entrées. No sooner had he seated himself in front of the television to catch up on some French evening news than his phone rang. He recognized it as François's wife's number.

"François?"

"Oui. I am in the lobby."

"What lobby?"

"Your lobby."

CHAPTER 10

CONSPIRACY

It took Christophe a moment to get over the shock of his unannounced visitor. "Give me five minutes, and I will come down." He straightened the apartment up a bit and spooned his spaghetti dinner into a plastic container to go back into the refrigerator.

When the elevator door opened, he saw François standing in the lobby. "François? What in the world are you doing here? How did you find me?"

"Your address isn't exactly a secret. It's at the bottom of your emails."

"How did you get here?"

"We drove," responded François nonchalantly.

"We?"

"Yes. Chloé and Biscuit are in the car." He pointed to an older-model Renault just outside. "I have something important to show you."

"You are parked in a loading zone. Why don't you pull into the parking garage? It's just twenty meters up ahead on the right. The code is 2266. My space is 403. I rent it out during the high season, but it should be vacant now. I will meet you down there."

The car had pulled into space 403 by the time Christophe arrived, and François was retrieving a cardboard box from the trunk. A woman was standing next to the car cradling a small dog that could only be described as "French lacking pedigree."

"I'm glad to see you, François, but isn't this a bit sudden?"

"I would like to introduce you to my wife, Chloé. I don't think you two have ever met."

"Enchanté." Chloé extended her hand in greeting. "And this is Biscuit." She moved his paw up and down as if to wave.

"Christophe, I need to show you something that is in this box. Can we come up to your apartment?"

"I tried calling you several times," Christophe interjected.

"I know, but we didn't know who might be listening in."

"Okay. Come on up. Have you had dinner?"

Christophe locked Minnie in the bedroom—not for her safety, but for Biscuit's. She didn't like dogs, and Biscuit was barely bigger than she. François headed to the dining room table and hunted for a nearby wall outlet. He unpacked a device that Christophe immediately recognized as a portal control valve and began setting up his personal computer. While this was going on, Christophe fetched a bottle of wine and glasses. He was not prepared to entertain guests, but fortunately he had purchased some crackers and cheese, which he laid out on a plate. He and Chloé went into the living room while Biscuit explored the apartment. Chloé was quite different from how he had pictured her. She was petite and not at all unattractive, sporting long hair in a high ponytail. He had always assumed that François and his wife were about the same age, but she was clearly younger by at least ten years. In all the discussions over the years, François had led Christophe to think he was henpecked. Although Chloé might have been high-maintenance, she was not at all what he expected. She was charming, speaking English with practically no accent at all. He set a glass of wine on the table next to François, who was too focused on his task to notice, and then poured wine for Chloé and himself. They sat in the living room waiting for François to get ready.

"Where did you learn to speak such perfect English?"

"I was an au pair for an American family in Colorado for several years. I got to learn English right alongside a two-year-old. It was like growing up in the family. Perhaps this is the best way to learn a foreign language, don't you agree?"

"Oh, no matter how hard I tried, French never really clicked for me."

"François told me you speak good French."

"I can understand most things, and I can read a French newspaper, but when I try to speak, it just comes out jumbled. Anyway, everybody speaks English these days, so I don't get much opportunity to practice."

"Hey, Christophe. Come look at this."

Christophe got up and went into the dining room. The vacuum control valve assembly was in the middle of the table with various cables running to an interface board connected to François's computer. "How did you ever manage to get hold of a VCVA?"

François flashed him a grin that spoke, *You really don't want to know.* Then, pointing to a tiny light-emitting diode built into the valve, he said, "You see it's not lighted, right?" Christophe nodded. "That means the valve is closed. It should be normally closed. Even when the power fails, it should remain closed." He unplugged the power connection and then plugged it back in. "See, still closed. There is no possible way for the valve to open without a specific software command." Then he hit a key on his computer to initiate a program. "This is the same code that is used on the portal system to activate the valve." The LED on the valve turned green when the valve made its characteristic *click* and remained green. "See, I have opened the valve with a command, and when I hit this other key, the valve closes. See?" The valve closed with a *clack*. François cycled the valve several times to be sure everyone understood exactly what he was doing, demonstrating that the valve was functioning properly.

Again, he executed the command to open the valve, and the green LED lighted to confirm this. "Now watch." He then unplugged the power cable, and the valve closed again just as it was designed to do. He looked up at

Christophe. "If the valve in the Paris portal had lost power, even for an instant, it would have closed automatically and remained closed until specifically commanded to open again. The fact that it didn't close led everyone, including me, to conclude that the valve got stuck in the open position."

Christophe said, "But of course. This is what we confirmed when we ran the defective valve on the ETU on Friday. The valve was cycling perfectly."

"Exactly. Now pay careful attention." François typed in some additional instructions and hit the return key. The green LED lit up when the valve opened. "Now watch." He unplugged the power connection again, and the light stayed on. The valve should have closed with the loss of power, but this time it did not. François looked up with a smile.

"I'm not sure I understand," said Christophe.

"The other night you sent me a message to look for a trapdoor. I have no clue how you even came up with this idea, but I decided to look for one. Since I wrote a lot of the code myself, if there had been a trapdoor anywhere in the code, I would have spotted it immediately. I saw nothing. If there ever were any trapdoors, I am pretty sure we would have removed them before releasing the programs for use.

"But your hint gave me an interesting idea. What about in the firmware? Each valve has a set of primitive instructions built in, basically to execute the command to open or close. Simple, right?" François dug something out of his briefcase. "It is not straightforward to read the firmware built in to the Sturgeon valves, and who would have even thought to do it, but on your hunch, Christophe, I downloaded the firmware. You will never guess what I discovered."

"A trapdoor?" said Christophe.

"No. There wasn't a trapdoor. There was a Trojan horse."

Christophe exclaimed, "What is a Trojan horse?"

"A Trojan horse is a segment of code built into firmware designed to run only when triggered by a specific command. When executed, it could override the normal operation of the valve. I figured out how to execute it." François looked around at Christophe and Chloé proudly. Holding up a sheet of paper with a few lines of primitive machine-language code, François said, "Once I located the segment of code in the firmware, I should have been able to determine what would cause it to execute, but I couldn't figure it out. Then I had one of the more brilliant epiphanies of my entire life. I went back to the event log where I had found the power bump at T-minus 493 microseconds, just as I told you before, and deconvoluted the waveform. An ordinary person would have thought it to be just noise. But I am not an ordinary person. It wasn't noise at all. It was a signal! Christophe, it was a signal designed to cause the Trojan horse in the firmware of that particular valve with that particular serial number to latch open. It was deliberate! It was sabotaged, and it was sabotaged in such a way as to convince everyone, including me, that the valve was defective."

The apartment went silent except for the noise of Biscuit scratching at Christophe's bedroom door to meet Minnie. François finally took a sip of his wine and suddenly realized he was hungry. He walked over to the plate of cheese and crackers on the kitchen counter. "I really need a cigarette," said François. "Do you mind if I step out on your terrasse for a smoke?"

"No problem," said Christophe.

Chloé interjected, "I really wish you wouldn't, dear. You have been doing so well with your nicotine patch."

Just then, Christophe's phone rang. It was Henri. "Say, Christophe. I am sorry to bother you, but there are a couple of guys is a van parked down the street who seem to keep looking up in the direction of your apartment. I'm sure it's nothing, but I thought you might like to know anyway."

Christophe turned white as a sheet. "Thanks, Henri. Let me know if they leave." Hanging up the phone, he turned to the others and said, "We have a situation." François was standing in the doorway to the patio. "Come back in. I don't think you should risk being seen."

"What's going on?" asked François.

"There is a possibility we are being watched." After a moment of reflection, it occurred to Christophe that even though people would know he was in the apartment, it was quite possible that no one knew that François and Chloé were there unless they saw their car go into the garage, which was unlikely. "François, is there any chance you were followed?"

"All the way from Paris? Doubtful."

Chloé said, "What makes you think we are under surveillance, Christophe?"

"That was the apartment manager on the phone. He says there are a couple of guys in a van out front watching my apartment."

Chloé suggested, "Why don't you let me check it out? I need to take Biscuit for a walk. Even if they recognized François, no one would know what I look like. Is there a side door to the building?" By now Christophe began closing the window blinds. It would be easy enough to tell if there was more than one person in the apartment just from the shadows.

"That's a good idea. There is an emergency exit from the garage. I will go down with you. I suggest we take the stairs. François, you stay here and lie low. No smoking in my apartment, please. I will let Chloé out and then leave from the lobby with shopping bags to go to the market to get something for dinner. They will expect that. That way, Chloé will be able to tell if I am being followed."

Christophe, Chloé, and Biscuit went down the stairs to the basement garage. Chloé got a coat out of the car, which had a hood that she pulled over her head, and a scarf. It was only possible to go out of the emergency exit of the garage, so Christophe found a brick to block it open so that Chloé could slip back in later. It was just before eight in the evening and dark. He opened the door and motioned to Chloé, saying, "There's a path on the left that leads up to the street. Turn left, and you should see me come out of the lobby door in just a minute. The van will probably be down on the right."

Christophe went into the supermarket and bought some bread, cheese, and sliced turkey and a jumbo bag of potato chips. This was about the best he could do on the spur of the moment. He also picked up a couple of bottles of Bordeaux wine from Fredrick's vineyard. They were on special, but even so, it was twice as much as he was used to paying. He returned to his apartment trying to appear as unwary and carefree as he knew how to be. His heart was pounding.

Chloé and Biscuit arrived at his apartment door after about fifteen minutes. The wait was excruciating. "You are definitely under surveillance. One of the men got out from the passenger side and followed you into the market. The other one stayed behind in the driver's seat. He was listening to the radio, and it was not French."

Christophe set the food out on the kitchen counter. "You need to make your own sandwiches. I am a bit shaken up by all of this." Turning toward François, he said, "There can be no one who knows you are here. Without you, we have nothing. There is a spare bedroom, but you won't be able to turn on the lights. Otherwise, they will know I'm not the only one staying here." Christophe fetched some pillows and blankets from the hall closet. "On the other hand, you may prefer sleeping on the couches in the living room. We will figure this out in the morning."

Christophe gave Chloé a spare key to his apartment and instructed them to make themselves at home. Chloé and François went to the car to get their suitcases, taking the stairs as before. Christophe contemplated reheating his spaghetti for one, but by that time he had lost his appetite. The Bordeaux remained unopened. Christophe went to bed before Chloé and François returned. Minnie was waiting patiently on his pillow. Both were exhausted.

CHAPTER 11

UNDER SURVEILLANCE

C hristophe had difficulty going to sleep because of all the excitement, not to mention that his biological clock was still out of sync, so he took a couple of sleeping pills. When he finally woke up the next morning, it was after nine o'clock. He showered. It was nice to finally have hot water again in the morning. He dressed and went out of his bedroom. Biscuit was waiting eagerly at the door to meet the mysterious cat. The minute Minnie caught a glimpse of the dog, she ran away and jumped up to the top shelf in the closet for safety. Biscuit showed no particular interest in the cat thereafter. He followed Christophe, tail wagging, to the kitchen.

François was sitting at the dining room table typing away on his computer. Chloé greeted Christophe and said, "I made breakfast." She had prepared a tray with a glass of orange juice, hot coffee—brewed and not instant—scrambled eggs, slices of blue cheese, and fresh croissants with butter and jam.

"Where did all of this come from?" Christophe inquired as she handed him the tray and he sat down on the couch. The coffee was particularly welcome.

"I picked up a few things at the market this morning." Chloé continued cleaning up the kitchen. "I took Biscuit out early through the side door just like last night, and I walked by the van. Both men were sound asleep. I let Biscuit chase squirrels in the park for a while, and by the time I got back, there were two new men in the van—the day shift, I imagine. Anyway, they hadn't seen me before, so I smiled when I went by, giving them a good chance to check me out. I just waltzed right into the lobby as if I lived here."

François must have been listening in because this caught his attention. He looked up from his computer. She continued, "I ran into a bald guy in the lobby who asked me who I was and what I was doing there."

"That's Henri, the apartment manager," Christophe said. "What did you tell him?"

"Oh, I just held up your key and told him I was your girlfriend." Christophe and François exchanged glances. "It's the perfect cover, don't you think?"

François had been preparing a detailed report of all his findings. "I should be done with this by tonight. It will be encrypted so that no unauthorized person will be able to open it. I will give each of you the key and a copy on a memory stick for safekeeping. It would not be wise to leave any files on your computer, Christophe.

And obviously don't try to send it to anyone. I don't think we can trust anybody, and there is a pretty good chance your phone and data lines are bugged. The fact that you are under surveillance is a pretty good indication that somebody doesn't want this to get out." François reflected further and said, "Let's just hope no one intercepted the call I made to you the night before last from Chloé's phone. If anyone did, they will know that we have figured out almost everything."

The thought of his apartment being bugged had not occurred to Christophe before this, and it caused him a brief moment of panic. "Do you think someone may be monitoring the wideband?" He shrugged in desperation. "Even so, we can't just keep this to ourselves. We have to let someone know what you found out."

"Who? There's no way to know how deep this conspiracy goes."

"How about contacting Bernice?"

"No way!"

"Think about it. She's your boss. If she is mixed up in this, it ought to be easy enough to figure it out."

"I surely can't contact her," said François.

"But I could," responded Christophe. "I have no cover to blow. I will just call her and ask if she knows where you are."

"Perfect," interjected Chloé. "Bernice knows that you and François are old friends. Just tell her you called to say that you are sorry for getting everyone in trouble."

The three looked around at each other for a dissenting opinion. There was none. "Okay then. Let me give it a try." Christophe selected the number from his contacts. He now knew this call might be monitored, so he chose what he planned to say carefully in advance.

"Allô. Bernice Lille speaking." Her voice was shaky and insecure, as if she had been crying.

"Bernice, this is Christophe." There was a pause, indicating she was reticent to talk to him. Then she slowly said, "Do you have any idea how much trouble you got me into?"

"I am really sorry," replied Christophe. "That's why I called. I regret asking you to stick your neck out like that. I wanted to tell you it was a foolish stunt, and I shouldn't have proposed it." The last sentence was a lie, but he used it as a way to get her to lower her defenses.

"You can't imagine what has been going on around here. A group from the agency showed up this morning and confiscated François's and my computers. They wiped clean the data record on the ETU and yanked out the memory cards. On top of that, François has gone completely missing. He won't answer his phone, and the police told me his apartment is dark. I'm scared, and I don't know what to do."

"Again, I am so sorry," said Christophe. "If I hear from François, I will let you know."

"It's not for my sake. I just wanted to tell him that I think he may be in some danger."

"Danger?" relied Christophe. "What kind of danger?" Christophe took this to mean Bernice could not possibly be involved in any conspiracy.

"I'm not at liberty to say any more than this. Just, if you hear from François, have him get in touch with me immediately."

"Okay, you have my number. I am at home in Beaulieu-sur-Mer. Please let me know if there is anything more I can do to help. Feel free to call me anytime. Goodbye."

Christophe put down the phone. Chloé and François were eagerly waiting to have him recount the other side of the conversation. "I don't think she is involved. You need to excuse me while I make another call." He went back into his bedroom and called Fredrick, who answered directly.

"Fredrick. Were you successful in that matter we discussed?"

"When you said 'over your head,' you were not kidding. It's all set. They are expecting you. By the way, Laurent wants to learn how to sail. You should give him a call."

Christophe knew that Laurent cared very little for boating, so he interpreted this as some kind of code.

"Thanks, Fredrick. I am really in your debt." Then, Christophe called Laurent. "Hello, Laurent? Your dad told me that you might be interested in going for a sail."

"That's right. I am coming to Beaulieu this afternoon."

The code seemed to be working. "I can't wait to see you. Will you be coming from Nice by taxi?"

"Yes. I have your address. I expect to arrive at your apartment around 3:00 p.m."

"That's wonderful. I have made up the guest bedroom for you, and we can go sailing first thing in the morning.

See you this afternoon, then." Christophe hoped that Laurent didn't take this invitation literally, since the guest room was already being used by François and Chloé. "Goodbye."

Christophe went back out to the others. "There will be someone coming here this afternoon whom I want you to meet. He speaks your language, François."

Laurent took the maglev from Bordeaux to Nice. With intermediate stops at Toulouse, Montpelier, and Marseille, the trip took just over an hour. In front of the station at Nice Ville, there was a line of autonomous taxis. Some had two seats, and some had four. Laurent got into one of the two-seaters. He typed in his credentials and the address of Christophe's apartment. In a moment, the screen replied, "Confirmé." Laurent pressed the button reading, "C'est parti." These taxis had axles that pivoted so that they could move out of their parked positions along the curb perpendicular to the line. As soon as Laurent's taxi left the line, the others automatically closed rank. The screen displayed the route, with the option to modify the destination or cancel the trip entirely, in which case the taxi would return to the train station.

The driverless taxi was soon caught up in the normal Nice traffic congestion. Some things never change. Traffic would always increase up to the point where people would just decide not to go at all. It didn't matter how many roads or tram lines were built, the amount of traffic remained constant year after year.

Laurent's taxi finally pulled up in front of Christophe's apartment building. There was no need to tip the driver. There was no driver, and the fare had already been deducted from Laurent's account. He proceeded up to the panel outside the lobby and pressed the button for C. Conally—403.

"Hello?"

"Uncle Christophe, it's Laurent."

"Hold on. I will buzz you in. Just take the elevator to the fourth floor."

Christophe was waiting in the hallway outside the elevator door when it opened. They hugged. "Thank you for coming." An enthusiastic Biscuit was also on hand for the greeting. Entering the apartment, Christophe addressed his friends, "This is my nephew, Laurent. He is a computer genius whom I invited to come help us." To Laurent he said, "I would like you to meet François and Chloé. You already met Biscuit." Laurent was surprised when he saw that his uncle had other houseguests or that Christophe had not yet disclosed to anyone the reason for Laurent's visit.

"Here, Uncle Christophe. This is for you from my dad." It was an unmarked envelope with a card inside that simply said "134 rue Masséna."

Chloé made espresso for everyone. Laurent had a dim notion of the reason for his coming to Beaulieu, but after briefly taking with François, everything was becoming clearer. François and Laurent sat down at the dining room table to review the evidence for the discovery. They were speaking mostly computerese with its own eclectic lexicon. This gave Christophe and Chloé a chance to catch up and start hatching a plan for the next step.

Chloé could now come and go as she pleased with the perfect cover. Laurent would not expect to attract attention, but Christophe would be tailed everywhere he tried to go. More importantly, they could not take the risk that François would ever be discovered. Christophe's hope was that Laurent could learn enough of the technical details from François to relay them to the right party when necessary.

The plan was mostly worked out. Laurent would return to Nice after dinner by taxi, and Christophe would sneak out the next morning with Chloé's help, walk to Villefranche, and catch the train to Nice. Then Christophe and Laurent would meet up at Pierre Fabré's home around ten o'clock the next morning. It sounded like a solid plan.

François and Laurent worked together on the report until the evening. François was just glad to have fresh eyes looking at the data. Finally, Christophe stood up and said, "I think it's time for dinner. I want to take you all to my favorite restaurant."

"Of course, François can't go out," replied Chloé.

"That's okay," said François. "I need to finish the report tonight anyway."

"Laurent, then I guess it will be just you and me."

"I suggest we include 'Auntie' Chloé. This would give it the appearance of a social occasion, and it might look suspicious if you went to dinner without your girlfriend, don't you think?" Laurent said this with a wink.

It was agreed. Christophe closed the blinds and drew the curtains so that there would be no indication that another person was still in the apartment. François promised not to try to sneak a smoke on the patio while they were gone. Christophe opened one of the bottles of Château de Pommerance for François to enjoy while they were at dinner. Christophe knew that François would not appreciate the irony, but it was not lost on Laurent, who immediately recognized his father's label.

The three put on coats and scarfs, exiting the apartment into the cool evening air as if they were going to celebrate a birthday. It came as no surprise to Christophe when one of the men from the van got out and followed them as they walked into town. He pretended not to notice.

CHAPTER 12

THE SLIP

The following morning, Christophe got Henri to call the police to report the van, which had been parked illegally all along. In the winter, no one generally cared, but when the police showed up, Chloé went out holding Biscuit and made a big fuss in her most obnoxious American accent. The police had no choice but to chase them off, if for no other reason than to get Chloé to shut up. The ruse worked perfectly. Christophe slipped out the side door and disappeared unnoticed down the pedestrian walkway that led to the waterfront. In no time, he had made the short walk to the Villefranche train station and boarded the train to Nice. Once outside the Gare de Nice-Ville, he considered taking a taxi but decided to walk instead. The thought had crossed his mind that since he did not know the extent of the electronic eavesdropping, it might be best not to have an automatic taxi transaction that could place him in Nice. Anyway, his knees were not bothering him, and he felt good after the walk from Beaulieu to Villefranche.

The address 134 rue Masséna turned out to be the street entrance for an apartment building. Christophe pushed the button for Pierre Fabré.

"Allô?"

"Yes. This is Christophe Conally, wishing to see Mr. Fabré."

"Come up, please. Second floor." The buzzer on the door sounded, and he went in. The door to the elevator on the second floor opened directly into a spacious apartment. Laurent was already there, sipping coffee. Several people who appeared to be staff were standing around, and Pierre Fabré was seated in a wheelchair with a woolen throw over his knees and a little white dog in his lap. "Christophe. Is that you, my son?" Pierre was smiling broadly. Except for needing a wheelchair, he seemed in remarkable health for a ninety-one-year-old.

"Yes, Mr. Fabré."

"Non, non. Please call me Pierre." Christophe took his hand for a shake, but Pierre drew him in and wrapped his arms around his neck, kissing both cheeks. "I have missed you so."

Christophe was overwhelmed and began to gently sob in Pierre's hug, which went on for some time. Then, after regaining his composure, he said, "When Monique died, I just could never bring myself to face you again."

"I always understood. That was such a painful time for all of us. Fortunately, your sister, Sandra, has kept me up to date about you. And now you have finally come home. What a joy for me to see you before I die." He signaled to the attendant. "Get Christophe a cup of coffee, and see if he wants something to eat." He turned his wheelchair to head into the sitting room. An attendant showed up behind him and directed the chair to his favorite spot next to the fireplace. The apartment was already warm, but Pierre liked the ambience and additional heat of the crackling wood fire.

An attendant brought coffee and a plate of pastries to Christophe. "Sucre ou lait?"

"Just cream, thanks."

Then Pierre took a sip of his coffee and began to speak. "Laurent has been telling me a very interesting tale. It seems you have uncovered some kind of conspiracy."

"Mr. Fabré—um, Pierre—I stumbled into something I never expected. All I wanted was a quiet retirement in the South of France. I was not looking for trouble. Now, I'm being watched around the clock. I didn't know whom to trust. You are the only one I could think of."

"This was a very good decision, Christophe. You can trust me with your life. I'm not sure how much you know about me. I always had to be pretty secretive because, as you know, I worked in the Intelligence Ministry—the French equivalent of the CIA in the United States."

"I had some inkling," said Christophe, "but I was so enthralled with Monique at the time that I really didn't pay much attention to anything else."

"Well, I actually ran the ministry before I retired, and I have a lot of friends in high places. Not many are still alive at my age, mind you, but still there are people I trust. Laurent tells me you have a colleague at the Portal Authority in Paris who is in some kind of danger."

"Oh, where to begin?" Christophe sighed. "I don't know how much Fredrick or Sandra may have related to you about me and my career at Ashleigh."

"Actually, Christophe, I ran the Intelligence Ministry. I know a lot more about you than you can imagine."

This statement was pregnant with implications, but Christophe pressed on. "I was heading home to Beaulieu-sur-Mer last week." Christophe began to retell the story of the previous days. "The initial conclusion was that a piece of hardware, a valve, had failed, basically getting stuck in the open position. I know those valves well, and it is really unlikely for such a thing to happen. I was suspicious of the report almost from the beginning. I arrived in Paris late last Friday, so I decided to stop by the Portal Center at Gare du Nord to take a look. My security access had expired, so I persuaded an old friend to sneak me in to take a look at the valve."

"That wasn't by any chance a woman named Bernice Lille, was it?" interrupted Pierre.

Christophe stared at him in astonishment. "How in the world did you know that?"

"As I told you, I have lots of friends in high places. Go on."

"Well, anyway, I convinced Bernice and a guy named François Benoit, whom I had worked with for many years, to run the defective valve that was suspected of causing the shutdown of the portal through a battery of tests

129

on an environmental test unit. Basically, this is a very sophisticated piece of equipment designed to give detailed diagnostics of vacuum control valve performance in real time. As I suspected, there was nothing wrong with the valve. We provided the test data to Bernice Lille and thought the matter was settled."

"Apparently, you have no idea the can of worms you opened, Christophe."

"So I discovered the next morning."

"Oh no, Christophe, my son. You don't know the half of it."

Christophe looked puzzled but continued. "In any event, I had a couple of hunches while I was in Bordeaux with Fredrick and Sandra, and a big revelation thanks to Laurent here. I sent an inquiry to François to look for a particular signal on the event log."

"A power bump?" Pierre asked.

"How much do you know, really?" said Christophe, totally flummoxed.

"Almost everything," replied Pierre. "Remember. I know a lot of people in high places. What I did not know until this morning when Laurent told me, though, was that Mr. Benoit and his wife are actually staying in your apartment in Beaulieu. You have done a very nice job of concealing that."

"The men in the van?"

"No, they are not ours. They work for some very nasty characters in the syndicate."

The more they continued, the more confused Christophe became. "Okay. François and Chloé drove from Paris to Beaulieu because he had discovered that it wasn't a software glitch that caused the valve to malfunction, as I had been assuming. The cause turned out to be a pernicious piece of firmware code built into the valve itself, called a Trojan horse. Basically, this meant someone that knew this code could send a command to cause any valve to open at any time in any portal at will."

At this point, Pierre held up his index finger in the direction of the man standing next to him on his right. "Stefan, we always suspected there was a mole at Sturgeon." He then clapped his hands together and said, "I am getting hungry. Let's eat." The attendant wheeled him into the dining room and set him at the head of the exquisitely set table. "What are we having? Looks like veal."

"Yes, sir. Just the way you like it."

Pierre gently pushed the dog off his lap and said, "Time to get down, Woofy."

The comment about a mole in Sturgeon put Christophe's mind into a frenzy. He was well acquainted with the US company and had personally had a hand in choosing it as the company with the winning proposal to produce the vacuum control valve assemblies. He knew almost everyone at the company. A mole? Impossible!

"Christophe," Pierre began after the entrée had been served. "There is something you need to know. I have to be a bit careful, because much of what I am about to tell you is probably classified. If I get out of line, Stefan here will shut me up." Pierre took a sip of wine to clear his throat. "I know you spent your career with Ashleigh and probably assumed they were just an ordinary bloated bureaucratic multinational corporation. Nothing could be further from the truth. Even as a vice president in the company, you would not have known of their true nature, as it would have been obscured from you. The president doesn't even know what the board of directors is up to. In reality, Ashleigh is part of a conspiracy run by a group of very powerful people based in Genève called the syndicate. It is not a multinational company at all. It is what we call a *supranational entity*. They have no loyalty to anything but the pursuit of global power and influence. I spent my entire career trying to understand them and their underlying motivation. They have absolutely no respect for national sovereignty, and they consistently subvert French national interests to further their own agenda. The intelligence agencies in most countries started getting alarmed about forty years ago—about the time you went to work for Ashleigh—when the syndicate's global power was starting to rise. But by the time the threat was fully appreciated, it was too late, and we were all on the defensive. It seems they exert influence and control by means of a supragovernmental agency that operates anywhere in the world with impunity. They control Ashleigh and a number of related companies."

Christophe interrupted, "Is that the agency that Bernice mentioned, the one whose representatives confiscated the computers at the Paris Portal Center?"

"Yes," replied Pierre. "Their ability to walk in and confiscate computers and data records attests to their power, but that is only a minuscule manifestation."

"But I was always led to believe that the Portal Center was run by the French government."

Pierre looked up from his meal at Christophe and simply smiled.

"More salad, Mr. Fabré?" asked the attendant.

Pierre went on. "There is something very sinister going on at Ashleigh. We are not sure what, but the Paris portal incident is probably just the tip of the iceberg. Someone has gone to a great deal of trouble to ensure that the cause of the incident looks like a simple mechanical failure. Obviously, no one anticipated that you would show up at the center, and no one expected this Bernice woman to give you unauthorized access. Even then, they might still have been able to sweep it under the carpet. That is, until you sent the message to Mr. Benoit to look for a trapdoor."

"I don't understand," said Christophe. "How does anyone know about that?"

Pierre looked over at Stefan. "Let's just say, at least one interested party was monitoring your communications with Mr. Benoit." He paused while the plates were cleared and dishes of crème brûlée were served. "Ah, my favorite!" he said. Then, staring right at Christophe, he said, "You need to know, Christophe, if one interested party intercepted your messages, it is likely that other interested parties did as well. You need to be extremely vigilant. They will do whatever it takes to get their hands on Mr. Benoit. They know he is probably the only one astute enough to piece everything together. Stefan will be arranging safe passage for him. No one except the people at this table know that he is in your apartment, and it needs to stay that way. Our only chance of being able to figure out what the syndicate is really up to depends on keeping them convinced that there is no one who knows about the problem with the Sturgeon valves. Do you understand?"

When lunch was nearly over, Pierre suggested that Laurent return directly to Bordeaux. There was no need for him to be involved any longer, and so far, he was probably not in any real personal danger.

Turning to Christophe, Pierre said, "Stefan will take you back to Beaulieu. You can trust him. Do not discuss any sensitive matters on the phone, and do not send any messages to anyone. Your apartment is bugged. The electrician who showed up at your apartment yesterday morning to fix your water heater was not actually an electrician. He works for the syndicate. He was sent to bug your apartment. Just lie low and keep Mr. Benoit out of sight."

"Bugs?" exclaimed Christophe. "My apartment is bugged?"

"Well, yes, but the second electrician, who came yesterday, was actually Stefan. He installed some countermeasures."

Christophe looked across the table at Stefan, who said with a grin, "It's true. I actually am an electrician, and I did indeed fix your water heater while I was at it."

"Countermeasures?" demanded Christophe.

"Well, it's not all that difficult," replied Stefan. "We just patched into the microphone signals and have the ability to filter out anything other than the normal background noises you make when you are alone in the apartment. Except for the three-second delay, they will never know." Stefan paused momentarily while Christophe tried to assimilate the implications. "Actually, the camera was a bit trickier."

"What camera?" exclaimed Christophe.

"The one they put in the chandelier in your living room. For that we had to improvise some closed-circuit video to match the audio. It is amazing what we can do with augmented reality these days."

"Don't worry, Christophe," said Pierre. "In a couple of days this will all be over, and you can return to a normal life."

As Pierre was dismissing the group, he hugged Christophe again and told him he wanted to have him come back often once things blew over. Woofy jumped back onto his lap as everyone said goodbye in the foyer, and the guests got into the elevator.

Christophe's days were becoming stranger and stranger. Stefan drove him back to his apartment in an electrical service truck. He had him put on some orange coveralls and a hard hat.

"No one will ever recognize you in that," Stefan said.

"What if we run into the apartment manager in the lobby?"

"Henri? Oh, he knows all about you. Just pay attention to messages he passes to you or things showing up in your mailbox."

The service truck pulled up in front of the apartment building, and Stefan got out first to place orange rubber construction cones in front of and behind the vehicle. When Christophe got out to enter his building, Stefan said, "By the way, I contacted Henri and told him that Chloé is not really your girlfriend. He suspected as much."

Stefan grabbed a large tool chest on rollers from the back and locked the truck. He accompanied Christophe on the elevator to the fourth-floor apartment, and Christophe let them in with his key. François and Chloé were more than a little surprised to see him show up in bright orange coveralls with another strange man. "This is Stefan. You can trust him."

Minnie and Biscuit both came out to greet them, while maintaining a safe distance between them. The two had more or less made peace during the morning. One hiss and a swipe of the cat's paw at Biscuit's nose was all it took to establish which one was the boss.

Stefan removed his work gloves and shook the Benoits' hands. "François. I know this is rather sudden, but I need to get you out of here immediately. You are not safe as long you stay here." Stefan was walking around the apartment looking for anything that could result in a security breach. "No one can ever know you were here."

François and Chloé were looking at each other with obvious terror in their eyes. "I have a plan," Stefan continued. "The men in the van down the street saw two guys in orange coveralls get out of the service truck and come into the building. It is important that two guys get back into the truck. Except for the beard, François, they won't be able to tell that a different guy in orange coveralls got back in. It's probably too much to ask you to shave, so if you pull up the collar, I will just screen you with my body, and we should be able to pull this off."

By this time, François was panicked and perspiring. This cloak-and-dagger stuff only took place in the movies. "Don't worry. There is a private jet waiting for you at Côte d'Azur International Airport. They will take you to a safe place."

"A private jet? Where?" said François.

"I can't tell you. Anyway, I don't even know myself."

"What about Chloé?"

Stefan looked at Christophe. They hadn't discussed this before. "She stays here and keeps up the charade that she is with Christophe. So far this has been working very nicely."

François looked over at his wife. "Chloé?"

"If you are really in danger as this man says, what choice do we have?" Then to lighten the mood, she added, "Anyway, I have become rather fond of this apartment. I could really get used to this lifestyle."

"Is that all right with you, Christophe?" asked Stefan.

"Sure. Anyway, she's a terrific cook."

"Okay, then. It's settled. Take off the coveralls and give them to François to put on."

"What about my things?" said François.

"You won't really need much, but I brought up this empty tool chest to put your stuff in." François went back to the guest bedroom to get his duffel bag and started pulling on the coveralls.

"How about my computer and the valve hardware? I will need them as evidence," said François.

"Just put the computer in the tool chest, and pack everything else back into the cardboard box. We can just put it on top of the tool chest and roll it out." Stefan opened up the chest. "Oh, one more thing." He took out two French license plates and handed them to Christophe with the instruction, "Have Henri put these on the car in the garage. Here is the fake registration for the glove box. Everyone in France, especially the police, is looking for the Benoits' car."

This was all a bit much for Chloé, who began to sob. "When will I see you again?

"Don't worry, Chloé. As soon as he is in a safe place, he will call you." Stefan reached in his pocket and handed her a mobile phone. "Just don't download movies on this."

Then he said, "I think it's time to go. Please stay here in the apartment for at least an hour, until the jet gets off the ground." Then looking directly at Christophe, he said, "Remember—check your mailbox regularly. It is the only safe way to pass you messages."

François and Chloé hugged, and just that fast, Stefan and François disappeared with the tool chest into the elevator and were gone. The entire encounter had barely lasted twenty minutes. Henri was in the lobby to see them off. "Thanks again for fixing the lighting," he said loudly as the truck sped away.

CHAPTER 13

THE GRAY YACHT

Christophe stood in the hallway trying to process all that had just happened. Biscuit was jumping up on Chloé, indicating that he needed to go out.

"Sorry, Biscuit. You will just have to wait."

Christophe was not thrilled by the prospects of an accident on his carpet. "Give me the leash. I will go down to the lobby to see if Henri will take him out."

Henri was still in his office and was happy to do it. "I will bring Biscuit back up to the apartment in a few minutes. I just love dogs," he told Christophe.

When Christophe returned to the apartment, he found Chloé standing on the terrasse sipping an espresso. She turned and said, "I made you coffee. It's on the kitchen counter." Christophe joined her on the terrasse after fixing himself a cup of coffee. It was the first time either of them had noticed that it was a truly magnificent day on the French Riviera. The sea was calm and sparkled with a million flashes of light from the sun, which was low in the sky at that time of year. Neither of them spoke as they watched a few sailboats on the horizon brightly illuminated by the setting sun.

After a while Christophe's doorbell rang. "That's probably Henri with Biscuit." He left Chloé on the terrasse to let Henri in. Henri was at the door with a very relieved Biscuit. "Come on in. Coffee?" said Christophe. Chloé is out on the terrasse. I don't think the two of you have been formally introduced." The three stood on a portion of the wraparound terrasse, which was not visible to the men in the van below, enjoying the extraordinary view.

"So, Henri. How long have you been a spy?" asked Chloé finally.

"Oh, I'm not actually a spy. I am merely part of the network."

"The network? What is that?" asked Christophe.

Henri paused for a moment as if reluctant to disclose his secret. "The network is a group of French nationalists with roots going all the way back to the French Underground during the Nazi occupation of World War II. We are just ordinary people with an informal alliance trying to preserve France from the threat of globalization."

"How did you meet Stefan?" asked Christophe.

"Some strange things were going on around here starting about Monday while you were out sailing. This guy showed up claiming to be an electrician wanting access to your apartment. He showed me the service request. Apparently, you were having some issues with your new water heater turning off in the middle of the night. This would have been routine, except I could tell this guy was no electrician. I tried to keep an eye on him when he was in your apartment, but he was clever. I knew he was up to something, but I couldn't quite figure out what. So, I called my contact. I have no idea who that is. I just have a phone number I call and then enter my password. I got a call back after a few minutes, and a voice told me someone was looking into it. Stefan showed up shortly thereafter. He was obviously much more than just an electrician."

"That's all?" said Christophe.

"That's when the strange car showed up in your parking space. I pay close attention to everything going on in the garage, so I assumed it was another tenant borrowing your space for a guest. Just in case, I ran the number of the license plate, and when it came up as an all-points, priority one, I knew the police were looking very hard for it. Either it belonged to criminals or something else was going on. I don't trust the police. They have been infiltrated by sinister elements at the top, so I called the network number again. They told me someone would be looking into it. That's when Stefan showed up the second time."

Henri finished his coffee, "Of course, there was my strange encounter with Chloé in the lobby when she claimed to be your girlfriend. I thought I had heard everything, but that one deserves an award."

Christophe went into the apartment to get the fake license plates. "Henri, would you mind putting these on Chloé's car and putting the others somewhere for safekeeping?"

"I would be delighted. I don't like the idea of having a car in my garage that everyone thinks belongs to felons."

The afternoon had completely slipped away. It was dark when Chloé's special phone from Stefan rang. She didn't immediately recognize the ringtone and fumbled in her purse until she found the phone. "Chloé, it's François. I'm off. I don't know where we are going, but I seem to be in good hands. I will call you when I land." Just like that, the call ended. Chloé had no chance to respond. She looked at Christophe for some reassurance. She had had more excitement in the last twenty-four hours than in the previous fifty-two years of her life.

"Should we go out for a bite to eat?" asked Christophe.

"That's a nice idea, but frankly, I am starting to crash from all the adrenaline. I'm not very hungry. If you don't mind, I think Biscuit and I will just retire for the evening. I barely slept last night on the couch, so I am looking forward to sleeping on the real bed in your guest room. As you can probably tell, I have made myself at home here."

"That's just fine. I made spaghetti for dinner last night, which I never got a chance to eat. Staying in is a good idea for both of us, I think."

Christophe woke up early the following morning, refreshed from his first good night's sleep in days. He made instant coffee and proceeded out to his favorite lounge chair on the terrasse to watch the sky awaken.

Minnie jumped up into his lap. There were no clouds to announce the arrival of the sunrise, and the sun breached the horizon without warning. After a while, M. and Mme. Onze-heures showed up for breakfast. Biscuit also came out to see if he could arouse any interest in having Christophe take him out. After a while, Chloé also showed up, slightly groggy, but considerably more relaxed than when she had gone to bed the night before. "You look like you had a good night's sleep," said Christophe.

"Yes, except for the call at 3:00 a.m. from François. He is somewhere in the Middle East but couldn't tell me where. He thinks I may be able to join him in a couple of days." Then looking out at the sea and taking a deep breath, she said, "What a glorious morning. We never have weather like this in Paris in November."

"I was thinking of going for a sail today. Would you care to join me?"

"Oh, Christophe. What a kind offer. But even the thought of boats makes me seasick. François persuaded me to go on a river cruise up the Rhône to Avignon a couple of years ago. He said it would be completely gentle. I spent the entire cruise in our cabin wishing I were dead."

Christophe chuckled. "Then do you mind if I go? Sailing and being on the water just has a way of calming my soul. The last few days have given me a lot to think about."

"That would be fine. I will pick up some groceries and cook a good French dinner for us." Biscuit was starting to whine. "Okay, Biscuit. I get the message."

Christophe took his usual route to the marina. He figured that he did not need to worry if he was followed because soon he would be out to sea, and they wouldn't be able follow him there. *Monique II* was waiting for him. He stopped by the fuel dock to top off his ethanol tank and then headed out to sea. Conditions were perfect. His plan was to sail east and dock in Monaco, where there were many good places near the marina to have lunch. With the gentle wind and a little help from his electric drive, the trip took just under an hour. He pulled into the marina below the Palace and had no difficulty at all finding a guest slip. This late in the year, there was hardly ever the need to reserve one in advance. He tied up and closed the hatch. He was in the mood for fresh Mediterranean dorado.

He started strolling down the pier and ran into a rather burly man blocking his way. "Monsieur Conally, please come with me." It was immediately clear to Christophe that there was no option to decline the invitation. The man motioned him into a waiting inflatable speedboat, jumped in behind Christophe, and cast off the ropes. The driver sped out across the marina to the area where the big yachts were tied up. They pulled up to the fantail of a very large gray yacht, and the burly man motioned for him to disembark. Another burly man dressed in the same type of black knit long-sleeve pullover motioned for Christophe to follow. They entered some sort of lavish stateroom where an important-looking man in a dark suit was seated. He did not get up but pointed to a nearby chair. "Have a seat, Monsieur Conally." He spoke English with a strong accent, but Christophe couldn't place it.

"What's this all about?"

"Oh, I think you know."

"No, really. What's this all about?"

The man spoke deliberately and slowly with a syrupy intonation. "We are interested in the whereabouts of a certain gentleman by the name of François Benoit. I believe you know him."

"Of course I know him. We worked together for years. He lives in Paris."

"Is that so?" The man was dark-complexed with a full black beard, but otherwise he was almost totally bald. He snapped his fingers, and someone standing by handed him a piece of paper. He read it as if seeing it for the first time. "It seems you sent him a message last Saturday evening requesting that he look for something called a 'trapdoor.' What would that be, Monsieur Conally?"

This caught Christophe totally off guard. He had nothing to reply, so he simply remained silent while he tried to review in his mind the exact contents of his message to François. How much did they actually know? "It was nothing. I just had a hunch that there was a glitch in the software that might have corrupted some test data we ran."

"And the power bump, Monsieur Conally? This is not a laughing matter. We are quite serious. Where is Monsieur Benoit? We know you have been in contact with him."

Christophe had regained his composure by now and began to have a clearer sense of what was taking place. He tried to stall. "I don't even know you. Why should I tell you anything?" Christophe realized that if they had known that François and Chloé had been in his apartment, that would have been clear by now. Also, the man did not seem to know about the discovery of the Trojan horse.

"Monsieur Conally, we know about the phone call and the message regarding a 'power bump.'" The voice was getting more and more irritated, making Christophe feel like he was in the coils of a boa constrictor.

By now, he was pretty sure that they had not intercepted the call from François on Chloé's phone or his call to Fredrick. "Well, we talked, but he never got back to me, and I haven't heard from him since."

The man flashed a disbelieving look at the others and said, "Okay. You are free to go. Dmitri will take you back to your sailboat." *Dmitri! Of course,* thought Christophe. *These guys are Russians.* He looked back over his shoulder at the yacht as he was pulling away and realized it was the very same one he had encountered two days earlier when he was sailing out of the rade of Villefranche.

Christophe forgot all about lunch. All he could think about was getting away from Monaco as quickly as possible. He didn't really begin to shake until he was well out to sea. Up to that point, he had not been all that scared, but now he was terrified. The wind had picked up a bit and blew from his stern, so it was only about thirty minutes before he pulled back into his slip at the Beaulieu-sur-Mer marina.

Chloé was watching TV when he finally scrambled back into his apartment. He recounted to her every detail of his ordeal. "What should I do now?"

Chloé thought for a minute and said, "Why don't you see if Henri has some advice?"

Christophe found him in the utility room in the basement of the garage mixing paint. He related the adventure again. Henri said, "I will call the network. Maybe they will know what to do."

Within two hours, Henri brought a sealed envelope up to Christophe's apartment. "This was in your mailbox." All that was on the outside was "C. Conally." Christophe opened it and read the contents:

> We know all about these Russians. Don't worry. They are basically harmless. They probably won't bother you again. It sounds like you handled yourself very well. Good job.
>
> Stefan

He passed the letter to Chloé to read.

CHAPTER 14

THE SYNDICATE

Things settled down considerably over the next few days, with life returning more or less to normal for Christophe. The guys in the van had finally gone away, and he could come and go freely. Chloé had been summoned to join François, but the location was never disclosed. She needed to leave Biscuit behind, but this was fine as Christophe had become rather attached to the dog. Minnie also seemed to like having Biscuit around but drew the line when it came to him sleeping on "her" bed with Christophe. At night, Biscuit would slip away and spend the night on Chloé's bed, waiting for her to come back. Christophe began taking Biscuit with him everywhere. He even took him sailing one morning. Unlike the cat, Biscuit loved going out on the boat.

One evening there was a sealed envelope in Christophe's mailbox, just like before. It read as follows:

P.F. wants to see you again. Tomorrow at 14h00. You know the place.

—S

Christophe understood that P.F. was Pierre Fabré and S. was Stefan.

The following day, he called for a taxi. It was waiting out front at exactly half past one, as arranged. He got into the two-seater and entered his credentials and the destination, 134 rue Masséna. The autonomous taxi pulled away from the curb and drove the short trip to Nice. Pierre was expecting him. Stefan was in attendance, and another man with long thinning hair and a full gray beard was also standing in the foyer when the elevator door opened.

"Good to see you again, Christophe," greeted Pierre. "Glad you could make it. I want to introduce my old friend Abraham." The two shook hands. "I think the three of us have a lot to discuss. Coffee?"

"Yes, please, with just a little cream," replied Christophe.

"Why don't we all go into the sitting room?" said Pierre.

"Forgive me, but I have other matters to attend to," Stefan said for Christophe's benefit. "I won't be joining you."

"Later, perhaps?" Christophe asked rhetorically. He knew that this mercurial acquaintance would probably never become a friendship.

Pierre sat in his wheelchair next to the fireplace with his little white dog, Woofy, on his lap, while Christophe and Abraham sat on opposing sofas. The coffee arrived along with a tray of small sandwiches, which pleased Christophe because he hadn't eaten anything since breakfast, and he'd been unsure whether or not the invitation was for a late lunch.

"Abraham and I go back a long way," Pierre began. "We spent many years together trying to untangle the true intentions of the syndicate. He probably knows more about them than any other living person. I mentioned to him what you may have uncovered about the Paris portal incident, and he took up an immediate interest." Pierre motioned to Abraham that it was okay to talk freely.

"Christophe, from what Pierre has told me, it is quite possible that you have stumbled upon the very key to unlocking the mystery of the syndicate's Paris activities. Somehow you hit a nerve, and they are desperate to cover it up, whatever it is. I am eager to hear the full story of your recent adventures at the Portal Center, but first I thought you might be interested in hearing a little historical background of the syndicate." At this point, Abraham embarked on a lengthy discourse.

"Bear with me. I really should start at the beginning. From the dawn of recorded history, human civilization has been defined by its great empires. Throughout the ages, empires became ascendant by subordinating and annexing neighboring states, subjecting people to a common hegemony. These same empires then went into decline once they overreached their ability for self-management, which was more often than not the direct consequence of rampant corruption. An empire is characterized by the geographical concentration of power in its capital city; therefore, maintaining an empire requires the ability to project power and influence from a centralized location. Managing an empire is expensive. An empire ultimately fails when the cost to maintain it exceeds the value it brings to those who run it. But as long as the value afforded to those in control of an empire is greater than the cost to maintain it, the empire will prosper and grow in power and influence. This was true of Babylon, Persia, Greece, Rome, and all significant empires around the world until fairly recently, when a fundamental geopolitical change occurred.

"So, let me explain. The reach of an empire is determined by the distance at which power can be projected. Empire building requires conquest, and conquest requires the ability to project power at a distance. The strongest empire was invariably the one that could project the most power the farthest distance in the fastest time. That is, from ancient chariot armies to Panzer divisions, conquest was determined by speed. If a Roman outpost in Britain came under siege in the second century, it took some days for the news to reach Rome and some weeks for reinforcements to arrive. The news of Napoleon's return to France from Elba Island reached Paris in an hour because of an ingenious network of semaphore towers for communication before the telegraph was invented. By the end of the twentieth century, these times were collapsed down to minutes. The ultimate goal of global domination requires the ability to project power anywhere in the world almost instantaneously. Intercontinental ballistic missiles and space-based lasers afforded this, but at a huge price.

"The last and final attempt at empire building by this old-world paradigm was carried out simultaneously in the 1930s and 1940s by the Axis powers in Europe and Imperial Japan in Asia. In both cases, the time-honored Napoleonic approach was employed to try to create empires by projection of military might and conquest along with forced hegemony. Both these empires used a virulent new weapon—airpower—that shrank the size of the battlefield immeasurably, and radio communications were used for the first time for command and control, which dilated the time scales of warfare. As was always the case, annihilation of the enemy, if necessary, was an acceptable cost of gaining ascendancy. The Battle of Britain was carried out not so much with annexation in mind but with the intent to wipe London off the face of the earth. The Allies responded in kind by employing airpower to decisively defeat the Axis empires. But unlike all previous wars throughout history, the intention was not to replace one empire with a new one—although this was what actually did happen—but simply to crush the Axis empires. It was under the pretense of altruism to "serve the better good of humankind" that German cities were firebombed and atomic bombs dropped on Japan.

"What ensued was the ascendency of two new empires, the United States and Soviet Russia. The Americans referred to Russia as the 'Evil Empire,' and so it was, but the term *superpower* is probably more accurate. A standoff between the superpowers, called the Cold War, ensued. This was unprecedented in human history. The prospect of true global domination was in reach, but neither of the superpowers could ever figure out how to achieve it. The consequence of the Cold War was that it became much more difficult to expand an empire by invasion and armed aggression. Both superpowers, joined subsequently by China, entered into a nuclear arms race, not for the purpose of projecting power—that would have been nearly impossible—but for the sole reason of ensuring mutual annihilation. Their respective attempts at jostling for global power were always tempered by the risk that everyone would lose. The cost of empire had become enormous in the nuclear age.

"The Soviet Union came apart first. This left the United States as the sole global superpower, except absent was any real understanding of what that actually entailed. The United States had no burning desire for empire status and no real interest in global domination. It didn't really want to rule over everybody. It simply wanted to have the means to look out for its own strategic interests around the globe, which inevitably became a euphemism for controlling crude oil supplies to support its growing addiction to petroleum. The United States was ambivalent about its role on the world stage. It thought it could usher in a benevolent 'New World Order.' Nothing could have been farther from the truth. It led a coalition of military forces against an Iraqi despot that proved to be the last and final military invasion by land of the modern era. It used the very weapons built in anticipation of a land invasion of Europe by the Soviet Union. What was thought to be an exercise in liberation, along the same lines as the Allied invasion of Normandy in World War II, turned out to be something quite different. The 'liberated' country, Iraq, splintered into a number of warring factions, plunging the entire Middle East into turmoil for decades, leaving the United States with a sense of responsibility to 'clean up the mess.' This American adventurism ended up heaping an enormous debt on the country that it could not afford to repay. The United States reached the tipping point around 2020, when the cost of its empire exceeded any potential benefits.

"The US debt crisis in the first quarter of the twenty-first century, combined with growing corruption in Washington, DC, and political paralysis, contributed to the breakup. The state of Texas was the first to secede, followed shortly by California. California subsequently broke up into two parts, each becoming a sovereign state. Surprisingly, unlike during the American Civil War, this was all accomplished without much violence or bloodshed. The will to keep the states 'united' had gone away. The country had lost its traditional cohesive force. As you know, the United States ultimately fragmented into more than fifteen independent principalities by the natural process referred to as 'Balkanization,' which got its name from the breakup of Yugoslavia in the 1990s. The European Union was the last desperate attempt to revitalize the Roman Empire and prop up the Old World Order, at least on this continent, but the new global interconnectivity proved to be so dynamic and facile that any attempts at 'control from a distance' could no longer master it.

"The geopolitical forces of Balkanization were also global. Nation after nation broke up into smaller pieces when it was realized that a centralized government no longer served any useful purpose. At the beginning of the 2020s, when the United Nations moved from New York to Geneva in order to get away from the political turmoil in the United States, it had fewer than two hundred members. By 2040, there were over one thousand. The preeminence of small countries was following the model of nation-states like Monaco and Lichtenstein, which had already demonstrated that countries did not need huge populations and modern armies to defend their sovereignty. This was the true New World Order. The value of empire building was gone forever. But," Abraham said, pausing for effect, "the desire for control was still alive and well.

"Two fundamental and irreversible factors precipitated this global disaggregation trend. First was the acceptance of English as the de facto international common language. The net effect was that international dialogue in English virtually eliminated any need for isolationist nationalism by making it possible to maintain local dialects, customs, and cultural values, while external communications could be carried out simultaneously in a common language. English-speaking people in every sector found themselves on equal footing with anyone else in the world by virtue of this common tongue, independent of their mother tongue. By virtue of an accident of history, British imperialism two centuries earlier had planted the seeds of a common language from Singapore to Timbuktu, which ended up making the English language the great equalizer in the world. No one could claim supremacy over another on the grounds of linguistic snobbery. Provincialism could coexist in harmony alongside globalism for the first time in history.

"The second fundamental change was the creation of the internet. Never before had a single technology infused itself so rapidly and so completely into the fabric of society in all places. The internet was impartial to regional customs and peculiarities despite numerous attempts by governments to control it. It served everyone equally. Besides simply accelerating communications, it enabled international banking. More correctly, it crushed the power of international banks. Local currencies were gradually replaced by digital currency, making it almost impossible for central banks to manipulate local economies. International commerce was carried out as effortlessly by small players as by big ones. A dairy in Corsica could purchase cheesecloth directly from Vietnam and have it delivered the very next day.

"Empire building, as practiced for four thousand years, was over. All the elements that favored empire building were wiped out almost overnight. Central governments no longer served a useful function. They did whatever they could to retain control, but without success. Influence and control drained steadily out of the world's commercial centers, and geopolitical power no longer rested with the large metropolitan centers. The internet and the English language connected every human on the planet directly to everyone else without the need any longer to have a power broker in the middle.

"This is when a completely new type of empire emerged—an empire not based on military strength, but an empire intermingled seamlessly and imperceptibly with the New World Order. The syndicate was born. It is no accident that the syndicate is based in Geneva. It is the home of the United Nations, a body that, even though it no longer has any real power, has managed to become the de facto seat of world government."

Pierre commented under his breath, "As if the world actually needs a world government." Then he took over from Abraham, saying, "The UN provided the perfect vacuum into which a new type of influence on global affairs could be interjected. It could have never coexisted with another global power base. I am convinced that the syndicate seeks to ultimately subordinate the UN. The syndicate has changed into an entity that seems to thrive in an environment of perceived localized autonomy that can be manipulated by the influence of an overarching international body like the UN."

Abraham jumped back in. "This is the part we don't fully understand. Somehow, the syndicate has managed to disguise their globalist agenda."

Abraham paused while another round of coffee was served. Christophe held up his cup up to one of the servers. "Could I please have some more coffee?" Turning back to the conversation, he said, "Tell me then, Abraham, how did the syndicate come into being?"

At this point Pierre commented, "No one really knows for sure. As with any secret society, they are shrouded in mystery. We don't know who they are or where they come from. We don't even know how many there are. The only way we know they exist is that their influence shows up in strange and unexpected places. They seem to be pursuing an agenda of global domination, but we have no idea how they plan to pull it off."

Abraham added, "Our theory is that they originated sometime after the fall of Rome. They have been observed in various embodiments throughout the ages, some you may recognize, but most you will never have heard of. Every so often one of their members breaks away. This is believed to be the case with Benito Mussolini. He apparently got it into his head that he was descended directly from Julius Caesar, and he conned Adolf Hitler into joining him to re-create the Roman Empire. More recently, we think they were behind the petroleum cartel, OPEC, of the 1970s. OPEC was designed to control oil supplies in an era of rising demand. It was enormously effective, and it could be argued that it was the most powerful entity in the world for a period of time. OPEC was ultimately the victim of dwindling supplies and alternative sources of energy, forcing the syndicate to find new ways to meddle in world affairs."

"Christophe," added Pierre, "the most curious thing about these people is that they do not employ ordinary means of communication. We think every aspect of their business is conducted in person at their Geneva headquarters. But no one ever sees them come or go. Very strange, don't you think?"

This last comment by Pierre caused Christophe to reflect on some elements he had been trying to piece together in his mind. This, combined with recent thoughts about inconsistencies in the explanation for the Paris portal shutdown, triggered a hunch. "Pierre, I have a theory about how they might be meeting without being detected. I need to run an idea past François as soon as possible."

"Please tell us."

"Not yet. The idea is really crazy, and I need to give it some more thought. Can you arrange for me to see François?"

Pierre replied, "But he is in—" Then he stopped himself. He glanced over at Abraham, who shrugged his shoulders to give his consent to disclose the location. "He is in Israel now, but I think there is a plan to transport the Benoits back to a safe house in Paris the day after tomorrow."

CHAPTER 15

THE TRAPDOOR

Stefan showed up at Christophe's apartment the following morning wearing his orange coveralls. He wanted to check on the countermeasures to be sure they were still effective and to deliver a message in person. He informed Christophe, "Chloé and François are safe and sound in the outskirts of Paris, hidden away in a safe location. His work is nearly complete, so we were able to bring them back a day earlier than planned, but he is still being debriefed. Pierre told me you want to meet with him."

"Yes," said Christophe. "I think it is urgent."

"The two of you are still too 'hot' to be seen together. You can't just hop on the TGV and drop in on him."

Christophe considered this for a minute and then said, "Okay, but why can't I drive?"

"Drive?"

"Yes, drive their car that's in the garage. With the fake plates, even if I am stopped by the police, I will just show them the fake registration and say I borrowed it from a friend."

"Do you even know how to drive?"

"Well, it's been awhile, but yes. It's a perfect plan. I will load up Biscuit and look to the world like I am just returning from holiday. Anyway, surely the Benoits would like to have their car back at some point," he said, pausing, "and their dog."

Stefan thought about it for a minute and finally said, "It might actually work. I need to discuss the idea with others. I will be back shortly." Then he departed. He returned in about fifteen minutes and said, "Okay. It's agreed. When were you planning on going?"

"Early tomorrow morning. If I drive straight through, it will take me about nine hours. I want to get an early start so I don't have to drive in Paris after dark."

Stefan reached in his pocket and handed Christophe a slip of paper. "Here is the address of the RER station at Lieusaint-Moissy, southeast of Paris." He reached in his other pocket and handed Christophe a pack of cigarettes.

"No thanks. I don't smoke."

"These cigarettes are not for smoking," replied Stefan.

"They sure look to me like real cigarettes."

"That's the point. There is a transponder buried inside. We will be able to track your position everywhere you go. Keep it in your pocket at all times, and don't let it out of your sight. When you get to the RER station at the address I just gave you, pull into the parking lot. Someone will meet you there. One more thing: Don't decide to take up smoking. If you remove one of the cigarettes from the pack next to the empty space, the transponder will send out an emergency signal, meaning you are in some sort of trouble."

"Will I see you in Paris, Stefan?"

"Probably not. Remember: no smoking unless you need to be rescued, and please don't offer a cigarette to François either." Stefan always seemed capable of some dry humor during stressful times. Without even so much as a goodbye, Stefan was gone.

The following morning, Christophe packed up enough things for a few days, taking along a warm coat because the forecast said it was supposed to be cold and rainy all week in Paris. He checked on Minnie's supply of food and water, closed the blinds, and double-locked all the doors to the patio. The last thing in the world he needed was a break-in while he was gone. With Biscuit on the leash, he got into the car. Chloé had left the keys with him just in case. It was a small two-door Peugeot with an old blanket spread over the back seat for Biscuit. Christophe took some time to become familiar with the features of the natural gas–electric hybrid. The pressure gauge indicated that he would need to fill up the liquid natural gas tank sometime before he got to Aix-en Provence. He left the garage at about six in the morning and was pleased to discover that he still knew how to drive a car. The sun would not be up for another hour and a half.

The drive to Paris was uneventful, and the traffic was unusually light. He pulled into the RER parking garage as instructed. No sooner had he turned off the engine than a man hopped into the passenger seat. Biscuit growled with disapproval. "It's okay, doggie. I'm on your side." Looking around to be sure he hadn't been spotted, the man said, "Pull out of the garage and turn left." He gave Christophe directions as needed for the ten-minute drive to an area that appeared to be filled with abandoned warehouses. The man punched some sort of code into his phone, and a large shipping bay door went up. "Turn right and go in there." There were two armed guards standing just inside the door. As soon as they recognized the passenger, they waved Christophe on. "Pull into that space there," he said, pointing to the desired spot. "Turn off the car and follow me."

"What about the dog?"

"Bring him."

They walked up a flight of stairs to find François and Chloé eagerly waiting for their arrival. Biscuit went crazy with excitement when he saw Chloé and jumped right into her arms. Everyone embraced. After doing a little catching up, Chloé requested permission to take Biscuit out for a walk. Christophe pulled François aside. "We have a lot to talk about."

François led Christophe to a brightly lit windowless room. A man and a woman in uniform stood up when they entered. François introduced everyone and then said to them, "Would it be possible to finish the debriefing later? Christophe and I have some important matters to discuss."

"As you wish, Mr. Benoit." They pulled the door closed as they left.

François seated himself at the table and offered Christophe coffee and a tray of croissants.

"I think I have figured it out!" exclaimed Christophe.

"No. Me first," replied François, not giving Christophe any further opportunity to talk. "Do you remember that night at your apartment when I was demonstrating the VCVA operation?"

"Of course."

"You asked me how I managed to get hold of one of the valves, and I didn't tell you at the time. That's because I took one out of the stockroom without signing for it. That alone would have been grounds for getting fired."

"Bernice might have authorized it."

"Well," said François, "I was intending to sneak it back into inventory on Tuesday morning before anyone had a chance to notice that it was missing." François leaned back in his chair and placed his hands behind his head. "Do you remember that I told you the valve I brought with me to your apartment was from the very same production lot as the valve retrieved from the portal?" He stared intently at Christophe. "I just can't believe I had been so blind. It didn't occur to me until I was in Israel to check the blasted serial numbers."

Christophe was about to explode with curiosity. "Well? Tell me. Tell me!"

François spoke more slowly at this point. "The serial number of the VCVA I brought to your apartment from the stockroom was the very next one in the sequence to the one delivered to me from the Paris portal." Christophe shook his head a little. He did not understand. "Christophe, the valve purported to come from the portal—the one we tested in my lab—didn't come from the portal at all. It came from our stockroom." Both men stared at each other in stunned silence. Christophe still did not fully grasp what François was saying. "There never was a defective valve. It was a total ruse all along."

Finally, Christophe said, "What does that mean then?"

"First of all, someone very high up in the company knew this and needed to cover it up. Second, it wasn't a faulty valve that caused the portal to go down, and they knew this too."

"Then where does this leave us, François?"

"The Trojan horse is real enough. Any valve in the portal could have been commanded to latch open, and the signal I found on the power bus did, in fact, cause a valve to latch open. The command signal I executed to latch up the valve in your apartment was for the valve with the serial number I brought with me. Stick with me here. I know this is complex. It wasn't until I was in Israel that I actually checked the serial number coded into the command signal I found on the power bus in the event log. For some reason, I was given a perfectly good VCVA to send to Toulouse for destructive testing. If you hadn't come by that Friday, no one would ever have known."

Christophe was still puzzled. "Christophe, the valve in the Paris portal did not stick open. It was only made to look that way."

François took a gulp of coffee. "There's more. The valve is not what triggered the emergency recompression that brought the portal down."

"Okay, François, now you have completely lost me."

"It is good that you are sitting down. The command signals on the power bus are being used to override the system in such a way as to make something happen that no one would ever suspect. I began studying event logs for the prior days, and I saw that very same signal showing up every once in a while holding that particular VCVA open for a longer time than normal. Something else went wrong last Thursday that brought the portal down, and somebody needed to cover it up in a hurry."

Christophe's brain was now playing over and over again the image of the ducks going around in the water channel of his grand-nephew's game when the recirculating pump stopped working. What had he seen? He buried his head in his hands on the table and let out a loud exhale. Things were just beginning to make sense. After a minute he raised his head and stared intently at François. "Okay, now it's my turn. I assume you heard about my run-in with some Russians in Monaco." François nodded. "They kept grilling me about the 'trapdoor.' Why were they so interested in this? They surely have no idea what a trapdoor is. Anyway, as it turned out, you showed that there never was a trapdoor in the code, and they seemed to have no knowledge of a Trojan horse or any other sophisticated piece of computer firmware. But it was my use of the term *trapdoor* that caused all the commotion." Christophe paused midsentence to organize his newest thoughts.

"Two days ago, I met a guy named Abraham at Pierre Fabré's home."

"Oh, I think I met him in Israel," François interrupted. "It must be the same Abraham."

"Anyway, Abraham and Pierre explained to me about a subversive organization called the syndicate and how they are able to meet in Geneva without anyone ever seeing them come or go. The thought occurred to me that they have constructed a private portal into their headquarters building. This is what I came to Paris to tell you. Until a minute ago, I thought I needed to go looking for it. But now I think I know what has actually been going on."

"Please tell me," cried François.

"The 'trapdoor' does not refer to some arcane piece of computer code. The trapdoor is a switch in the portal that allows a capsule to be diverted into another portal. Years ago at Ashleigh I worked on this technology until the project was abandoned." The two men stared at each other incredulously. "You know, François, by figuring out this secret, we would be able to tell who is going to the syndicate headquarters and when simply by watching for the control signal on the power bus and seeing which capsule gets redirected to the second portal."

"You realize, Christophe, that we are the only two people alive—at least for the time being—who know this secret."

"Yes. And this also places us in real jeopardy. We must be very careful whom we disclose this to." They sat in silence for a few moments, trying to contemplate the ramifications. Christophe finally said, "Something just doesn't add up, though. Can you hand me a piece of paper and calculator?" Christophe scribbled, "Distance equals velocity squared divided by two times acceleration." He punched some numbers into the calculator. "The maximum safe speed for switching from one portal to another is about fifty meters per second. In the Paris portal, I am going to guess this speed will be reached about five hundred meters from the end." Christophe paused for a moment to reflect.

François interjected, "You are right; something doesn't add up. There is a problem with this. The incident report said that the defective valve was thirty kilometers in. I verified this from the serial number I was given. The capsule would still be moving at well over five hundred meters per second. There is no way a capsule could be switched at that speed."

"But how can you be sure which valve was actually switched? You just assumed the serial number from the incident report," said Christophe.

François was furiously thumbing through the specifications for the Paris portal, checking the locations of the various VCVAs by serial number. He looked up and lowered his reading glasses to the bridge of his nose. "Oh, Christophe. Why didn't I think of this before? The serial number is encoded into the control signal that triggers the Trojan horse. When we tested the valve at the center,

I just assumed it had the right serial number. But you are right. There is no way a switch could happen at that speed. Guess where the valve with the serial number that activates the switch is located?"

"Five hundred meters from the end?"

"Four hundred meters, to be exact," responded François with satisfaction, as if he had just solved a murder mystery.

"I think we need to keep this just between the two of us, François. Until we have a chance to confirm it, we don't really know whom we can trust at this time." François concurred.

"You know, Bernice could not possibly be involved in the conspiracy. If she had known that the serial number on the valve in the shipping container destined for Toulouse did not match the number from the incident report, she would never have allowed you to do the test for fear that you would notice the discrepancy."

"On the other hand," François replied, "if I had been diligent in my job, I would have double-checked the serial number before doing the ETU test, and the discrepancy would have been known then and there. I would have accepted that somebody made a clerical mistake, Bernice would have reported the error, and that would have been the end of it."

During the intense hour that Christophe and François spent together, they had pieced together a working hypothesis of what was actually taking place in the Paris portal right under everyone's noses. Both men were mentally exhausted but invigorated. They walked out into the main lobby to see Chloé holding Biscuit and surrounded by half a dozen people laughing and listening to her relate the story of pretending to be Christophe's girlfriend. One of them stepped forward to introduce himself. "Hello, my name is Guillaume. I am in charge of this unit. Chloé just asked me if she could go home, and I see no reason why not."

"Is that what you want?" François asked his wife.

"Yes. I am really ready to be home now."

Guillaume looked at François, "André can drive her home in your car. With your hat and his beard, and the cover of darkness, he will have no difficulty passing off as you." André was the guy who had gotten into the car at the RER station and led Christophe to the safe house.

"What about the plates?" asked Christophe.

Guillaume smiled wryly. "Your apartment manager is a very shrewd fellow, Mr. Conally. He hid the real plates in the door panel. They have already been put back on the car." He turned to Chloé and said, "Madame Benoit, tomorrow I expect the police will pay you a visit. They have been looking everywhere for your car since François was reported missing. Just tell them François slipped out for a cigarette. Their only concern is for your well-being. Once they determine that you are okay, they shouldn't bother you any further."

CHAPTER 16

THE SWITCH

The following morning, François was already busy with his debriefing by the time Christophe emerged from his room. François was not kidding when he said it wasn't five stars. The tiny windowless room consisted of a cot and a desk. The community bathroom was down the hall. The only thing that distinguished it from a prison cell was that he didn't have to call for someone to unlock the door to let him out. It was clear why Chloé wanted to go home. He walked out into the break area and inquired where breakfast was being served. A couple of people sitting around the breakroom laughed and pointed at a bank of vending machines along the wall. This would never do. In his whole life, Christophe had never eaten breakfast served from a machine. He got directions to the group manager's office and poked his head in. Guillaume was sitting at his desk reading reports. "Excuse me." Guillaume looked up and motioned for him to enter. "Forgive me, but I have forgotten your name."

"Guillaume."

"Guillaume. I don't think there is any need for me to stick around all day. Would it be possible for me to step out for a bite to eat?"

"Sure, but the nearest café is several blocks away—in fact, right next to the Lieusaint-Moissy RER station. I can have André drive you if you like."

"So I don't need to stick around?" asked Christophe.

"Certainly not. You are completely free to go anywhere you like."

The feeling of being in prison was starting to subside. "In that case, perhaps I will grab my things and check in to a hotel in the city, if that's okay."

"Of course. That's a very good idea. Mr. Benoit should be finishing up by noon, and we were planning to let him go back home."

"Aren't you worried about his safety?"

"We will have his apartment under twenty-four-hour surveillance. So far, the information he has given us is certainly useful, but I don't think it poses enough of a threat to place him in any real danger. If the situation were to change, we could always bring him back here if necessary."

Christophe wanted to blurt out, "But what about the new stuff we figured out last night?" But that would not have been wise. Apparently, Guillaume was unaware of what he and François had pieced together, and Christophe didn't know whose side Guillaume was really on. He packed up his things and headed down the stairs to where André was already sitting in a car waiting for him.

Christophe caught the RER and headed northwest into the city. His plan was to get off somewhere near Place de la Bastille and explore a little, but it was raining, and by the time the train reached the right stop, Christophe's adventurous spirit had dissipated. He decided instead to stay on the train all the way to Gare du Nord, where he knew all the hotels and restaurants in the surrounding blocks. It was also not totally by accident that he wanted to return to "the scene of the crime." There was a magazine kiosk in the station that he knew. He wanted to see if it still carried tourist maps. Paper maps were pretty much a thing the past, but happily the kiosk still had a street map of Paris and a decent folding map of northern Europe, both of which he purchased.

The only hotel that still had any vacancy turned out to be the very same hotel he had stayed at the week before. It was a decent four-star hotel that he had found to be a good value for the money. It was directly accessible from the station by an underground walkway, so he wouldn't even have to go out in the rain. Furthermore, they served a marvelous European-style buffet breakfast. Christophe checked in and headed to the breakfast area while he waited for his room to be prepared. He still had fifteen minutes before the breakfast closed at ten.

As he was piling food onto his plate, it dawned on him that all he had eaten in the past twenty-four hours was a chicken sandwich and chips that he had purchased at a filling station on his drive to Paris, and a croissant at the safe house. The adrenalin of the past day had apparently suppressed his appetite, but now the sight of all the food choices reminded him that he was famished. The strong hot coffee also revived his senses. He began to review in his mind the things that he and François had figured out the previous evening.

When he had finished his breakfast, he opened up the two maps, starting with the map of northern Europe. He drew a straight line between Belmullet, Ireland, and Le Gare du Nord. This would have been the path of the Paris portal. Then he took out the Paris street map and found where the route of the Paris portal crossed the same bend in the Seine on both maps. Then he drew a line on the Paris map from that point on the Seine to Le Gare du Nord. Lastly, he consulted the legend to determine the scale, and estimated the location of a point four hundred meters from the terminus of the Paris portal at Le Gare du Nord back toward Belmullet. He marked the spot and wrote "Location of switch" beside it. The calculation was crude, but he was probably within 50 meters of the exact location. The x fell close to the Barbès-Rochechouart metro station. This had to be it. Christophe could barely contain his excitement.

His room was still not ready, so he checked his backpack at the reception desk, took out his raincoat and umbrella, and headed toward the metro station on foot. There it was—an elevated portion of the Blue Line that had been in service in Paris for more than one hundred years. Christophe first took the escalator up to the track level. He saw nothing unusual. Then he took the elevator back down to the street level. The button only permitted this one stop, but he also observed a numeric keypad, which he thought was unusual for an elevator that only went between two floors. He stepped out into the street and observed the elevator for several minutes. Almost everyone took the escalator, but a few took the elevator from time to time if they had luggage or were disabled. He then observed a perfectly healthy man without any luggage get on the elevator alone at the street level and watched for him to exit at the track level above, but the elevator door never opened. After a minute or so, the elevator door opened again at the street level, but the man was nowhere to be seen. Christophe concluded that he must have entered a code on the keypad to command the elevator to descend to some level below ground.

He was understandably intrigued. There was a café across the street. He sat at a table outside with a good vantage point of the elevator, ordered coffee, and just watched. Every so often, a solo person would enter the elevator and disappear, and sometimes a solo person would exit the elevator at the street level when it was clear that no one had gotten on at the track level. *What is down there?* he wondered. He then observed a man with a Day-Glo yellow vest pushing a trash can open a door next to the elevator with a key and push the trash can inside. When the door closed, it did not close completely. The man failed to notice it because he was busy trying to light a cigarette as he walked away. Christophe quickly paid his tab and walked across the street. He opened the door and went inside. It took a moment for his eyes to adjust to the dark. There was a staircase going down, just as he had anticipated. He carefully inched down the two flights to the space below. It was a cavernous dimly lit room. He was able to conceal himself behind some crates while he took in the sight. There was an open crate on the floor nearby that contained several portal capsules. He was now positive that he had found the location he was looking for.

"What are you doing here?" Christophe turned around to see a very agitated security guard pointing a gun at him. Christophe was speechless. "Vous venez avec moi," he demanded. The guard led him into a side room and ordered him to take a seat. He took a two-way transmitter out of his utility belt and tried to report in. All he could hear was static. The guard let out a string of expletives.

Christophe took the pack of cigarettes out of his pocket and removed one, asking the guard, "Do you have a light?"

"You can't smoke in here, you idiot!" Christophe was actually relived because he wasn't sure he could puff on a lighted cigarette in a convincing manner. He put the cigarette back in the pack and then put the pack back in his pocket. Almost that fast, two men in masks appeared out of nowhere. One slipped a hypodermic needle into the guard's neck while the other stood guard. The security guard was out cold in an instant. By the smile left on his face, others would conclude he had been sleeping on the job when they discovered him. The drug was short-lived and would leave him with only a headache and no recollection of the preceding hour.

One of the men in a mask signaled for Christophe to follow—something he was all too happy to do. They went back up the staircase to the street level. Prior to opening the door, they both removed their masks. "Stefan?" said an astonished Christophe. The three slipped out the door and disappeared into the crowd unnoticed. Stefan led the way back to Christophe's hotel without saying a word. The other man followed, turning around occasionally to look for any sign of being tailed. Once back in the hotel, Christophe and Stefan sat down in the lounge area. The third man stood guard near the door.

Christophe looked at Stefan, totally bewildered. "You told me you weren't going to be in Paris."

"Things changed."

"How did you find me?"

"Besides the location transponder in your pocket? Guillaume called me the minute you left the compound in Moissy-Cramayel."

"Guillaume?" responded Christophe.

"Yes, Guillaume. He had me tail you."

"Why?"

Stefan paused to consider how much he was at liberty to say. "We had a pretty good hunch what you would do. We figured you would go looking for the location of the switch."

"The switch?" Christophe exclaimed. "How in the world do you know about the switch?"

Stefan paused again staring at the ceiling. "Did you really think the room where you and François were in last evening wasn't bugged?"

"You mean you heard everything?"

"Everything. We knew you would lead us to the location of the switch. We just never dreamed that you would be crazy enough to actually go down there. When we saw you go in that door, we knew there was going to be trouble. By the way, that business with the cigarette was nicely done. It was just a good thing we were right outside the door when you set off the alarm."

Christophe was still bewildered. "You knew everything all along?"

"You were never in any real danger. The biggest gamble was that the syndicate might be tipped off. If they ever discovered that we had figured out how they were getting people in and out of Geneva undetected, they would shut the whole operation down, and we would lose any chance of identifying the members. This is why the run-in with the security guard was so dicey. There can be absolutely no hint that anyone ever penetrated their operation."

Christophe was still quite rattled from his ordeal. "You look like you need something to drink?" said Stefan.

"Just some water, please. *Gazeux.*"

Stefan hailed the server and made the request, then pulled up a little closer, displaying a more serious expression, if that was even possible. "So, Christophe, tell me about the switch."

The server arrived with a bottle of Perrier and a glass with ice. Christophe's throat was parched, and the fizzy water felt good going down. "Some years ago—about twenty—when the hyperspeed transcontinental portal was being constructed across North America, the question of intermediate stops kept coming up. The portal extended from Los Angeles directly to Chicago. Chicago is the hub where portals to Goose Bay and also New York, Atlanta, and a dozen other cities originate. There was no portal to Denver, and this did not sit well with them. Denver was the capital of a newly recognized principality that included Wyoming and parts of New Mexico, Nebraska, Kansas, etcetera, and they wanted to be connected by portal to the rest of the world, but the cost to bore an additional tunnel under the hard granite of the Rocky Mountains was more than anyone was willing to pay. The Los Angeles–Chicago subterranean portal actually passes some three hundred kilometers south of Denver. A compromise was reached whereby capsules destined for Denver could be switched to a second portal, while the capsules going through to Chicago would continue on in a straight line. The problem was that it is impossible to redirect the trajectory of a capsule going one thousand meters per second without ripping apart the capsule and its occupant. It would be necessary to slow the capsule down to a speed below fifty meters per second, which is about the maximum safe switching speed. It was thought that capsules headed to Denver could be switched out of the main portal, but this meant timing everything perfectly so that the capsule could be slowed down and switched out before the next capsule, which would be going one thousand meters per second, closed in on it. In theory, the idea actually might have worked, but it was soon realized that if for any reason there should have been a malfunction in the switch—if it didn't get locked back into position in time—there would be an unpreventable disaster. The idea of installing a switch in a portal was, thus, abandoned, and all the capsules would, instead, be brought to a complete stop at the intermediate station south of Denver. This added thirty minutes to the Los Angeles–Chicago trip, but I guess that is a small price to pay for the added safety. This actually turned out for the better, because the terminal just south of Colorado Springs ended up serving as an important redistribution hub for destinations not well served by Chicago. As far as I know, however, Ashleigh never stopped doing research and development on the idea of switches."

Stefan said, "But what does this have to do with what is going on below the Barbès-Rochechouart metro station?"

"Ah. What's the best way to transfer people from one portal to another? You install a switch. But in this case, you install it a point where the speed of all the capsules is slow enough—near the end of the trip. That would be about four hundred meters from the terminus."

Stefan sat back in his chair. He was beginning to get the picture. Christophe went on. "Let's say there is someone in a capsule whom you want to send somewhere different than where the portal is going, and you want to do this in a secret fashion so that no one will suspect it. How might you do that? You could install a secret switch to route the designated capsule out of the portal, but then this creates a problem. The portal operators at the terminus would know immediately that there was a missing capsule, and more importantly, they would know who the missing passenger is. The way you solve this dilemma is to switch a duplicate capsule back into the portal at the same instant. The new capsule would need to have the same serial number and designation so that the receiving sensors would not detect anything amiss. Every capsule is closely monitored, but no one ever checks the identity of an arriving passenger, do they?" Christophe flashed a huge grin because it was clear that Stefan now got it. "The capsule arrives. The passenger pops out and walks away, except that this passenger is a paid employee of the syndicate who got into the capsule just four hundred meters from the end of the line. He walks out of the Gare du Nord terminal and makes the short trek back to the Barbès-Rochechouart metro station, goes down in the elevator, and waits for the next syndicate bigwig to come along."

"Then how do the syndicate 'bigwigs,' as you call them, actually get to Geneva?" asked Stefan.

"I am going to guess that there is a second, secret portal connecting the metro station to the basement of the syndicate headquarters."

"How about when they leave Geneva? How do they get back?"

"Simple. They just return to the staging area under the metro station. In this case, another paid syndicate employee would need to have been dispatched to Belmullet in advance, in order to take the portal back to Paris. Just like before, but in reverse, the capsule with the paid employee is switched out and the bigwig is switched in. Five minutes later, he or she pops out of the capsule and goes about his or her business in Paris. No one would ever know that this person had been to Geneva, never mind for how long."

"Are you kidding me? That's absolutely brilliant!" exclaimed Stefan.

"Yes, brilliant, but incredibly sinister." Christophe was pleased with himself. The more he thought about this idea, the more sense it made to him.

"Did you ever figure out why the portal went down?" asked Stefan.

"No, but I have a pretty good theory. If for some reason the replacement capsule wasn't ready to launch in time, they would have had no choice but to trigger an emergency recompression. Otherwise there would be a missing capsule at the end, and obviously this would cause quite a stir. An emergency recompression would mean that all the capsules would come to a complete stop so that the replacement capsule could still be switched in to the portal without arousing suspicion. The only evidence would be that the spacing between the capsules near the exit end would be off."

Stefan exhaled with a whistle. "Christophe, how did you ever figure all this out?"

"Simply by watching a little boy pluck rubber ducks out of a water trough at the fair."

Stefan shook his head in disbelief. "Christophe, you are completely insane."

There was so much about Stefan that Christophe was dying to know. There were so many questions regarding this enigmatic fellow that kept turning up unexpectedly. Stefan leaned forward in his chair and said quietly, "There are a few loose ends to tend to." He signaled to the other man standing by the door, who nodded and went out. "Christophe, we have a unique opportunity to bring down the syndicate, but only if we can fabricate a credible story. We need to convince the syndicate that you and François never met up in Beaulieu and never figured out anything important. We have created a travel itinerary for François and Chloé for the past week showing them on a vacation in Normandy, complete with bank card receipts and the hotels they stayed in." He paused. "You get the picture. Other than the message you sent him from Bordeaux, we are pretty sure now that the syndicate doesn't know anything more."

"What about the call I got from him on Chloé's phone?"

"As far as we can tell, this was never intercepted." The other man returned at that moment and handed Stefan a shopping bag containing a box neatly wrapped in shiny gold paper with a large gold ribbon bow and a small gift card attached.

"A Christmas present?" exclaimed Christophe.

"Well, not exactly," said Stefan. "The box contains the VCVA that François took from the stockroom. It is essential that we smuggle it back in before anyone misses it. That means today."

Christophe looked intently at Stefan, "And you think I am the crazy one." Then after some reflection, he added,

"You know, there is only one person who could pull this off."

"Yes, we know." Stefan handed Christophe the bag. "Be here in this lounge at three o'clock." Stefan started to get up to leave. "One more thing, Christophe. François has no knowledge of anything that has gone on today, and it needs to stay that way. You must not ever try to contact him."

"What will happen to him?" asked Christophe.

"He has been reassigned to a new duty at the agency, where he will be able to work happily until he retires with full pension. Remember—right here, three o'clock sharp."

CHAPTER 17

CLEANING UP

A courier pressed the doorbell of Bernice Lille's apartment and waited at the door. When she answered, he handed her a small sealed envelope, waited for her acknowledgment signature, and left. Inside was a plain card that read, "Please meet me in the lobby of the InterPlaza Hotel at 3:00 p.m. today. It is extremely urgent. —Christophe."

"The nerve!" said Bernice as she walked back into the kitchen and dropped the note in the trash. She sat back down to finish her lunch but couldn't get the message out of her mind. It had certainly piqued her curiosity. She decided at last to go see what this was all about.

Christophe got up to greet her when she entered the lobby. He pointed her toward a chair in a quiet area of the lounge. He could tell by the fire in her eyes that she was not at all happy to be there. She saw the bag with the "gift" next to his chair and said, "You think you can make peace with me by just offering me a present?"

"Bernice," Christophe said apologetically, "I need a big favor."

"Doing favors for you, Christophe, has been rather costly for me lately."

"I know," said Christophe. "This is the last time. I promise. Anyway, the favor is not for me. It's for François."

Bernice sat down. "Okay. I will hear you out."

"François did something really stupid last Monday that will probably get him fired. He desperately needs his pension, and you are the only one whom I trust who can fix this."

"Okay. I'm listening."

"He took a spare VCVA from the stockroom."

"He what!" Bernice exploded loud enough to turn some heads in the lounge area.

"François needed a real valve on which to perform some diagnostic tests, so he took one home with him."

"Wow! I don't know what to say," she said. "That is a very serious infraction."

"I know. François knows. He was planning to return it on Tuesday but then you told him not to come in. He is really in a bind now. I know you are kindhearted and compassionate, and I know you wouldn't want him to lose his job over this, just before he becomes eligible to retire."

Bernice sat back in her chair. "I need something to drink."

"Sit tight. I will get it. What would you like?"

"A glass of Chablis."

Christophe went up to the bar to place the order and returned to his seat. Bernice was staring into space with an expression that spoke that this whole business was completely out of control. She sat without saying a word. When the wine arrived, she took a sip. "Okay. But this is the last time."

"Bernice, I owe you my life."

"You already owed me your life from the last favor," she said sarcastically.

Christophe handed the shopping bag to Bernice. "The VCVA is in here. It is wrapped to look like a Christmas present, so you shouldn't have any trouble getting it past the security guard. I will be in my room when you get back. Just call me on the house phone."

Bernice took the bag and headed to her office at the Portal Center. She had a growing dislike for her job that predated the incidents of the prior week. She had had her fill of working for the French government, and she was in discussions with a private defense contractor that was thinking of offering her a job. The work was top secret, requiring a security clearance and an extensive investigation into her background. Now she was about to commit a crime that would probably get her fired and make it impossible to be employed by the new company. She had a sick feeling in the pit of her stomach. She managed to convince herself that what she was about to do would be okay. She kept repeating to herself, "It's all for François. It's all for François." She entered the lobby as if it were just another ordinary day, but she worried that the fear in her eyes would give her away.

"Bonjour, Mademoiselle Lille," said the security guard at the desk. "What brings you in on a Sunday?"

"Oh, I have a big day tomorrow, and there is a report I need to finish," Bernice replied as she walked past him toward the door. She fetched her security badge from her coat pocket and held it up to the reader. Her heart was pounding so hard that she was sure the guard could hear it.

"What's in the bag?" he asked. If Bernice had had a weak heart, that question would have triggered a heart attack. She was hoping he wouldn't require her to put it through the x-ray scanner.

She turned with a disarming smile and reached into the back. Holding up the package for him to see, she said, "I just did a little early Christmas shopping. Do you need me to open it?"

"No. Of course not. Have a nice day." The door opened. It took all her willpower not to run to the safety of her office. There was no one else around. All the lights were off, but they turned on automatically as she walked down the corridor. She sat at her desk for several minutes just staring at the wall and waiting for her heart rate to subside.

She untied the bow, unwrapped the box containing the VCVA, and headed down the corridor toward the stockroom. She swiped her badge to open the door, which she knew meant that her entry would show up on the access log. Hopefully, there would never be any reason for anyone to check it. She placed the valve back on the shelf in its proper position, after instinctively double-checking the serial number to be sure it was in the right order. There were four other valves on the shelf. She looked at the number on the label of the last box on the shelf to be certain that the one she'd gotten from Christophe was the next one in the sequence. To her horror, she discovered that the number on the box behind was not in sequence but was two numbers lower. The prior one in the sequence was also missing.

She went to the logbook to see who might have checked it out, but there was no entry. She panicked, not knowing what to do next. Her immediate thought was that François had taken two valves but only returned one to her. She thought she had been duped by Christophe, and this made her really angry. She hurried back to her office, grabbed her coat, and stormed out. The security guard commented, "That sure didn't take long."

Bernice looked at him and managed a smile. "The file I was looking for turns out to be in the vault. I can't get access until the morning. *Bonne journée.*"

"Mademoiselle Lille, you seem to have forgotten your Christmas present." Bernice nearly passed out with terror. "Oh, I left it in my office. That's okay. I will get it tomorrow."

Bernice rounded the corner and began to sob with fear. After regaining her composure, she stormed back to Christophe's hotel and called him on the house phone. "You duped me, Christophe."

"What?"

"You duped me." Bernice began to sob again.

"Wait. I will be right down. Don't move."

Bernice was in the lounge crying softly when Christophe arrived. When she saw him, she said, "You ruined my career."

Christophe ordered her a glass of Chablis and sat down next to her. "What do you mean?"

"François took two valves, but you only gave me one to return. When they do inventory tomorrow, they will figure out that there is a missing valve and see that I was the last person to enter the stockroom."

All the color drained out of Christophe's face. Bernice did not know that the other missing valve was the one that she had shipped to Toulouse. He wasn't at liberty to tell her, because that would require disclosing the conspiracy.

"Are you going to just sit there and stare at me?" blustered Bernice.

Christophe didn't know what to do, so he reached in his pocket and took out a pack of cigarettes. "Would you care for a smoke?"

"No thanks." She looked at Christophe quizzically. "I didn't know you smoked."

"I don't." Bernice looked puzzled. Christophe pushed the cigarette back into the pack. At that moment, the waiter brought glasses of wine for both of them, and she eagerly took a sip. Christophe could see that her fragile state of mind was starting to subside.

Out of the blue she started unloading on Christophe. "I really hate my job, Christophe. I have been with the agency for just under ten years. It's the only place I have ever worked. In the beginning it was fun and exciting, but over the past couple of years it has become more and more dark and oppressive. I don't know what has changed. It is almost as if the people I work for are marionettes being manipulated by dark outside forces. Everybody is suspicious of everybody else. I never expected that working for the French government would be like that. I am thirty-three and have no life of my own. I have no friends, no relationships. All my family is in Lyon. I hate Paris!" She paused for a moment. "I feel like they have been trying to force me to quit for the past few months. It's just subtle things: extra scrutiny of my reports, suspicion, glaring and untrusting glances in meetings. You know what I mean. Surely you experienced this in your career with Ashleigh?"

Christophe nodded, thinking to himself, *If only she knew.*

Christophe was sympathetic and a bit surprised at her sudden frankness. She then confessed, "I am planning to quit. I have submitted a job application to a company headquartered in Lyon. I have been called back for a third interview next week, which I interpret as serious interest on their part. I will need a background check and security clearance, and apparently that is the only holdup. Until today, my record was squeaky-clean. Now I am embroiled in a conspiracy and cover-up. I am ruined." She started to cry again.

Stefan showed up at that moment, looking a bit irritated. "You know, Christophe, that pack of cigarettes is only for emergencies."

"This is an emergency. I want to introduce my friend Bernice Lille."

"Enchanté." Stefan pulled up a chair to join them.

"Bernice, this is Stefan. I apologize, I don't know his last name. He knows all about you sneaking the valve back into the stockroom on my behalf."

Stefan took Bernice's extended hand. "Just Stefan will suffice. So, what is the emergency?"

Christophe looked over at Bernice to signal that it was safe for her to begin.

She started out, "I work for the agency Le Centre des Portals de Paris."

"Yes, I know. I have seen your dossier," said Stefan.

Bernice glared at him. "I beg your pardon? My dossier?"

"Apparently Christophe failed to tell you about me," Stefan said, looking over at Christophe. "I am with the French Intelligence Ministry. I have been reviewing your application for a security clearance." This caused Bernice to sit straight up defensively in her chair. "Don't worry. I'm a friend, more so than you realize. And so is Christophe."

Christophe said, "Stefan, we have a situation, something I did not anticipate. When Bernice returned François's VCVA to the stockroom, she noticed that there was a second missing valve." Then he added, "This is the one with the serial number that François and I tested in his lab, supposing it had been removed from the Paris portal."

Bernice's eyes opened wide at this. "Wait a minute. What did you just say?"

Christophe looked across at Stefan to be sure it was okay to go on. Stefan nodded. "The VCVA we unpacked from the shipping container in François's lab was presumed to have come directly from the repair crew in the portal. Everyone believed it to be the defective valve that supposedly caused the portal failure. We had no reason to think otherwise. When we ran it through the ETU tests, it checked out, as you know." Christophe looked over at Stefan again to be sure he could tell the rest of the story. "François took a VCVA from the stockroom on Monday morning without telling anyone, as you know, because he was hoping to figure out at home why the ETU failed to pick up the fault reported by the VCVA that brought down the Paris portal."

"This much I know," said Bernice. "But what's this about the second missing VCVA?"

Christophe continued, "In the lab on Monday morning, François entered the serial number on the defective valve that came from the Paris portal in order to run the ETU diagnostic and thought nothing more about it. He didn't actually notice until a couple of days ago that the serial number on the valve he had taken from the stockroom was the next number in the sequence after the one he presumed to have come from the portal. Well, of course, that's not possible. The VCVA installed in the portal would have had a much lower serial number because no valves in the tunnel have been replaced in years."

"Wait a minute," Bernice interrupted. "Are you are telling me that the valve I received from the repair crew actually came from the stockroom? That's impossible. François and I are the only two people with access. Nobody could have pulled off a switch like that without me knowing it."

Stefan and Christophe exchanged glances. It was abundantly clear by now that Bernice was not involved. Stefan looked deeply into her eyes. "Bernice, something took place in the Paris portal that Thursday that resulted in an emergency recompression, as you know. But it was necessary for the agency to cover up the exact cause." He let the impact of this sink in and then said, "Bernice, if you aren't involved, then we need to find out who is."

Bernice looked around the table. "You think I am involved? That's crazy."

"We are sure you were not involved in this," said Christophe. "But we need to find out who actually did take the other VCVA from the stockroom."

Bernice's expression slowly transformed from one of despair to one of near triumph. "A lot of curious and unexplained things at the agency are now beginning to make sense." She took another sip of wine. "Christophe, when I went into the stockroom just an hour ago, I noticed something unusual that didn't fully register in my mind until now. The computer display on the inside of the door shows a log of everyone who comes and goes. It shows the exact time they enter and the exact time they leave. I glanced at the screen when I left, hoping that by some miracle my entry had not been logged. No such luck. But I noticed that François was the last person to enter. That would have been Monday morning, as you said. Guess who entered the stockroom on Friday morning?" She looked at the other two with a grin. "Me!"

Christophe and Stefan exchanged confused glances.

"Do you know where I was on Friday morning? Not at the center. I was at the dentist." She slapped the table. "Someone forged my credentials. I'm being set up."

Stefan, Christophe, and Bernice ordered dinner from the lounge menu. Over the course of the next two hours, in the privacy of their little corner of the InterPlaza Hotel lounge, Stefan and Christophe explained everything they knew about the activities going on below the Barbès-Rochechouart metro station and all they knew about the syndicate. Bernice was a sponge. This was all starting to make a great deal of sense to her.

Stefan was also formulating a new strategy. He had seen Bernice's security dossier, which included a psychiatric evaluation, and had already reached the conclusion that she would make a terrific spy.

CHAPTER 18

THE MOLE

When they were done, Christophe went up to his room, and Stefan and Bernice went out into the street, where the rain had picked up notably. "Can I offer you a ride home?" Stefan said to Bernice as she was fumbling to open her umbrella.

Her first thought was that Stefan was being a bit forward. Her defenses always went up in the presence of men her age. "No thanks. I'll take the metro."

A car pulled up to the curb, and the driver stepped out and opened the rear door. Stefan motioned in with his arm. "Are you sure? It's really starting to rain hard."

Who is this guy? she wondered. "Okay, if you insist." Stefan went around to the other side and got in. The car sped away.

"Do you mind if we make a stop along the way? There is something I would like to show you," he said.

Bernice perceived this as a rhetorical question and did not answer. The car pulled off the boulevard and descended into a parking garage through a door that went up just as they arrived and closed immediately after they were inside.

"What is this?" asked Bernice.

"This is where I work. There is someone here I would like you to meet." The car pulled to a stop, and the driver got out and opened Bernice's door. Stefan and Bernice took an elevator to the fifth floor, where there were dozens of people scurrying about, apparently oblivious to the fact that it was nine o'clock on a Sunday evening. Stefan ushered her into an office where an older gentleman with thinning hair and a full gray beard sat behind a huge desk. He stood up immediately and embraced Bernice and kissed her on both cheeks as if he had known her for years. "I am so delighted to finally meet you. I have heard so many good things about you."

Stefan said, "Bernice, meet Abraham, our director."

Stefan stepped out of the room so the two could get acquainted. Bernice had absolutely no idea what this encounter was all about, but she would soon be finding out. Meanwhile, Stefan walked down the corridor to the computer center to find Cédric, the French Intelligence Ministry's master hacker. He described the nature of the mission and then went to the break room to make himself a cup of coffee and wait for Abraham to finish up with Bernice.

After a while, Bernice and Abraham emerged from his office, laughing together as if they were old friends.

"Stefan," said Abraham, loud enough for everyone in the complex to hear, "Mademoiselle Lille is a remarkable young lady. You were absolutely right in your assessment."

Stefan snatched her away, and the two headed back toward the computer center. "Bernice, this is Cédric. Cédric, Bernice." They shook hands, and Cédric swiveled back around to his computer console.

"Everything is set. All I need is her log-in credential."

Bernice gave Stefan a puzzled look. Stefan explained, "Cédric has hacked into the agency computer. He has gained access to the entry–exit data log on the stockroom door and will delete the last two entries. That would be François's entry last Monday morning and yours from this afternoon. If he does this without using your credential, it would be possible for the agency to detect that they had been hacked. Using your credential, we will leave no trace."

"What about the fake entry using my name earlier on Friday?" asked Bernice.

"If we erase that one, then they will for sure know the log was hacked because the perpetrator somehow got hold of your credential in order to falsify the entry. Presumably that is someone high up in the organization. All we need to do is erase any trace that François removed a valve and that you returned it today," explained Stefan.

"Okay, then. Here—let me type it in when you are ready." Cédric rolled his chair aside to give Bernice access to the keyboard.

Cédric then typed a few keystrokes and swiveled back around. "Done!" He had the amused look of someone fully appreciative of his own brilliance.

Stefan walked with Bernice back down the corridor. He said to her, "Is it all right if I call the driver to take you home now?"

"What's next, then?" she asked.

Stefan took both of her hands reassuringly and said, "You realize that nothing in your life from now on will ever be quite the same. Are you okay with that?" Bernice gave a slight nod. "For you, it needs to be business as usual. Go to work tomorrow, do the things you normally do, and pretend like none of this ever took place." The elevator door opened, and the same driver as before was standing to take her down to the car. She stepped into the elevator and turned around. Stefan could tell she was working hard to manage her fear. "Don't worry," he said. "We will be watching over you every minute."

Christophe went to bed at ten, but he was too wired from the day's excitement and from drinking too much coffee to be able to sleep. He decided to go out for a walk and maybe even take another look at the Barbès-Rochechouart metro station. He was bundled up in anticipation of the cold. As he passed the front desk, the night desk clerk said, "Bonsoir, Monsieur Conally. I have an envelope for you."

It was a familiar plain sealed envelope with "C. Conally" handwritten on the front. Christophe opened it while the clerk watched.

Christophe:

You need to trust me that everything is now under control. It is time for you to go home to Beaulieu-sur-Mer. The biggest risk to our operation at this point is that you might be spotted. It is critical that no one ever finds out that you were in Paris today. Your hotel room has been paid, and you will find a train ticket to Nice leaving tomorrow at 0625. There will be a car out front at 0600 to take you to Gare de Lyon. You will notice that the ticket is not issued in your name. There is also in the envelope a false French identity card to match the name on the ticket. Hold on to the card. It might come in handy someday. Also, hold on to the pack of cigarettes. You just never know when the urge to pick up that nasty habit may come over you.

—S

Christophe removed the ticket and the photo ID: "Sam Houston." *Very original,* he mused. He started for the door, and the desk clerk said, "Um, Monsieur Conally? May I please have the message back? I need to destroy it."

Christophe said under his breath, "Is everyone in this blasted country a spy?" The desk clerk must have read his lips, because he flashed a broad grin. Christophe returned the envelope and put the ticket and ID into his pocket. "I am going out for a beer."

"We have a wonderful selection of draft beers in our lounge," said the clerk, swiftly coming out from behind the desk to show him the way. Obviously, Christophe knew where the lounge was, but this maneuver was intended to convince him that if he headed out the door, he would probably have been tackled.

"Good idea. I think I will just have a beer in the lounge, then." Then, turning back to the clerk, Christophe said, "Yesterday all of the other hotels in the vicinity were completely booked. How is it that the InterPlaza just happened to have a room available?"

"We always keep a room available for special clients," said the clerk with a grin.

At Gare de Lyon early the next morning, Christophe scanned his ticket and handed his ID to the attendant at the gate, who scrutinized it carefully. The likeness was not very good, but apparently it was good enough to convince him that Sam Houston was indeed the passenger. Christophe was waved through. He had only five minutes before the train was due to depart. It was a modern high-speed maglev. The trip to Marseille, including several stops, would take only two hours. He tossed his backpack in the overhead rack, took his assigned seat next to the window, and settled in for the pleasant trip south through the heartland of France along the Rhône.

As the train pulled out of the station, he began to reflect on the fact that an American named Sam Houston was leaving Paris but another man named Christophe Conally would be arriving in Marseille. This was only possible because no one bothered to check the identity of an arriving passenger anymore. The ease with which someone could pretend to be someone else was a curious thing. True identity was almost irrelevant. He looked around at the other passengers and wondered how many of them might be traveling under false identification. The thought gave him a chill.

Christophe used the time to begin doing some reading about identity checking and border security. He found a few relevant articles, the most interesting of which had to do with Switzerland. He learned that there was a time in the not-too-distant past when identity verification was required at most international border crossings. It was necessary for all disembarking passengers to go through a retinal scan. In those days, it was nearly impossible to travel under an assumed name. It became a point of international debate—whether it was actually necessary to verify identity both upon departure and upon arrival. By international cooperation, the arrival check was deemed to be unnecessary and was subsequently phased out. After all, if the identity of a passenger was verified upon boarding, then obviously that very same person would disembark. Most countries did away with immigration control once the country of origin was able to demonstrate strict adherence to the international protocols for passenger identification.

Switzerland was a notable exception. It was not possible to enter the country without a retinal scan. This caused a huge outcry when the UN relocated its headquarters to Geneva. Diplomats refused to submit to an additional screening, which they considered degrading, and ultimately got the Swiss government to relax the requirement, but only for credentialed diplomats. The consequence was that Geneva became the international meeting place for subversive and shadowy groups because the UN failed to maintain tight control over the issuance of diplomatic credentials. For a price, nearly anyone could buy fake credentials. This is how the syndicate was able to get together in the early days. Their members could travel to Geneva using fake diplomatic credentials.

After a while, the Swiss government got wise to the practice and implemented random checks of diplomats. The penalty for trying to enter Switzerland with forged documents was up to two years in prison. Diplomats, of course, would merely be deported, but besides the personal embarrassment, they would be blacklisted from ever returning to Switzerland. This pretty much put an end to the practice. The syndicate considered moving their base of operations to another city, like Paris, where there was no scrutiny given to arriving passengers. However, it was their ability to influence the UN that was central to their effectiveness at manipulating global geopolitical affairs. Christophe was convinced that the syndicate had constructed a secret portal for smuggling syndicate members in and out of Geneva in order to circumvent any identity checks on the Swiss side. This would have required that a controlling interest in Ashleigh Systems be acquired by the syndicate, with its members posing as an outside consortium of investors.

Christophe vividly remembered the event. At the time, he was busy managing the North Atlantic portal project. When it was announced that Ashleigh had been purchased by a group of investors with no prior experience in portal technology, it precipitated a shock wave through the company. Christophe had feared that since the North Atlantic portal was way over budget, the new owners would either pull the plug on the project or start cutting corners. Neither of these concerns ever materialized. In fact, the cash began to flow more freely than ever. New portals were announced, and it seemed that senior Ashleigh management had made a very prudent decision in selling the company. The consortium also had holdings in shipping, telecommunications, airlines, and railroads. One of the most interesting acquisitions was that of the freight juggernaut UPX. The consortium seemed to have found a way to control virtually the entire gamut of global commerce without ever giving the appearance of trying to monopolize any particular sector. It looked to everyone like a solid multinational global enterprise. Even though Christophe had been focused on transoceanic portals, he had been aware of most of the portal projects being managed by Ashleigh, which included a portal between Paris and Geneva. This portal was particularly high-profile because it would become the primary route for people coming from and going to the UN.

As the French countryside slipped past his window, Christophe started giving some thought to the possible existence of a secret portal based on what he had learned over the past twenty-four hours. Something that had been very troubling to him, however, was how it would even be possible to construct such a second, secret portal without anyone finding out about it. For one thing, excavation of a tunnel generates a lot of debris that has to be dumped somewhere. This would only have been possible if both portals were constructed simultaneously and if the debris from the second, secret tunnel was removed through the legitimate primary tunnel. Such a feat could only be carried out with a high degree of conspiracy involving careful orchestration of multiple parties. It would not have been possible in any of the projects he had managed, so it was worth doing some checking to find out who at Ashleigh had been responsible for managing the Paris–Geneva line. He would look into this as soon as he got back to his apartment.

Bernice showed up at work at her normal time of nine in the morning. There was nothing out of the ordinary. The only action item on her desk was a request for transfer for a Mr. François Benoit to another division, requiring her signature. There was no need to find a replacement. Her branch of the agency was winding down, and any opportunity to reduce head count through attrition was always welcome.

Meanwhile, Cédric had written a program to give an alert each time the coded signal on the power bus to override the VCVA in the Paris portal was detected. It soon became routine to identify the occupant of the capsule passing under the Barbès-Rochechouart metro station. Within a few days, the identities of several passengers participating in the switch were known.

CHAPTER 19

BEDROCK

Christophe was deep in thought about the Paris–Geneva portal as his train was descending through the Rhône Valley. He had lost track of the passage of time when he felt the train come to a stop. He glanced out the window to see that he was at the Gare d'Avignon. An idea struck him like a bolt of lightning. He grabbed his backpack from the overhead rack and dashed for the door, managing to slip out just as it was closing. When the train departed, he was filled with the feeling that he had probably just lost his mind. Spontaneity was one of those things that often tended to get him into trouble. He went to the curb, hopped into a cab, and entered the destination as Université d'Avignon. Several options popped up, and he selected Accueil. The console came back with the trip duration and fare and requested his password. The taxi pulled up at the administration building twenty-three minutes later.

Christophe had visited many French universities but never this one. At the reception desk he asked for directions to the earth sciences department. It was clear across campus and took him ten minutes to walk there. Just inside the front door of the building that housed the department he was looking for was a directory listing the names and office numbers of all the professors in alphabetic order. The one he was looking for was the top entry, Professor P. Aubrey, room 202. He located the office, but the door was closed and the lights were off. He popped his head into an office across the hall occupied by several graduate students. "I'm looking for Professor Aubrey. Does anyone know where I might find him?"

"He is teaching a class right now. He should be back in about fifteen minutes," replied one of the students without looking up. Christophe went back downstairs to wait. At 9:50 there was a scurry of activity signaling the end of the period. Christophe went back up to room 202 to wait at the door. Philippe showed up soon thereafter.

"May I help you?" he said, juggling books from one hand to the other so he could fetch the key out of his pocket.

"Philippe?" Christophe said for confirmation. "My name is Christophe Conally."

"Dr. Conally. What an unexpected surprise. Come in, come in." Philippe unlocked the door and threw the books on his desk. He cleared more books from one of the chairs. "Please sit. What brings you to Avignon?" There were stacks of books and papers everywhere.

"I was on my way to Marseille this morning, and when the train stopped at Avignon, on a whim I got off to see if perchance I could meet you in person."

"What a welcome honor! It is so good to see you again. What has it been, twenty years? Coffee?" He didn't wait for an answer. He started down the hallway to the commissary, with Christophe following. "So, tell me, Dr. Conally, what is the reason for your visit?" He typed a code into the espresso machine and indicated for Christophe to make his selection. "Are you going to accept my invitation to speak in Lausanne?"

Christophe took his brewed coffee out of the machine. "Actually, I haven't made up my mind about that yet. My life has been unexpectedly hectic lately." He took a sip in anticipation of changing the subject. "I was hoping to discuss another matter with you."

"Fine." Philippe took his coffee and motioned toward a table to sit down. "Tell me what's on your mind."

"Do you happen to know what type of rock exists at about one hundred meters down between Paris and Geneva?"

"Not offhand, but it would be easy enough to find out. I would suspect limestone. But what an odd question. Why do you want to know?"

"I am interested in locating where debris from the boring machine that made the Paris–Geneva portal might have been deposited," said Christophe.

Philippe stirred more sugar into his coffee. "Why?"

At this point, Christophe was not sure how much to say. "I presume the tailings from the tunnel would have been used as landfill?"

"Of course," replied Philippe.

Christophe paused, cautious about how he phrased things. "It would have been necessary to extract the tailings from an access tunnel in some remote section somewhere in the middle, no?"

"Yes, I suppose."

"What if I wanted to find the location of that fill?" For Christophe to say any more would have required divulging information beyond what he was comfortable sharing.

"The location would be a matter of public record. There would be an environmental impact affidavit. Is this all you want to know?"

Christophe paused, looking around the room. "Philippe, would it be possible to access those records in secret?"

"In secret? Why in the world would you want to do such a simple inquiry in secret?"

Christophe finished his coffee and leaned back in his chair. "Let's just say that Ashleigh may have done something during the construction of that portal that they would not want to be made public."

At this, Philippe leaned forward in his chair. "Oh, I do hate that name."

"Why is that?" asked Christophe.

"Surely you are aware that the company defrauded my father out of millions of euros in royalties they agreed to pay for licensing the Aubrey technology."

"No. That's not possible. I personally signed off on all the royalty payments for the tunnel segments used on the North Atlantic portal," said Christophe.

"My father said he got the runaround from some attorneys in Geneva who worked for the consortium. I doubt that anyone at Ashleigh was really at fault. Ashleigh was just a cog in their business empire. There's no reason you would have known this. The company stalled and stalled for years until my father finally passed away, and I had no desire to continue the battle against an army of corporate lawyers." Philippe paused, then said, "If you know a way to get even, count me in."

What Christophe failed to tell him was that if he could locate the tailings, it might provide the evidence for bringing down the entire syndicate empire. "I have a theory that Ashleigh constructed a second, secret tunnel next to the other one. The size of the tailings landfill could prove this."

"Definitely," said Philippe, pulling up the calculator application on his phone. "How long is the Paris–Geneva portal?"

"Four hundred seventy kilometers."

Philippe began the calculation. "Assuming a one-meter radius times pi times two for a bidirectional portal, times four hundred seventy thousand meters—that comes out to almost three million cubic meters. It would be nearly impossible to hide that. It would even show up in the satellite images." He looked up at Christophe. "You want to do this in secret?"

"If possible," replied Christophe.

Philippe flashed a grin. "This will take me some time, but I should be able to estimate the landfill volume from satellite images and preexisting topographic maps. It will take a couple of weeks, but I have the perfect graduate student to assign to the task. His research is in assessing environmental damage to underlying strata due to landfill overburden. It's perfect." Phillip stood up from the table. "Do you have time for a quick tour?"

"Sure."

Philippe led the way down three flights of stairs to the basement. "I want to introduce you to Karl." He scanned his badge to enter the High-Pressure Rock Physics Laboratory where Karl was working. "Karl, this is Dr. Christophe Conally."

"Dr. Conally! What an honor it is to meet you."

"You have heard of me?" asked Christophe, sure he was being mistaken for someone else.

Karl glanced over at Philippe with a puzzled look. He reached up on the bookshelf above his desk and handed Christophe a book entitled *Physics of Strain-Induced Phase Changes in Crystals at Ultra High Pressure*, the PhD thesis of Christophe C. Conally of UCLA, written in 2034.

"Really? I thought the only person who ever read that old thing was my thesis adviser," said a shocked Christophe.

"No need for false modesty, Christophe," said Philippe. "You basically invented the field."

Karl added, "And your pioneering work on the North Atlantic portal is the foundation for almost everything we do here." Christophe was genuinely surprised. Forty years of climbing the corporate ladder at Ashleigh had shielded him from finding out that he'd ever done anything of lasting value.

"Karl is Swiss, from Berne," said Philippe. "Why don't you show Dr. Conally what you are doing?"

Karl showed Christophe an amazing array of scientific equipment for measuring the properties of mineral samples in various atmospheres at high pressures up to several thousand atmospheres. Compared with the equipment he had had available to him aboard the control ships, he was astonished at how far the state of the art had advanced.

"Come over here," Philippe said when Karl was finished. "I want to show you an interesting instrument we have been developing with a start-up company that my son-in-law founded. The principle of operation is based on the fact that the speed of sound in a material is different depending on the composition and state of stress." Philippe opened up a specimen hatch. "We originally developed the equipment only as a means to measure the applied pressure being exerted on a rock sample. An ultrasonic impulse is directed at the specimen, and the resonance response is picked up by ultrasensitive hydrophones and analyzed by the spectrum of sound velocities. Originally, we were using a single quartz crystal as a way to calibrate our high-pressure equipment. One day, a graduate student loaded a piece of granite into the sample chamber just to see what would happen. What he got was just a jumble of responses. But he had had some training in digital signal processing, so he decided to see if he could deconvolve the signal. What he found was that not only does the entire specimen resonate at a frequency that is characteristic of the applied pressure, but also each individual component in the granite specimen resonated with its own characteristic frequency. What we had discovered, quite by accident, was a way to do nondestructive analysis of the different phases contained in a specimen with micron-scale resolution, just by measuring the speed of sound."

Christophe understood the physics pretty well, but he never would have believed it possible to actually build such an instrument.

Philippe took an old US penny from a box of samples and placed it on the specimen stage. He closed the hatch and entered a few keystrokes on an adjoining computer. After about a minute, he pointed to the analysis on the screen. "Voilà! The penny is actually copper-clad steel." He turned proudly to Christophe. "If you look carefully at the readout, you will see the exact alloys used and the thickness of each layer."

The tour ended up lasting more than two hours. Afterward, the three went to the cafeteria for a late lunch. The experience at the lab and the collegiality made Christophe nostalgic. He sensed that he had been carrying an emptiness in his heart all his life for not having pursued an academic career. Perhaps if Monique had not died, everything might have been different. But as it turned out, so much of his life had been spent plastering over the walls of those empty chambers rather than actually trying to fill them back up. The time in Philippe's lab had somehow satisfied a deep need. He realized the time had come for him to have a new beginning.

CHAPTER 20

ALIAS

The instant Minnie heard the key in the lock, she scrambled to the front door to greet Christophe. Cats seemingly have no awareness of the passage of time, so it didn't matter if he was gone for five minutes or a week. She was just as happy to see him in either case, which she expressed by purring loudly while weaving in and out between his legs. Christophe was just as glad to be home as she was to have him home. He laid the plain white envelope from his mailbox on the table in the entryway. This time would be an extended stay, so after he raised the blinds and opened the glass doors to the terrasse, he decided to tackle the most pressing chore of doing a load of laundry. M. and Mme. Onze-heures showed up on his railing, cooing particularly loudly to announce their arrival for dinner. Christophe served himself a glass of rosé from the box in the refrigerator and then headed out to the terrasse to watch the changing color scheme play out over the Mediterranean Sea while the sun was setting. There were only a few fluffy clouds on the horizon, which were just beginning to glow orange. In a few more minutes, they would go pink and then dull red like the last glimmer of light from a dying fire in the hearth. He fell sound asleep. The night chill and the high-pitched whine of his washing machine on spin cycle finally woke him up.

A quick look around his kitchen for something to eat was all it took to discover that Chloé had straightened all his cupboards and stocked his pantry with food. Christophe took some pride in being able to fend for himself, but there was something about a woman's touch that made a welcome difference. He hardly ever became lonely, but seeing the care with which Chloé had found a place for every item made him wonder if he had made the right decision never to seek female companionship again after the pain of Monique's death had faded. Now he was sixty-six years old, and the thought of the time approaching when he would become more and more dependent on others settled on him like a dark mist. He stared aimlessly at the collection of microwavable dinners that Chloé had purchased for him and placed in his freezer drawer. A sense of melancholy suddenly overwhelmed him. What was he going to do for the rest of his life?

He pulled out a frozen *quatre-fromage* pizza. He was aware that it would become soggy in the microwave, but he didn't feel like waiting for the oven to heat up. Chloé had purchased a packaged brie and some crackers, so he changed his mind and decided to spend some time preparing a proper dinner, starting by preheating the oven. He sliced up a ripe tomato, laid the crackers and cheese out on a plate as if he were expecting guests, poured another glass of rosé, and turned on the television to catch up on some French news while he waited for his pizza. He had not actually watched any news or read a newspaper since he had left California. He had been so busy that nothing going on in the outside world had much relevance. Any big news he would have known about, so apparently the past two weeks had been rather eventless. One of the feature news stories dealt with the disturbing trend of the increasing spread between the price of physical gold bullion and digital currency. The trend was inflationary and had been going on for some months, but no one knew exactly why. International monetary policy, as set by the United Nations, required that all digital currency be backed up by genuine gold reserves. This practice had virtually eliminated the currency speculation that had caused fiscal instability in the days when paper money was printed recklessly by almost every country. Digital currency backed by gold had become the international standard for commerce. Currency exchange rates had become a thing of the past because every transaction in the entire global economy was based on the worldwide supply of gold held by the respective member countries of the United Nations. The relative wealth of each country was more or less determined by its gold reserve and not by its ability to print paper money. The world gold supply was stabilized by the increase in reserves resulting from mining and by the decrease due to consumption, mostly by electronics manufacturers. The fact that the value of digital currency had been steadily declining against gold supplies could not be easily explained, because this would mean that gold was being consumed at a faster rate than was being reported—less gold would mean a tightening of the supply of digital currency, making everything more expensive. Somehow, the world gold supply was being depleted, but no one knew where the extra gold was actually going. International transport of gold bullion resulting from trade imbalance between countries was allowed, which had the effect of balancing out local differences in productivity. But all transfers of gold were carefully regulated by the United Nations to prevent laundering and fraud.

The timer on the oven sounded to inform Christophe that his pizza was ready. He sprinkled on some spicy pizza oil. It was delicious, as it turned out, and had been well worth the wait to cook it properly in the oven. The French comedy show that came on after the news was too subtle for him to follow, so he watched a rerun of an overdubbed American crime drama instead. The quality of television shows had been steadily going downhill for years, so some of the best programs were more than thirty years old. On his way to bed, he remembered the envelope on the table by the front door. He was tempted to leave it until morning, but curiosity got the best of him, and he opened it.

Christophe:

Take *Monique II* to Monaco, guest slip number 43. Be there at 10:00 a.m. tomorrow.

—S

It was a good thing that he had opened the envelope when he did, because if he were to be in Monaco by ten, he would need to depart fairly early. The weather prediction was for calm seas with a light onshore breeze. The trip would only take about an hour. "Why Monaco, of all places?" he asked himself as he switched off the lamp next to his bed.

The following morning, Christophe sailed east out of Beaulieu. He motored past the breakwater and into the Monaco yacht harbor, finding slip number 43. Stefan was nowhere to be seen, but it was still twenty minutes early. This gave him an opportunity to use the water hose on the dock to do some much-needed cleaning of *Monique II*. At ten o'clock, there was still no sign of Stefan, so he began to wonder if he had gotten the day wrong. He started walking down the pier to find a cup of coffee and ran into the same burly Russian he had encountered the week before. The man pointed to the inflatable powerboat with the very same scowl, giving Christophe no opportunity to decline the invitation. He sat in the back seat, petrified with fear. No! He couldn't go through this again! Had Stefan set him up?

The inflatable pulled up to the fantail of the same gray yacht—a sixty-five-meter boat with five decks. Christophe was ordered to the open lounge area overlooking the landing pad where he had been interrogated before, except this time he was alone with just the burly Russian, who removed his jacket to reveal a handgun in a shoulder holster.

"Do you mind if I smoke?" asked Christophe.

Christophe removed a cigarette from his pack and put it awkwardly between his lips. "Do you have a light?"

"Sorry." The burly Russian turned and went up the staircase to the bridge, leaving Christophe alone with his unlit cigarette. He placed it back in the pack, relieved that on top of everything else, he was not going to have to figure out how to smoke. The yacht pulled away from the dock and headed out to sea. If Stefan had received his distress signal, there was no chance now for a rescue.

After about an hour, the burly Russian returned with a tray of croissants and a mug of americano coffee with cream, just the way Christophe liked it. "Where are you taking me?" Christophe demanded.

"Just keep your eye on that tiny dot on the horizon," the Russian responded, pointing to a barely visible speck off the starboard side. Then he disappeared up the stairs again. Christophe watched the dot get bigger and bigger as it approached the yacht. It was a four-pod hovercraft flying directly toward them at a high rate of speed. As soon as it got close to the ship, the pods swiveled and the craft settled gently onto the aft landing pad, making surprisingly little noise. It was a two-seater. Once the turbo fans stopped rotating, the right-hand canopy popped open and a familiar man got out. Christophe was totally astonished when he recognized the man to be Stefan.

The burly Russian accompanied Stefan to where Christophe had been watching. Stefan flashed him a broad smile as if he had just pulled off a huge caper. "So, I see you have met Dmitri." Observing the speechless Christophe, Stefan said, "I apologize for his demeanor. Pay him no attention. He has romantic notions about the spy business, and sometimes he gets a little carried away, imagining himself in the KGB fighting the Cold War." Dmitri grunted.

Christophe remained speechless as Stefan gave him a big hug. *Whose side is Stefan really on?* he wondered.

Stefan turned to Dmitri and asked, "Is the video link ready?" Dmitri nodded. Stefan led the way down to a windowless stateroom below water level with a large television screen. By the time Christophe realized he was still clutching his mug of coffee, it was stone-cold. Dmitri brought him a warm one in an attempt to make amends.

Stefan pointed Christophe to a sofa and seated himself. He said jokingly, "So Christophe, it appears you almost took up that bad habit of smoking again today." He looked over at Dmitri, who was standing in the doorway.

"Don't worry. I wasn't about to let him light that thing, Stefan!" exclaimed Dmitri.

Finally, Christophe blurted out, "What's going on here?"

Stefan said, "There are probably a few things I need to explain."

"A few things? This is the yacht where I was interrogated last week, and that guy," he said, pointing at Dmitri, "is the guy who kidnapped me in Monaco."

"Ah, yes," responded Stefan, looking down at his feet. "That whole business with Dmitri and the interrogation was really just a ploy. We needed to know for sure which side you were really on."

"Stefan, that whole episode, including the last two hours, has taken ten years off my life!"

Stefan chuckled. "We just needed to know what stuff you are really made of."

"And the guys surveilling me from the van outside my apartment?"

"Those were not ours," replied Stefan. "They were real bad guys." Then looking back over his shoulder at Dmitri, he said with a nod, "Rather than having me explain any more, it might be best to hear it from the top."

The television came to life with Abraham seated next to Pierre Fabré on the screen. Pierre started out, "Good morning, Christophe. I am told that Dmitri managed to scare the wits out of you again this morning. He can get a bit carried away. I apologize, but something urgent has come up that we needed to discuss with you in absolute secrecy. It was necessary to abduct you to international waters so we could employ a scrambled satellite video link.

It was too risky to try to meet you anywhere in person. Are you okay with that now?"

All a bewildered Christophe could manage was a simple "Yes, sir."

Abraham took over the briefing. "Do you know this man?" A photograph appeared on the lower right-hand side of the screen.

"Of course. That's Fred Simms."

"Are you sure?" asked Pierre.

"Yes. That's Fred Simms. He runs the North American Division of Ashleigh Systems. He is also the director of the Portal Safety Board, of which I was a member until last week, when I was summarily dismissed."

Abraham continued, "With Bernice Lille's assistance, we have been able to identify many of the people believed to have been in capsules switched out of the Belmullet–Paris portal. Basically, she managed to give Cédric access to all the activity data logs going back more than a year. Once we knew what to look for, based on the discovery you and Mr. Benoit made, it was pretty easy to figure out who was actually traveling in the switched capsules. So far, it does not seem that they are on to us."

"Was there anyone important?" asked Christophe.

"Surprisingly, not really. They are mostly just ordinary salaried Ashleigh employees. We haven't been able to piece together a plausible connection yet. But Bernice recognized the guy in the photo you just saw. She also identified him as Fred Simms. But his name is not Fred Simms. It turns out that his real name is Trent Lachmann."

"Trent Lachmann? That's not possible. I have known Fred for twenty years," said Christophe.

"Bernice had the same reaction, but the name associated with the retinal scan in Belmullet when he got in the capsule is Trent Lachmann, a shady character with well-known underworld connections," replied Pierre.

"That's just not possible, Pierre. The shadiest thing that Fred Simms ever did was to sneak away with one of his girlfriends to his cabin in Big Bear. He's a mild-mannered career corporate bureaucrat and playboy. The only thing he knows how to do is sign reports and hand them back to his secretary—usually doubling as one of his girlfriends."

"Christophe," Abraham said, "his real name is Lachmann, and he is notorious. He doesn't own a cabin in Big Bear."

Pierre added, "Something else we have discovered. The capsules that are switched out of the portal are usually in clusters of up to ten, and they generally arrive in Paris at times of low use, when the portals are operating at about half capacity, which lengthens the interarrival times."

"There's more," said Abraham. "You will never guess who was in one of the capsules that got switched just prior to the moment the Paris portal went down." At the thought, Christophe became pale. "You got it. Trent Lachmann, alias Fred Simms."

"That's just not possible. He called me several times that evening from Big Bear."

"He wasn't in Big Bear. He was actually in Paris," said Stefan. Christophe became sullen. This was all too much for him to take in.

Abraham added, "We have no idea yet what is going on, or what Lachmann is up to, but something big is cooking, and we need to get to the bottom of it."

Pierre said, "Christophe, we have been formulating a mission that would require you to return to Santa Monica. Are you up to that?"

Christophe sat quietly in shock as he tried to process all that he had just learned. Abraham and Pierre waited patiently for his response. "Yes," he finally answered, pausing, "probably. What do you have in mind?"

"Just pay attention to Stefan. He will tell you everything you need to know."

Christophe interjected, "Pierre, do you remember a college classmate of yours by the name of Philippe Aubrey?"

"Vaguely," replied Pierre. "Why do you ask?"

"His son, Philippe, is a professor of geophysics at the University of Avignon. I visited him yesterday on my way back from Paris. He has an idea how we might be able to locate the tailings landfill produced from construction of the secret Paris–Geneva portal. I think that if we can prove the existence of that tunnel, we can expose the syndicate and shut it down."

"Christophe," cautioned Abraham. "You are trying to think like a spy again. This will get you into trouble. You must stop trying to solve these things on your own.

226

Promise me you will coordinate your activities with Stefan."

"I promise," said Christophe. The video screen went dark.

Stefan said, "We are now heading for the port at Bonifacio on the island of Corsica. Do you have your Sam Houston ID with you?"

"Yes."

"Good. Here is a plane ticket to Monaco. Sam Houston just spent a wonderful weekend at the Grand Palacio Hotel in Bonifacio and is heading back home tomorrow afternoon on a commuter VTOL jet. We should be arriving in Bonifacio early tomorrow morning. Dmitri will show you to your stateroom. Enjoy the cruise."

Stefan headed back out to the landing pad. He gave a thumbs-up to the pilot, and as soon as he was strapped into the craft, the four engines spun back to life. The hovercraft departed like a giant dragonfly.

The principality of Monaco was never connected to the outside world by portal for a number of reasons, not the least of which was its proximity to Nice, making the travel distance too short to require hyperspeed travel. Monaco did, however, always desire to have its own airport, but there was simply not enough room to build one. With the advent of vertical takeoff and landing (VTOL) commuter jets, the idea of constructing a floating airport just outside the harbor breakwater gained traction. Large concrete slabs, constructed using the same neutral buoyancy technology developed by Aubrey for submarine tunnels, were joined together and tethered to the seafloor with dynamic anchors that adjusted automatically for tides and storm surge. It could hardly be called an airport in the modern sense, but it was big enough to handle up to four VTOL aircraft and a few helicopters or hovercrafts at one time.

Christophe's flight from Bonifacio was on a ten-seater VTOL commuter jet. Such airplanes had become the backbone for short-hop travel to places not otherwise served by portals or high-speed trains—that is, for people who could afford to take them. Since the Monaco "Aerodrome," as it was called, was adjacent to the marina, Christophe had no difficulty getting back to his sailboat. He made the short voyage to his home marina of Beaulieu-sur-Mer, securing *Monique II* in her slip. Two days that he had anticipated to be dull and empty had unexpectedly turned into a wild adventure beyond anything he could have imagined. He could not seem to see clearly how he was going to spend the rest of his life, but somehow each individual day was unfolding with new and unique challenges and surprises. He had not slept well on the yacht, so by the time he got into his apartment, he was bone weary. There were no messages in his mailbox. In fact, there was nothing exciting awaiting him at all, and the prospects of having to just wait around for Stefan to make contact depressed him. Minnie, as always, was glad to see him all the same.

To make matters worse, the weather had turned cold and overcast. Christophe passed an entire week in relative boredom waiting for an envelope in his mailbox and his new assignment. He had come to the sober realization that he had no friends in Beaulieu. Dining out alone was getting old, and he was drinking a bit too much. The days were short and dark, the sea was too cold for swimming, and the weather was not conducive to his one true passion, sailing. Boredom and lousy weather conspired to mix a toxic brew that was making him stir-crazy. He had begun to question whether or not he had made the right decision to move out of Marina del Rey. There, if not exactly close friends, he at least had a circle of acquaintances.

CHAPTER 21

12.5 KG

Beatrice returned to work as instructed by Stefan. She was anticipating consequences, but it was as if nothing at all from the prior week had ever taken place, except that François had been reassigned to work on the Paris–Rome portal that was experiencing some intermittent problems. This portal, as with most routes heading to the southeast, started at Gare de Lyon, so François had to relocate his office, which was fine with him since Gare de Lyon was much closer to his apartment. The Belmullet–Paris portal had been returned to service and was completely operational once again. The explanation of the defective valve was made official. It had supposedly been repaired, and as far as anyone knew, that was the end of the story. After helping Cédric gain access to the portal activity data logs, Bernice assumed a low profile at the agency and settled back into her old routine.

One morning upon arriving at her office, she found a purchase request in her in-basket needing her signature. It was for a replacement of a defective digital scale. Ordinarily, this would have been routine, as the amount was well below her authorized spending limit. But she found this particular request to be rather odd. The request came from the foreman of the work crew in the capsule servicing area responsible for removing the ballast from each capsule after arrival. The ballast consisted of bags of lead shot of differing weights—100, 500, and 1,000 grams. It was essential that each capsule weigh 250 kilograms before being launched into the portal at Belmullet. Once the weight of the capsule was determined with the passenger on board, the ballast bags were added through a hatch in the side of the capsule to adjust the final gross weight to 250 kilograms. Upon the capsule's arrival at its destination, the bags were removed and recycled for the next launch. By sheer chance, a foreman in the unloading bay had noticed that occasionally the ballast weight on the capsule manifest did not match the combined weight of the ballast bags removed. Of course, he knew that this was impossible. The weights had to match, so he said that the scale was defective and requested a replacement. Bernice, on the other hand, knew about the possibility of a capsule switch. But the weight of the exchanged passenger should not have mattered. The capsule was not weighed at the exit. The weight of the passenger being switched out of the portal, including his or her things, would typically be different from the surrogate passenger, but this would never be detected.

This caused Bernice to begin wondering why the ballast weights were off. *Is it possible that something is being smuggled in the ballast compartment?* she wondered. She began looking for an excuse to go talk to the foreman in the capsule servicing bay. This was not a simple matter of just waltzing out onto the shop floor. The loading and unloading bays were highly secured areas that required special authorization to enter. She decided to make up the excuse that the replacement scale was no longer available and that in order for her to certify the updated model, she needed to make sure it was compatible with the installation. This worked. She received authorization with no questions asked. She donned her hard hat and grabbed the specifications for the replacement scale. Surprisingly, in her ten years with the agency, this was the very first time she had ever ventured out onto the shop floor. She was familiar with how it all worked but had never actually watched people doing their jobs there. The task of interfacing with the workers had always been assigned to subordinates.

It took her quite some time to locate the right place. She was familiar with the passenger disembarking area from the numerous times she had traveled on the portal. It was bright and cheery to greet arriving passengers. On the other side of a wall was where the capsules were serviced for reuse. It was anything but bright and cheery. The noise and pungent odor of disinfectant were overwhelming. In production line fashion, first the seat was popped out and passed through a wash line; next the ballast was removed from each capsule; then the interior was dry-cleaned with high-pressure supercritical carbon dioxide; and finally the seat was placed back in, and the entire capsule was fumigated with the canopy closed. Half a dozen men worked furiously to keep up. At peak operation, it was necessary to turn a capsule around every thirty seconds or so. During slow periods, they would sometimes have a minute. Bernice was shocked. She had never imagined that this is what it took to keep a portal operational.

She found the shop foreman, who had requested the replacement scale, sitting in a tiny office near the seat-cleaning conveyor doing paperwork.

"Hello, my name is Bernice Lille. I need to discuss the specifications for the replacement scale with you." She extended her hand for a handshake. The foreman smiled, holding up his palms to show that his hands were filthy.

"Sorry, I just replaced one of the driveshaft belts on the seat cleaner." Bernice understood the gesture.

"Tell me why you think your scale is defective."

The foreman led the way to the area where bags of ballast were being removed from a compartment under the seat. She watched one of the workmen pull the seat up and toss the various bags into respective buckets marked 100, 500, and 1,000. "Pretty routine, no?" he said to Bernice. "The capsule manifest says how much ballast was added at Belmullet, but we never used to check it. After the portal incident two weeks ago, I decided to start weighing the ballast bags on that scale over there." He pointed to a digital scale on the floor nearby. "I just wanted to check that the guys in Belmullet weren't messing up and getting the ballast compensation wrong. Something like that could well trigger a portal failure."

"But I thought they determined the failure to be the result of a defective VCVA," said Bernice. She knew otherwise, but she repeated the official story, assuming the foreman believed it.

"Unlikely," said the foreman. "Really unlikely. I know this system like my own wife." He grabbed some ballast bags at random and dropped two bags marked 1,000 grams, one marked 500 grams, and one marked 100 grams on the scale.

"Twenty-six hundred grams, see?"

"It looks to me like the scale is working just fine," said Bernice.

"Precisely," said the foreman. "There is nothing at all wrong with the scale."

"Then why in the world did you order a new one?" queried Bernice. The foreman appeared reticent to answer. "It's okay. You can trust me."

Then he said, "Do you have any idea what would happen to me if I accused the Belmullet crew of messing up the ballast calculation? I would lose my job. That is what would happen." He turned and walked back to his office, signaling for Bernice to follow. Grabbing a clipboard from the wall, he looked intently at her. "I was just hoping that someone like you would come check this out. I need to show you something interesting." He turned the clipboard toward her and scanned down a column of handwritten numbers. "The column on the left is the manifest ballast weight," he said. "The column on the right is what we determined from the ballast bags we removed. Do you see it?"

Bernice went slack-jawed. Most of the time the weights matched, but every so often, a cluster of between five and ten sequential weights were exactly twelve and a half kilograms too low. "How do you explain that?" said the foreman. "I hope I did the right thing in showing you this. I just didn't know what else to do."

"Oh, trust me, you did the right thing." Bernice looked at him intently and said, "Promise me that you won't breathe a word of this to another soul." She handed him a card. "Call me at this number if there are any further problems. I will go ahead and order you a new scale. Just blame everything on the old one." She started to leave and then turned around. "I don't even know your name."

"Maury. Everybody knows me as just Maury."

"Thanks, Maury."

It took all of Bernice's focus to walk calmly back to her office. The minute she saw the ballast weight deficits, she knew exactly what was going on. She sent the four digits, #5608#, on her mobile phone, which was the secret code to Abraham that she needed to meet as soon as possible. Almost immediately the code #5609# came back, which meant that pickup would be arranged for that evening after work.

Bernice left the office at five o'clock sharp and proceeded south on foot along Boulevard de Magenta toward her apartment. A black Mercedes with tinted windows was parked along the way, and as soon as she went by, the rear door opened. She recognized the driver and got in. The car sped away and entered the underground garage of the Intelligence Ministry. By this time, the whole procedure had become a familiar exercise.

Abraham and Stefan were in the conference room waiting for her arrival. Bernice grabbed a cup of espresso from the machine and went into the briefing room, which was a sensitive compartmented information facility, or SCIF, where top secret matters could be discussed freely. The code #5608# indicated the highest possible priority for exchange of sensitive information.

Bernice sat down at the conference table, and the door closed automatically with a loud click, indicating that the room was secure. "I know what they are up to!" she exclaimed.

Abraham and Stefan looked at her eagerly without saying a word.

"I know what's going on. This is not about people at all." She paused momentarily to finish her espresso, tormenting Abraham and Stefan, who were eager to hear her report. Then, flashing a huge self-confident grin, she said, "They are smuggling gold!"

"Gold?" said Abraham. "How do you know?"

"It was by total accident," she said, recounting the complete story of her day's adventure into the capsule refurbishment facility.

"The twelve-and-a-half-kilogram weight discrepancy is exactly the weight of a standard gold bullion bar. It jumped right off the page at me."

Abraham and Stefan exchanged looks that said they understood this was a total game changer.

"You see," she continued, "there is no way to get into France with a twelve-and-a-half-kilogram brick of gold in your travel valise. Besides being illegal, it would light up on x-ray like a Christmas tree. No! The bars are somehow being brought to the Belmullet terminal and then used as ballast in capsules. When a particular capsule reaches Paris, it is switched out of the portal, the gold bar is removed, and the capsule is switched right back into the portal. The reason the switches are carried out in clusters is to reduce the effect of the time lag. No one would notice if a capsule was a few seconds late once in a while. But if there were too many discrepancies, someone might notice. By sending capsules in clusters, it would only be the first one that would show up late. The rest would show up at normal intervals. I estimate that the whole process can be carried out in about twenty seconds. All anyone would have to do is pop the hatch on the ballast compartment, pull out the gold bar, and close the hatch again, and then the capsule would be accelerated and switched back in at the correct location."

"That sounds like a pretty complex operation if you ask me," said Stefan.

"Incredibly complex!" replied Bernice. "Only the portal operator could pull it off—in a company like Ashleigh Systems."

The three sat in silence contemplating the implications. Finally, Bernice started again. "You can imagine what would happen if someone failed to switch out a capsule containing a gold bar in time. At a bare minimum, it would cause a commotion in the capsule servicing area, don't you think? I am going to guess that no one actually wanted to find out what would happen. I suspect that a bar slipped through by mistake that particular Thursday night and someone panicked, triggering the emergency recompression. This would have brought all the capsules to an immediate stop. It took more than thirty minutes before the first capsule was retrieved out of the portal after the shutdown, which would have given someone plenty of time to crawl into the portal and extract the bar."

Finally, Abraham spoke up. "Assuming someone— the syndicate, I suppose—is going to all that trouble to smuggle gold into France, and then presumably to proceed on to Switzerland, it's not all clear to me why. You can't just deposit gold bullion in a bank. Where is the gold coming from, and why hasn't any gold been reported missing? Is the United Nations complicit in this? If no one knows they have the gold, they can't issue digital currency against it, so what good is it?"

None of the three knew how to connect the dots any further at this point. Abraham spoke up again, asking Bernice, "What about all the people we have been assuming were being switched out and rerouted to Geneva through the secret portal? And what about Lachmann?"

"I think they must all be mules," she replied.

"Mules?" asked Stefan.

"They can only smuggle one bar at a time," said Bernice. "This means there must be a lot of people shuttling back and forth to Belmullet. Any more than once a week for any Ashleigh employee would surely draw attention. I suspect that Lachmann was just doing 'mule duty.' It must have just been a coincidence that Lachman was in one of the capsules of the cluster when the portal was shut down."

"If that's the case," said Stefan, "then we should start flagging all employees of the syndicate consortium."

Abraham said, "You are talking about more than fifty thousand employees."

"Yes," replied Bernice, "but obviously not all fifty thousand are dirty. At least this way we would know which ones are clean and which ones are dirty. It would be particularly useful to know which executives are involved and which companies they work for. Anyway, I don't think there is another secret portal. This isn't about shuttling high-ranking syndicate operatives into and out of Geneva."

"It still doesn't answer the question why no one is reporting missing gold or what they plan to do with it," said Abraham.

CHAPTER 22

WC

Three weeks had passed since the Paris portal incident, and Christophe was becoming increasingly restless. He had still received no word from anyone regarding a trip to Santa Monica. He mostly stayed in his apartment and puttered around. This routine suited Minnie and M. and Mme. Onze-heures just fine, but Christophe was about to lose his mind, particularly in the evenings when it was already dark by four, as Christmas was approaching. Finally, he had received a message from Philippe Aubrey that he had the results from the study and was wondering if Christophe could come to Avignon to see them. By mutual agreement, they had decided only to communicate about anything of substance in person, so Christophe replied that he would come to the university the following day. He stopped into Henri's office on his way to the supermarket. "Henri, do you think you could arrange to have our electrician meet me in Avignon?"

Christophe was extremely eager to see Phillippe's findings. The next morning, he decided to take the train from Beaulieu-sur-Mer, even though he had not yet heard back from Stefan. The direct train from Nice to Avignon followed the Var river from Nice to the north into the Maritime Alps, before entering a long tunnel connecting Digne and going down to the Rhône Valley to the west. He had packed his backpack with provisions for two nights, thinking he would go on to Paris to tell Stefan and Abraham in person the good news about confirming the secret portal to Geneva.

Traveling by train and taxis, it only took Christophe an hour to reach Philippe's office. Philippe and Karl were expecting him. The three went into an adjacent conference room, where Karl unrolled a topographic map of northern France on the table. It had a straight line drawn between Gare du Nord in Paris and the United Nations headquarters in Geneva, the latter of which is where Christophe had told them the portal would probably terminate. Shaded in on the map was the landfill area obtained from the environmental impact affidavit. Karl pointed out the features of the landfill and launched into some technical aspects that were over Christophe's head. Then he overlaid the map with a high-resolution satellite transparency at the same scale. The image was taken in the infrared spectrum in order to add contrast to the underlying limestone tailings, which would otherwise have been obscured by revegetation. Karl looked up at Christophe. The conclusion was unmistakable.

"Are you telling me there is no difference?" asked a very disappointed Christophe.

"It sure looks that way to me, sir," replied Karl.

"Do you concur, Philippe?"

"I'm afraid so," said Philippe. "We estimate the resolution to be on the order of about one hundred cubic meters. If a second tunnel was bored, we can find no trace of the tailings anywhere along the route."

This was not at all what Christophe was hoping for. He had become totally convinced of the existence of a secret portal. He stared at the map for a long time. Philippe said, "Is there perhaps something else we should be looking for?"

"No," said Christophe. "This is not what I was expecting, but I guess I have my answer. This is pretty conclusive. Nice work. Thanks."

Karl gathered up the map and overlays and disappeared down the stairs. Philippe and a pensive Christophe went to the cafeteria for coffee.

Philippe said, "I need to go to Lausanne this afternoon to check out the hotel facilities where the earth sciences conference is going to be held. I haven't been there before, and I must be sure it is everything I expect. There is nothing worse than having to deal with two hundred angry colleagues at a lousy conference venue. Say, why don't you come with me? Perhaps I can twist your arm to give the keynote address along the way."

Christophe's characteristic spontaneity was often in direct conflict with his desire to stick to established plans, and this invitation proved to be a good example. It took him a couple of minutes to rewire his brain from planning to go to Paris to tell the ministry that he had firm evidence for the existence of a secret portal to going through Paris for another reason altogether—to take the one and only portal to Geneva.

"Sure. Why not? I was heading to Paris anyway. My meeting there can wait. Sounds like fun. It has been a long time since I last visited Lausanne."

"Great," said Philippe. "We can drop by the department office to book your tickets and a hotel room for tonight. Hopefully, there is still availability on the Geneva portal. Normally, it would be nearly impossible to get a reservation on the same day, but the United Nations is on recess until the first of the year. Let's see if the school can pull some strings."

Philippe led Christophe to the office. "This is Chantal. She will take care of you. I need to go by my office to tend to a few things. I am supposed to be watching my twelve-year-old granddaughter while her parents are away for a couple of weeks in the Brazilian jungle. They didn't want to take her out of school, so I need to be sure she made it to her aunt's house."

Chantal was able to book Christophe's hotel room without any difficulty. For the train and portal tickets, she needed his travel credentials. He had planned to go to Paris as Sam Houston, but that would have been difficult to explain. He hoped Stefan would not be too upset if he traveled this time as Christophe Conally. He handed her his true credentials. After a few phone calls, Chantal succeeded in booking a portal capsule fifteen minutes before Philippe's. "I hope you don't mind waiting a few minutes in Geneva for Philippe, but this is the best I could do." She handed Christophe the confirmation. He thought to himself how nice it would be to actually have an efficient secretary like this to manage his travel again. This was the first time he had missed this perk since he had retired from Ashleigh Systems.

The high-speed maglev ride to Paris was slow by portal standards, but it gave passengers an opportunity to ride together and engage in conversation. Philippe was an interesting person. He was sixty-two and divorced. He was able to fill Christophe in on a lot of details regarding his father's company and the acrimonious relationship with Ashleigh.

"My father was a mining engineer, you know," said Philippe. "But at heart, he was an inventor and entrepreneur. His first start-up company developed the auger head that revolutionized the tunnel-boring business. Before his invention, a boring machine was capable of no more than ten to twenty meters per day through hard rock. With his revolutionary auger head, this was increased to about one hundred meters per day. He sold the invention and plowed all the proceeds into Aubrey Industries."

"What was the secret behind the auger?" Christophe inquired.

"It was so simple as to be almost silly, but I guess most good inventions are that way. The augers in the boring heads use replaceable WC inserts."

"WC?"

"Oh, sorry. Tungsten carbide. WC is just the chemical formula."

"Of course. For some reason my brain switched to thinking of a water closet. It's been awhile since I did any chemistry," Christophe said with some embarrassment.

"Tungsten carbide is quite hard, as you know, but also very brittle. It is necessary to use a lot of coolant water to keep the boring head from getting too hot. My dad developed a device for making microscopic bubbles in water using ultrasonic energy. He found that the heat transfer property of coolant water with these tiny bubbles was much better than ordinary water. The rest is history. He built the first ultrasonic boring heads and patented the invention. Besides improving boring speed, the new augers improved carbide life. He sold the invention for twenty million euros. It was worth ten times that, but he was a humble guy, as you probably figured out from working with him. He ended up using the same ultrasonic technology for introducing bubbles in concrete. This was the basis of the neutral buoyancy submarine tunnel segments."

"Do you take after your father as an inventor?" asked Christophe.

"I do invent things from time to time. That's the fun part," replied Philippe. "But it is the whole process of building a business around it that I don't care much for. This is what my father loved to do: filing the patents, dealing with lawyers, raising venture capital. But these things really don't appeal to me. Now, as for my son-in-law, Pascal, this is another matter. He thrives on this stuff. He is a genuine entrepreneur, following directly in my father's footsteps. When he learned about the ultrasonic analysis technology I showed you in our lab, he wasted no time commercializing it. He formed a start-up company in Paris called Sonilyzer Systems, which has just rolled out the first commercial units onto the market. This is really good for me because the university will be receiving a royalty income, which will help support my graduate students."

"Is your daughter in the business?" asked Christophe.

"Absolutely. Pascal is a technical genius, but my daughter has the head for business. They went to Brazil together to demonstrate a higher-power version of the system that we think can identify mineral deposits for a large mining company. Pascal told me this could be the largest gold and platinum discovery of all time. But the ore is deep, and it is hard to do core sampling in the jungle over a wide area. Pascal thinks they can map out the deposit using this modified Sonilyzer. There is no telling how big a business opportunity this could become for Sonilyzer Systems. There's a company to keep an eye on if you are into investments." Christophe filed this tip away in his brain near the top of his to-do pile.

From Gare de Lyon, the two men took an autonomous taxi to Gare du Nord, where the Paris–Geneva portal originated. It was the most lavish and advanced portal in the world. One of the conditions that the Swiss government required when they agreed to host the United Nations in Geneva was that access to and from the city be exclusively by means of a single bidirectional portal to Paris. There were certainly other ways for people to enter Switzerland, but the Paris–Geneva portal—the PG, as it was called—was by far the most convenient. The trip took a mere thirty-two minutes, which was less than the time it took to go from Gare de Lyon to Gare du Nord by taxi. The departure hall had been built specially to showcase the PG. It was opulent with fountains, statues, and high-end boutiques.

Christophe proceeded on ahead of Philippe through the retinal scan before boarding. Philippe went looking for a sandwich. The whole loading procedure was fast and smooth, in contrast to either Goose Bay or Belmullet. Also, the PG was one of the few portals in existence using custom capsules. They were roomier and more comfortable than standard capsules, with ambient lighting and additional conveniences for the traveling dignitaries, such as live television news and a selection of wines and beers. When he arrived in Geneva, after what seemed like barely a minute, Christophe passed through a second retinal scanner with all the other "ordinary" passengers. Switzerland just did not trust the French to screen out people traveling under fake identities. The diplomats went on to a separate screening station of their own.

Christophe found a seat in the arrivals hall to wait for Philippe. He became fascinated watching the people going through the retinal scanners. They all seemed so ordinary. Even those credentialed diplomats from every corner of the globe all seemed completely ordinary. They had lanyards around their necks, which they swiped through some kind of reader, and were waved on by the border guard, who seemed to recognize most of them. Every once in a while, one of them was chosen for a random retinal scan, but even this was efficient. He began to wonder if he could actually spot a "seedy character." He had generated a stereotype in his mind of someone in a gray trench coat with collar turned up, wearing dark glasses and peering out from under a trilby hat. No one he saw that day fit that stereotype. *How about the notorious Trent Lachmann?* he mused. Fred Simms was as ordinary as it gets. He would fit in with any crowd.

As Christophe was watching people going through the scanners, he saw a man who looked a lot like Fred Simms. He looked more closely. It was Fred Simms! Christophe's heart stopped beating while he ducked his head and snuck away, hoping he hadn't been spotted. He went outside and stood in the shadows to watch the man who looked just like Fred Simms enter a taxi and speed away. By the time he got back to the arrivals hall, he found Philippe wandering around looking for him. The two took an autonomous taxi to the hotel in Lausanne. It was twenty minutes before Christophe's heart started beating normally again. The cab ride to Lausanne took half an hour.

While Philippe was checking out the hotel conference facilities, Christophe went for a walk by himself along the lake. The hotel was truly exquisite, built around an ancient castle right on the water's edge. It was very cold, and the moist wind coming off the lake made his bones ache. The Alps rising from the other side of the lake were brilliant with fresh snow. He had not dressed for such conditions, but the brisk walk gave him a chance to clear his head. By this time, he was beginning to doubt that the man he saw in Geneva really was Fred Simms, and the absence of a secret portal caused him to begin thinking that his wild imagination was getting the better of him. All his notions of spies and subterfuge were a composite of old movie villains and their activities. The idea of a bunch of evil men sitting around a table in a smoke-filled room in the basement of the syndicate headquarters in Geneva, plotting to take over the world, was starting to seem preposterous. Christophe began to worry that he was losing his grip on reality.

He had walked much farther along the lake path than he'd realized, so by the time he got back to the hotel he was frozen. He waited for Philippe in the lobby in front of a roaring wood fire. They had arranged to have dinner together in the hotel restaurant so Philippe could see if it was suitable for the conference.

The restaurant could accommodate at most about thirty guests. Philippe had discovered that the hotel was smaller than he had imagined and that the manager had overstated its true capacity. Even considering arrangements made with other nearby hotels, two hundred conference-goers would be a real stretch for this hotel. The rooms were really lovely, and even though Philippe had negotiated an amazing room rate, it was becoming clear that the hotel was probably not the right choice. Christophe could sense Philippe's disappointment.

After dinner, the two sat in an old hall of the original castle in front of a fire making small talk and drinking Limoncello digestifs. They agreed to meet for breakfast at eight. Christophe retired to his room and soaked in a hot bath below a picture window overlooking Lake Geneva, with Mont Blanc glistening in the distance under a nearly full moon.

He fell asleep by nine while watching a French cooking competition, and woke up early the next morning wondering why he had not agreed to meet Philippe earlier for breakfast than eight o'clock. He was one of the first to sit in the breakfast room, which opened at six thirty. He ordered a mushroom-and-swiss-cheese omelet, and the server brought him a thermos of hot coffee. The breakfast room had a commanding panoramic view of the lake, dotted with lights, which he could see all the way to Geneva, fifty kilometers away in the distance. He got up to go to the buffet, and when he returned to his table, there was a man sitting across from his chair.

"Stefan?" said Christophe, more than a little surprised.

Stefan simply nodded.

"How in the world did you find me?" asked Christophe.

"Did you forget that there is a GPS transponder in your cigarette case?"

"Cigarettes! Oh no." At that instant Christophe remembered that he had forgotten to remove the cigarettes from his pants when he washed them the day before. He patted the seldom used zippered pocket to discover that it was soft and squishy. Unzipping it, he found tobacco fragments and paper wads. There was also a shiny cylinder about the size of a throat lozenge. He fished it out and held it up.

"Yes. That's it," said Stefan with a chuckle. "At least the transponder is waterproof. I guess I will have to issue you a new pack of cigarettes."

"Stefan, you will never guess whom I think I saw yesterday getting off the PG," said Christophe excitedly.

"Fred Simms," said Stefan nonchalantly.

"Is there anything you don't know?" This was a rhetorical question since Christophe already knew the answer. "Yesterday, I found out there is no secret portal."

"Yes, I know."

"You know that I found it out or that there is no secret portal?"

"Both." Stefan poured himself a cup of coffee from Christophe's thermos. "Do you know a woman named Bridget Anderson?"

"If you mean the Bridget in the Ashleigh office in Los Angeles, the answer is yes. She's Fred Simms's secretary, and until a couple of weeks ago, I assumed she was his mistress."

"Oh, for sure, she's not his mistress. She works for SCIP." Stefan slowly sipped his coffee the way only a real spy knows how to do.

"Who's Skip?" asked Christophe.

"Not who, what! SCIP, Southern California Intelligence Prefecture. Surely having lived in Santa Monica you have heard of them. She's one of us."

"Bridget is nice to be sure, but she's not the sharpest knife in the drawer, if you know what I mean. She's no spy."

This comment made Stefan smile. "One more thing. What do you know about tungsten?"

This was the second time in two days the subject of tungsten had come up. Christophe said, "Hardly anything. But Philippe, the guy I am here with, seems to know a lot about it. I am supposed to meet him here at eight."

"I need to be gone by then. When are you planning to return to Paris?" asked Stefan.

"Sometime early this afternoon."

"Good," said Stefan. "I will send a car to pick you up outside the PG Paris arrival."

"How will you know when I arrive?"

Stefan pointed to the bulge in Christophe's zipper pocket.

"Stefan, tell me, how did you know it was Fred Simms?"

Stefan glanced at his wrist watch and leaned forward in his chair. "We knew Trent Lachmann was in Europe somewhere, but until he passed through the retinal scan at the PG departure area in Paris, we didn't know where. It was actually because of you that I happened to be in Geneva at all. We saw your reservation, so I took the PG just a few minutes ahead of you to see what you were up to."

"You were spying on me?" exclaimed Christophe.

"In a word, yes. But you tried to contact me to meet you in Avignon. I couldn't make it, so I thought I would just meet you here instead." Stefan took another sip of coffee. "I was standing right next to you in the magazine kiosk while you were watching the arriving passengers in Geneva. I knew Trent Lachmann would be going through the scanners right after you. I was just about to jump out into the middle of the concourse to fake an epileptic seizure as a distraction when you had the good sense to slip away, unseen." He drank the last of his coffee and stood up. "We have much to discuss, but we can't do it here. Learn as much as you can from Dr. Aubrey about tungsten. I have to go now." Just like that, Stefan was gone.

Christophe had time to check his messages. There were none.

Philippe showed up for breakfast as planned. He was in better spirits but had resolved to stay over one more night to work with the conference staff. They had assured him that they could handle the number of people he was anticipating, and he had decided to try to make things work. Christophe decided to depart for Geneva by train around ten, so he had a couple of hours to learn all about tungsten.

It turned out that Philippe was quite knowledgeable about the metal. China had a virtual monopoly. They produced about 80 percent of all the tungsten in the world from indigenous ore called wolframite, which is a nickel–iron tungstate ore. Almost all of the tungsten is converted into tungsten carbide for cutting tools, but some of the refined metal is also cast into bars. Philippe mentioned that one of the interesting properties of tungsten is that it has almost the same density as gold. There had been many attempts to make counterfeit gold bullion from it. Pascal's Sonilyzer could apparently tell the difference between gold and tungsten with ease. Another thing that Christophe learned was that it was Ashleigh's tunneling division that had acquired the boring auger patent rights from Philippe's father. This actually made perfect sense, because it catapulted Ashleigh into the position as world leader in portal boring technology. One last bit of information that he picked up was that thanks to the company's ambitious portal boring operations around the world, Ashleigh generated hundreds of tons of tungsten carbide scrap each year from broken and worn-out inserts from the boring augers. There was so much scrap, in fact, that Ashleigh created a company in Torrance, California, to recycle tungsten carbide back into metal ingots. Christophe happened to know that this company in Torrance was one of the companies Fred Simms was responsible for running.

Christophe took the escalator up from the arrivals concourse of the PG in Paris, and as promised, a car was waiting for him. It took him to the Intelligence Ministry. Abraham and Stefan were sitting in the SCIF along with another, unexpected guest. Bernice greeted him and said, "I

am here on my lunch break. Help yourself to a sandwich."
The SCIF door locked behind them, and the four began
comparing notes. Once Christophe accepted the premise
that they were dealing with gold bullion counterfeiting
and smuggling and not transporting seedy characters
to syndicate headquarters through a secret tunnel, the
various pieces were starting to fall into place. He was able
to bring in the new information about tungsten and the
operation in Torrance. After about an hour, the working
hypothesis emerged that counterfeit gold bullion bars
were being fabricated and replacing genuine gold bars.
The genuine bars were then being smuggled into France.
How the real gold was being obtained was still a mystery,
but it was pretty clear that the economy of any country
caught holding counterfeit bars would likely collapse.

They estimated how much gold might actually be at
stake. At about ten to twelve bars per day for ten years,
it would be possible to smuggle forty thousand bars. At
twelve and a half kilograms each, this would amount
to almost five hundred metric tons. Twelve and a half
kilograms of pure gold, which is one-eightieth of a metric
ton, was the international standard. The gold standard
dictated that any national currency is set equal to exactly
one thousand units of currency per gram. A standard
twelve-and-a-half-kilogram bar was, thus, worth exactly
twelve and a half million euros, or dollars, or pounds, or
rubles, or any other currency. It did not matter which;
five hundred metric tons were worth five hundred billion
euros. Furthermore, this was their estimate of how much
gold might have been smuggled into just France over ten

years and did not include the possibility of how much gold might have been smuggled through other portals.

At that point, Abraham, Stefan, Bernice, and Christophe, and soon to include Pierre Fabré, were the only ones in the world who knew the secret of what the syndicate was really up to. It was no longer about conquering Europe by force. It was about commandeering its economies.

Abraham spoke up to try to bring closure to the meeting. His commanding presence left no doubt why he was the director of the Intelligence Ministry. His wisdom and experience were echoed in every carefully chosen word. "Here is what we are looking at as of this very minute. We have credible evidence for a large-scale international gold smuggling operation. We must assume that some large but unknown fraction of the world's gold bullion has been replaced by counterfeit bars. Since the International Banking Division of the UN closely tracks the serial numbers of every gold bar and certifies all new gold production, unless the IBD has been corrupted— something I find unlikely—this means that the genuine bullion bars are being stashed somewhere in Europe and that they have been replaced with counterfeit bars in the foreign repositories—probably in North America. The genuine bars obviously cannot be circulated because they would have been stamped with the real serial numbers, and the counterfeit bars would need to be stamped with a duplicate serial number. In a sense, the real gold has no value because the national currency has already been secured by the supposed value of counterfeit bars in repositories around the world. As long as no one were to know their bars are counterfeit, there would be no problem. This could, obviously, go on for years and years until virtually all of the world's gold was stolen." Abraham looked intently into each face around the table. "If news of this were to leak out of this room, there would be global economic pandemonium. There can be no leaks or even rumors until we know for certain where the real gold is being stashed. Does everyone understand this?"

All heads around the table nodded agreement. "I need to be very clear on this." Abraham said this looking directly at Christophe. "No more rogue operations. I beg you." Abraham paused to take a sip of coffee. "I am going to disclose to you a very sensitive piece of new intelligence. This must not leave this room. We have been tracking a fresh fish delivery truck to a fish market across the street from the Barbès-Rochechouart metro station. Tubs of fresh fish packed in ice are dropped off every day. There is nothing at all unusual about this. But then they also load supposedly empty tubs back into the truck. The problem is that moving the 'empty' tubs requires the use of a handcart." Abraham looked around the table to be sure everyone understood the significance. "The next delivery, believe it or not, is always another fish market in Versailles!"

"Versailles!" exclaimed Christophe. "That's where Ashleigh's French Research Center is located. I spent five years working there. I know that fish market. I ate there all the time."

"Precisely," said Abraham, smiling broadly. "We think we know the location of the vault where the gold is being stashed, and it does not seem, at least as best as we can tell, that any gold is being shipped out. Of course, this could change at any minute if they were to get spooked."

"Why don't you just move in and seize it then?" asked Christophe.

Abraham glanced over at Bernice. "Bernice has been working with Cédric in our cyber division. They have found that the same Trojan horse signal you and Mr. Benoit uncovered on the Paris portal also shows up on the Rotterdam and Frankfort portals. It is likely now that gold is being smuggled to at least three European destinations from Belmullet—perhaps more. We don't know the extent of the operation. It is essential that we take down the entire syndicate network all at once, which will require a great deal of international coordination."

At this point, Abraham looked back at Christophe and said, "This is why we brought you here today. We need your help. We have reason to believe that most of the stolen gold bullion has been coming from the former United States. As you know, the United States held the majority of its gold reserves at Fort Knox, Kentucky. When the country broke apart, the gold reserves were redistributed to each of the new principalities. That is, fifteen new gold repositories were created, but unlike Fort Knox, these repositories were initially housed in banks, where the security was considerably less stringent. The syndicate would have had no difficulty substituting counterfeit bars for real ones during this period of confusion. What we think this means is that the American principalities are unknowingly holding an unknown quantity of counterfeit bars, while the real gold has been stashed somewhere to be smuggled into Europe."

Christophe's extensive executive training told him that he was about to be handed a new assignment. "Christophe," said Abraham, "we need you to move back to Los Angeles. Since you are an American, you have the perfect cover. In the past, we would have just gone to the CIA, but there is no CIA anymore—just fifteen autonomous intelligence agencies. The one based in Los Angeles is the Southern California Intelligence Prefecture, or SCIP. I know the director, and I think you know a woman named Bridget Anderson, who is working undercover there."

CHAPTER 23

SCIP

C hristophe settled back into his reclining seat feeling the gentle tug of the acceleration of the capsule as he departed west from the Ivory Coast. He found it difficult to relax. He had spent most of his career ensuring the safety of submarine portals in the North Atlantic, but someone else had built the one he was now taking that connected the west coast of Africa to the east coast of South America. There was just something about traveling four times the speed of sound through a tunnel two thousand meters down in the ocean that he would never get used to. The consolation was that if anything were to go wrong, any trace of his existence on earth would be obliterated in about ten milliseconds. It certainly beat the alternative, however, of drowning while trying to pass through the Strait of Magellan during a winter storm in a sailing ship just three hundred years earlier. Actually, it was widely believed that submarine portals were safer than subterranean ones because they were not susceptible to shearing faults during an earthquake. This actually happened once in the portal going between Seoul and Nagoya where a big earthquake caused a kink in the subterranean tunnel portion near Kyoto. Fortunately, the submarine portion in the Sea of Japan was unaffected. There were quite a number of fatalities, and the portal was out of service for several months while the tunnel was rebuilt between Kyoto and Nagoya.

Christophe would have preferred not to have to travel to North America in December, but the urgency of the situation demanded it. Henri agreed to watch over Minnie and his apartment, and he had been able to put a winter cover over *Monique II*. The only real casualties were M. and Mme. Onze-heures, who would need to find somewhere else to dine out for a while.

He sat in the darkness of his capsule listening to the *click-clack* of opening and closing VCVAs. There were some aspects of the Paris portal incident that still did not make sense. For one thing, why was Fred Simms in a capsule when the emergency recompression was triggered? Was this merely a coincidence? Where did he get off, at the metro station? Or did he go all the way to the Gare du Nord terminus? Why, then, did he travel to Geneva as an ordinary passenger on the PG? Something else even more troubling was percolating in the back of Christophe's brain. A sudden switch out of a portal at a speed of 50 meters per second, or 180 kilometers per hour, would feel like being T-boned in an automobile at a highway intersection. Although survivable, it would be very unpleasant. Fred Simms was not the kind of guy to submit to such torture willingly.

Then it struck him. Christophe couldn't imagine why it had not occurred to him before. He had been assuming the maximum switching speed of 50 meters per second based on the Colorado study, but in that case, a capsule would be switched out at a shallow angle and decelerated slowly. A gentle switch like that would not be possible on approach to Gare du Nord, because such a maneuver would require more than 1,000 meters. The capsules would have to be traveling much more slowly in order to execute a switch only 420 meters from the terminus. Christophe had an application on his mobile phone that could measure his acceleration. It contained a miniature accelerometer for keeping track of his movements in the absence of a GPS signal. He had used it quite often in the past but had completely forgotten about it. He retrieved his phone from his vest pocket and started up the program. By the time he was due to arrive in Belem, in about thirty more minutes, he would have a complete record of the deceleration profile, which he could then use to calculate his velocity and distance using some simple integral calculus.

Christophe had a clean data set by the time he popped out of his capsule at the portal terminus in Belem. As he was waiting for his capsule for the next leg to Houston, he ran the data through a least squares polynomial fit and entered the coefficients into a numerical integrator on his device. As he was en route somewhere along the

Belem–Houston portal, one hundred meters below the Amazonian rain forest, he had his answer.

Not too far away on the surface, Philippe Aubrey's son-in-law, Pascal, was listening to seismic echoes through sensitive hydrophones for evidence of precious metal mineral deposits. He could clearly hear the click-clacking of the portal deep below. The noise was a real annoyance that complicated his task of data analysis.

Christophe's velocity at 420 meters from the terminus at Belem was only 5 meters per second—the speed of a fast sprinter. Switching capsules out of a portal at this speed would be a breeze. All portals would follow about the same deceleration profile. Christophe had estimated the distance of 400 meters from the terminus of the Paris portal at Gare du Nord based on the assumption of a constant deceleration of 1 g. It was by sheer luck that he had guessed the location of the switch in the Paris portal to be under the metro station.

He stopped in Houston and then traveled on to the old Bradley International Terminal at LAX. The trip from Marseille had required four separate portal hops and had taken just under five hours. He had departed Marseille at two in the afternoon and crossed eight time zones, so he arrived in Los Angeles at eleven in the morning. One of the quirks of high-speed travel from east to west was that one arrived before the time of departure. Unfortunately, Christophe's body still thought it was seven in the evening.

Los Angeles was the capital of the Southern California Prefecture, which encompassed an area that included Santa Barbara to the north and Baja Ensenada to the south. The eastern border was the Colorado River, although borders between prefectures were largely meaningless. Mexico had devolved into a group of warring states. La Paz and the lower Baja formed an independent principality. San Francisco was the capital of the Northern California Prefecture. The flat-map notion of the world as a patchwork of different-colored interlocking tiles had become a relic of the twentieth century. By 2050, it had become a bitmap of prefectures and principalities with dithered transitions. With few exceptions, the whole idea of borders between nation-states was gone. This was the direct result of mobility, which had had the effect of homogenizing the globe, homogenizing not only races and ethnicities but also goods and services. It essentially became possible to carry out commerce on a global scale from virtually anywhere on the planet. There was also another important consequence: it rendered central governments irrelevant.

From the dawn of civilization, nationhood was characterized by the concentration of power and influence in a central location—the more power and influence that could be concentrated, the more powerful and influential the nation would become. This was the sole basis of the "Old World Order." The first cracks in the foundation could be observed in the Soviet Union in the aftermath of the Second World War. The whole premise of the communist empire was command and control of every aspect of the Russian society. Such old-world notions of a centrally planned economy never worked very well. The impact was felt most dramatically in declining farm production. The men in the Kremlin deluded themselves into thinking they knew farming better than the farmers. The consequence was mass starvation, which has a way of catalyzing rapid social unrest. Sadly, China followed the Soviet Union's dismal example. The Soviet Union finally came apart in the last decade of the twentieth century. The next empire to crumble was the European Union, which had been created with the utopian idea that the needs of Europeans would be best served by collectivization. Once again, it was agriculture at the root of the breakup. For example, bureaucrats in Brussels tried to control the price of dairy products in France in order to give Spanish dairies a fighting chance. The result was disastrous for all, with dairies in France and Spain ultimately collapsing simultaneously. Ultranationalism was blamed for the breakup of the EU, but in reality, it was finally realized that no European citizen was better served with the Union than without it.

The last holdout was the United States. Here the breakup was more difficult because the country had been founded on the notion of unification. In fact, the United States had fought a bloody civil war when unity was imposed by force on the breakaway Confederate States. But by 2030, it was widely realized that the only Americans actually benefiting from the union were those people in the capital city of Washington, DC. And DC's sole purpose had become to perpetuate itself. As with any empire, the end comes when the amount of energy spent trying to prop up the power base is greater than the value the empire brings to those being governed. The United States subsequently broke apart into an amorphous collection of prefectures. Over the course of just a few years, the power of the federal government dwindled away, and hardly anyone missed it. Otherwise, not much else really changed, because it became evident that there was practically nothing that could be accomplished in Washington that could not be done better elsewhere. The US capital was conquered not by force but by irrelevancy.

The best example of such a plunge into irrelevancy was the Central Intelligence Agency, with palatial headquarters just outside the capital. For fifty years, almost nothing took place in the entire world without their knowledge and consent. The agency had been created to fight the Cold War, but it lost its raison d'être with the collapse of the Soviet Union. After many years of attempting to reinvent itself, the agency ultimately devolved into a huge, bloated organism resembling Jabba the Hutt in the *Star Wars* movie saga, whose sole purpose had become just keeping itself fed. The CIA was designed to operate under the Old World Order. It was no match for the syndicate, which had adapted to operate effectively under the New World Order.

With the breakup of the United States, the need for intelligence did not go away, however. The function simply devolved to the prefectures. This was the origin of the Southern California Intelligence Prefecture, or SCIP. Beginning around 2060, the agency had reliable intelligence that a large-scale gold bullion counterfeiting and smuggling operation was taking place in the former United States.

The SCIP's ability to uncover the extent of the activity was hindered by an unwillingness to exchange intelligence with other prefectures. This was due to underlying suspicions that some of them might still be loyal to the CIA in Washington. It came as a welcome surprise when Abraham contacted his old friend the director of the SCIP.

One of the concessions for peaceful secession at the breakup of the United States was that the gold bullion stored at Fort Knox be distributed according to the population of the new prefectures. Fort Knox held 4,500 metric tons at the time, which represented more than 50 percent of the world's bullion, worth $4.5 trillion. Southern California Prefecture had the largest population, amounting to about 8 percent, which entitled them to 360 metric tons of gold, worth $360 billion. In addition, Southern California was also forced to take on 8 percent the $20 trillion national debt, or $1.6 trillion. The gold would secure less than 22.5 percent of the debt, so Southern California Prefecture was basically insolvent from its inception. Years of fiscal austerity had forced drastic cuts in the size of government. SCIP was one of those agencies forced to operate on a shoestring budget. One of the consequences was that many SCIP agents held real day jobs. Such was the case with Bridget Anderson, who was Fred Simms's personal assistant and the office manager for Ashleigh's Santa Monica headquarters.

CHAPTER 24

SANTA MONICA

C hristophe's condominium in Marina del Rey overlooked a portion of the extensive yacht basin. It had been his home for ten years and was close enough to Ashleigh headquarters in Santa Monica that he often rode his electric scooter to work. Really, the only downside was that it faced north so that it got practically no sun during the winter. He had planned to buy a yacht and retire there, until he fell in love with the South of France. In many respects, the Southern California coast and the Côte d'Azur were quite similar.

Southern California Prefecture was a sprawling megalopolis that extended from Ensenada in Baja to San Luis Obispo with about sixty million inhabitants. It had seen explosive growth when fusion reactors became commercialized, which made large-scale water desalination feasible. Southern California could never have remained inhabitable as long as it depended on

North California and the Colorado River for fresh water. With inexpensive desalination, they now had all the fresh water they would ever need. This sparked rapid growth along the entire Pacific coastline, extending to regions that had previously been uninhabitable for lack of water. Luxury resorts dotted the entire Baja California peninsula all the way to Cabo San Lucas at the tip. Despite the administrative chaos and growing pains associated with secession, Southern California thrived as an independent principality. Unburdened by federal bureaucracy, the prefecture was able to complete a high-speed maglev train between La Paz and Santa Barbara in 2053. The whole project only took five years to construct and eliminated much of the traffic congestion that had made life practically unbearable by 2040. A maglev was more practical than a portal for this route because it would need to make frequent stops along the way. The train was built as an elevated system adjacent to the old sixteen-lane Interstate 5. It did not take long for people creeping along in traffic and watching the train go by at three hundred fifty kilometers per hour to decide to abandon their automobiles. Ultimately, the interstate freeways were dedicated almost exclusively to autonomous container transports. Southern California had become one of the most vibrant and prosperous economies in the world. But for Christophe, as he got older, life in Los Angeles offered everything he was looking for except peace and tranquility.

When he came up the escalator from the LAX Bradley portal, he called his realtor to arrange to pick up the key to his condominium. Fortunately, it had not sold yet. Christophe had been considering offering it as a rental. He was now glad that he had left it furnished. The realtor had been telling him he needed to drop the price, but he knew it would not show well until spring, when there was more direct sunlight. Anyway, he did not need the cash from the sale, so the idea of some supplemental rental income was beginning to appeal to him. As it turned out, the realtor was on her way to the condo for a showing to prospective buyers and had agreed to meet Christophe there. It was just a short taxi ride from LAX, which was one of the principal advantages of the Marina del Rey location, since he had been traveling almost all of the time he had worked for Ashleigh.

The door to the condominium was open when he arrived. He observed an exuberant young couple oohing and aahing at everything. They kept saying to one another, "That's just perfect!" and "Oh, look at this! Isn't it wonderful?"

The realtor turned to Christophe when she saw him walk in and cupped her hand over her mouth. "Don't worry, Christophe. They can't afford it." The euphoric prospective buyers finally departed. They were delusional to think that Christophe would settle for 20 percent less than the asking price. The real estate agent gave him the key and assured him that there would be no more showings as long as he was still in California.

The condo was nicer than he had remembered. It had been completely repainted, and new carpets had been installed since the last time he was there. Also, new blinds on the sliding glass door to the patio seemed to brighten everything up a bit. He walked around, doing an inventory of the household supplies he would need to purchase for his extended stay. His suitcase would not arrive until that evening at the earliest.

Christophe was scheduled to meet with the director of SCIP at two o'clock. It was Saturday. From the Venice Boulevard address that Abraham had given him, it was a little more than five kilometers away. He was planning to take an autopod taxi, but when he walked outside into the pristine cloudless morning, he realized it was the first sun he had felt on his face in a week. He had forgotten how pleasant it could be in Los Angeles in December. He had plenty of time, so he decided to walk.

The address given to him by Abraham led him to a stand-alone medical office building where a certain dentist by the name of Petrovski was in suite B. Christophe assumed he had gotten the address wrong, so he went inside to get directions. There was a man holding his jaw at the receptionist counter, obviously in a great deal of distress. All Christophe could make out from the moaning was "oothache."

The receptionist was trying to explain to him that she was very sorry, but Dr. Petrovski was not taking any new patients at that time. She handed him a list of referrals and finally persuaded the man to leave. Christophe stepped forward and showed her the address he was looking for.

She reached under her desk to press a button, and a door behind her swung open.

"The director is expecting you."

In the corridor, the only room with an open door was the one at the end. He peeked in. It was a spacious, well-furnished office with a big oak desk at the far end with wall-to-wall bookcases behind it. A man who appeared to be about the same age as he was sitting on the far side of a conference table facing him. A woman was also seated with her back to him. When the man spotted Christophe, he popped up out of his swivel chair and rushed to the door to greet him.

"Dr. Conally, so good to see you. I am Tor Andersen, the director." He extended his hand as the woman turned in her seat. "I think you already know my daughter, Brigid."

"Bridget?" exclaimed a startled Christophe.

Christophe had only known this woman as a rather ordinary secretary. Her clothes never seemed to fit quite right. Her hair had always been tacked up on the top of her head awkwardly, and she had worn black-frame glasses that were always slipping down her nose. She had been pleasant to him, but he had never thought of her as being particularly capable in the office. The woman who stood before him was tall and rather striking. Her long blonde hair was neatly braided down her back. A well-fitting black pullover revealed the bulge of a handgun in her waistband. Surely, this was not the same Bridget. He had seen her résumé and had concurred with Fred Simms to hire her. "Bridget Anderson, born Modesto, California,

2045. Dropped out of junior college. Modest computer skills," and so on. Who was this woman who radiated a stunning beauty as a result of her physical appearance, as well as from the obvious refinement that Christophe had not previously noticed? Awkwardly, Christophe greeted this woman whom he recognized but apparently did not know. He said to her, "It seems we have some catching up to do."

The three returned to the conference table, and Tor began. "Christophe, I have heard a great deal about you from Abraham. He and I go back a long way. Your journey into our clandestine world was a welcome surprise. We have known about the bullion counterfeiting ring for quite some time, and we have been on the trail of Trent Lachmann for most of it. Our problem was that after the dissolution of the CIA, we didn't know whom we could trust. We suspected that the CIA had been infiltrated by the syndicate but could never prove it. The only reliable connections in the intelligence community I have are all in Europe—with the French Ministry, in particular."

At this point, the receptionist from the front desk showed up with coffee, soft drinks, and an assortment of doughnuts. Christophe made a habit of avoiding American junk food, but he hadn't eaten anything since Belem, so he chose to make an exception this time.

Tor continued, "Until recently, we were stymied in the undercover investigation. We knew that counterfeit tungsten bars were being cast at the Ashleigh Recycle Company in Torrance. Brigid went there undercover many times on behalf of Fred Simms and actually managed to sneak one of the bars out." Tor got up from his chair and fished a box out of his lower right-hand desk drawer. He removed a dull gray metallic tungsten bar that was packed in foam. "What is interesting about this bar is that it is smaller by about a centimeter in each dimension than a standard gold bar." He looked intently at Christophe. "I'll bet you can guess why."

Christophe nodded. "Because it gets gold plated. But why so much gold plate? Wouldn't a few microns suffice?"

Tor replaced the bar into its case and put it back in his drawer. "The answer is that it is necessary to stamp the serial number and seal of authenticity on the top. This requires about a half a centimeter of real gold thickness; otherwise, the tungsten could show through. Electroplating deposits a uniform coating of five millimeters on all the outside surfaces. I can assure you that neither you nor anyone else experienced in detecting counterfeit bars would ever know they were not real—the fakes are that good."

Christophe let out a quiet whistle. "It just occurred to me that such a thick veneer of electroplated real gold would consume a lot of gold from the industrial markets. This would be hard to disguise, wouldn't it?"

"Interesting that you picked this up, Christophe. You are quite right. You are probably aware that nonbullion industrial gold consumption has been higher than expected, which has been causing inflation in the world digital currency markets. Well, now you have the explanation. The gold has not been disappearing at all. It is simply being used to coat a lot of counterfeit bars, while the real bars are being smuggled out."

Tor walked around the table and reached for a cardboard box that was lying on the floor of his office. "We just received this new piece of equipment from Abraham. He claims it is the best, and maybe even the only, way to detect counterfeit bullion without having to drill holes into the bars." He pulled out the instrument and placed it on the table. The label on the side said Sonilyzer 2110A. "Apparently you know all about this instrument." Once again, Christophe felt he was living in some kind of time warp. He sensed that his every move had been anticipated. A lot of things were beginning to fall into place.

"We are not sure yet how to operate it," Brigid said, "so we were hoping you might be able to help us." She glanced at her father to be sure she could speak freely. "We have been quietly working with the authorities at the Southern California Repository in order to gain access so we can start identifying which bars are real and which ones are counterfeit."

Tor continued, "Christophe, you have no idea what a miracle it was that you stumbled onto what was going on with the Paris portal. We knew about the counterfeiting and most of the details of how the counterfeit bars were getting substituted into the gold repositories. We knew that Trent Lachmann was behind the operation. But until you came along, we had absolutely no idea where the real gold was ending up."

At this point, Brigid added, "Christophe, you can appreciate that taking on a globally entrenched cartel like the syndicate requires an international intelligence network and tight cooperation between countries. We have treaties with some foreign governments, but you are an American! This was pivotal to our investigation, to have an American show up when you did." She paused for a moment and then slowly added in a voice barely above a whisper, "We are now just inches away from being able to shut down the entire syndicate operation!"

After several hours of discussion, some detailed plans were laid out for how to proceed. The biggest challenge was to locate where the real gold was being stored in North America—assuming it was in North America. Moving gold bars around the continent by truck would be easy enough, so delivering the bars to Goose Bay would be straightforward. They now knew how bars were being smuggled from Belmullet into Europe as capsule ballast, but the question of how the bars were being moved across the North Atlantic from Goose Bay to Belmullet was still a mystery. Christophe had a hunch, but it was too soon to articulate it.

By the end of the afternoon, they were exhausted. Tor suggested that the three of them go to dinner at a quiet place he knew of in Malibu. Even if they were spotted together, there would be nothing out of the ordinary about Bridget Anderson and her dad having dinner with an old friend from work. It was Saturday night, so the receptionist had to pull some strings to make the reservation.

Tor, Brigid, and Christophe sat at a table outside in a quiet corner of the deck with a propane heater to cut the chill. Brigid was wearing her familiar droopy glasses and "Ashleigh attire." There was no reason to suspect that they might be watched, but they needed to talk softly when using certain delicate key words and phrases such as *gold bullion* and *syndicate*.

"So, *Bridget*, tell me about the real Brigid," inquired Christophe.

"What do you mean?" she responded.

"You could start with Modesto."

"Oh, I guess you mean my fake résumé. Well, for starters, I was not born in Modesto." She took a sip of wine. "I was born in Bergen, Norway. When I was little, Papa taught me how to shoot. From as far back as I can remember, all I dreamed of was becoming an Olympic biathlete. My parents encouraged this and enrolled me in training camps. By the time I was seventeen, I was competitive and could hold my own against the boys my own age anywhere in Norway. I was particularly good with a rifle and aspired to compete in the 2062 Winter Olympics with the Norwegian Team. Then I did a really stupid thing. I fell off a horse and fractured my collarbone while fooling around with some guys from the team. We had all been drinking. It took me out of action for six months and dashed to pieces my dream of competing in the Olympics that year. I had always been a bit wild, but this time it caught up with me. Anyway, I never lost my love for firearms."

Tor jumped in at this point. "She had been a good student, but the only thing that really got her going was speed—fast cars, motorcycles, wing suits—"

"Wing suits?" asked Christophe.

"Yes. Her mother and I only found out after the fact that she had plunged off Trolltunga in a wing suit with a parachute. It was her first jump!"

Brigid shrugged her shoulders and smiled. "Anyway, I enrolled at the National Technical University of Norway in Trondheim. I was getting stir-crazy at home while I was recovering and had to get away. University seemed to be a perfectly good excuse. The surprise came when I discovered that I actually liked mathematics and engineering. After I graduated from NTNU, I went into the army for the obligatory two years, which turned into ten. I made lieutenant in two years and captain in eight. I was the youngest female ever promoted to captain in the Norwegian Army. This led to a stint as the head of security for the king and queen in Oslo, which is where I got my first exposure to the intelligence business."

"That's when my daughter became a spy," Tor said proudly.

"All that time growing up, I thought Papa was working for a North Sea natural gas company. I never had any inkling that he was in Norwegian intelligence. Do you know how I finally found out?" She looked over at her father lovingly. "There was a group of ultranationalists in Norway who wanted to overthrow the monarchy. The king asked me to go undercover and join the group. When the bust came, you will never guess who burst into the room wearing a SWAT uniform. Papa!"

This caused a good laugh.

"I could not tell her that my team had been surveilling her all along, for fear of blowing her cover," said Tor.

Brigid looked seriously at Christophe. "Working undercover was the most exciting thing I ever did, Christophe. The adrenaline rush of pretending to be someone else become an addiction."

"That's a healthy thing, I suppose. Isn't it?" inquired Christophe.

While Brigid was thinking about how to answer the question, the server came to take their dinner requests. Up to that point, no one had bothered to look at the menu. As they were fumbling through the pages, the server said, "Let me make this easy on you. We received a magnificent ahi tuna caught just this morning off Port Hueneme. As the specialty of the house, it is served lightly seared and topped with our world-famous spicy cilantro."

"That sounds wonderful," said Brigid.

"I agree," said Tor. "I will have the same thing."

"Make that three," said Christophe. "And bring us a bottle of white wine that you recommend with the main course, please." As the server was walking away, Christophe stood up and said quietly in his ear, "And please be sure to bring me the check for dinner."

The wine steward poured a little Riesling for Christophe to taste. It was a bit fruity but satisfactory. Wine was served around.

Christophe looked back at Brigid, eagerly awaiting to hear the rest of the story. "Oh, you asked whether or not it was a healthy thing." Brigid became a bit somber as she continued. "Actually, no. The months I spent with the ultranationalists really messed with my head. I became so good at playing the role that after a while, I lost the ability to tell which world I was living in. It became like parallel universes, where I weaved in and out between the two, never knowing which one I was in. To be honest, it was horrific. When I came out in the open, I nearly had a nervous breakdown." Tears formed in the corners of her eyes.

Tor jumped in. "Undercover work takes a toll." The dinner salads arrived as a welcome break. "Brigid's mom and I had no idea what she was going through. She was just sullen and despondent. To make matters worse, Brigid's mom became terminally ill and died rather suddenly in the midst of all this. This was an incredibly difficult time for us. When my name came up as a potential candidate for the position of director here at SCIP, I saw it as a chance for Brigid and me to make a new start. They wanted someone who had never worked for the CIA. I was a pretty good choice, don't you think?" Tor took a bite of salad and mumbled with his mouth full. "It was actually because of Abraham that I was offered the job. I had practically nothing to do with it."

Brigid entered back into the dialogue, saying, "I was pretty much done with the whole spy thing by that time. After Papa and I moved to Los Angeles, I took up surfing rather seriously and did practically nothing else. I just couldn't find anything to do that really made me happy. Then one day I came across an advertisement for an office manager job at Ashleigh. I simply wanted to do something radically different. My real résumé would never have gotten me in the door. What, Norwegian engineer, former spy, sharpshooter, hell-raiser? So, I fabricated my résumé to become a simple girl from Modesto. That's when I met you for the first time, Christophe."

Christophe said, "You have to admit, Brigid, that it is a bit ironic that you tried to get away from working undercover and jumped right back in."

"That was not my intention at all. I liked the idea of underachieving for a change and of being a simple girl from Modesto. I listened to cowboy music nonstop to master the American redneck accent. I even spent a month in Modesto so that if I ever actually encountered someone from there, I would be able to pretend like I grew up there. I never dreamed that the identity I created for myself would become the very cover for my clandestine work at Ashleigh. Who would have ever thought that I would be working for an international gangster?"

"I presume you mean Fred Simms?" asked Christophe.

"Oh, Fred Simms! His playboy act was very convincing at first. I actually found him charming, if you can believe it. But certain things he did started to set off alarm bells."

Tor volunteered, "She came to me one night and said, 'Papa? I am working for this guy, but I don't think he is who he claims to be. He has this flamboyant California partygoing flair, but I think he is actually cold-blooded. For one thing, he claimed to have all these beautiful girlfriends. That type of woman would want to be seen with him in public, but I never saw one, Papa.' I told her I would look into it."

"In ten years working with Fred, I never got a hint that he was phony," said Christophe.

"That's because you are a man," volunteered Brigid. "It takes a woman to see these things."

Tor said, "I ran the name Fred Simms through the intelligence database, and he checked out—squeaky-clean, only a couple of speeding tickets on his record. But when I started looking a little closer, I discovered that his birth certificate had been reported lost. It was particularly strange that he apparently traveled a great deal but there was no record of a Fred Simms in the retinal scan database. Apparently, Fred Simms was a pseudonym and he traveled under different credentials."

"This is when things started to get really interesting at work," said Brigid. "Fred used to have me go quite often to courier documents between headquarters and the recycling company in Torrance. Papa checked the company out, and it proved to be totally legitimate. It is not a small operation. Tons and tons of discarded tungsten carbide auger bits from tunnel boring operations were shipped in from around the world. One day they proudly gave me a tour when I expressed an interest. The carbide is crushed and reduced to metal powder. The powder is melted in some sort of a high-temperature, high-pressure furnace and cast into bars in a reducing atmosphere. There were stacks and stacks of ingot bars on pallets being loaded onto trucks, presumably to be shipped off to China to be turned back into more tungsten carbine. It was really interesting and very high-tech."

At this point, dinner arrived. Tor continued the story. "Well, there was no picture of any Fred Simms on file anywhere, which seemed more than a little odd for a high-profile senior executive in a huge international conglomerate. I asked Brigid to take a picture sometime when he wasn't looking. When I submitted the picture to facial recognition, guess who came up?"

"Trent Lachmann," said Christophe.

"Bingo. And Trent Lachmann was well-known for being involved in a lot of shady deals. It turns out that he had been caught up in a gold coin scandal some years ago. He was found to be in possession of a quantity of counterfeit one-ounce gold US eagles, and he said he didn't know they were fakes. He claimed he was just the victim of fraud."

"Nothing ever came of it," said Brigid, "but at the mention of gold counterfeiting, I immediately thought of Ashleigh Recycle. When I was in college, a metallurgy professor had said one day in class that if anyone ever wanted to counterfeit gold coins, just electroplate gold onto tungsten, and no one would be able to tell the difference without actually cutting them open, because tungsten and gold have almost the same density." Brigid took a sip of wine. After a long pause she said, "Guess what was under the gold plating of Lachmann's coins? Then it dawned on me that the tungsten ingots I had seen at the Ashleigh Recycle plant were about the same size and shape as a standard twelve-and-a-half-kilogram gold bullion bar. Not bad for a simple girl from Modesto, don't you think?"

Tor talked at some length about the necessity of locating and securing the stashes of real gold before exposing the existence of counterfeit bars. He and the directors at a few other American prefecture agencies whom he trusted had concluded that the switch was being carried out right under everyone's noses. Under the agreement of the Acts of Secession, the Fort Knox gold was being delivered to the various repositories in the prefectures. The serial numbers on the bars were carefully checked and logged when the bars were removed from Fort Knox and then rechecked when the bars arrived at their new repositories. They used an armed courier to transport the bars—a courier that was none other than a wholly owned subsidiary of the global freight giant UPX. UPX was, of course, a wholly owned subsidiary of the conglomerate based in Geneva, otherwise now known as the syndicate. Once en route, the trucks in the armored convoy with the real bullion simply drove off the highway at some remote prearranged rendezvous, and the guards got into identical armored trucks with the counterfeit bars, neatly stamped with the same serial numbers as the real bars, and drove on to the destination repository. Meanwhile, the real gold drove away. The last of the Fort Knox gold had been transferred only the year before. Several of the banks had suspected that they were holding counterfeit bullion, but if they admitted it, they would be ruined. They needed to keep the fact secret until all of their real gold was recovered. So far, it had vanished without a trace. The first sign of its possible reappearance showed up in Versailles, thanks to the work of Abraham's team in Paris.

Christophe was dying to express his theory about how gold was being smuggled into Ireland. But while he was listening to Tor, he realized that he now also knew where the rest of the Fort Knox gold was probably located—the bullion that had not yet been smuggled into Europe. Fifty-five hundred metric tons of gold bullion had been removed from the national repository at Fort Knox. Versailles could not possibly account for more than 10 percent of this. If Rotterdam and Frankfurt received similar amounts, then there had to be roughly thirty-eight hundred metric tons remaining in North America somewhere, or more than three hundred thousand bars. All of this gold needed to be smuggled into Europe through Belmullet by one of those three portals. At thirty bars a day, this would take another three to five years.

Christophe could hold it in no longer. "I know where it is and how it's getting to Ireland. It's at the airport in Goose Bay."

They stared at him in wonder. "How in the world do you know that?" asked Tor.

For Christophe it was morning and he was just starting to come to life. "I have been puzzling over how the gold bullion was getting to Belmullet for quite some time. Obviously, once it gets across the Atlantic to Ireland, it gets stashed in the capsules as ballast, and now we have figured out how all that works. But how did the bars get to Belmullet in the first place?" Christophe didn't need any more coffee, but he ordered some for his friends because he wanted them alert when he explained it.

"As you know, the North Atlantic portal is unidirectional. All the capsules travel from west to east. You might ask, why not smuggle gold in capsules coming from Goose Bay then? The answer is simple. There was never a possibility to construct a capsule trapdoor switch like the one in the Paris portal, because if they had, I would have known about it. I ran the whole construction project." Christophe paused to catch his breath. "There's a much better way. I can't believe it didn't occur to me sooner. They are smuggling the bars in the empty capsule transport containers."

By this time, the after-dinner coffee had arrived and the effects of the wine were wearing off, but the expression on Tor's and Brigid's faces spoke that neither had the faintest idea what Christophe had just said.

"The containers," Christophe repeated for emphasis, to be sure they heard him. "The containers." Still neither had any idea what he was talking about. "Capsules arriving on the North Atlantic portal fan out to a dozen European destinations. Some of the empty capsules are returned to Dublin and loaded into special containers, and then they are taken by train to Belmullet, where they are put onto jumbo jet freighters for transport back to Goose Bay."

Tor interrupted, "That doesn't make any sense. Why would they be smuggling gold back to North America?"

"No," said Christophe. "The empty containers need to be flown back from Goose Bay to Belmullet to be offloaded before being sent back to Dublin by train. The containers collapse. I know this because this is how I designed them. There wasn't any point in flying empty containers back to Belmullet. They take up too much space, so we made them collapsible. The walls fold down, allowing them to lie flat. A typical jumbo jet can carry about two hundred fifty of these folded containers on the return flight." Tor and Brigid were still lost.

"There are plenty of nooks and crannies that could accommodate gold bars. At the airport in Belmullet, the returned containers are not handled as ordinary freight. There is no manifest or waybill or anything. They just get offloaded directly onto railcars. When we originally designed the system, we had proposed that planes also be allowed to carry freight along with the folded containers, but powers high up in Ashleigh vetoed the plan. Now I know why. They didn't want anyone searching the planes for contraband. After all, they were just folded containers, they argued, and didn't need to be subject to import inspection." At this point, the light went on for both Tor and Brigid.

"You want to know where the rest of the gold from Fort Knox is stashed?" asked Christophe. "Just look in the hangar at the Goose Bay airport where the containers full of capsules are being delivered from arriving jets and then folded up to be shipped back to Ireland." Christophe finally exhaled and took the last sip of wine. He turned to the waiter. "Could I please have the check now? I think we are ready to leave."

CHAPTER 25

THE CONTRACT

It was after one o'clock on Sunday morning by the time they finally left the restaurant. As they were preparing to depart, Christophe asked Tor, "What's next?" Tor handed him a keyless entry fob for a Toyota. "You want me to drive somewhere?"

"No," replied Tor. "It's not for a car. The button marked 'panic' is just what it means. Don't push it unless you are in a life-or-death emergency. If you need to contact me, just push the 'door unlock' button, and someone from the SCIP will come find you. There is a GPS transponder inside, so we will know where you are at all times."

"Am I in some kind of danger?" inquired Christophe.

"No. We will be keeping an eye on you. But just in case." Then Tor added jokingly, "This is probably a bit more practical than a pack of cigarettes, since smoking is illegal in California."

The three had agreed to take separate cabs from the restaurant in Malibu. There were taxis waiting out front. These were called autopods. About the size of a golf cart, each had four wheels and a guide pin that extended into a slot in the track for power and control. The autopods swarmed all over Los Angeles like columns of ants on tracks, mostly raised on pedestals, running down the middle of major streets. They were switched in and out automatically to side streets, and depending on traffic, the whole network was balanced dynamically to reduce congestion. Autopods were ideal for short trips of less than ten kilometers. For longer trips, there were high-speed trains and, of course, portals for even longer distances. The system worked so well, in fact, that fewer and fewer people even bothered to own a car. It was always possible to rent one if necessary. This freed up an enormous amount of space in the city that had formerly been dedicated to parking lots and garages.

Christophe hopped into his autopod, and an androgynous voice said, "Good evening, Christophe Conally. Where would you like to go?" The system used facial recognition, and there was no console for typing anything.

Christophe spoke, "Yacht Haven, unit 202, Marina del Rey."

"Got it. Yacht Haven, unit 202, Marina del Rey," repeated the androgynous voice. "Your trip will take twelve minutes and thirty-six seconds, and you will be charged $4.21. Shall we go?"

"Yes," replied Christophe. His autopod, which had been switched to a siding in front of the restaurant, merged into the main track on the Pacific Coast Highway heading east.

As the pod neared Marina del Rey, the voice came on saying, "The exit to your destination is currently blocked. What would you like me to do?"

The system worked well most of the time, except when there was a mechanical failure on one of the tracks. Christophe gave some thought to this unexpected annoyance and finally said, "Get me as close as you can, and I will walk from there."

After a few moments, the voice came back. "That would be the intersection of Lincoln Boulevard and Bali Way. Is this acceptable?"

"Yes," replied Christophe.

The autopod slowed to pull off onto a siding that was currently occupied by several other autopods with disembarking passengers. Despite the late hour, apparently others had also made the decision to disembark at this platform. "I apologize for the delay," said the voice.

Christophe got out and walked down the staircase from the platform and soon realized that traffic on Admiralty Way, the quickest route to his condo complex, was completely blocked off. As he turned the corner to enter the locked gate of Yacht Haven, he saw flashing red and blue lights everywhere and a great deal of commotion. A fire hose extended from a hydrant outside the complex. Christophe asked the security guard at the gate, "What's going on?"

"Apparently some sort of explosion and fire," said the guard as if it were a daily occurrence.

Christophe continued through the main gate to discover that the fire engines were right in front of his building.

A fireman was carrying the remains of a blackened and shredded suitcase. "Hey! That looks like my suitcase," exclaimed Christophe. He checked the name tag, which was still intact. "Yes, that is mine!"

The fireman replied without emotion, "Sorry. It's evidence now," and walked away.

Christophe could not believe his eyes. A big yellow X covered a gaping hole where his front door used to be, and yellow tape was everywhere with the words Keep Out—Crime Scene.

A fireman approached him, who appeared to be in charge. "Is that your condo, sir?" he asked, pointing to unit 202. By this time, Christophe could tell that a large portion of his entryway was missing. "Was that suitcase yours?" the man asked.

"Yes," replied Christophe, still in shock. "I just arrived from France this morning. The freight courier was supposed to deliver it this evening."

"Apparently there was a bomb in it."

"A bomb?" exclaimed Christophe.

The chief fireman pointed to a black bag about the size of a human on the landing. "If you had shown up any earlier, that would be you in that bag."

"Someone died?" asked Christophe, in shock.

"Yes. We have identified him as the cat burglar we have been trying to catch for quite some time. I suppose that's not how he expected his life of crime to end." He spoke into his radio. "I have the owner here. Do you want me to bring him in?" The response was too garbled for Christophe to make out.

"Would it be possible for me to fetch my backpack from the back bedroom? It just has my toiletries and some clothes."

"It's an active crime scene, sir," said the fireman. He looked at Christophe with pity and finally said, "Let me see what I can do. Stay here until I get back."

Christophe was at a total loss for what to do. He pulled the Toyota key fob from his pocket and pushed the panic button. After about fifteen minutes, the man returned with Christophe's backpack. "There is a person in that car over there who has vouched for you. He has connections that are way above my pay grade. We are releasing you into his custody."

Christophe walked over to the parked car, and the back door opened. "Quickly, get in," said a man in the shadows. "You are in grave danger."

"Stefan?"

The car pulled into the underground parking lot at Dr. Petrosvki's dental practice. Stefan and Christophe went upstairs to Tor's office. Brigid was not there. Tor had turned on the espresso machine in the lunchroom. The coffee was welcome to all. It was now three thirty in the morning. The men sat at the conference table relishing the coffee, trying to decide who would be the first to talk.

Christophe had not noticed it before, but the office was windowless. No one on the street below would know that any lights were on in the building. More importantly, the walls of Tor's office were impregnated with wire mesh, creating a secure Faraday cage. Finally, Christophe spoke up, saying, "Stefan, how did you get to LA before me?"

Stefan glanced over at Tor for approval to speak. "I was already here when you arrived. I flew in yesterday." He looked again at Tor and asked, "Is it okay if I tell him?" Tor nodded. "We started receiving intelligence reports last week that the syndicate was getting edgy. There were some early signs that they had gotten wind that we were on to them. As you know, we had Versailles under surveillance, but we also located the portal switches in Rotterdam and Frankfort, and since we knew their modus operandi, it was straightforward to locate the bullion stashes and put those locations under surveillance as well."

At this point, Tor chimed in. "Something we did not fully appreciate, literally until dinner with you tonight— rather, last night—was that you would be able to solve the mystery of where the bullion was stashed in North America so quickly and how it was being smuggled into Belmullet. I presume you figured it out because you had been a key employee at Ashleigh. Fact and possibility together make for an interesting combination. You might be the only person alive with enough knowledge of the North Atlantic portal system to figure it out."

"Apparently, some people at Ashleigh also knew this and came to the same conclusion," said Stefan. "We got word that a contract had been put out on your life."

The color drained from Christophe's face. "A contract?" he said weakly. He looked over at Tor. "Did you know?" Tor looked at Stefan to continue.

Stefan said, "I was dispatched immediately to LA. We didn't want to tell you about the contract for fear that you might shut down. We would never have allowed you to be in any personal danger." Stefan glanced over at Tor again. "We had a plan to use you to get to Lachmann. We thought maybe he could be turned if threatened." There was a long pause before Stefan added apologetically, "But I have to confess that the business with the bomb in your suitcase caught everyone by surprise."

Tor added, "Lachmann arrived in Los Angeles yesterday shortly after you. Perhaps it was coincidental, but now it seems likely that he was going to personally clean up his mess, which included getting rid of you."

Mild-mannered, flamboyant Fred Simms, a murderer? thought Christophe. *That's pretty far-fetched.* He finally spoke up: "What does all this mean?"

"For one thing," said Stefan, "we no longer need you to turn Lachmann. We found the gold in Goose Bay, just where you told us to look."

Christophe glanced at his watch. "I only told you about that three hours ago."

Tor and Stefan looked at each other with amusement. Tor volunteered, "We have good friends in Newfoundland."

Stefan then said, "Lachmann is in his office right now shredding documents. Brigid is monitoring his every move using a surveillance camera. By 6:00 a.m. Pacific time, the syndicate gold operation will be completely shut down."

"Then I am no longer in any danger, right?" said Christophe.

Stefan replied after a long pause, "Christophe, you just cost the syndicate about five hundred billion euros. The contract on your life is no longer about shutting you up; it is now a matter of seeking revenge."

Tor added, "We need to find a safe place for you until this blows over. We think it would be best if you disappear for a while."

Thierry's phone rang in the barn late on Sunday afternoon. He was in the middle of repairing the pump on one of his sugar syrup transfer tanks and had his hands full. Sophie was standing by the door. "I think the call is from Southern California." She picked it up. "Allô?"

"Hello. May I speak with Thierry?"

"Il est occupé en ce moment. C'est Sophie parant. Est-ce-que je vous aider?"

"Sophie, this is Christophe Conally. We met last month in an Irish pub in Belmullet."

"Christophe?" she exclaimed. "What an unexpected surprise to hear from you." Hearing Christophe's name got Thierry's attention. Sophie handed him the phone.

"This is Thierry speaking."

"Thierry, this is Christophe Conally. I was wondering if you could use some extra help on the farm for a couple of months."

CHAPTER 26

THE FARM

C hristophe was wide awake before dawn as he had been having difficulty sleeping. He bundled up and slipped out the side door with Thierry's golden retriever following close behind, tail wagging enthusiastically. The other dogs preferred to stay huddled in front of the gas heater. In the courtyard, it was totally quiet. Even the rooster was still asleep. The morning mist hung frozen in the air as tiny crystals sparkling in the yard light, too small to fall as snowflakes. He and the dog walked down what was a now familiar footpath, dimly illuminated by diffuse moonlight, to his favorite spot, a wooden bench on the bank of a small pond on Thierry and Sophie Monfort's farm in the northeast corner of France. Here he would wait for the sun to rise. The only sound was the tumultuous clamor of his own thoughts, which he was unable to silence. The only movement was the swirling of condensate in his exhaled breath.

His gracious hosts had opened their home to him without asking any questions. Christophe felt safely hidden away deep in the French countryside, but even after six weeks since leaving Los Angeles, the posttraumatic stress still stalked him relentlessly. He just couldn't shake the dark oppression of knowing that someone actually had tried to kill him. He shuddered again and forced the fear back into its place in his subconscious. Thierry's dog Bounder lay quietly at Christophe's feet. The two had become inseparable friends.

The first faint streaks of daybreak began to appear in the distance beyond the far side of the pond. Christophe paid close attention to the surface of the totally still water as it was trying to decide whether or not to freeze all the way across. Already ice crystals anchored at the shoreline were jutting out, each trying to be the first to reach the center. He watched the needles penetrate outward until further growth was arrested upon encountering another ambitious ice crystal. The dynamics were fascinating as the delicate balance between the liquid and solid phases of water played out with the air temperature exactly at the freezing point. Every so often a gentle breeze would spread over the surface of the pond, and the leading edge of the ice crystals would retreat before reengaging in their urgent pursuit to be first. Christophe reflected on the subtle competition between ice crystals as a perfectly natural thing. Everything in nature seems to continue to grow until external forces step in to stop it.

Earlier in the week, he had walked with Thierry and Bounder into the fields to check on the condition of the planted sugar beet seeds. Thierry dug up several from the furrows to check for mold. Christophe, having found it interesting that the seeds were planted exactly twenty centimeters apart, asked Thierry why he didn't just sow the seeds closer together to get more plants. Thierry explained that this was a matter of years of experience. He knew the ideal growing conditions in every square meter of soil on his property. He had explained to Christophe that if the plants were too close together, the beets would be smaller, and if they were too far apart, weeds would crowd them out. It was all a delicate balance to ensure that the right combination of water, nutrients, and sunlight existed to produce the best yield. Each of his fields was slightly different, depending on slope and orientation, requiring the personalized touch only an experienced farmer could bring.

Thierry had waited too long the previous year before planting. The spring had been very wet, raining almost every day in March and April, so that by the time the fields were dry enough for him to go on them with his tractor, it was almost May. This shortened the growing season substantially, so his yield was below expectation. This year he had decided to try a new hybrid seed that could be planted in the fall. According to the agricultural supplier, these seeds were encapsulated with a new type of time-release fungicide to keep them from molding over the winter. The weather this January had been unseasonably warm, and besides mold, Thierry was now worried that they might germinate prematurely. Farm life was always lived on the knife-edge between abundance and ruination. It took a special type of person to keep at it year after year and generation after generation.

"You know, Christophe," Thierry had said, straightening back up and sweeping his outstretched arm across the horizon, "this farm has been in my family for three generations. Originally, all the land you can see around you was part of a vineyard belonging to a German duke. When Napoleon conquered this region, he ordered that all of the grapevines be dug up and the land replanted with sugar beets. Tradition has it that his generals at the eastern front advised him that his troops in Russia needed French pastries a lot more than they needed German wine. At the time, the British had blockaded all sugarcane molasses imports from the Caribbean, and making sugar from sugar beets became a national priority. Personally, I think Napoleon just had a grudge against the German duke, but who knows?"

The sunrise was magnificent, warming both Christophe's body and his soul. It was going to be a rare cloudless February morning in northern France. As soon as the first shaft of sunlight pierced the horizon, the ice on the pond was vanquished for that day. Rising from the bench, Christophe proceeded around the pond and followed one of the two ruts that was the service road for the farm's two largest fields. The smell of the black earth was pungent with compost and manure. Christophe had passed his days wandering along the numerous paths and trails around the farm with Bounder at his side. The therapy had been working wonders.

He walked with Bounder to the far edge of the 120-hectare farm, which was large by French standards. Two enormous wind turbines stood motionless at the end. There was no characteristic *whoosh, whoosh, whoosh* of the 50-meter-long airfoil blades this morning. On a normal day, with only a modest breeze, the turbines would spin slowly, generating 5 megawatts of electric power for the town of Saint-Quentin, 8 kilometers to the southeast. Thierry did not own the wind turbines. Rather, he received about €2 per megawatt-hour as compensation for placing them on his land. This provided the farm with about €38,000 of supplementary annual income—much more, on a per hectare basis, than growing sugar beets brought in. He was in negotiations with the electric utility to install two more, but the proliferation of microfusion reactors, which operated continuously, was steadily eroding the demand for intermittent power from wind turbines and photovoltaics.

A drainage ditch and hedgerow separated Thierry's farm from the neighbor's. Christophe walked along the footpath that would be ablaze in wildflowers in a few more weeks. On the near side of the Monfort compound stood two buildings, a large barn and the smaller sugar beet processing shelter, where the sugar beets were crushed and the juice was concentrated into syrup. A pile of unprocessed beets, as well as several sugar syrup holding tanks, stood nearby. The other prominent feature of this portion of the compound was a thirty-thousand-square-meter array of sun-tracking solar panels. Thierry did own these—at least, they were financed by the bank. They could produce an additional seven and a half kilowatts of electric power, which was mostly used to power the sugar beet processing equipment. During the periods when there were no beets to process, Thierry was able to sell the surplus power for about forty euros per megawatt-hour, which helped cover the interest payment on the solar array.

The balance of the Montfort farm was used for growing sugar beets for producing fuel ethanol. There were about one hundred hectares under cultivation that yielded six thousand metric tons of beets in a normal year—enough to produce about two hundred thousand liters of 95 percent bioethanol, worth about one euro per liter. Thierry received about fifty cents per equivalent liter from the local distillery for the syrup he shipped out. The field—now occupied by solar panels—used to be where Thierry pastured two dairy cows. In prior generations, it was expected that any French farmer worth his salt would keep some livestock. It had dawned on Thierry one bitter-cold winter day several years earlier that hand-milking two stubborn cows for about ten euros worth of milk was not such a great value proposition when he could generate ten times more revenue on the same plot of land without getting up every morning at four in the morning. Anyway, the composted sugar beet residue, when properly treated, turned out to be almost as good a fertilizer as cow manure.

The Monfort farm was a typical energy farm. They produced no food at all except the prize vegetables from Sophie's garden, and apples and pears from their orchard.

Such specialization had become commonplace, but it was not without controversy in traditional French farming communes. Pricing pressure on French food producers from imports, however, had precipitated the transition to energy farming because growing crops for energy was simply more profitable than growing food. This, too, was a matter of delicate balance. But energy crops, including wind turbines and solar arrays, gave farmers more options for how to best utilize their land. Unfortunately for Thierry, microfusion reactors and plentiful natural gas were precipitating a return to food crops.

During numerous journeys along the hedgerow separating the Monfort farm from the neighbor's farm to the north, Christophe had taken note of the different colors of the planted beet field on his left, compared to the neighbor's field, which was white with barley stubble. The stark color contrast accentuated the appearance of the region when zooming in on a satellite image. He had been reflecting on the significance of borders for quite some time and had been studying satellite images of the surrounding French countryside because he was fascinated by the interlocking irregular polygons. They fit neatly together with hardly any unused space. He had observed the uncanny similarity between the mesostructure of French farmland, as viewed from ten kilometers up, and the microstructure of polycrystalline solids. During construction of the North Atlantic portal, he had spent countless hours studying scanning electron micrographs of polish sections of the mineral specimens removed from the anchor holes drilled on the seafloor. In both cases, whether parcels of farmland in ten square kilometers or crystallites in ten square microns in the micrographs, they shared an interesting common feature: even though there was a variety of shapes, the sizes always seemed to bunch around an average value with relatively little variance. For the microstructure of solids, pattern recognition software was used to do the exact determination of the distribution, but the human eye could detect this phenomenon with ease. Grain boundaries and cracks in the polycrystalline microstructure were replaced by roads, streams, and ancient hedgerows in the farmland mesostructure. Large parcels such as towns and parks were easily identified as outliers. Similarly in a micrograph, inclusions and foreign bodies could be easily detected because, with their size and shape, they did not fit into the pattern. The science of grain growth kinetics in polycrystalline materials was a well-established discipline, but as far as Christophe knew, there were not any models for what determined the size and shape of French farms. The polygons tended to have four sides, with a few having three or five, but there was no obvious explanation for the angles of the four corners. He finally concluded that the size of a field had something to do with how much land could be plowed or planted in one day, but this was a question he would have to pose to Thierry.

Of more interest to Christophe at that moment, however, was why the Monfort farm was 120 hectares and not 12 or 1,200. What determines the optimal size? Did farms tend to become bigger and bigger over time by gobbling up surrounding regions the way empires grow?

The land on which Christophe was standing—not far from the German border—had changed hands dozens of times over the centuries, but the size of the fields had hardly changed at all. The only significant change had been urbanization, which caused cities to expand at the expense of farmland. Much of the traditional farmland to the south of the Monfort property was already now converted to factories, warehouses, and apartment buildings, and this trend would consume the Monfort farm before too long. Nevertheless, the size of individual French fields had changed very little over the centuries. Over the course of the time that Christophe had spent there, he had begun to appreciate the forces that dictated the optimum size of a field. Like the growth of ice crystals on a pond, or microcrystals in igneous rocks, fields tended to fall in line with the natural order of things, because the driving forces—just like with the solidification of crystalline solids—were distributed and uniform. From time to time, neighboring properties came up for sale, causing Thierry and Sophie to consider pursuing the acquisition. Ultimately the decision hinged on deciding if the marginal value of the increased size of the farm was greater than the marginal cost. The invisible hand of microeconomics was always at work at the level of the family farm. The forces behind urbanization, on the other hand, like the growth of empires, resulted from centralization and concentration of power.

Christophe had learned a fundamental lesson during his stay on the Monfort farm: farms generate wealth by converting resources into something of value. He mused on the fact that empires, as embodied by governments, cannot create wealth. The best they can do is redistribute some of the wealth to others. Just like with King Louis XIV and the Palace of Versailles, which precipitated the French Revolution, the syndicate was the worst type of empire. The people at the top simply wanted to confiscate wealth for themselves without any intention of sharing it with anyone else.

By the time he returned to the house, the sun was well up in the sky. Sophie was in the kitchen, and she explained that the electricity had gone off. "Thierry is out in the barn fixing the generator, if you are looking for him," she said.

Christophe walked across the courtyard to the barn and popped his head around the sliding door. It was dark inside, so while he allowed his eyes adjust, he called out for Thierry.

"Over here," came the muffled voice from somewhere on the far side beyond the tractor. The front panel of the generator control cabinet was off to the side, and Thierry was lying on his back trying to position his flashlight so he could see. "There is a thirteen-millimeter open-end wrench in the toolbox over there. Would you mind getting it for me?"

Christophe handed him the wrench and remarked on the logo at the bottom of the removed panel. "EthoGen. That's the same company that made the fuel cell in my sailboat."

"I'm not surprised," said Thierry. "I think they make the best fuel cells on the market." There was a thousand-liter polyethylene tank standing on a pedestal next to the generator with a large yellow warning label with black letters on the side reading, "Flammable: Bioethanol." A feeder tube coming from the bottom led to the area where Thierry was working. "I have had almost no trouble with this system until just recently." He grunted while he tried to loosen a stubborn nut on the supply hose fitting. "There is a pump here that meters the flow of fuel to the cells. It has some rubber O-rings that apparently dissolve after some time in alcohol. The factory service desk sent me some Teflon replacements. I just need to remove the pump so I can take it apart to replace the seals." After a while, Thierry stood up, proudly holding the pump, and walked over to his workbench. It took him almost no time to make the repair. He was a capable mechanic, which was a prerequisite for any farmer. He reinstalled the pump, opened the fuel gate valve, and replaced the cover panel. When he flipped the power switch, a green status light came on with the sound of the faint whir of the pump as it went back into service.

"We should have power in about thirty minutes," said Thierry as he returned his tools to the toolbox. "Until then, I'm afraid it's going to be cold cereal for breakfast."

As they were going back into the house, Thierry remarked, "You know, Christophe, I actually got a chance to meet the inventor of that fuel cell. It was while I was studying agricultural engineering at the university in Dijon. I was taking a course in biofuels, and he delivered a guest lecture to my class. That was my first exposure to direct alcohol fuel cells."

Sophie had placed a container of granola, a pitcher of milk, and glasses of orange juice on the kitchen table. The sunshine was streaming in, so it didn't matter that there was no light coming from the fixture overhead. The three sat down at the table for breakfast.

"It's pretty interesting how those things work," Thierry continued. "The electrochemical cells use a thin ceramic membrane that conducts protons. The fuel cells must operate at a high temperature, which is why we won't have electricity for a while. The system in the barn shut itself down this morning and needs to come back up to temperature."

"It's the same on my boat," said Christophe, "but I can run on batteries while the fuel cells heat up. I never gave much thought to what was inside, though." The mention of proton conductors led him to reflect briefly on his discovery that this phenomenon was what made reduction of carbonate minerals to make methane possible—essentially the fuel cell process in reverse. This thought then triggered him to remember that he still owed Philippe Aubrey an answer about giving the keynote address at the Earth Sciences Convention coming up in June.

"More orange juice?" asked Sophie. "I'm sorry there's no coffee yet."

"Apparently, it takes high temperatures to break down ethanol into hydrogen," Thierry continued. "The hydrogen somehow goes through the membrane and reacts with air on the other side to make electricity. It's a scientific marvel and much more efficient than burning fuel in an engine. The EthoGen system has sure made a big difference for us, compared to the old standby diesel generators we used to use. These days we don't even need power lines anymore. The farm is completely off the grid," he said proudly.

The phone rang in the back bedroom, and Sophie got up from the table to answer it. She came back into the kitchen, handed the phone to Christophe, and said in a soft voice with a big smile, "I think it's that nice girl from Modesto."

"Hello?"

"Hi, Christophe, it's Brigid. I'm just checking up on you. How are you doing?"

"I'm so glad to hear from you, Brigid. I'm fine. Sophie and Thierry have been wonderful to me. Thierry has been trying hard—but without success—to turn me into a sugar beet farmer."

"I just wanted to give you some news," said Brigid. "There was a top-level restructuring at Ashleigh. The company threw a very nice retirement party for Fred Simms after closing down his division. Also, the carbide recycling division is up for sale. And you know what else? I got laid off!" She chuckled. "They laid me off three days before Christmas. Can you believe that? Anyway, the queen begged me to return to work for her, and I just couldn't say no."

"Are you moving back to Norway, then?" asked Christophe.

"Actually, I am in Oslo now. Papa had no trouble convincing me that life as an office manager was not challenging enough for me. He encouraged me to take the job. Anyway, the queen and I get along pretty well. I am her new personal bodyguard."

"I don't know what to say," said Christophe. "Congratulations!"

"Oh, Christophe, one more thing. Your condo in Marina del Rey has been fixed up. Papa asked me to take care of it for you personally. But I have to say that your insurance company is a real pain to work with. I will be in touch. Goodbye for now."

Christophe's story had been dribbling out over the course of the previous six weeks, so Sophie and Thierry had learned all about Brigid. At that moment, their son, Bruno, walked through the door. "I just stopped by on my way to work to check up on the syrup dehydrator. The solar panels are really cranking this morning. I expect that we will have the last of the beets juiced by the end of next week." Bruno had developed a new type of dehydrator that was interfaced directly to the low-voltage direct current output of the solar panels. The design was so successful that he had started a company in Saint-Quentin to manufacture them. He was now starting to sell units around the world, which meant he had less and less time to spend helping his dad on the farm.

"Dad, I think it's time to start thinking about hiring some help," said Bruno.

Thierry looked over at Christophe, who said shaking his head vigorously. "Don't even think about it."

"There is a potential problem," continued Bruno. "All the syrup holding tanks are nearly full, and the distillery has not come by to empty them. I called them this morning, and they said they were out of storage capacity and all of their tanker trucks were full. I guess the warm weather has everyone stepping up production so the beets don't rot in the piles. I checked on ours, and the nights are still cold enough that we don't need to be concerned. But if the weather stays this mild and you can't schedule a pickup from the distillery, we may lose some beets."

The power had come back on. Sophie handed Bruno the first cup of coffee, saying, "Well, I guess the silver lining of production being down 30 percent this year is that there aren't as many beets to spoil. Hopefully 2077 will be a better year for us."

Up to this point, Christophe had not sensed that the farm was facing any serious financial difficulties.

"Thanks, Bruno. I will look into buying another holding tank. We'll talk later," said Thierry. Christophe could tell by the way he said this that it wasn't a serious proposal.

After Bruno left, Christophe started in. "Thierry and Sophie, there are no words to express how much it has meant to me to be here these past six weeks and to share Christmas with your family. You know I was in pretty bad shape when I came, and you have kindly kept my presence here a secret. The two of you have saved my life. I will be forever grateful. Who would have ever dreamed that a chance encounter in an Irish pub in Belmullet would lead to such a friendship? But I think the danger has passed, and it is now time for me to move on with my life and get out of your hair."

Sophie said, "We are not surprised. We knew this day was coming soon."

"I just heard Bruno tell you there's not a lot of work left to do for a while, so I had an idea." Christophe fished in his pocket and pulled out the set of keys to his condo. "You know, the beets won't even be sprouting for at least two months, and March is a lovely time of year in Marina del Rey." Handing the keys to Thierry, he said, "It is likely that they have changed the locks since the bombing, so I will need to make arrangements for you to obtain new ones."

Thierry said, "I don't understand."

Christophe continued, "Brigid just told me that my condo in Marina del Rey has been all fixed up. I had been trying to sell it, but after the bombing, I pulled it off the market. I don't really want to sell or rent it out anymore. If I knew that the two of you would go there from time to time, I would hold onto it." Christophe sipped his coffee while Sophie and Thierry looked at each other, stunned.

"I don't know what to say. Surely, you are not serious," said Thierry. "Santa Monica is our favorite place in the world. We were sure after last year's trip that we would never be able to afford to go again." Tears were welling up in Sophie's eyes.

Christophe finished packing his suitcase and straightened up the guest bedroom as best he could. Ordinarily, Bounder lay by the side of the bed, but this time he was lying across the threshold in an attempt to block the exit. He sensed that Christophe was leaving and would not be coming back. Sophie and Thierry had insisted on driving Christophe to the train station in Saint-Quentin. Christophe went out to their awaiting car with a very sad Bounder trailing close behind. He put his suitcase in the trunk, gave Bounder a big goodbye hug, and hopped into the passenger seat behind Thierry. The car headed down the long driveway with Bounder in hot pursuit. The dog did not stop when Thierry turned right onto the road heading into town. Thierry watched him through the rearview mirror running as fast as he could to keep up. Finally, Thierry pulled over to the side of the road. "This is ridiculous!" he exclaimed, looking at Sophie in the seat next to him. Bounder was sitting outside, panting heavily. Then, turning around in his seat, Thierry looked at Christophe and said, "Sophie asked me this morning if I would consider letting you take Bounder with you."

Sophie swung open the door, and Bounder jumped into the seat next to Christophe, giving him a slobbery kiss in his right ear. Christophe wrapped his arms around him and buried his head into the soft fur of his beloved dog's neck, sobbing quietly.

CHAPTER 27

BOUNDER

Bounder, sitting in Christophe's lap the entire trip to Beaulieu-sur-Mer looked out the window and took in every scene. On the way to the train station in Saint-Quentin, Thierry had stopped by the pet store to pick up a leash. He told the proprietor, with a wink, that Christophe was visually impaired and that Bounder was actually his service dog. He could plainly tell that Christophe was not in the least bit seeing-impaired, but he and Thierry were old friends, so he issued him a bright red harness that said *Chien d'assistance*, along with the necessary papers, so Bounder could ride on the train with Christophe.

Minnie rushed to the door the minute she heard Christophe's key go into the lock, but at the sight of Bounder, she disappeared to her safety perch above the bedroom closet. Christophe was glad to be back. As

313

usual, while he was gone, Henri had been placing his mail in a basket on the table in the front hall. And judging by the absence of any odor, it was clear that Henri had been looking after the cat as well. Christophe had sent him a generous Christmas bonus. After opening up the apartment and giving Bounder a chance to explore, he needed to tend to the first order of business. He went downstairs to the supermarket to buy dog food—a task that was completely new to him, but Thierry had given him some instructions on the proper care for a rambunctious two-year-old golden retriever. He found the right brand and the feeding and water bowls in the pet section. He picked up more cat food and kitty litter while he was there. He scanned the items at the checkout and paid by debit card without giving any further thought to the complexity of the financial transaction that had just taken place.

Behind the scenes, 0.087 grams of gold had just been transferred from his bank in Santa Monica to the supermarket's bank in Lyon. No physical gold actually changed hands. The transaction involved a note of credit extended by the bank in Lyon to the bank in Santa Monica. Christophe's account in Santa Monica was debited 0.087 grams of gold on credit, for which Christophe was charged a small handling fee. The 10-kilogram bag of dog food cost €14.2, or 0.0142 grams of gold. If someone had an account with the bank in Lyon and wanted to buy a bag of dog food at a pet store in Santa Monica, the reverse would occur, and the two transactions would balance out. If that person wanted to purchase the same French dog food in Santa Monica, it might have cost $18, or 0.018 grams of gold, the difference of 0.0038 grams resulting from the cost to import dog food from France. On the other hand, that person might have been able to purchase dog food made in Los Angeles for only $12.50, or 0.0125 grams of gold. Then the difference between the cost of dog food in France and dog food in Santa Monica would reflect differentials in the relative productivity of the two economies. By the simple act of buying a bag of dog food, in essence Los Angeles would become wealthier than France by the minuscule trade imbalance of 0.0142 less 0.0125, or 1.7 milligrams of gold. Billions of such purchase decisions, and the resulting transactions executed around the world every minute, kept the global financial system in perfect balance. The transactions were all carried out by blockchains, so the potential for hacking and fraud were practically eliminated. Local banks merely provided the service of supplying the buffer required between the gold in the repositories and the account balance of its depositors. This was the genius of the gold standard.

Before the international gold standard was implemented by the banking division of the United Nations, this balancing was taken care of by currency exchange rates. Once the gold standard took effect, exchange rates became irrelevant. The equivalent value of a dollar, or pound, or euro, or yen was the same. More importantly, currency speculation and money markets went away. The only groups that opposed the system were central governments themselves, because they had to relinquish their ability to fund inflated operations by printing more money. The gold standard, in effect, eliminated fiat money and deficit spending. Local governments could no longer micromanage their economies by controlling the supply of money, because the supply of money was fixed by their gold reserve. The relative economic strength of a domestic economy became a true measure of a country's wealth and its ability to generate wealth. Under the gold standard system, wealth traveled freely and seamlessly around the globe.

The most dramatic example of wealth mobility was seen in the 2050s, when petroleum reserves in the Middle East were being exhausted. Enormous gold reserves had been accumulated by oil-producing nations by virtue of the trade imbalance. But once the ability was lost to generate wealth at a faster rate than it was being spent abroad on luxury villas and yachts, much of the gold drained out of those countries, plunging them into the same poverty that existed there before petroleum was discovered.

Gold bullion actually did change hands, but moving tons of gold around the world from one repository to another was no easy task and took a lot of time. Unlike the commercial transactions like buying dog food, which took only microseconds, every 12.5 kg gold bullion bar in the world was registered by serial number with the UN Bank. In order to physically move a bar, each transfer had to be approved and recorded. The UN Bank knew exactly where every bar in the world was kept, and the issuance of local currency was therefore closely scrutinized, leaving practically no room for gaming the system.

In addition to the registered gold bullion, it was estimated that about 80 percent of the world's gold was held privately in the form of everything from coins to jewelry to industrial reclaim salvage. It was not known how much gold there actually was in these various forms. In addition, gold mining operations added gold to the international reserve, but unlike during the days when the price of gold fluctuated wildly, the gold standard meant that mining could only be carried out profitably when the value of the gold extracted exceeded the cost to produce it. The net effect was that gold consumption by industry and individuals tended to exactly offset the production of new gold from mining, and the total amount of gold remained more or less the same year after year.

Nonbullion gold could be exchanged freely without upsetting the balance imposed by the gold standard. Cash and banknotes did not entirely disappear. Anyone privately holding gold coins, bars, or even jewelry could always redeem it for the cash value in the local currency. Surplus gold collected this way could be turned into new registered bullion, subject to registration with the UN Bank. The increase in the total amount of registered gold bullion was, thus, a direct measure of the rising standard of living around the world.

The designers of the global gold standard never imagined that the registered 12.5 kg gold bullion bars in the twelve hundred repositories around the world might not actually be made of pure gold. The large-scale counterfeiting scheme attempted by the syndicate, if successful, would have plunged the world into financial chaos. Even rumors that there might be phony bullion could destroy confidence in the gold standard system. Known affiliates of the syndicate had been lobbying the United Nations Bank for years to abandon gold-backed currency in favor of all-digital currency. They argued that currency deregulation would result in a more open market system. Christophe had become convinced that the syndicate's counterfeiting scheme was intended to create panic and usher in a new digital currency regime—a regime the syndicate would then be able to easily monopolize and control.

Minnie came down from her perch atop the closet once she was satisfied that Bounder was not all that much of a threat. It would take a couple of weeks, though, before the two would actually become friends. M. and Mme. Onze-heures were not so welcomed. When they finally showed up on the railing, Bounder growled and chased them away. It took some patient scolding from Christophe to convince him that the turtledoves meant them no harm. The trio settled into a routine, with Christophe waking up early each morning, assuming his usual place on the terrasse wrapped in a blanket with Minnie on his lap, and having a large cup of coffee and a pain au chocolat purchased from the boulangerie the night before, with Bounder lying quietly by his side. It was typically two hours before the sun would finally peek over the eastern horizon, but the sunrise was starting to get noticeably earlier. Bounder was proving himself to be quite the gentleman when at first light he would rise up and gently nudge the dozing Christophe's forearm, being careful not to startle the cat, who watched him closely with a wary eye. "Okay, boy. Let me get dressed."

Christophe's brief career as a spy had come to an end. He missed the intrigue and the sense of having been part of something important, but he was actually content now to be living a more settled life. He and Bounder passed the days exploring the South of France together on foot. He had tucked the new pack of cigarettes that Stefan had given him in a pocket of his backpack that was stored away in the front hall closet and had forgotten all about them. But still, every time he saw a black van, he thought it might contain syndicate thugs. Also, he peeked out occasionally to see if a van was parked out on the street. Christophe's paranoia had mostly subsided, but it had not completely disappeared. Had it not been for Bounder, he would not have gone out at all. He had also declined the invitation from Philippe Aubrey to address the Earth Sciences Conference in Lausanne. Previously, the exhilaration of speaking to a crowd of people would have motivated him to invest the necessary time to prepare such a talk, but after the ordeal he had just been through, being in the limelight just did not appeal to him anymore.

One particular morning in early March, it was looking like it would be a very good day for a hike. Christophe had lost five kilograms during his stay on the Monfort farm, which was partly the result of Sophie's insistence on serving only healthy food and partly a direct consequence of the endless walks with Bounder. The inflammation in his knees and hips that he had been blaming on arthritis had largely gone away. When Bounder returned from chasing squirrels in the park across the street from Christophe's apartment building, Christophe informed him, "Today, we conquer Èze Ville." Christophe and Bounder took the SNCF train from Beaulieu to the next stop, Èze-sur-Mer, just three kilometers to the east. The SNCF, or Société Nationale des Chemins de Fer Français, operated the electric commuter railroad that ran between Cannes and Monaco. It had changed very little in a century, remaining the preferred mode of travel for short trips in the region. The trailhead for Le Chemin de Nietzsche was just across from the train station. The popular serpentine footpath led upward along a pristine valley ridge, four hundred meters up the mountain to the ancient village of Èze. The trail got its modern name from the German philosopher Friedrich Nietzsche, but it had served as the main trail connecting the ancient fortified village of Èze to the seaport for centuries. Countless hikers had discovered that the moderately strenuous climb, combined with stunning vistas of the Côte d'Azur, was always rewarding, allowing lots of time for reflection.

Christophe let Bounder off the leash. Later in the spring, the trail would be packed, but in early March, there was hardly another soul. Bounder would run ahead until Christophe disappeared out of sight, and then the dog would return to try to figure out why his master was walking so slowly. Bounder had energy that Christophe could only dream of at age sixty-six, but at least the latter's health was sufficiently improved that he could attempt the climb. Halfway up, he sat on a bench to catch his breath. It was an exceptionally clear day, and he could just make out the top of the mountains on the island of Corsica, two hundred kilometers away. He reflected that the last time he had sat on this particular bench, he was with Monique. She was the one who introduced him to the trail, and they had climbed it together several times. He had not been back for forty years. Christophe was slowly learning how to use those happy memories to begin entering some of the dark chambers in his psyche that he had been avoiding most of his adult life. Somehow, having Bounder close by as a sentinel made this easier.

Two men came up the trail after them, and Bounder let out a muffled growl as they passed. Christophe's tranquility was once again shattered as the irrational fear that he was still being stalked overwhelmed him unexpectedly.

After a while, he resumed his climb to the top. For Christophe, this meant taking slow, methodical steps with deep breaths. For Bounder, it meant trotting up and down and side to side. What was for Christophe a 1.6-kilometer hike, when all was said and done, was at least 5 kilometers for Bounder. They passed the restaurant the Chèvre d'Or as they entered the old village from below. Fond memories of having had lunch in the warm sunshine on the patio with Monique flooded Christophe's thoughts. The village was nearly deserted. A bustle of activity suggested that the shops and artist galleries were preparing for the tourist season soon to arrive. The only restaurant open for lunch was a small pizzeria. The weather was pleasant enough to eat outdoors, so Christophe seated himself at one of the tables, and Bounder lay down at his feet. The two men who had passed him along the way were already seated at another table nearby. When they greeted Christophe, it was clear that they were only tourists and posed no threat. The server came out with a bowl of water for Bounder and took Christophe's favorite order, a glass of rosé and a quatre-fromage pizza.

Christophe and Bounder made it back to the apartment in the middle of the afternoon, just ahead of a torrential downpour. The climb had cleared Christophe's head sufficiently that he resumed working on a puzzle that had been plaguing him ever since he had figured out how the gold bullion smuggling operation was being carried out. Numerous unanswered questions still circulated in his mind. What good was real gold bullion if the UN Bank would know it was stolen? Was there collusion between the UN and the syndicate? If so, why was the syndicate lobbying to go off the gold standard? Perhaps they planned to melt down the gold and wait for the free market price to take effect. Even then, wouldn't questions arise as to where the syndicate's gold came from? And what would happen when it was finally discovered that the bullion in American repositories was counterfeit? Once the world abandoned the gold standard, the gold repositories would surely start trying to sell it to make coins and jewelry, and then they would find it was just gold-plated tungsten. Christophe worked along all the logical pathways he could think of, but none of them led to a satisfactory conclusion. One thing did pique his curiosity, however. He thought it would be interesting to know which serial numbers on the counterfeit bars in American repositories matched the serial numbers on the real gold bars at Versailles. At least this way it would be known where the real gold bars were headed when hijacked by UPX coming out of the vault in Fort Knox. It was certainly worth posing the question, but given the imposed secrecy, he would probably never get an answer. Stefan had been very clear to Christophe that he was now officially retired from the spy business.

The following day, Christophe decided to hike around the perimeter of Saint-Jean-Cap-Ferrat. The footpath hugging the jagged coastline went past the Grand Hotel at the tip and the old lighthouse, and ended up at the public beach in Villefranche-sur-Mer. There were a few brave souls in the frigid water in March, but the air temperature was almost hot. Of all the walks that Christophe took, this one was Bounder's favorite because he could go for a swim at the end. It was only eleven o'clock by the time they got to Villefranche, so it was too early to have lunch. Christophe was not ready to go home yet, so he decided to take the train to Nice. The train was nearly empty on that Sunday morning, which was a good thing because Bounder still had the wet dog smell. From the Gare de Nice, Christophe and Bounder walked down Avenue Jean Médecin toward Old Town, where quaint restaurants were abundant. Even though it was only early March, anticipation of the approaching spring was in the air, and preparations were under way for the Festival of Flowers, which was to begin soon.

After lunch, they started walking back to the train station when it occurred to Christophe that they were only a few blocks from Pierre Fabré's apartment, so on a whim, he decided to drop in to say hello. He pushed the button outside the apartment. "Bonjour," came a female voice over the speaker.

"Oh, hello. My name is Christophe Conally. I was wondering if Monsieur Fabré might be available to see me."

"Veuillez patienter," she said. After about a minute, the buzzer sounded to let him in the door. He boarded the elevator with Bounder, who fortunately was dry by then. When the elevator door opened, he saw Pierre's smiling face from his wheelchair in the entry. The dog on his lap perked up at the sight of Bounder.

"What a pleasant and unexpected surprise, Christophe," he said. "I hardly ever get visitors anymore. And it looks like you brought a friend with you."

"This is Bounder. I apologize for showing up unannounced, but I don't know your phone number. Otherwise, I would have called ahead. Is it okay that I brought my dog?"

"Absolutely! Come in. Come in." The attendant wheeled Pierre into the sitting room next to the fireplace. Bounder obediently remained behind in the foyer by the elevator. Christophe sat in the now familiar sofa, and the attendant showed up shortly with a cup of coffee prepared just the way he liked it. Christophe had no way to know how much Pierre actually knew about what had taken place over the previous months, but it was a good bet that the latter was probably up to speed.

Christophe felt awkward, not knowing how to initiate a conversation with someone he knew practically nothing about. "I'm glad to finally be done with the gold bullion business," Christophe said. "I haven't heard any news in weeks, but apparently the syndicate counterfeiting operation has been shut down and everything has returned to normal." He said this in an attempt to fish for some confirmation.

Pierre simply nodded.

Getting no response, Christophe continued, "Bounder and I have really been enjoying retired life. In fact, yesterday we hiked the Nietzsche Trail to Èze. Monique and I used to hike it all the time, but this was the first time I have hiked it since then. It has not changed one bit in all that time. As I recall, your dog's name is Woofy."

Pierre manipulated his wheelchair so he could open the drawer of the table next to him. He retrieved a tattered children's book about a dog named Woofy titled *Woofy doit garder un secret*. He stroked the cover gently and handed it to Christophe. "This belonged to Monique when she was a little girl. Yes, my dog's name is Woofy."

After a pause, Pierre said, "Fredrick and Sandra came by for a visit a couple of weeks ago. They said you were staying on a farm north of Paris. Otherwise, they would have dropped by to see you. They brought little Julien with them. He is such an adorable child. When your name came up, all he wanted to do was tell me how

Uncle Christophe helped him win a Concorde jet. He and Woofy sure took a liking to one another."

"Bounder and I are hoping to go to Bordeaux soon." Christophe had made no immediate plans, but the mention of his sister suggested to him that such a trip might be a good idea.

Pierre picked up a glass of water from the table and settled farther back in his wheelchair after taking a deep breath. Woofy jumped down from his lap to go check on Bounder in the foyer. "Christophe, my son, there is something I have been wanting to tell you for a very long time. I have kept it from you all these years. I couldn't say anything because of my role as ministry director and the sensitive nature of the information." Pierre took a long drink of water before continuing. "So, retired spy to retired spy, it is time to clear the air. I can tell you now." Pierre took a long pause in order to compose his thoughts. "Before I became director, I headed up a covert unit that was on the verge of unmasking a particularly unsavory top-level member of the syndicate. I began receiving threatening letters that said if I did not back off, there would be very unpleasant consequences." Pierre's voice began to break. He took another deep breath and exhaled slowly. "Monique's plane was not brought down by terrorists, as you were told. The bomb was placed by the syndicate." Pierre's voice trailed off, and tears began to well up in his eyes. He was unable to go on. Christophe realized at that moment that the pain he had felt over the loss of his fiancée paled in comparison to that of Pierre, whose daughter was murdered—not in a random act of violence, as Christophe had always thought, but as a target of retribution for her father's own actions.

The two men sat quietly together for a long time. The only sound was the crackling of the wood fire. Finally, Pierre said, "You understand why I couldn't tell you? You are the only one outside the ministry whom I have ever told." Both men had subverted the painful memory in their own private ways, but now that the secret was revealed, the proper healing could begin. Neither would have to suffer alone any longer.

Meanwhile, Bounder and Woofy had become friends. They came into the sitting room together, looking as if they both wanted to go outside.

"Pierre," said Christophe, "it is a beautiful day. Why don't we take the dogs out for a stroll along the Promenade des Anglais."

Thereafter, strolls along Le Promenade des Anglais became a regular event that both men and their dogs looked forward to. Christophe would try to manage the two dogs on leashes while the nurse pushed Pierre's wheelchair along. On nice days, which was most of the time, Christophe would show up in the morning with Bounder and ring the doorbell. Pierre did not have a phone, and for security reasons, Christophe was never offered another means of contacting him in advance except to show up at the door at predetermined times. The walks gave both men an opportunity to share intimate aspects of their private lives that had been left unattended by the years spent pursuing the demands of their careers—Pierre as the former director of the French Intelligence Ministry, and Christophe as vice president of Transoceanic Portal Construction. In a perverse way, it was the syndicate that had brought them back together after forty years. Together they were able to begin unlocking some of the dark chambers in their souls that neither dared to enter alone. Even though he was confined to the wheelchair and showed signs of increasing frailty, Pierre's mind remained sharp, and his grasp of world affairs was striking. The two spent hours discussing the evil intentions of the syndicate, without ever really reaching a clear understanding of what motivated them. The concept of exercising control over others just for the sake of being able to do it was alien to freethinkers like them. They both viewed one's purpose in life as bringing about a brighter future, where each individual was empowered to reach his or her potential. The syndicate had a darker view, seeking to keep humankind in slavery.

One overcast but rainless morning in May, Christophe and Bounder rang the doorbell to Pierre's apartment to see if he and Woofy would care to go for a stroll. There was no answer. He rang it a second time, and still there was no response. This had never happened before, and Christophe became concerned that perhaps Pierre's caregiver had failed to show up for work. He turned to walk away when he heard the door open behind him. It was Stefan. He waited for Christophe to return and quietly said, "I am so sorry to tell you, Christophe, but Pierre passed away last night."

Christophe was not prepared for a shock like this; he was caught completely off guard. He was confident that Pierre would live into his hundreds. "Oh, Stefan. I just can't believe it," replied Christophe, sighing deeply.

"His nurse was with him. She said he died peacefully in his sleep. I expect the medical examiner to be here any minute. Would you like to come up?"

Christophe and Stefan went up to the apartment. Bounder remained quietly behind in the foyer. Stefan showed the way to Pierre's bedroom. His lifeless smile radiated as if he had just been told "Well done, good and faithful servant." The nurse was sobbing, and Woofy was lying down in the empty wheelchair where he always slept while Pierre was in bed.

Stefan placed his arm around Christophe's shoulder. "I am so sorry."

"Thank you. As sad as it is to lose him, it is not tragic. He led a good life. I will just miss him."

"Me too," said Stefan. After several minutes of silence, Stefan said to Christophe, "I need a huge favor."

"Anything," responded Christophe.

"The dog is rather upset, as you can see. He growls at anyone who comes near his master, and I am afraid he will try to bite the medical examiner. Would you please take Woofy with you until we find a new home for him?"

"Of course." The nurse clipped on his leash and handed it to Christophe. He tugged the end, but Woofy was not about to budge from the wheelchair. "Wait a minute. I have an idea." Christophe went out to the foyer and brought Bounder back with him into the bedroom.

At the sight of Bounder, Woofy jumped down to greet his friend. The team of medical examiners got off the elevator when Christophe and the two dogs got on.

"I will be in touch with you about the memorial arrangements," said Stefan.

"I appreciate everything you have done. You know how to get hold of me." The elevator door then closed on one more chapter of Christophe's life.

CHAPTER 28

LONGYEARBYEN

Pierre Fabré's memorial service was held at the Basilique Notre-Dame de l'Assomption in Nice. The church could hold about four hundred people, and there was not an empty seat to be found for the service. People came from all over the world. It was amazing to Christophe that a man who lived his entire life in the shadows could have so many dear friends. Christophe hardly knew any of them, but Fredrick and Sandra came from Bordeaux, along with Laurent, Audrey, and little Julien. The biggest surprise was seeing Tor and Brigid Andersen. Abraham was unusually stoic, but it was clear that the departure of his closest friend weighed heavily on his heart.

At the reception and ministry-sponsored luncheon that followed, Brigid and Stefan seemed to spend a lot of time together. It was their first opportunity since Los Angeles to interact in person, and it was obvious that there was more chemistry between them than simply a professional relationship. Other than the phone call from Brigid in Thierry's kitchen, Christophe had received no other news about the progress of the counter-counterfeiting operation.

"Is there any news you can tell me?" Christophe asked Stefan.

Stefan glanced at Brigid. "Well, I am pleased report that we have managed to keep you alive," he said with a grin.

"No, I mean about the gold," said Christophe.

At the mention of the word *gold* Stefan and Brigid both looked around to see who might be in earshot. The noise in the reception area was otherwise sufficient to cover up their conversation. Stefan finally said, "Christophe, this is not a game. It is very dangerous for you to keep dabbling in this affair." Stefan looked around for anyone who might have been listening and said, "I can tell you that we have only recovered a fraction of the missing bullion so far. You can imagine what this means. But I warn you, stay out of this. We have everything under control."

"Does that mean that there are still counterfeit bars in the repositories?" said Christophe. Stefan simply glared at him.

Realizing that he would get nothing more from Stefan, Christophe changed the conversation. Addressing Brigid, he said, "I received an invitation from Ashleigh to attend the formal commissioning of the Paris–Longyearbyen portal next week. The invitation said that the queen of

Norway would be doing the ribbon cutting. Can I assume you will be there as well?"

"Are you planning to attend?" asked Brigid, dodging the question.

"Of course. I hear this portal is a technological marvel. And my invitation said that I would also be given a tour of the tunnel preassembly facility for the Arctic portal. I am actually more interested in seeing that since I had a hand in setting it up."

Right then, Abraham and Tor joined their group. Abraham's normal overpowering demeanor had been tempered by a little too much wine to help him cope with grieving the loss of his friend. On this occasion, he seemed just an ordinary French gentleman. Brigid had never actually met Pierre, so Abraham and her father launched into a series of humorous anecdotes about some of the tight spots they had managed to get in and out of with him.

Following the reception, Fredrick and the rest of the Pommerance clan went to Christophe's apartment. Laurent had visited there the previous year, when François and Chloé were staying there, but Fredrick and Sandra had never seen it. Julien was eager to see Woofy again and was the first to barge through the door into the enthusiastic embraces of both Woofy and Bounder. A curious Minnie was perched atop the table in the entryway. Christophe opened the door to the terrasse so everyone could take in his extraordinary view.

"Now I am really sorry I didn't take you up on your offer to visit sooner. I had no idea you had such a beautiful place," exclaimed Fredrick.

"Sadly," replied Christophe, "I haven't had much opportunity to enjoy it. Every time I try to settle down into a lifestyle appropriate for a retired old man, I seem to get sucked into something that draws me away."

Sandra said, "Perhaps this time will be different with summer fast approaching."

"The only thing on my plate at the moment is to attend the grand opening of the Paris–Longyearbyen portal next week. As you know, I had quite a lot to do with the Arctic portal project, and Ashleigh invited me to attend the gala affair as a VIP and former company executive."

"That's very nice," said Sandra. "Maybe you will finally get the recognition you deserve."

"That's unlikely," said Christophe under his breath.

Julien showed up trying to carry Woofy in his arms. Bounder was worn out by all the excitement and by Julien trying to pick him up. He had escaped into Christophe's bedroom with Minnie. "Woofy and I are the best friends ever," Julien said excitedly.

Christophe looked over at Fredrick. "You know, Fredrick, Woofy needs a home."

Audrey and Laurent both blanched simultaneously. Julien said, "Can I have him, Mommy? Can I have him?"

They exchanged reluctant-parent looks. Julien had Woofy in a full embrace. Christophe said, "Otherwise,

Woofy goes up for adoption. I just can't manage two dogs."

"Laurent and I discussed getting Julien a pet, but we were thinking more along the lines of a rabbit," said Audrey.

While everyone was thinking through the feasibility of taking Woofy home, Christophe pulled Sandra aside. "I need to go to Svalbard Island next Wednesday. I don't really want to leave Bounder in a kennel, so I was wondering if Bounder and I could stop by on my way to Paris. Then, I would leave Bounder with you and pick him up on Friday or Saturday on my return."

"Oh, Christophe, that would be wonderful. But isn't Wednesday your birthday?"

Christophe nodded.

"We can celebrate your birthday when you get back then. We would be delighted to watch Bounder. It would also be good for Woofy to have a friend to help him get used to living in Bordeaux."

"Does that mean Julien can keep Woofy?" inquired Christophe loud enough for everyone to hear.

Sandra looked over at Audrey, who was nodding her head in affirmation.

Sandra then gave Christophe a long embrace without saying anything more.

He arrived at the departure concourse for the Paris–Longyearbyen portal at Gare du Nord at nine in the morning on Wednesday. He handed the receptionist his invitation. "Dr. Conally, we are so glad to see you. Please come inside and join the other guests." He was ushered into a large hall with Ashleigh banners everywhere and displays along the walls. A large video showing the highlights of the portal construction was running continuously on a screen overhead. Most of the other guests were in formal attire. Christophe was just in a sports jacket without a tie and was carrying his backpack. He had had no idea this would be a formal affair. There was no indication of this on his invitation. A waiter promptly met him with a tray of champagne, and he gladly took a glass. Nine o'clock in the morning was a bit early for champagne, but it would give him something to occupy his hands while he walked around looking at the exhibits trying to look inconspicuous. He surveyed the crowd for any familiar faces. The last person in the world he expected to bump into was Fred Simms, but there he was nonetheless. When Simms caught sight of Christophe, he came over and gave him a big hug.

"I didn't expect to see you. What brings you here?" was all Christophe could manage. He was looking right into the face of the man who had just hired syndicate thugs to blow him up, and now he acted as if they were best friends. Was it possible that Fred was unaware that Christophe knew his true identity?

"Didn't you hear?" said Fred jovially. "I retired at the end of last year, so just like you, I am an emeritus Ashleigh executive VIP. It is nice that the company arranged this gala event for us, don't you think? You probably know a lot of the people here." Thankfully the loudspeaker interrupted their conversation at that point.

"Ladies and Gentlemen, *Mesdames et Messieurs*, welcome to the grand opening of the newest and most advanced Ashleigh Systems portal ever built. Before we begin with the ribbon-cutting ceremony, I would like to take this opportunity to bring to your attention a few of our distinguished guests." The announcer introduced several current and former Ashleigh executives, a few of whom Christophe knew either personally or by reputation. There was a round of applause at the mention of each name. "Fred Simms, recently retired executive vice president for American Operations, and—"

Finally, the dreaded moment arrived. "And Dr. Christophe Conally, retired vice president for engineering for Transoceanic Portals." There was some warm applause that Christophe did not notice. He was still trying to deal with the shock of running into Trent Lachmann.

"Now, I would like to introduce our president and CEO, Monsieur Jean-Luc Galatin." Mr. Galatin stepped up to the microphone and waited for the applause to die down.

"Before I begin, I want to give special thanks to all the exceptional men and women of the Ashleigh team—past, present, and future—who have made this moment possible. We could never have accomplished any of this without you. I toast you." He held out his champagne glass to the crowd and said, "Santé."

"You know, this Paris–Longyearbyen portal is really a marvel. It is quite possibly the most significant technological achievement in all of history. From the time of Marco Polo, humankind has sought a northwest passage to Asia. Longyearbyen is just thirteen hundred kilometers from the North Pole. It is the ideal hub for a network of portals fanning out across the Northern Hemisphere. At this very moment, currently under construction are two hyperspeed portals that will connect Longyearbyen to cities all over Asia and North America. Imagine traveling to Seattle in two hours, Shanghai in three and a half hours, Tokyo in three hours, or Sydney in four hours. Travel to these places at four times the speed of sound was not even dreamed of thirty years ago. Think of it. You will be able to leave Paris after breakfast, have a one-hour business meeting in Beijing, and be home in time for dinner.

"Today, we are celebrating the formal christening of the long-awaited Paris–Longyearbyen portal. This portal has been built with a host of breakthrough technologies. It is faster and safer than any mode of travel ever conceived. We have deployed the new twin one-point-six-meter submarine tunnels for the very first time, which permits the use of four-person capsules. Most importantly, this is the first capsule-powered portal ever built for distances of greater than one thousand kilometers. This has allowed us to break away from ballistic trajectories on long trips. The speed of each individual capsule is controlled electronically. Gone are the days of pressure control. This also means that we can use a higher vacuum—one-millionth of an atmosphere, to be exact. This is equivalent to flying in low earth orbit more than one hundred kilometers up. Also, because the capsules are propelled by linear motors in the maglev track, we have succeeded in mastering the Coriolis effect, so polar trajectories no longer need to be unidirectional. Today you will all be traveling at a top speed of more than thirteen hundred meters per second. That is almost four times the speed of sound. Think of it: if you were to blow a whistle the instant you depart from Paris, you would have to wait two hours in Longyearbyen before you would hear it. That is, of course, if you have really exceptional hearing." This brought a chuckle from the adoring crowd. Mr. Galatin was exceedingly charismatic, and his manner of public speaking was upbeat and spellbinding.

"The Paris–Longyearbyen portal is the same length as the North Atlantic portal, yet it will handle ten times the passenger traffic—and all this while going in both directions."

Christophe was completely unaware of most of these advancements. He needed to come to grips with the realization that his life's great achievement was based on twenty-year-old technology that was becoming obsolete.

Mr. Galatin continued, "In a few minutes you will all have an opportunity to travel to Longyearbyen, Svalbard Island, a place that now belongs to every citizen of the world. The thirty-four-hundred-kilometer trip will take you a mere forty-three minutes. We have planned a lovely luncheon at the brand-new Northern Lights Resort and Spa, and after that we will have you all back in Paris in time for dinner." This last comment also came as a shock to Christophe, who had assumed that everyone was planning to stay overnight in the new hotel. "Now with no further fanfare, for the formal ribbon cutting, I am honored to introduce Queen Camilla, the queen of Norway and the UN ambassador to Svalbard Island."

The applause was thunderous. Christophe nearly fainted when it dawned on him that Brigid would be accompanying the queen with the security detail. Surely she was aware that Trent Lachmann, alias Fred Simms, was in the audience, and she would stay out of view in the wings. He hoped and prayed that Fred Simms would not spot her. It was doubtful that he'd ever found out that she had been working undercover in his office.

The red ribbon was cut, more champagne corks were popped, and people began forming a cue for the ride like excited children waiting to get on a brand-new roller coaster at an amusement park. Christophe hung back at the end of the line, hoping, if possible, to have the last capsule all to himself. He watched Fred Simms interact with his former comrades. He was outgoing and gregarious, making everyone feel like long-lost friends. How many of them actually knew he was Trent Lachmann? For that matter, how many of them were also operating under an alias? This thought gave Christophe a chill. Was everyone around him living a double life? He knew many of them, and a few he thought he knew well. They had interacted on various projects over the years. Christophe looked out at the crowd of familiar faces in the line. They were joking together and catching one another up on the status of their kids and their life's triumphs or difficulties. He came to the sad conclusion that he didn't really know any of them. He knew about them, but he didn't actually know them. The flamboyant Fred Simms was certainly in character that day, but inside, he was a ruthless lieutenant of the syndicate. Even the scatterbrained office manager from Modesto turned out to be someone else. In his now sixty-seven years, Christophe concluded that the only person he had ever really known was Monique. Everyone else seemed to be pretending.

Christophe, having gotten his wish, boarded the final capsule by himself. It was every bit as plush and spacious as advertised. Just as the canopy was about to close, another man hopped into the seat next to him, panting. He extended his hand to Christophe with a huge smile. "Bonjour. Je m'appelle Jean-Luc." He looked at the attendant closing the canopy and said, "Thanks for holding the capsule for me."

Once Christophe got over the initial sock of finding himself seated next to the president and CEO of Ashleigh Systems, he introduced himself as well.

"Dr. Conally. I know who you are by reputation, but it is an honor to finally meet you in person. I saw your name on the guest list, and I was hoping we would get a chance to talk. You are in for a real treat today." Christophe was seldom at a loss for words, but suddenly he could not think of a single thing to say.

After the checkout sequence, which lasted only about thirty seconds, the capsule was launched into the portal. The acceleration was so smooth and quiet that Christophe was sure they were still waiting in Paris to be launched.

"Here, you can monitor our progress on your screen." Jean-Luc reached over and pushed a button on

Christophe's console. By the time the map came up, they were already passing the French coastline.

"I can't hear the VCVAs opening and closing," Christophe finally said.

"You are probably thinking of the *click-clack* sound in the old ballistic portals. This portal does not use them. Our speed is not controlled by varying vacuum pressure like your North Atlantic portal. The magnets in the track also provide a little propulsion along the way." He paused for a moment and looked over at Christophe, whose first thought was that maybe Jean-Luc wanted to know why he wasn't wearing a tuxedo. "You know, Christophe, your transatlantic portal was a magnificent piece of engineering in its day."

Christophe replied, "I also worked some on the Arctic portals for a while, but almost everything on this one is new to me."

Jean-Luc pointed to their location on the map. "We will be hugging the western Norwegian coastline for most of the way to stay in shallow water. We are only three hundred meters down. It must have taken nerves of steel to build a portal at two thousand meters—and crossing the Mid-Atlantic Trench! I find it miraculous that there hasn't been a serious incident in twenty years. This is a tribute to you, Dr. Conally."

"Oh, I worried plenty. We both are aware that a breach in the tunnel at that depth would cost a couple thousand lives."

"You probably don't know this, and please keep it between us, but Ashleigh is planning to take the North

Atlantic portal out of passenger service as soon as the Arctic portal becomes operational. Here, let me show you something. Do you see those square boxes on your screen? Those are emergency escape blockhouses staged every twenty-five kilometers along the route. Each one is equipped with a gate valve that can close off the tunnel in the event of an emergency. If there were to be a complete failure of any portion of the tunnel, that section can be isolated just like the watertight compartments on a submarine. Of course, this would not be good news for anyone unlucky enough to be within that particular twenty-five-kilometer section, but everyone else in the portal could be safely evacuated. This is only possible if the portal runs at a shallow depth near land, because such systems require a great deal of electric power."

"As I recall, the Arctic portal will pass through some pretty deep water," said Christophe.

"You mean the one that was planned to be routed directly over the North Pole?"

"Yes."

"I guess you never heard. How long has it been since you retired?" asked Jean-Luc.

"Two years ago—from today, in fact."

"Ah. Is today your birthday?"

"Yes. Sixty-seven. Old age has a way of catching up with you."

"Stop! At sixty-seven you are just getting started." Jean-Luc looked intently at Christophe with an approving smile. "Anyway, Ashleigh abandoned that deep tunnel concept as being too risky. Instead we decided to build two separate Arctic portals that pass closer to land—one above Canada and a second above Siberia. That is the primary reason why we converted this portal we are now in into a four-seater—to handle the increased traffic through Longyearbyen."

Christophe was soaking all of this new information up like a sponge. It surprised him how much things had changed in just two years and how little he actually knew about the extent of the rapid advancement in portal technology. The two men sat quietly for a while. Jean-Luc was looking at his phone and was preoccupied with messages.

Christophe began thinking about what might be involved in smuggling gold bullion in such a capsule. "How do they add the ballast?"

Jean-Luc looked over at him in bewilderment. "There is no ballast required on this type of portal. You are still thinking of the old-style portals. In that case, yes, it was necessary that each capsule be the same weight. This portal we are on is powered. The capsule is propelled electromagnetically. It doesn't matter how much the capsule actually weighs."

"You speak of the old-style portals in the past tense. Are they really obsolete?" asked Christophe.

Jean-Luc hesitated as if choosing his words carefully. "Don't get me wrong, the long transoceanic portals like yours and the one connecting the Côte d'Ivoire and Belem were hugely successful. They blazed the trail for intercontinental hyperspeed travel. But we have always known that if there ever were to be only a single bad accident—just like with the supersonic Concorde jet—no one would venture into a capsule again. Those portals are getting old. They served their purpose well. It's not possible to install power blocks in two thousand meters of ocean far from land. This is precisely why Ashleigh has gone in the direction of routing submarine portals along littorals." After a pause Jean-Luc said, "I am a bit surprised you didn't know this."

Christophe thought about this for a minute, trying to decide how forward he was prepared to be, but when would he ever get another chance to have the president and CEO as a captive audience? He responded, "You know, Jean-Luc, Ashleigh is a very compartmentalized and secretive organization. One division hardly ever knew what another was up to."

Jean-Luc nodded knowingly.

Then out of the blue, Christophe asked him, "Have you ever heard of someone named Trent Lachmann?"

Jean-Luc did not answer immediately. He had resumed looking at his messages. Either he was distracted by an important one or he was not sure how to answer the question. "No, I don't believe I have ever heard that name," he said nonchalantly without looking up. In hindsight, Christophe wished he hadn't asked that question. Either Jean-Luc was part of the conspiracy or he wasn't. In either case, the answer would have been no.

He had a great many more questions he wanted to ask, but the encounter was interrupted when the canopy popped open in Longyearbyen. On this trip, Christophe had not even felt the deceleration from the top speed of thirteen hundred meters per second. The experience made him feel as if he had spent his entire life traveling on propeller-driven airplanes and had just walked off his first jetliner. Portal technology had changed radically right under his nose without his knowledge.

CHAPTER 29

THE FOUNDRY

Passengers arrived in Longyearbyen in a spacious hall with an escalator that led directly up to the lobby of the Northern Lights Resort and Spa. A reception had been arranged where the guests could socialize for a couple of hours until lunch was served at one in the afternoon. Christophe's invitation had mentioned an option to tour the foundry and tunnel preconstruction facility, and he assumed that all the guests would participate. But of the more than thirty guests, only a handful chose to go for the tour. They were mostly younger employees who appeared to be aspiring executives, none of whom Christophe had met before. He attributed this general disinterest in technical matters to the drifting of senior management at Ashleigh Systems away from a focus on engineering and toward "bean counting." He thought this was a shame, because the company had been founded on engineering excellence. It was engineering excellence that had allowed the company to grow and prosper for half a century. Ashleigh had always been the first to introduce the most advanced innovations. However, more recently the company had become increasingly focused on the bottom line. Fewer and fewer engineers and scientists held top positions, and this was one of the primary reasons why Christophe had felt a growing sense of isolation from the corporate mainstream in the years leading up to retirement. For most of his working career, he had been proud to work for Ashleigh. The company's pursuit of excellence had always been what motivated him. Fewer and fewer of the other executives shared his passion toward that end, and this was reflected in the fact that only five other people joined him on the tour.

His brief encounter with Jean-Luc Galatin caused him to reconsider that perhaps things were changing for the better. Although Galatin had no formal technical education, he seemed to have a keen sense of the value of technical innovation. He had become CEO just about the time that Christophe had retired. The previous succession of CEOs had all risen up through the Ashleigh ranks and had been contaminated by the good old boys' network. Galatin was brought in from a sister company that revolutionized the international shipping business, but any resulting cultural change hadn't had a chance to trickle down to Christophe's level before he retired. Nevertheless, he sensed that Galatin was just the right kind of man to revitalize Ashleigh. The new CEO seemed to have genuine interest in advancing portal technology, and the new Paris–Longyearbyen portal provided clear evidence of this. It would probably take Galatin many years to turn the ship around and change the company culture. Christophe was anxious to see firsthand what innovations in portal construction technology had taken place recently.

An usher approached Christophe as soon as he entered the lobby to direct him toward the shuttle bus for the factory tour. Christophe dropped his backpack off at the front desk and followed the usher, along with the five other participants, to the waiting bus. There was a howling spring blizzard outside, and those going on the factory tour were provided with winter coats and gloves.

The preconstruction facility was adjacent to the port, about five kilometers away. It was an enormous building that appeared out of nowhere in the near whiteout conditions. The shuttle bus drove into the building and pulled up to a curb, where the passengers were greeted by a tour guide and directed inside to a warm staging area. There was a group of factory workers waiting to get on the bus to return to the station. Even though the Paris–Longyearbyen portal was not officially open to the public, it had been in operation for more than a year to transport workers and employees to and from the remote island. With the ribbon cutting, Svalbard would be officially open for business as a tourist destination.

Each participant for the tour was issued coveralls, a hard hat, safety glasses, and headphones since they would be going right out onto the factory floor. The tour guide did a quick audio check to be sure everyone could hear her clearly, as many of the areas they planned to visit were very noisy. She also gave a safety briefing and showed everyone the button on their lapels to push in the event that they needed her assistance. She made everyone aware that the tour would last about an hour and would involve a good deal of walking and some stair climbing.

Once everyone was ready to go, she led the way down a long corridor into a cavernous area of the foundry where tunnel sections were being fabricated. They walked up a flight of steel stairs and followed a catwalk that overlooked the entire operation. The tour guide turned around and did a quick count to be sure she had not lost anyone along the way. "Okay. We are now in the tunnel liner extrusion facility. The process begins with that large furnace on the far side. Titanium metal is brought into the port by ship and staged in a warehouse on the other side of that wall. Each lot of metal is subject to a rigid quality conformance test prior to being introduced into the vacuum furnace, where it is melted at seventeen hundred degrees." She paused for a moment for the group to take in the sheer magnitude of the operation. She then pointed to a region near the bottom of the furnace where a large-diameter pipe was slowly emerging horizontally. "What you see there is the extruder. The nearly molten metal is being squeezed out through the die under high pressure to form the seamless one-point-six-meter-diameter tunnel sections with a wall thickness of just twenty millimeters. You can see the joining flange on the leading edge moving outward. As soon as the length of fifty meters is reached, you will be able to watch a laser cut the tube, and the trailing joining flange will get forged." After about a minute, a clamshell device descended on the tube, and just like that, the end flange was formed. The huge fifty-meter-long tunnel section proceeded along a conveyor, disappearing through a door into what the tour guide said was the annealing furnace. At the same time, the stub of another tube section began emerging from the extruder. The leading end of the red-hot metal was flared outward to form a right-angle flange.

Christophe had seen many factories in his career, but never anything quite like this one. He was completely overwhelmed by the scale and precision of the completely automated process taking place right before his eyes. Such a procedure could never have been designed by a company that had lost its commitment to engineering excellence. He had been told by other engineers that the Longyearbyen foundry was worth visiting, but he was not prepared for what he saw. Was this really the same Ashleigh Systems where he had spent his career working? This was the first time in years he had actually been proud to be associated with the company. This was certainly not the work of a company that had become corrupted by the pursuit of counterfeiting and gold smuggling.

The tour guide gave everyone a chance to savor the impressive sight, and then she signaled for them to follow. They went back down the staircase and through double sliding doors into an adjoining room. Whereas the foundry area was dark and noisy, this area was brightly lit and spotless. The scent of metal-cutting fluid was strong in the air. A couple of workers wearing white coveralls were monitoring the automated process. One of the fifty-meter tunnel segments was rotating on a huge lathe. "This is where the joining flanges are machined," said the tour guide. Christophe watched in amazement as the flange was faced off perpendicular to the tube axis. A precision groove was then machined into the face of the flange with a circumference of about ten centimeters larger than the inside diameter of the tube. Finally, a bolt circle of thirty-six axial holes was drilled around the circumference beyond the groove. "The groove is for the sealing gasket, and the holes are for bolting the segments together," the tour guide continued. No sooner was the enormous tunnel segment completed and moved along a conveyor out of the room than a new segment appeared through an opening in the wall to be mounted in the lathe.

The tour guide continued, "This operation goes on around the clock, seven days a week, three hundred sixty-five days a year. The production line produces a new tunnel segment once every ten minutes, which translates into an annual production of about twenty-five hundred kilometers. I know this seems like a lot, but it constitutes what is actually required for the construction schedule of two new Arctic portals. The current production rate is limited by how fast the construction vessels can assemble and lay down portals. Due to pack ice in winter, construction won't resume again until June, so all the segments being produced right now are going into inventory." She looked around the group to judge if the interest level was holding up. "Does anyone have any questions?"

Someone piped up, "Why titanium? Isn't it really expensive?"

"That is such a good question," the tour guide replied. "I am so glad you asked. Titanium is not as costly as you might think—only about twice as much as steel—but there are three important reasons for using titanium. First of all, it is very strong for its weight. The wall thickness of the tubes only needs to be two centimeters. This makes the tunnel segments much lighter to handle than if they were made of steel. The second reason is that titanium does not corrode in seawater. This is important considering that the Arctic portals are designed to last for fifty years." She looked at the person who had asked the question, and asked, "Can you guess the third reason?" He shrugged.

Christophe knew the answer, but he wanted to hear how the guide handled it. She continued, "It turns out to be the most important reason of all, and the portals could not operate without it. Does anyone know?"

Christophe finally said, "Because titanium is nonmagnetic."

"Okay, then. Apparently, we have a scientist among us. That is correct. Since the portals use electromagnetism to levitate the capsules, the walls of the tunnel must be made of a nonmagnetic material. That means ordinary steel won't work. Aluminum is not strong enough, and anyway, it would corrode in seawater. And stainless steel would be too expensive. Does that answer your question?" The man nodded, but the blank expression on his face suggested that he probably did not even know what magnetic levitation was. Christophe allowed himself a secret moment to feel proud of himself. The choice of titanium for portal construction was largely due to him. It was an engineering decision that he had proposed years before his tour guide was even born. It was based on his study of declassified Soviet submarine technology that he had obtained in the 2030s and had managed to get translated from Russian into English. At that time, titanium was used in a few niche applications, but Christophe was the one who could easily claim the credit for developing the technology to such scale necessary for making portals. He had adopted the technology from the giant titanium tube extruders that had been developed by Russian submarine builders and were subsequently abandoned after the Cold War. There is no way the tour guide would have known this. Ashleigh believed that innovation was always a collective affair, so accomplishments were attributed to teams and recognition for actions by specific individuals was never granted. Like so many innovations in almost any corporate culture, the long battles Christophe had waged advocating the use of titanium were long forgotten. All that mattered was that titanium ultimately emerged the winner.

For the next leg of the tour, the group entered a separate climate-controlled building that felt like a tropical rain forest. "You have undoubtedly noticed by now that this room is hot and humid," said the tour guide. "This is where the signature Ashleigh concrete shroud is applied." She pointed to a bank of huge oval-shaped molds on a conveyor. When the top half of the mold closest to them was flipped open, an overhead gantry crane delivered two titanium portal sections. These were carefully lowered into the mold side by side. The top half of the die was pivoted to the closed position, and the loud sound of viscous material filling the mold under pressure could be heard. The process resembled a huge plastic injection molding machine. Then the filled mold disappeared into an adjoining room. The tour guide waited while everyone had a chance to watch the complete cycle.

"In this process, the portal segments are being fabricated as a shroud of neutral buoyancy concrete is injected into that enormous mold, which takes about thirty minutes to set. The portals are bidirectional, as you know, so each segment contains two 1.6-meter tunnels encased in a 2.5 × 5 × 50 meter concrete ellipsoid. Each portal segment will weigh in at about 860 metric tons when finished. On the other side of that far wall, the parts are removed from the molds and placed on curing racks for forty-eight hours. We won't be going in because the atmosphere is tightly controlled."

The process was mesmerizing to watch, and the tour guide finally had to insist that they move on if they were to be done with the tour in time for lunch. Christophe was awestruck with the realization that Ashleigh had been able to retain its technological edge, although no mention of Philippe Aubrey, the inventor of neutral buoyancy concrete, was ever made.

The guide then led the group into the final area of the tour. "This is where the flat copper gaskets are fabricated," she said, pointing to a machine designed for making the huge vacuum seal rings. "I know it is not as impressive as the molding operation, but it is no less important." She pointed to a spool of large-diameter wire feeding the machine. Picking up a segment of the wire to pass around, she said, "I know the wire looks like gold, but don't be fooled. What you are actually looking at is a very thin electroplated gold layer of about ten microns on top of a copper core. The gold coating prevents the gasket from corroding if it were ever to come into contact with seawater. If you look at the wire at the end, you will see only the dull copper color."

When the giant die opened, a robot arm fed the wire into a rectangular groove in the base of the die with a circular diameter of 165 centimeters. At the point where the two ends joined, there appeared a bright glow for a couple of seconds while the ends were butt-welded together to make a solid ring. The top cavity of the die then came down, and after it was raised again, a beautifully formed flat gasket could be seen. "This gasket is what lies in the groove you saw being machined into the ends of the tube segment flanges. When the tunnel segments are bolted together, the soft copper of the gasket gets squeezed out to form a vacuum-tight seal." At this point she passed around a sample of a joint that had been cross-sectioned and polished to show the two flanges bolted together with a gasket, rectangular in cross section, filling the groove in the middle. Christophe made a mental note that the compressed gasket was about two centimeters wide and one centimeter thick. He studied the sample carefully, noticing that this joining method was a huge advancement over the way the tunnel segments had been joined together on the North Atlantic portal.

For the final operation, Christophe watched an aluminum supporting ring with adhesive on one face being placed on top of the gasket. The delicate copper gasket, attached to the supporting ring, was lifted up out of the die mold with the robot arm and added to a stack of gaskets on a pallet nearby.

"Besides being incredibly reliable, this joining method means that portal segments can be assembled and fully pressure-checked at the surface aboard the construction ships before being lowered to the seafloor as a continuous finished tube. This way, no seawater has to be pumped out of the tunnel during construction, and no further work needs to be done on the inside." During construction of Christophe's North Atlantic portal, evacuating the water from the tunnel while simultaneously adjusting buoyancy had been the single greatest engineering challenge. Even though it would never have been possible to lower air-filled segments two thousand meters to the worksite below, he wished he could roll back time, regretful that he hadn't had the chance to use this method for constructing his portal. It was clear to him why the type of portal that used this joining method had to be laid in shallow water along the coastlines.

The tour group moved on to the same staging area where the tour had begun. "This ends our tour of the Ashleigh Longyearbyen foundry and preconstruction facility." The tour guide began collecting the hard hats and safety glasses. Everyone stepped out of their coveralls, hanging them on a rack by size. "If you will direct your attention to the screen, I will start a short video that shows one of our Arctic portal construction vessels. You will be able to see what happens to the segments once they leave this facility. Thank you for your attention. I hope you all have a wonderful day."

Christophe and the rest of his tour group returned to the luncheon. On the shuttle bus, he noticed that none of the other people on the tour was wearing formal attire. He asked one of them, "Did your invitation say this was supposed to be a formal affair?"

"No," the man said without emotion.

It was clear by the time Christophe entered the luncheon hall that the alcohol had been flowing freely. He went through the buffet line and seated himself at a table in the back by himself. He was joined almost immediately by his comrades from the factory tour. He still had no idea who they were and was not sure he ever wanted to find out. He hated small talk. On the other hand, they seemed to know who he was, and they appeared to be pleased just to be sitting at his table. Jean-Luc Galatin came by and placed his hand on Christophe's shoulder, asking, "How did you all like the tour?" Everyone agreed it was formidable. Then he addressed Christophe directly. "Aren't you in the least bit curious who these people are?" It was evident that Jean-Luc had not been drinking.

Christophe looked up at him, trying to figure out the significance of such an odd question. After a curious pause, Jean-Luc finally said, "You are looking at the future of Ashleigh Systems. I asked them to follow you around and to learn as much from you as possible." That's all he said before he went away to interact with the other guests. Christophe looked around the table at the now smiling faces. The scene was totally surreal. They all seemed to be younger than thirty.

One of the men finally said, "Dr. Conally, we would like to hear everything—the whole story from the beginning."

Christophe did not know how to respond. Which story? The story about how he had uncovered the gold counterfeiting operation within Ashleigh? Finally he said, "What story do you want to hear?"

"We want to hear about the construction of the North Atlantic portal, of course," one of them responded. Christophe exhaled a huge sigh of relief and began recounting the details of his career with Ashleigh Systems, beginning with the construction of the London–Paris portal.

CHAPTER 30

THE SEALS

C hristophe had assumed that a block of
rooms had been reserved at the hotel
for the other dignitaries. Apparently, this was not the case.
The other guests, including his luncheon companions,
headed back to Paris after eating. Svalbard Island was a
magical place that Christophe had always wanted to visit,
but before the new portal had been constructed, it was
a hard place to get to. The Northern Lights Resort and
Spa was brand new. It was intended for tourists whose
final destination was Svalbard or who planned to lay
over on their way to other places once the Arctic portals
became operational. The resort operator hoped that four-
seater capsules would start attracting families on holiday.
So far, only one hundred rooms in the hotel portion
and one restaurant were open, but fourteen hundred
rooms were planned. In addition, a casino, conference
facilities, several restaurants, an outdoor activities center,

an indoor shopping mall, and an amusement park were under construction. The hotel was officially open only for special guests, and there was a room reservation under Christophe's name.

Christophe pretty much had the entire hotel to himself. His room looked out on a glacier, featureless in the dim glow of dusk. By next month the sun would not be setting at all. The desk clerk had recommended that whatever he did, he needed to be sure to visit the spa. On this advice, he made a seven o'clock dinner reservation, put on his swimsuit and a bathrobe provided in his closet, and headed to the top floor. The elevator opened up into a place that was beyond anything he had ever imagined. There was a large circular swimming pool, a fitness center, and a series of hot tubs built as grottos from natural glacier-smoothed boulders, each maintained at a different temperature. In the center of the swimming pool, water jets circulated the water for swimming in place or just relaxing, making the bather feel as if he or she were being carried along by a river. The entire facility was enclosed by an enormous hemispherical glass dome that provided an unobstructed 360-degree panorama. The blizzard had passed, and the North Star twinkled brightly directly overhead from cloudless skies. Other stars came in and out of view through the dim glow of the aurora borealis on the horizon. It was already too late in the year to be able to see the full effect. Christophe could only imagine what it must be like to be swept around the pool under the luminous glow of the northern lights in January. This was going to be a place he would try to visit often.

Christophe was the only person in the spa. He surmised that once the portal was fully operational, the hotel would be booked for months in advance and there would be standing room only in the pool. After a brief swim, he tested the water in the lowest hot tub grotto. Finding it a bit cool, he worked his way upstream, like Goldilocks, until he found the one with the perfect temperature. He lay submerged up to his neck, hoping the day's stress would dissolve. He had been trying, without success, to make sense of his strange encounter with Fred Simms. He wondered how it was even possible for someone so corrupt to become a senior executive at Ashleigh without the cover of a deeper conspiracy. How many Fred Simmses were there? On the surface, Ashleigh Systems had every appearance of being a normal successful corporation, even though it was a part of a conglomerate thought to be controlled by the syndicate. Was it possible that large corporations, like people, could be capable of living double lives? Was Ashleigh merely the Fred Simms front for the Trent Lachmann syndicate? Christophe's encounter with Jean-Luc Galatin and everything he had observed on the factory tour argued against this. The Ashleigh Systems he had always known was a good and reputable company that he had been proud to work for. Was there another Ashleigh Systems hidden from view that was involved in gold bullion counterfeiting and smuggling? Or had the company just become so big that corruption could hide undetected, like a cancer consuming its unsuspecting host? Then there was Jean-Luc. How much did he really know, and how much control did he really have?

Christophe's troubled thoughts drifted over to his curious lunch companions. After a full two hours, he had learned practically nothing about them. Every time he tried to probe into their motives, they simply asked him more questions about his work experiences. This made absolutely no sense. Why did they want to learn about constructing a portal that was nearing obsolescence?

The thought of the word *obsolete* pushed Christophe into an even darker state of mind. He knew that innovation rarely outlives its inventor, but this realization made him morose. It forced innovators like him to dwell in the past. There was a hollowness about describing his former accomplishments, which everyone knew were fast becoming irrelevant. Perhaps he was being too harsh on himself, but who could possibly find any lasting value in achievements that had lost their usefulness? Everything meaningful he had done in his career was about figuring out how to span the North Atlantic at the shortest crossing—the same problem that had faced mariners for centuries. Portals operating at extreme pressures anchored to the seafloor seemed to be a good idea at the time. Millions of people had made the crossing in less than an hour in that system. But the simple solution of just building portals in shallow water along littorals had never entered his mind. And yet this was precisely why the London–Paris portal on the seafloor of the English Channel was so successful, and why it would remain open for decades while the deep transoceanic portals would be closing down. In his zeal to solve the deepwater challenges, he had completely overlooked the obvious and more elegant solution of routing the portal in shallower water.

He felt sad for all the fellow engineers and scientists like the ones who had invested more than twenty years of their lives designing and constructing the Concorde supersonic transport, only to witness the project's steady descent from glory to ignominy. The sole evidence of their effort that remained was in museums and in toy models at amusement fairs. There were countless examples of technological devices whose half-lives could be measured in months before the next generation overtook them and sent them to the salvage crusher. The contribution of every incremental innovation, enabled by its inventor, was forgotten, and the memory was subsequently erased from history. Just as Jean-Luc had said, the North Atlantic portal had been an engineering triumph in its day, but now it was soon to be converted from passengers to freight. Others would receive the fleeting credit for the newest portals until the next newest technology came along. For Christophe, entertaining fond memories of past innovation was like a child trying to grab a greased pig at the state fair.

The thirty minutes spent in the hot tub should have revived his spirits, but instead it had left him depressed. He was profoundly lonely, and he now longed to get back to *Monique II*, Bounder, Minnie, and Monsieur and Madame Onze-heures-deux.

Christophe had dozed off in the warm grotto's hot tub waters. When he awoke, it was time for dinner. He went to his room and changed. The dining room was lovely, but every delightful nuance and detail was lost on him as he sat alone by the light of a candle. A single red rose adorned his table. The restaurant was clearly intended for couples. He wasn't particularly hungry, but he ordered a cheese plate starter and a bottle of red wine. The wine would ensure that he would have almost no recollection of the evening until he awoke at three in the morning with a splitting headache.

"May I join you?" The voice was familiar, but the room was sufficiently dark that he did not recognize the speaker right away against the moonlight glare from the glacier behind her.

"Brigid?" he said. "Is that you? Please. Come, please sit. I didn't know you were in Longyearbyen."

"I have been watching you for a while. You seemed a bit melancholy. Is everything okay?"

"Oh, perhaps I was feeling blue, but seeing you has really cheered me up. Will you join me for dinner? I ordered more wine than I have any business drinking by myself. Tell me about your new job. How is it working out?"

She sat down across from him and replied, "I love being back in Norway, and I like what I do for the most part. You have to forgive me if I can't tell you some of the things I do."

"Is the queen here?" Christophe inquired.

"That's one of those things I can't talk about. As you know, I was hired to be part of her security detail. When she was appointed UN ambassador for Svalbard, I got reassigned to handle the interface between the monarchy and the Norwegian government. Svalbard has raised some interesting fundamental questions about the actual meaning of national sovereignty. I am currently embroiled in another issue that hasn't received much attention until recently, namely, who actually owns the Paris–Longyearbyen portal. Ashleigh claims they do, but it runs for the most part along the coast of Norway in its territorial waters, so Norway says it belongs to them. The matter is going to be taken up by the World Court sometime this year. I have been deposed to represent the interests of the monarchy. To be honest, Christophe, I really don't care much for the geopolitical stuff." After a pause she said, "There are times when I wish I was just that simple girl from Modesto. Do you know what I mean?"

"The undercover spy part or the pretend office manager part?" asked Christophe.

She laughed. "I'm not sure I ever knew the difference."

The server brought the cheese plate and a basket of fresh hot bread, and asked if they were ready to order dinner. Christophe told the server, "We haven't looked at the menu yet. Could you come back in a few minutes?"

"Oh, I have already eaten," said Brigid.

Christophe noticed that she had not touched her wine. "Won't you at least stay to have some cheese and wine with me?" he said, offering her the cheese plate.

"I am just glad to just sit with you for a few minutes. I am working tonight," she responded.

"Working?"

"Yes. When Norway ceded Svalbard to the United Nations, it was agreed that the civil government would be managed by the ambassador, Queen Camilla in this case. Svalbard has a small police force that she oversees. The task of setting that up has been assigned to me."

Christophe sat back in his chair, holding his wineglass. "So, I guess it is your job to make sure that Longyearbyen doesn't turn into a sanctuary for international gangsters."

"Oh, Christophe," she said, leaning forward, "you still don't get it. You don't comprehend the threat you pose to the syndicate."

"Threat? What threat? I am just a retired has-been," he replied pathetically.

Brigid took a moment to choose her words carefully. "Do you really think Fred Simms showed up today just to glad-hand with some old working buddies?"

"Come on, Brigid. He was completely plastered by ten o'clock. He's finished. Washed up. It was embarrassing just to watch him. How did he ever make it to be an executive vice president?"

"Did you ever actually see him take a drink?" asked Brigid.

A chill went down Christophe's spine at the sudden thought that Fred had merely been acting.

"I have news for you, Christophe. Trent Lachmann was here today to keep an eye on you."

This seemed a bit far-fetched to Christophe. He took a big sip of wine. After a long pause, he asked, "Those guys who sat with me at lunch?"

Brigid replied, "No. They weren't Lachmann's. I don't know who they were, but I suspect they were trying to keep you preoccupied. They were shrouding you everywhere. It was very strange to watch. It was as if they were trying to prevent you from interacting with any of the other guests."

"Brigid! That's ridiculous! You are still living in some sort of spy world fantasy. We busted the syndicate's gold-smuggling operation. It's over." Christophe was agitated. He didn't want anything more to do with the whole affair.

Brigid paused long enough for Christophe to settle down. "Do you remember at Mr. Fabré's memorial that Stefan hinted that not all the gold had been recovered?"

"Yes, but I interpreted that as meaning he was still in the process of cleaning up," replied a calmer Christophe.

"Actually," said Brigid, "the situation is far more serious. We did find a large stash of gold bullion at the Goose Bay terminal, just where you said it would be. But only about a ton. We also found a few hundred bars at Versailles and Rotterdam. That's a lot of gold, to be sure, but there is still about one thousand tons missing. The stash in Frankfort had been cleaned out by the time we got there. Apparently, they knew we were on to them."

"But I thought the gold bars from the Paris portal were being stockpiled in Versailles. You had them under surveillance. How did they get the bars out?"

Brigid sighed. "Everyone assumed that the fish delivery truck was going straight to Versailles, but apparently it was making an intermediate stop in an industrial park along the way. At some sort of electroplating facility. We only just discovered this."

Christophe was in shock. "Does this mean that the counterfeit gold bars are still in the repositories in North

America?" Brigid nodded. His first thought was that his entire retirement savings was based on the supposed gold bullion in the Los Angeles repository. If word ever leaked out that the bars were counterfeit, he and millions like him would be financially ruined. The selfish urge came over him to start wiring his life savings to a bank in France as soon as possible. His brain went into overdrive as he began contemplating the ramifications. Could the syndicate really hijack the entire global financial market after all? He was staring past Brigid at the glacier in the distance, which was glowing brightly in the moonlight. "The seals!" he shouted.

Brigid turned around in her chair to look. It would have been unusual for seals to venture on to the glacier at night because they would become easy prey for the polar bears. "I don't see any seals."

"No! The gasket seals!" Christophe looked around for a sheet of paper to write on. He hurriedly did a quick calculation of the volume of the 1 cm × 2 cm metal seal rings based on an average diameter of 1.65 meters, arriving at a volume of 660 cubic centimeters. He looked up the specific gravity of gold on his phone as 19.32 grams per cubic centimeter, and multiplied the two numbers: 12.7 kilograms. He stared at the result for a long time and then looked up at Brigid with a broad grin as if he had just rediscovered his purpose in life. "I know where the gold is stashed."

Brigid was completely puzzled. They just stared at each other for a long time. Finally, Christophe said, "Do you have access to the preconstruction facility I visited today?"

Brigid's official title in Svalbard was commissary-adjunct to the UN ambassador, a position that carried no real power but allowed her access to everything, including an overpowered four-wheel-drive police vehicle, which Christophe and Brigid took from the parking garage in the hotel. Christophe led the way. The security guard at the portal preconstruction facility waved them through without making them stop to show identification. Brigid commented to Christophe that Ashleigh needed to correct its lax security protocol. Anyone could steal her truck and just waltz right in. Rather than going to the main entrance, Christophe suggested that they drive around to the back. They could see a door that was propped open with a rock, apparently so that workers could step outside for a smoke. Brigid commented again on the sloppy security out back.

"I don't suppose you have a pair of bolt cutters in the back, do you?" asked Christophe.

Brigid smiled. "Of course. They are for cutting off padlocks."

It was –5°C outside, and Christophe was wearing only a light jacket. Brigid parked the truck out of sight of the door, and the two dashed in the shadows the one hundred meters to the propped-open door. A quick look inside by Brigid showed that there was no one in sight inside the building. She did a quick scan for security cameras and saw none.

Christophe remembered the layout from his tour earlier in the day. "The gasket machine is through that door." Fortunately, the machine was not running. All of the required seals could be produced on the day shift. While Brigid stood guard, Christophe snuck over to the wooden spool that was holding the wire feeding into the robot arm. He had to figure out how to cut a piece of wire from the spool in such a way that nobody would be able to detect it. He hunted around to find the loose end. On the back side of the turntable he found it. It was attached to a device that sensed when the wire was used up so the leading end of the next spool could be welded in. He could see a piece of wire sticking out, no more than five centimeters long. This would suffice. He snipped off a piece and tossed it in the air from his palm to assess the heft. "Voilà!" he said loud enough to capture Brigid's attention. The two returned to the truck unnoticed. On the way back to the hotel, Brigid commented to Christophe that she had looked all around for security cameras that might have captured their presence in the foundry. She hadn't seen any. Their break-in had been entirely too easy. This would all be covered in the plant security analysis report she planned to submit to explain their presence in the facility, if necessary.

They got back to the hotel just before ten. By this time, Christophe was aware that he had not eaten. Brigid joined him at the restaurant.

"Ah, Mister Conally," said the maître d'. "I am glad you are back. You left earlier without settling your bill."

Christophe looked over at Brigid and back at the man. "I am so sorry. An emergency came up, and I simply forgot."

"No problem. Would you like to return to your same table? I corked your bottle of wine, thinking you might return."

"That would be very nice. I am ready to order dinner now," said Christophe. His heart was still beating fast from the escapade.

Brigid sat quietly across the table from him as he went through the process of decompressing from the evening's excitement. "You know," she said jokingly, "you just committed a felony."

Christophe was perplexed. "What do you mean?"

"You just broke into the Ashleigh foundry and stole a chunk of gold. What do you suppose it is worth? A few hundred euros? That's felony theft." She held out her hand. "Cough it up." Brigid was having a hard time keeping a straight face.

Christophe reached in his pocket and took out the piece of gold, cradling it in his palm. "At least ten grams, I would say. That's more like ten thousand euros." He handed it over to Brigid.

"You realize that I need to turn this over to the queen. This is now a UN matter."

"Of course," replied Christophe. "You know, Brigid, that was the most fun I have had in months."

She smiled back at him, seeing that his former gloominess had completely vanished. "Let's order dinner. My shift is over, and now I want to hear all about growing sugar beets." They talked until the restaurant closed at one.

CHAPTER 31

ABRAHAM

Christophe had consumed more than enough coffee to keep him awake for the rest of the night. The last few hours he had spent with Brigid had been invigorating. He had gotten a taste of what it was like to feel that he was doing something important. Figuring out about the gold seals had given him a renewed sense of purpose, but otherwise he feared that his life was largely behind him now. Brigid had told him that it was his character that really mattered, not his accomplishments. It was who *he was*, not *what he did*, that people would remember. These were wise words, spoken as if by the daughter he had never had. She had given him a sense of belonging. The feeling of belonging anywhere, other than in his office at Ashleigh, was something he had not experienced in forty years with the company. This was a radical thought. When Brigid finally left, he decided to return to the spa pool to spend some time reflecting on the realization that his role in bringing down the syndicate was finally completed. He spent the balance of the night sitting in front of the gas fireplace in the hotel lobby and contemplating his future. He was beginning to feel ready to take on the challenge of retirement and getting plugged in somewhere.

He checked out of the hotel and made a reservation for a return capsule to Paris. The earliest capsule departed at six in the morning. The other three seats were occupied by Ashleigh employees. They wore headphones and showed no interesting in engaging in conversation. It caused him to wonder what the purpose of a four-seater capsule was if the passengers all just wanted to be left alone. Thankfully, the trip was brief.

Christophe took the escalator up from the Gare du Nord terminal. It was a pretty day typical of springtime in Paris. He decided to take the Metro to the Louvre, where a new exhibition hall on science and innovation had recently opened. This was quite a departure from their traditional focus on works of art. He wanted to find out for himself if works of science were being afforded equal standing as works of art. As he started to cross the street, a black sedan stopped in front of him and the back door opened. Stefan was seated inside, hailing him to hop in. Spending time with Stefan was about the last thing in the world Christophe wanted to do at that moment. Reluctantly, he got in.

Christophe looked at Stefan in dismay. "I knew I should have left my cigarettes at home."

"I hear you have been a busy fellow," said Stefan, grinning, as the car sped off.

The car went into the familiar garage of the Intelligence Ministry a few blocks away. "Abraham is waiting upstairs. He is eager to talk with you."

Christophe knew the way. He took the elevator up and decided he would use this opportunity to officially resign from the spy business. Abraham was seated behind his desk, and another man was seated with his back to the door. Abraham waved Christophe in with his customary warm welcome. "I think you have met Jean-Luc."

Christophe was exhausted from lack of sleep, and his state of mind was still fragile. The shock of seeing Jean-Luc Galatin sitting in Abraham's office at the French Intelligence Ministry nearly put him into cardiac arrest.

"Please join us," said Abraham, pointing to a vacant chair. He stood up and walked over to his desk, punching the intercom button. "Please bring Mr. Conally a cup of americano coffee, light cream." Christophe sat down as instructed.

Still standing, Abraham started in sternly, "Christophe. Do you by any chance recall the promise you made to me not to meddle anymore in this gold smuggling affair?" All Christophe could manage was a simple nod of the head. "And do you remember I told you this was a very dangerous business?" Christophe gulped.

Abraham sat back down in his chair and paused for theatric effect. "Well, it turns out I was wrong. It seems you just broke the case." He and Jean-Luc laughed. They were enjoying the joke a lot more than Christophe was, who had thought he was about to be sentenced to life in prison. "Jean-Luc and I have known for some time—thanks in large measure to your rogue adventures—that gold counterfeiting and smuggling was going on at Ashleigh, but until last night, neither of us had a clue where the gold was ending up."

Christophe was really glad to receive the mug of coffee at that moment. He buried his face in it to smell the aroma and wait for the color to return to his face.

Jean-Luc entered. "Christophe, one of the areas of the foundry that wasn't on your tour yesterday is the wiredrawing room. This facility is highly secured and off-limits except to a few select persons with authorization. The reason that people in management were given for the restricted access is that it contains cyanide baths for electroplating gold onto the copper wire, and breathing the fumes could be potentially fatal. Frankly, I always found this reason to be a bit specious. There have been some things going on at the foundry that just never seemed quite right. Upstream from the plating baths, the wire is drawn out from ingots. When the facility was set up, it was decided that wiredrawing and electroplating needed to be carried out in the same locked room to avoid contamination."

"Sounds to me like the perfect cover," said Christophe.

"Ah, yes. And here's the catch. The wiredrawing machines were designed for drawing ductile metals—any ductile metal," Jean-Luc said with a wink. "The spools of gasket wire look identical whether the wire is gold-plated copper or pure gold. The only people who would ever know the difference are the ones authorized to work in that room."

"Surely, anyone handling the gasket seals would be able to tell the difference just by the weight," said Christophe.

"One would think," said Jean-Luc. "But as it turns out, the gaskets are supported on a fairly heavy aluminum retainer. Once installed onto the titanium flanges, the gaskets are held in place and covered up by this temporary metal retainer to protect them from damage until the segments are finally joined aboard the construction vessel. It is the perfect setup. As you know, every detail of such an engineering project requires a lot of signatures. Someone has gone to a lot of trouble to make everything look totally legitimate."

Jean-Luc allowed some time for Christophe to soak up the information. "In all my years in business, I would never have dreamt that it was possible to build such a perfect factory within a factory. It seems that the very facility Ashleigh built to produce the best and most advanced portals has been subordinated for the purpose of stashing away a significant fraction of the world's gold reserves."

"I have been thinking about this," said Christophe. "What I find interesting in hindsight is that there is a precedent at Ashleigh for this. The idea of using all-gold gasket seals actually did come up years ago in one of my engineering review meetings. We always knew that gold seals would be better than copper, but after a simple calculation of how much gold this would take, the idea was rejected out of hand as ridiculous. When the thought occurred to me last night that there might be another reason for wanting to use gold seals, that's when the light switched on. In essence, they would be able to kill two birds with one stone."

Abraham nodded, and said, "Christophe, you seem to have a knack for lights switching on. We appreciate this more than you can imagine."

Christophe replied, "I also have a vested interest in this. My life's savings is now backed by practically worthless gold-plated tungsten bars in a Los Angeles repository." He looked over at Jean-Luc. "By the way, what was the deal with those five guys sitting with me at lunch yesterday?"

"They are part of an executive transition team. I dispatched them to follow you around to learn as much as possible about portal technology," replied Jean-Luc.

"It still puzzles me, then, why your five guys and I were the only ones on the factory tour. Surely there were lots of others who would have liked to see the foundry," said Christophe.

Jean-Luc replied, "Actually, Christophe, the tour was only for your benefit. No one else was invited."

Abraham jumped in at this point. "We needed fresh eyes on this. I convinced Jean-Luc that if there was something amiss in the foundry, you had a gift for seeing things that no one else notices. I got him to arrange a private tour without any distractions."

"But it wasn't a private tour. There were those other five guys who were basically clueless about portal technology," responded Christophe.

After glancing at Abraham for permission to speak freely, he said, "When you asked me on the capsule if I had ever heard of Trent Lachmann, that was a very risky thing for you to do. You didn't know whether or not I was part of the conspiracy. You could easily have ended up as fish food for North Atlantic salmon. I contacted Abraham right away because I was worried that you might try to interact with some of the other guests. Lachmann we know, but we still don't know how deep the conspiracy goes. Those guys on your tour and at your table work for me, and I trust them. I simply asked them to keep you occupied."

"Does that mean they weren't really interested in hearing my life story?" asked Christophe jokingly.

"Oh, I'm sure they found it interesting, but that wasn't their main purpose," said Abraham. He stood up again and started to leave the office. "You two keep talking. I have an urgent matter to tend to. I will be back shortly."

Abraham was gone for more than an hour, but this gave Jean-Luc a chance to catch up on some of the corporate history of Ashleigh's portal division. Having been in his current position for only two years, the only people he really trusted had been brought in from other divisions, and none of them had any corporate memory of the portal business.

Abraham finally returned, looking worried. Jean-Luc asked, "Is everything okay?"

"Oh," replied Abraham, "I just got off the phone with the UN Bank. They are getting nervous. They are concerned that the counterfeiting story will leak out and panic the global economy."

"Is that all?" said Jean-Luc sarcastically.

"How did they find out about the gold seals so quickly?" asked Christophe.

"I just told them. They weren't aware of it before, but I couldn't keep it from them any longer. They want positive confirmation by next week that we know where the gold is, or else they intend to start taking corrective action to stabilize the currency. You need to know, Jean-Luc, that there is serious talk of commandeering all the Ashleigh portals."

"That would ruin Ashleigh!" exclaimed Jean-Luc.

"Surely all the portals don't have gold seals," said Christophe. "Is there any possibility that Ashleigh has other facilities making gasket seals?"

"I think Longyearbyen is the only one," said Jean-Luc. "Anyway, only the newest portals use this gasket seal technology." He looked back at Abraham. "If they start commandeering our portals, the company is finished."

"Perhaps," said Abraham, "but Ashleigh is certainly culpable, and the repositories are going to want their gold back."

"By tearing out the portals?" Jean-Luc said, exploding.

The room went silent. The desire for safe and convenient travel was now in direct conflict with the need for international financial stability. Either way, they all knew that the syndicate would come out the only real winner in the end. The three men sat quietly, occupied by their thoughts.

"What if we were able to certify the existence of the gold in situ in the portals?" inquired Christophe. "No one could steal it. Think of it. The portals make the perfect repository."

Abraham and Jean-Luc sat expressionless. Such an idea was preposterous.

"No. Think about it," said Christophe. "My life savings doesn't exist anymore in Los Angeles." He paused to be sure the other two were listening. "What if my gold was held instead in the Paris–Longyearbyen portal?"

"Surely you are kidding," said Abraham.

"Seriously," responded Christophe, "what's the difference? What does it matter who owns the repository, or where it is located, as long as it is secure?"

The look being exchanged between Abraham and Jean-Luc slowly transitioned from total dismissal to intrigue. They both began considering it. "Could such a plan actually work?" asked Abraham.

"Even if such an idea were feasible," said Jean-Luc, "how could you ever certify the existence of gold that no one would ever be able to access without tearing out the portal? It would be like gold ore buried in the ground. It doesn't have any intrinsic value if you can't hold it in your hand."

"What is it that makes gold valuable?" replied Christophe. "Scarcity. What's the best way to make it scarce? Put it somewhere that everyone knows where it is but where no one can easily get to it. In fact, isn't that the whole purpose of a repository? The only reason gold ore deposits have no intrinsic value is because either you don't know where they are or the gold is in a place that costs too much to get to it." As Christophe articulated the case, it was becoming increasingly evident how brilliant the suggestion was. His confidence was growing that he could pull this off. He started to get an inkling of how he might want to spend the next few months of his life.

Christophe could sense that Abraham was not fully convinced. He looked directly at the director and said, "What better place is there to store gold than in the gasket seals of a submarine portal? The portal provides a vital service to humankind." Christophe looked at Jean-Luc. "You said it yourself just yesterday: Shanghai in three and a half hours. And you well know that the cost to rebuild the portal would bankrupt the company. All Ashleigh needs to do is convince the UN Bank that the gold is safe and secure—at least for the time being."

"All right," said a skeptical Jean-Luc. "Suppose I am the UN Bank and I hold up a 12.5-kilogram gold bullion bar. It has a certificate seal on it and a registered serial number. How are you going to convince me to accept a 1.6-meter diameter gold ring weighing 12.5 kilograms lying at the bottom of the North Sea as being equivalent?"

Christophe responded, "Suppose I hold up a fake bullion bar from the Los Angeles Repository. It also has a UN Bank certificate seal and a registered serial number. You tell me. Given the choice, which would you rather own?" This sealed the deal. Abraham and Jean-Luc hopped on board.

"Okay," said Abraham. "How do you intend to certify the existence of the gold in the gasket seals?"

"The same way they are testing for counterfeit bars in the Los Angeles Repository: by using QBUR, quantitative broadband ultrasonic resonance analysis. I need to pay a visit to Sonilyzer. I think their company is located here in Paris at the incubator in Station F."

"Before I carry this line of discussion to the UN Bank," said Abraham, "I need to take it up with Queen Camilla. Longyearbyen is under her jurisdiction. I will leave it to the two of you to figure out the technical details."

Jean-Luc looked over at Christophe and said, "Now are you ready to come out of retirement?"

Christophe and Jean-Luc took over the conference room and began sketching out the action plan. The first order of business was to estimate how many gold gasket seals might have been deployed. Jean-Luc contacted his secretary at headquarters to courier over all the production records for Longyearbyen. He was pretty sure that the foundry was the only possible source for the gold seals, but in the meantime, he was able to determine with certainty that all the gasket seals used in the Paris–Longyearbyen portal came from the foundry in Longyearbyen. Christophe estimated that if all the seals were pure gold, this would account for about 68,000 seals, or 850 tons of gold, worth 850 billion euros. The sheer magnitude of the number came as a huge shock to both men. If true, this would account for a large fraction of the missing 1,000 tons.

When the production records arrived, they determined that 2,125 kilometers of the Western Arctic portal had been completed, accounting for an additional 42,500 seals, or 531.25 tons. The portal-laying operation was shut down for the winter because the construction vessel was still encased in pack ice, so tunnel segments were being stockpiled in the yard behind the factory. There were 358 segments according to the production records, or an additional 4 tons. Construction of the Eastern Arctic portal had not yet begun. If all the seals turned out to be pure gold, then 1,385 tons of gold was tucked away in the Ashleigh portals—more than was known to be missing at that time. Either there was more gold taken than was previously thought, or some of the seals were actually copper. This would be the fundamental challenge to determine. Christophe had to work quickly to come up with a convincing method for confirming the existence of gold seals without actually tearing apart the portals.

Christophe asked Jean-Luc if it would be possible to obtain the display sample of the cross section of the joined flanges that had been passed around during his tour the day before. He left Christophe alone to work for an hour while he took care of a few things. Christophe made an appointment to visit Sonilyzer later in the afternoon. He called Bordeaux to let Sandra know he would be delayed in his return. She told him that Bounder was following Fredrick around everywhere he went, and both seemed perfectly content.

When Jean-Luc returned, he said to Christophe, "I would like to relocate our war room to the executive wing of headquarters in La Défense. I think you know Stefan. I had him perform a thorough sweep for bugs, and he actually found several. Apparently, I have been under surveillance by the syndicate for quite a while. Stefan disabled all of the bugs and assures me that it is now safe to work there. I have assigned three of my top engineers to you. None of them knows very much about portal technology, but Christian, in particular, is a quick learner. I have also assigned you a personal executive assistant. Anything you want gets top priority. Just ask. Finally, I have arranged for you to stay in the visiting VIP apartment. It is really lovely and just a short walking distance to the office. Just don't get too attached.

"Oh, by the way," he added, "the flange section you asked for will be on the desk in your office by the time you move in. I also requested a full gold gasket seal and matching end flanges. They are too big to fit in a capsule, so I have arranged to have them flown in. They should be here tomorrow. You will have to work with Christian on setting up a suitable laboratory at the headquarters building."

Christophe didn't know what to say. For the first time in his life he had clear direction from the top without any apparent obstacles. Jean-Luc looked at him and said, "Are you okay with this? I need you. If we fail to pull this off, Ashleigh is finished, and we both know that would be the greater tragedy."

At that moment, a page entered the room. "Mr. Galatin, I have a message for you from the police commissary in Svalbard. She says that the facility has been secured and that the general manager has been taken into custody. She asked, since there is no jail in Longyearbyen, where she should take him."

"Actually, I have no idea who has jurisdiction. I presume he has not been charged with anything yet. Just tell her to bring him to Ashleigh headquarters in La Défense."

Jean-Luc glanced at Christophe without commenting further on the news. He had been standing up to that point, and now he decided to sit down to catch his breath. A lot had taken place in a very short time. "You know, Christophe," he said pensively, "I still can't get over the elegance of the scheme. The syndicate is the perfect parasite, and Ashleigh is the perfect host. We needed reliable gasket seals, and they needed a place to stash the gold. As you said, both objectives were satisfied. The symbiosis of the two organisms was ideal. It is really astonishing when you consider it. I don't think anyone would have suspected a thing if you had not questioned the Paris portal incident report."

"Thanks, but it was a team effort," said Christophe. "One thing I don't get, though. Why didn't the syndicate just bury the gold bullion somewhere?" At that point, Abraham entered the room.

"That's exactly what Abraham and I thought they were doing. We have been searching everywhere for it. What we didn't fully appreciate until this morning is that the syndicate needed to stash the gold in a place where only they knew where it was, but where no single one of them could ever access it. I think that fundamentally, the members of the syndicate have a deep distrust for one another, and they realized that sooner or later one of them would get greedy and secretly try to go after it. In order to undermine the gold standard, they needed to make the gold vanish for a while without it actually disappearing."

Jean-Luc pulled a document from his briefcase and passed it to Christophe. The title read, "Company Confidential. Procedure for Repair and Replacement of High-Vacuum Gasket Seals on the Paris–Longyearbyen Portal."

"They were planning to use Ashleigh to access the gold as part of routine maintenance. All it would take is a worker who knew better than to throw the old seal in the trash." Christophe thumbed through the document. The procedure seemed to him to be completely legitimate.

Christophe looked up at Jean-Luc in disbelief. "This is incredible!"

Abraham chimed in, "Just like with a stolen Rembrandt painting, stolen gold has no value except to the one holding it. The syndicate had to figure out a way to make stolen gold valuable. What is the purpose of the gold standard currency anyway? To peg the value of currency to a fixed and regulated quantity of the scarce commodity—gold bullion. By undermining the amount of fixed gold held in registered bullion by means of counterfeiting, they hoped to undermine confidence in the gold standard. In fact, that is precisely what is going on right now at the UN Bank. As we speak, there are powerful voices arguing in favor of abandoning the gold standard. This would surely result in global financial chaos. The syndicate would relish that, but I no longer believe this is their underlying motivation."

Abraham sat in the chair next to Christophe. "Let me try to explain. This may seem a bit obtuse, but with the gold standard, the value—the purchasing power of currency, if you will—is dependent on a physical quantity of gold. Without the standard, things get reversed, and the value of gold becomes dependent on the supply of fiat currency, which can be easily manipulated. The syndicate—everyone, for that matter—knows that unregulated gold would be worth far more than one thousand euros per gram. As long as gold is regulated, it is not possible for anyone to make a killing through speculation. Deregulate gold, and everyone is suddenly going to want to own some, and the demand for gold will skyrocket. I estimate that the syndicate, sitting on one thousand tons, might have been able to go on a ten-trillion-euro shopping spree once the gold standard was abandoned."

CHAPTER 32

LA DÉFENSE

Brigid and the plant manager from Ashleigh's Longyearbyen facility were quietly sitting across the table from one another in Jean-Luc's office at Ashleigh headquarters when Jean-Luc finally arrived late in the afternoon. The plant manager said to him, "Mr. Galatin, am I really under arrest?"

"That all depends on how cooperative you are prepared to be," replied Jean-Luc.

"Of course. Anything you want." The plant manager showed no signs of belligerency.

"Okay. Let's start out by you telling us how long you have known about the gold smuggling operation."

"Smuggling!" exclaimed the plant manager, looking at Brigid with obvious terror in his eyes. "What do you mean?"

Jean-Luc nodded to Brigid, and she fetched a heavy box from her valise. She opened it and placed the contents, a dull copper-colored ingot, on the table in front of the plant manager.

Jean-Luc said without emotion, "There are stacks of these copper ingots in your warehouse in Longyearbyen."

"Be careful with that," said the plant manager. "That's not copper. It's copper-plated pure gold. It's worth twelve and a half million euros."

Jean-Luc and Brigid exchanged puzzled looks.

The plant manager peered around, confused. "What? Did you think we would just leave a few tons of gold lying around for employees to walk off with? We buy the bars preplated with copper so they just look like ordinary copper. Surely you knew this, Mr. Galatin."

"No, I am afraid I have no idea what you are talking about," replied Jean-Luc.

At this point, the plant manager was becoming panicked. "Mr. Galatin, you signed all the purchase requisitions. Who else at Ashleigh is high enough up to have authorized such huge payments?" Jean-Luc went to his desk and pushed the intercom button.

"Yes, Mr. Galatin?"

"Ask Maurice to come to my office immediately," said Jean-Luc. Maurice Trompet was the Ashleigh comptroller.

"Mr. Trompet called in sick today," said the receptionist.

"Then get him on the phone! Send Mme. Rouchart to my office immediately!" Jean-Luc was yelling.

Mme. Rouchart was the chief financial officer. "Mme. Rouchart went to New York this week, sir," replied the receptionist.

Jean-Luc went back to his chair at the table. "You say you have invoices for the gold that you claim I signed off on? With my signature?" said Jean-Luc to the plant manager. His voice expressed his growing alarm.

"Yes, sir," he replied.

"Where does the gold come from? How does it get to Longyearbyen?" demanded Jean-Luc.

"The copper-plated ingots are shipped from the port of Rotterdam. We use ordinary bulk shipment methods so as not to attract attention. The bars are electroplated with copper to make them look like ordinary copper ingot, which is also what the shipping manifest says. Pallets of two hundred fifty bars are shrink-wrapped so that no one can inadvertently try to pick one up. Obviously, if they did, they would know immediately it wasn't really copper, because the weight of a gold bar is more than twice that of copper. Trust me, the whole shipping process is carried out with undercover couriers and a great deal of security because each pallet is worth more than three billion euros. The minute they arrive in Longyearbyen, we verify the gold by weight and put the bars into locked inventory in the wiredrawing room."

Jean-Luc looked at Brigid. "I guess this explains the reason for the fish delivery truck stopping on the way to Versailles."

"Who all knows about this?" Jean-Luc asked, unable to conceal his growing frustration.

"Of course, me," replied the plant manager. "Our plant comptroller. A couple of shift supervisors. We carefully vet every employee who has any dealing with gasket seal production. We account for every scrap of gold, down to the milligram."

Jean-Luc took a deep breath. The story he was being told had all the earmarks of legitimacy. "Explain to me why you tell everyone on the factory tour, including me on several occasions, that the gasket seals are made from gold-plated copper. You even pass around a display sample that shows this. Why all the subterfuge?"

The plant manager looked over at Brigid. She could clearly tell he was beginning to feel entrapped. "Did you really want us to tell the world that each gasket seal was worth twelve and a half million euros? I can't believe you don't know any of this." He paused to take a sip of water. "The gold bars are not just copper-plated as a disguise. The copper is also an essential ingredient of gasket seal alloy," said the plant manager.

"The seal alloy?" repeated Jean-Luc, growing ever more agitated.

The plant manager was totally flummoxed at the realization that the president and CEO of the company apparently had no knowledge of basic portal technology. "Sir, pure gold is too soft, so we alloy it with one weight percent copper to make it more durable in handling."

Jean-Luc and Brigid were furiously exchanging glances, trying to make sense of the situation. Nothing they were hearing was what they expected. Finally, Jean-Luc said, "Didn't it bother you that the gold bars have registered UN Bank stamps?"

"Stamps?" This question again seemed to catch the plant manager by surprise. "There are no markings on the gold bars. Look." He pointed to the top surface of the bar in front of him. "If there were any markings, they would show through the thin copper plating."

Jean-Luc bowed his head into his folded hands for a moment in order to gather his wits. Raising his head again, he asked, "When did you switch from copper seals to gold seals?"

Once again, the plant manager expressed his complete dismay at the question. "Mr. Galatin, sir, in the five years that I have been running the foundry in Longyearbyen, Ashleigh never made a single copper gasket seal. We were told that corporate R&D had determined that they were not reliable enough, so the decision was made to go with gold from the very beginning."

"Are you trying to tell me that Ashleigh authorized a trillion euros to be paid for the purchase of gold for seals?" screamed Jean-Luc.

"Yes, sir," replied the plant manager. "They told us it was necessary for portal reliability. It always seemed a bit extravagant to me, so I kept a copy of every purchase authorization signed by you and by Mr. Himmel. They are in my office at the plant."

"My predecessor, Günter Himmel? The one killed in the plane crash in the Swiss Alps?" asked Jean-Luc.

"Yes, sir."

Jean-Luc went back to his desk and pressed the intercom button again. "Yes, Mr. Galatin?"

"Have you managed to track down Maurice Trompet yet?" said an exasperated Jean-Luc.

"No. He is not answering his phone. And Mme. Rouchart apparently never showed up at her meeting in New York." Jean-Luc sat back down, exasperated.

The plant manager looked over at Brigid for sympathy. "How is it possible that Mr. Galatin did not know about this?" He stared down at the gold bar in front of him. "Mr. Galatin, sir, I have told you all I know. There's nothing more I can do." The room was quiet. "I would like permission to go home to my family now, if that's okay? My wife was pretty upset when Commissar Andersen dragged me away in handcuffs."

Jean-Luc remained silent for a while longer, then said to the plant manager, "You work directly for Howard Schultz, don't you? Presumably he can back up your story. I asked him to be in this meeting, but so far, we haven't been able to track him down." He turned to Brigid and nodded. "Yes. Brigid can escort you back to Longyearbyen. But don't leave the island. We will have a lot more to discuss before this is over."

Brigid was glad to see Stefan sitting just outside Jean-Luc's office when she and the plant manager went out. She gave him a look that hinted at more than just a simple professional association. Stefan said, "Abraham asked me to accompany you back to Longyearbyen. He suspects that some added security may be in order."

Jean-Luc sat alone in his office staring out the window. He was a seasoned executive and had weathered many storms, but he was not mentally prepared for this one. He had suspected for a long time that some things were not quite right at Ashleigh. When he had been made aware of the tungsten counterfeiting operation being run by Fred Simms, it surprised him how easy it had been for a single high-level executive and a small cadre of loyal lieutenants to infiltrate and subjugate an entire division of Ashleigh. Now he suspected that Howard Schultz, executive vice president for European Operations, was similarly part of the conspiracy. Jean-Luc was responsible for fifty thousand employees worldwide, and the dark thought weighed heavily on him that he had no idea how many of them were taking orders from their syndicate masters rather than from him.

Christophe and Christian had gone to the headquarters of the Sonilyzer company. Headquarters would have been an overstatement. The company consisted of a small suite shared by several other start-ups in an incubator at Station F. They shared a common receptionist.

"Hello, my name is Christophe Conally. I am here to see Pascal Tiebot," he said, handing the receptionist a business card.

She dialed an extension, and said, "Yes, Pascal. There is a Mr. Conally up front to see you."

After a long wait, bordering on rude, Pascal appeared. "Dr. Conally. I am so glad to finally meet you. I am so sorry to keep you waiting. I am the only one in the office today, so I am a bit shorthanded."

This seemed to Christophe to be a rather inauspicious beginning to what could easily become a multimillion-euro contract. "Did your father tell you the reason for our visit?"

"Just something about copper-clad gold or gold-clad copper. He didn't really say very much. By the way, thanks for the nice lead. We have already shipped four 2160A's to your friends in California." Christophe gave Christian a concerned look. This was not at all what he was expecting. They followed Pascal into his office, which was piled with clutter. "Excuse the mess. I just returned from eight weeks in Brazil."

Pascal cleared some space on a workbench by dumping everything in a pile on the floor. "So, what can I do for you?"

Christophe placed a carrying case on the table and took out the display specimen of the joined titanium flanges, explaining that it was a section of a submarine portal. "Can you tell me what this metal is?" he said, pointing to the square slot where the gasket seal was visible in cross section.

Pascal studied it carefully, and after some consideration said, "It sure looks like some kind of copper to me."

Christophe and Christian exchanged another concerned look. "No," said Christophe with growing impatience. "Can your instrument analyze it by QBUR?"

"Quber?" asked Pascal.

"Q-B-U-R, quantitative broadband ultrasonic resonance," replied Christophe, unable to disguise his growing frustration.

"Oh," said Pascal, "of course. Let me get a Sonilyzer out of the stockroom." Miraculously, Pascal returned after only a little while with the instrument. He plugged it into the wall socket. While he was waiting for it to warm up, he rigged a coaxial cable across the room to an interface box next to his computer. He did some initial diagnostics and returned to the lab bench. "You need to forgive me. I shipped my last completed 2160A to California, so I have to improvise a bit."

"What were you doing in Brazil?" asked Christophe.

"That was an interesting project," he replied while bringing up a computer program on the screen. "It was for some mining company that contracted with us to develop a system to look for mineral deposits in the Amazon jungle. We had to pretty much develop a whole new method using a transducer array approach. It took more than two months in horrid tropical conditions, but they paid us a fortune. Interestingly, they sent me a letter the day before yesterday expressing an interest in buying my company. You wouldn't believe the offer." He picked up something that looked like a doctor's stethoscope and handed it to Christian. "Do you mind holding this up against the inside of the specimen where the two flanges meet?"

Pascal returned to his computer. "Don't move. This will take about ten seconds." Pascal typed some keystrokes, and a loud high-pitched squeal filled the air. When the noise stopped, he told Christian, "You can put the transducer down now." He scrolled up and down furiously on the computer screen, and after a while, he sent the results to the printer. "Let's take a look." He handed them one of the printouts. To their astonishment, they had in front of them a high-resolution two-dimensional color image of the entire specimen in cross section. Pascal pointed to a region of the plot. "This yellow area corresponds to the flanges. It is titanium with—" He looked over to consult a second printout. "It looks like about 1 percent aluminum and a little bit of molybdenum. I would expect that to be a very strong alloy. A good choice for submarine portals. Paris–Longyearbyen, I presume?" This triggered a surprised look exchanged between Christophe and Christian. Pascal looked at the printout again. "The bolts are titanium with 3 percent vanadium. No one ever has to worry about overtightening those babies."

He grinned at Christophe, who was obviously beginning to lose patience.

"But I guess you are mostly interested in the metal in the square groove." He consulted the printout again. "That looks like 99.9 percent pure copper, two centimeters wide and one centimeter in thickness, coated on all sides with thirty-five microns of electroplated gold."

As there was little remaining doubt that Pascal's Sonilyzer could do the job, Christophe left Christian behind to discuss the engineering details of constructing a capsule-mounted system. This would be an enormous task that was well beyond any Sonilyzer resources and that needed to be done quickly. Christophe returned to La Défense to report to Jean-Luc the good news that he was confident that QBUR would work. He needed to quickly put together a demonstration that would be compelling enough to convince the UN Bank that they could quantify the amount and location of the missing gold in the portals without actually taking them apart. For this, he would have to construct a full-size portal joint in the lab with a capsule to carry the equipment and sensors.

The demonstration was completed in a week. Christian and Pascal had designed a ring for the transducers that rotated just on the inside of the tunnel wall. Once the capsule was positioned with respect to the flange joint, the ultrasonic transducers were activated and rotated slowly around the circumference. The complete measurement required about sixty seconds per joint. In order to analyze all sixty-eight thousand joints in the Paris–Longyearbyen portal in a reasonable period of time, Christophe would need at least one hundred such test capsules. The portal could not be operated when the test capsules were being deployed, so he decided to test out the system on the Western Arctic portal first, since it was not yet fully operational.

For the time being, the UN Bank was satisfied. They would stay on the gold standard and certify the existence of the gold in the gasket seals in exchange for the counterfeit bullion in the repositories around the world. The panic in the financial markets was short-lived. Any gold owed to repositories by other repositories holding counterfeit bullion was guaranteed by the UN Bank. It soon became apparent that this was unnecessary, and markets settled down rather quickly—another testament to the robustness of the gold standard currency system. Once the UN Bank took possession of a counterfeit bar and confirmed the serial number and certification stamp, they would issue a warrant for the equivalent amount of gold at a designated position in the portal. Fortuitously, Ashleigh had designed the gasket seals to contain exactly 12.5 kilograms of gold plus 1,250 grams of copper plating. The Paris–Longyearbyen portal held almost 856,000 kilograms of pure gold—the equivalent of 68,457 standard 12.5-kilogram gold bullion bars. The gasket seals in the Western Arctic portal were also determined to be gold. Over time, including the gold reclaimed from the thick plating on the counterfeit tungsten bars, nearly all the gold was recovered. The big loser was Ashleigh Systems, who paid billions to purchase stolen gold they now had to write off their books.

Jean-Luc was able to corroborate the story of his plant manager. His forged signature was, indeed, on the invoice authorizations. Ashleigh Systems had apparently shelled out 1.27 trillion euros over five years to purchase stolen gold. Maurice Trompet and Francis Rouchart had disappeared without a trace. Jean-Luc and Abraham worked with Europol to try to track them down, but it was as if neither of them had ever existed. Jean-Luc never did find any record of corporate R&D having said that copper gasket seals would not be reliable enough. Sonilyzer grew to over 5 million euros in gross sales practically overnight.

Jean-Luc was standing in front of the window in his office looking out at the sprawling campus of Ashleigh International when Christophe entered. "Christophe, do you know what *bullionism* is?" he asked without turning around.

"Other than just the word, no," replied Christophe.

When Jean-Luc turned around, his face was drawn by mounting pressures. His mood was gloomy and philosophical. "Bullionism was a consequence of the mercantilist economic theories that were popular with the European imperialists prior to the nineteenth century. It was believed that the wealth of nations was determined by the amount of gold and silver bullion they held in their treasuries. The most conspicuous practitioner was Spain. Their Conquistadors extracted vast amounts of gold and silver from the New World on behalf of the Spanish Crown. Gold and silver were considered valuable in the Americas, to be sure, but also in the form of jewelry and artifacts distributed almost uniformly throughout the Western Hemisphere. The idea of melting these down for bullion to be hoarded in a central repository would never have occurred to the native populations." Jean-Luc motioned for Christophe to sit down, then joined him at the table, where the copper-plated gold bar was still lying untouched.

He continued, "The whole point of the gold currency standard was to distribute wealth. Anyone on the planet can own gold in any form, and if he wants, he can redeem it for cash from any repository at any time he wants. It is ironic that two centuries later, bullionism has resurfaced." Jean-Luc's personal assistant arrived at that moment with a mug of americano coffee for Christophe and an espresso for Jean-Luc, along with a tray of French pastries.

"How do you mean?" asked Christophe.

Jean-Luc downed his espresso in a single gulp. "I have been looking into the company you brought to my attention that contracted with Mr. Tiebot to do the survey in Brazil—a company called New World Exploration and Mining. It turns out that the company is a fifty-fifty joint venture between Ashleigh Tunnel Boring Company and a mysterious Russian mining conglomerate based in a remote Siberian town called Kitchera, about which I can find practically nothing. Ashleigh Tunnel Boring Company, as you know, bored the Belem–Houston portal, which we have both taken several times."

"What is special about Kitchera?" asked Christophe.

"Interesting. It is located at the midpoint of the Longyearbyen–Shanghai portal. It is a small mining town in the middle of nowhere that is booming because it will be the terminus of the Longyearbyen–Kitchera portal and will be the hub from which all the Asian portals fan out. This is obviously an enormous construction project for Ashleigh and a huge economic boom for the region. So, why the joint venture?" Jean-Luc went to his desk to grab a file folder and then returned to the table. "You have no idea how hard it is for me to get straight answers in this company that I supposedly run. But I was able to piece together a few details. First of all, during the boring of the Belem–Houston portal, they encountered a rich vein of gold ore under the Amazon rain forest close to Guyana. This was hushed up. One of my people encountered a confidential report in our archives by sheer accident. It seems that the Ashleigh people did not want to share the information with the Brazilian government, who maintains all the mineral rights for land traversed by our portals. Guyana, on the other hand, is a corrupt nation with ties to Russia going back to Soviet days."

Christophe was incredulous. Jean-Luc said, "You need more coffee. The story only gets better and better." He pushed a button under the table to call for his attendant. "Some people from the Ashleigh Tunnel Boring Company contacted dubious elements in the Guyanese government to formulate a plan to secretly bore tunnels from Guyana into Brazil to begin extracting the ore. This is where the Russian mining company got involved, because Ashleigh needed cover."

Christophe's coffee arrived just in time to give Jean-Luc a much-needed break. "I will be back in five minutes. Don't move."

Christophe stood up and stared out the window at the other buildings in the complex, each of the thousands of windows representing an office where some Ashleigh employee was dutifully conducting a small piece of the company's business. "How did you find any of this out?" asked Christophe when Jean-Luc returned, selecting a croissant and returning to his chair.

"Also in that file folder are the minutes of the Ashleigh board meeting where the New World Exploration and Mining Company was approved. Before that time, Ashleigh had been focused only on building portals, but the board was persuaded that the company needed to pursue other ways to exploit its tunnel-boring expertise. The joint venture was enthusiastically approved. No one bothered to look into the credentials of the nefarious Russian mining company, but with a simple set of signatures and some celebration, a completely legitimate company was announced as the result of a storied union between the world's premier hyperspeed portal builder—a company with two hundred billion euros in annual turnover and an unassailable reputation—and an unknown Russian mining company." Jean-Luc spoke this final statement with a great deal of sarcasm and then paused to give Christophe time to reflect.

After a while, Christophe asked, "Is that all?"

"Oh, no. There is much more," replied Jean-Luc as if in a daze. "This company, Sonilyzer, you have been working with? Their CEO, a Mr. Pascal Tiebot, was apparently hired by none other than New World Mining to do an ultrasonic survey of the ground above our Belem–Houston portal. They told the Brazilian government that it was routine, that they were only looking for faults in the rock that might compromise the integrity of the portal." Jean-Luc looked across the table at Christophe in near despair. "But that is not what you told me. You said Mr. Tiebot was conducting a mineral survey looking for precious metal deposits. I asked Christian to see if Mr. Tiebot could share the survey results. He obliged, apparently assuming that we all worked for the same company."

Jean-Luc opened the file folder and removed a sheet of paper. He slid it over the table to Christophe and pointed to a paragraph at the bottom of the page, which read as follows:

In our expert opinion, the mineral surveys conducted by Sonilyzer using an advanced distributed transducer technique called quantitative broadband ultrasonic resonance, covering an area of approximately one million hectares, has determined that approximately one thousand tons of gold, one hundred metric tons of platinum group metals, and in excess of ten thousand metric tons of silver exist at this site.

Signed,

Mr. Pascal Tiebot, CEO

Christophe slowly looked up at Jean-Luc. "You know, Christophe, it has really been bothering me why I wasn't fired at the emergency board of directors meeting last week when I informed them that Ashleigh would need to restate corporate earnings for the past five years to the tune of 1.286 trillion euros. They hardly flinched." Jean-Luc took another bite of croissant and sat quietly in his thoughts for a moment. "I have come to the conclusion that they realize that if they bring me down, they all go down with me."

He gathered up the papers and replaced them in the file folder. "You and I are the only two people on the planet who know the contents of this folder." He passed the folder across the table to Christophe. "I have no idea what to tell you to do with this information, but you are the only one left I trust who can figure it out."

Jean-Luc stood up and walked out of his office without saying goodbye.

EPILOGUE

It was dark by the time Christophe finally got back to his apartment in Beaulieu-sur-Mer. What was to have been just a few nights away ended up being a six-week absence. The apartment was hot and musty. Minnie did not come to greet him in the entryway, but by the time he opened the doors to the terrasse to let some fresh air in, she wandered into the living room, whining softly to let him know she didn't much appreciate being awakened. Henri had been looking after the cat, but she was noticeably fatter than Christophe remembered her being. He instinctively opened the refrigerator and closed it again quickly, his nose informing him that he had forgotten to ask Henri to clean out the perishable items. That unpleasant task would have to wait until the morning.

He thumbed through the mail he had retrieved from his box in the lobby. There was a bill from the marina stamped Past Due. It was for six months of slip fees and the repairs to his sailboat. It was the first time that Christophe had been hit with the harsh reality that owning a boat was not inexpensive. He would have to go to the marina in the morning to settle accounts. He got a bill from the syndicate "electrician" who had worked on his water heater. It gave him a chuckle that they actually expected him to pay to have his apartment bugged. He threw the bill in the trash. The rest was junk mail, except for a postcard from Marina del Rey. It had a picture of Thierry and Sophie standing together at the end of the Santa Monica pier, and it read,

Dear Christophe,

We had a magnificent time. Don't know how we can ever thank you enough. Give Bounder a kiss for us. Where do you want us to send your keys?

Love,
Sophie and Thierry

Christophe was planning to tell them to hold on to the keys, as they would be needing them again in the coming fall.

The sun was already up by the time Christophe awoke the following morning. He made instant coffee, which he had to drink black because the cream in his refrigerator had mutated into a hairy alien life-form. Minnie climbed up on his lap, and after a while, a single turtledove showed up on his railing. "Where's your friend?" asked Christophe. He finally deciphered from the frantic cooing and head bobbing that Mme. Onze-heures-deux was sitting on eggs.

The marina manager was glad to see Christophe and even happier to get paid. The winter covers were still on *Monique II*, which Christophe rolled up and stowed belowdecks. He sat in the captain's chair for a while, considering all the things that had to be done to get the boat ready to go out. The thrill he had always felt when anticipating going sailing was strangely absent that day. The marina manager walked down the dock toward him and said, "Say, Mr. Conally, there is a guy looking for a nine-meter sailboat to buy. He has had his eye on *Monique II*. If you ever decide to sell her, I think he might be interested."

Christophe's initial reaction was that he would never part with this sailboat, but as he continued to sit in his captain's chair, the idea began to incubate and merge with other thoughts he had been having about his future direction. He had rented a small apartment in Paris. Jean-Luc had asked him to work part-time as his personal adviser at Ashleigh. The newly discovered sense of belonging in Paris was causing Christophe to question the solitary life in Beaulieu he had once thought would make him happy.

The moment Christophe's taxi entered the driveway at Château de Pommerance, Julien burst out of the door with Bounder and Woofy close behind. Bounder was half barking and half howling with excitement. Woofy was simply yapping because Bounder was barking. Christophe stepped out of the taxi into Julien's hug. "Oncle Christophe! Oncle Christophe! Je suis si heureux de vous voir." When Bounder realized it was Christophe, he jumped up on him, nearly knocking him to the ground. Christophe fetched his things from the luggage hatch, and the autonomous taxi exited the driveway in search of the nearest recharging station to wait until summoned by the next passenger. The excitement in the driveway also brought Fredrick and Sandra out of the house. It was late summer. The clusters of Merlot grapes hung heavily on the vines. Their aroma was intoxicating.

After all the greetings were exchanged, the dogs took an interest in the kitty carrier on the ground next to Christophe's valise. Minnie expressed her displeasure at the unwanted attention by hissing loudly. Fredrick said to Christophe, "Follow me. There's something I want to show you."

Christophe said, "Let me just put the cat in the house first."

"No, just bring her with you," said Fredrick. The two men headed off across the driveway, with Julien and the dogs not far behind, to an outbuilding that had once housed the ancient winery's carriages. Fredrick opened the door and showed Christophe inside. The room was beautifully decorated. The smell of fresh paint was in the air, and a collection of antique restored harnesses graced the walls.

"This used to be a garage, but we just filled it up with junk, so Sandra nagged me for years to turn it into a guesthouse. It's yours for however long you would like. Why don't you go check it out?"

The downstairs had a sitting room with an open kitchen and an ample *salle de bain*. The bedroom was upstairs, which had once served as the hayloft. A spacious south-facing balcony had been added. Christophe knew immediately that Sandra had it built with him in mind. He burst into tears.

Sandra and Audrey served a banquet dinner for the complete family. They also celebrated Christophe's birthday belatedly. Even Laurent's two teenage daughters made a token appearance. Laurent informed Christophe of the exciting news that his company had just hired François Benoit as a senior computer analyst and that François and Chloé were in the process of relocating to Bordeaux. All anyone really wanted, however, was to have Christophe catch them up on his recent adventures. Julien, in particular, was spellbound by the story of sneaking into the basement of the Barbès-Rochechouart metro station and running into the security guard with the pointed gun. They did not afford Christophe much chance to eat his dinner, after which the others retired to the sitting room to watch the quarterfinals match with France in the World Cup. Christophe and Sandra were left sitting alone in the dining room.

Christophe finally said nonchalantly, breaking the delicious silence, "I sold my sailboat."

"*Monique II*?" she said. "I never thought you would do that."

"I just came to the realization that the boat had become my excuse for feeling sorry for myself," said Christophe. "Anyway, I will be spending more time in Paris, and it's time for me to begin a new chapter in my life." His sister bathed him with loving eyes. She did not need to respond.

"You know, Sandra," he continued after a long, reflective silence, "I always thought evil was localized like a cancerous tumor. Once you pinpointed where it was, you could operate to remove it. Like taking out Hitler in the Reichskanzler, which brought a clear and decisive end to the empire of the Third Reich. This is how I imagined bringing down the syndicate would be like. But now it seems that the syndicate is more like leukemia. It exists everywhere at once. Except, unlike leukemia, which weakens and ultimately kills the host, the syndicate is more like a parasite that thrives only to the extent that the host thrives. They feed off the host while being careful not to go so far as to actually destroy it. I think this makes them all the more dangerous."

Christophe poured himself another glass of wine. "Ashleigh has succeeded in making the world very small— practically a single village. I am proud to say I had a lot to do with this. I am convinced that the whole world is better for it. But the syndicate infected my company and subordinated the very things that make the world a freer and happier place. They did this in order to impose their will on everyone. They extended their reach throughout the globe without the need of an invading army. They never built a single tank, or a fighter plane, or a nuclear bomb. They simply tried to commandeer the world's economy by using the Ashleigh portals, the very portals I spent my life creating. Hyperspeed is just one of those things that can serve good and evil at the same time."

Everyone in the sitting room could be heard screaming at the TV, except Julien, who wandered back into the dining room and climbed up into his gramma's lap. Sandra didn't say a word as Christophe unloaded his burdens on her.

"Do you know the parable of the wheat and the tares in Mathew's Gospel?" he asked Sandra. She just nodded. Christophe continued, "I always found it enigmatic because any real farmer would never instruct his farmworkers to just let weeds grow alongside his crop. I mean, after all, when we walk through your vineyard, what do we do instinctively every time we encounter a weed? We pull it up by its roots, of course."

Christophe paused to take another sip of wine. "That was before I met a guy named Trent Lachmann. You see, Sandra, Trent Lachmann was really a tare masquerading as a stock of wheat in the form of a guy named Fred Simms. Apparently, in the field, wheat and tares look pretty much the same for a while. Fred Simms ran the entire North American division, which I was part of for twenty years up to the time I retired. He wouldn't have been my first choice to hold that position, but we got along. As it turns out, it was all an act. The real Fred Simms turned out to be a very sinister fellow who ultimately tried to have me killed. Sometimes it is just not possible to distinguish between the wheat and the tares until the heads of grain become visible in the end—just like in the parable."

Fredrick and the others returned to the dining room about that time. "France lost in the final seconds," said Laurent dejectedly.

Audrey gathered up Julien in her arms and said, "Just leave everything, Mom. I will be back in the morning to help clean up." They all departed with Woofy, leaving Fredrick, Sandra, and Christophe alone at the dining room table. Bounder lay quietly on the floor. Fredrick asked Sandra what they had been talking about, but there are some things that just cannot be recounted. "Christophe sold *Monique II*," she finally said.

Fredrick said to Christophe, "I just heard on the news that Brazil invaded Guyana today. There is some kind of a border dispute over a large gold discovery. Do you know anything about it?"

Christophe just shook his head. It confirmed to him that he had made the right decision in passing the file folder from Jean-Luc along to Abraham.

CPSIA information can be obtained
at www.ICGtesting.com
Printed in the USA
BVHW081120271118
534110BV00001B/23/P

9 781532 060199